72 Virgins

Avi Perry

Gradient Publishing

This book is a work of fiction. Names, characters, places and incidents are products of the author's imagination or are used fictitiously. Any resemblance to actual events or locales or persons living or dead is entirely coincidental.

Gradient Publishing
www.gradientpubishing.com

ISBN 13: 9780615280516
ISBN 10: 0-615-28051-X
LCCN: 2009923992
QBI PCIP: 1. Terrorism--United States--Fiction. 2. Jihad--Fiction. 3. Suspense-fiction.
I. Title. II. Title: 72 virgins.

PS3616.E7928S48 2009   813'.6
QBI09-600021

Visit www.gradientpubishing.com to order additional copies.

To my best friend,
the love of my life,
my wife, Shelly.

"We can forgive the Arabs for killing our children. We cannot forgive them for forcing us to kill their children. We will only have peace with the Arabs when they love their children more than they hate us..."

Golda Meir, Former Prime Minister of Israel.

ACKNOWLEDGMENT

Those who have never attempted their hand at fiction writing might not realize that a good quality novel requires a great deal of research, sustaining many of the fine points that shape the characters, the atmosphere, the scenes, the scenery, and the plot as a whole—keeping it real.

Much of the information imparted through *72 Virgins* required profound knowledge, some aspects of which were not within my grasp before moving the plot to the fore. In particular, story elements pertaining to law enforcement and intelligence agencies, types and attributes of chemical weapons, particular locations, places, and modes of worship, as well as aspects of science and technology that inspire modern spying techniques—were building blocks I brought into play, with the help of added insight from qualified mavens.

I was lucky to have generous people, connoisseurs in their particular field, who were enthusiastic about parting with their expert advice and more than willing to share some of their knowledge and information with me.

I wish to start by thanking Philip Edney from the FBI who guided me through the maze of the FBI building in Washington DC, providing me with a thorough analysis of the organizational structure and the roles played by the different divisions and the field offices. He also enlightened me on the methods, style and forms of cooperation with other security and intelligence agencies, thus keeping me honest.

I wish to thank my friend Motti, not his real name, from the Israeli *Mossad* who ran through stories, scenarios, culture, personalities and roles, typical of that legendary agency, thus making sure that I do not misrepresent it or its operating procedures.

On the chemical weapons and bomb making technology, I was briefed by Major Samuel Vitkin from the Engineering Unit of the Israeli Army. It was his humor-filled speaking style, encompassing sarcasm and weird but funny similes and metaphors, which not only helped me acquire a handle on the subject, but nonetheless, provided me with key attributes I employed while portraying Jerry, one of the main protagonists in the story.

My publisher's team of experts, Zach Coddington, Ron D., Helen Smith, Sandy Shalton contributed to cover and book design, editing and production.

Oliver James was the most enthusiastic, charismatic and supportive person when it came to having the manuscript see the light outside my laptop. He loved the story from the get-go, promoted it as a suspenseful and intriguing read from start to finish, then invested his publishing company's resources in having it published.

If there is one person whose contribution was above and beyond others, it is my dear friend, Dr. Ilan Halpern. His dedication, patience, and editing prowess helped me perk up an earlier draft. Not only did he help improve readability, he was also instrumental in identifying errors, which inevitably, squeezed through and snuck in, even when the guards were on duty.

My brother, Professor David Perry, was influential in helping me enhance one major plot-twist, and thus, added to the thrill that the story would offer the reader.

And of course, my wife, Shelly, I still consider marrying her—a momentous overachievement; she was first to read and comment on the initial draft. She had been the reason I gathered the courage and braved the commitment necessary to persevere all the way through this undertaking. Her early feedback, enthusiasm and encouragement granted me the energy required for spending lonely hours (that she was enduring as well) in front of the computer, trying to conceive subplots, achieve perfect flow, carry out meaty character development, employ proper language and clever lines, all embedded in the terrorism-filled reality that is today's world.

To all of you—my friends, colleagues, and family—I am eternally grateful.

Chapter 1

Sunday, October 27, 2002—Tel Aviv, Israel

It was noontime when the heaving bus entered the intersection across from the main entrance to the Dizengoff shopping mall in Tel Aviv. The cloudless blue skies painted a peaceful overture to an ordinary onset of another week. It was a beautiful autumn day. Dizengoff Street, one of the foremost symbols of the most vibrant city in Israel, home to many prestigious fashion designers, movie and theatre celebrities, authors and poets, as well as plain folk—was bursting with life. Office workers were out on their lunch break; shoppers were on the hunt for the usual bargains in and around the mall, and traffic was drawing near its customary gridlock that typified the first day of the working week in Israel.

The bus stopped at the traffic light, next to the main entrance to the mall, just ahead of King George Street. Then, in a flash, without warning, just as the traffic light was about to turn green, the sun turned dark. A Palestinian suicide bomber, sitting near the center of the bus, rose from his seat. His sad face cracked open in a sadistic smile; he looked up, filled his lungs, then shrieked, *"Allahu Akbar!"* (God is Greater (*than any other God and every human VIP*)) while igniting his explosives-filled belt.

The explosion went off inside the bus, blowing its top into smithereens, generating a massive fire throughout its interior. There were twenty-nine dead, all civilians, passengers and pedestrians, men, women, old, young, and younger. The enormous blast was heard throughout the city from the beachfront hotels to the Diamond Center in nearby Ramat Gan, and for a long, drawn out moment, the ordinary exuberance typifying life in this metropolis was brought to a standstill. The awful silence that followed the explosion was quickly interrupted by the screaming of urgent sirens. Ambulances and fire trucks converged on the scene as the local police force mobilized to cordon off the surrounding area.

Islamic University student, Abdullah Mansour from Gaza, the suicide bomber, was among the lifeless remains collected by the orange uniform-clad clean-up crew. One hour later, Mansour's picture was revealed on Palestinian TV. His mother was proud; his older brother was energized; his recorded will was recited by the young Palestinian kids who would follow in his footsteps. Abdullah Mansour's passage to Paradise was secured. It was paved with bloody and burnt corpses of innocent souls including his own—a prerequisite on the path to martyrdom. The moment he pulled the trigger was the happiest of his short life. Seventy-two virgins were awaiting his arrival in heaven. They'd be nursing his wounds and nurturing him forever. His place next to Allah's throne was now secured. He'd just become the latest martyr.

Chapter 2

Two days earlier—Gaza City

The few open stores in the Gold and Spice markets of the *el-Daraj* neighborhood were closing down early in preparation for the traditional Friday evening holiday prayer. The streets and alleys in the Gaza city center next to *al-Omari* mosque started filling with a massive crowd that was developing into an increasingly dense jamboree. Men wearing white and women dressed in black robes and white veils were rushing in from the nearby closed-down Antique and Gold market opposite the Pottery Quarter. There was still plenty of time, just about half an hour before the onset of the traditional evening prayer, but inside *al-Omari*, the largest mosque in Gaza city, there was no room left. Soldiers of Allah had already taken every spot.

Outside, in the backyard of the *el-Zahra* Secondary School, a two-story building that had been mistaken for Napoleon's castle, children ended their soccer game prematurely, leaving their improvised cotton stuffed football behind. It would be there tomorrow; they'd be picking up where they left off.

The local television crew was bracing for an upcoming live broadcast. Satellite dishes were placed inside and outside the mosque, and television cameras were positioned on location ready to transmit a critical sermon and the corresponding reaction to it over the airwaves. The audio would be fed directly to several radio stations for a live show.

It was time. The muezzin's call for the prayer service boomed out of the loud speakers positioned on top of the minaret. The traditional singing invitation included a special announcement confirming the scheduled and highly anticipated sermon by Dr. Ahmad

Abu Halabiya, member of the Palestinian Authority appointed *Fatwa* Council and former acting Rector of the Islamic University in Gaza.

Out in the *el-Zaytoon* neighborhood, Abdullah Mansour, a third-year student at the Islamic University, was getting dressed following his customary Friday afternoon nap. He'd overslept. It was the only time during the week he could enjoy a genuine break. The two-bedroom apartment in the Southern part of the neighborhood housed eight family members. In addition to his parents and one grandmother, he had four siblings, one older brother and three younger sisters. They were all hanging around inside *al-Omari* mosque, their traditional Friday evening routine. Except his old, ailing grandmother was sitting in the kitchen, sipping from a freshly made cup of bitter sweet, cardamom-filled coffee.

Abdullah Mansour loved his grandmother. When he was growing up, she used to tell him stories about her home in Palestine, her parents, her siblings. He'd never met them, but he held them close in his thoughts. They were all martyrs, and he regularly imagined chatting with them, sharing cigarettes, sipping coffee together. One day he would walk in Jaffa, his grandmother's hometown next to Tel Aviv, proud and free, after the predictable victory over the criminal Jews.

Mansour rubbed his eyes for a full minute. When they finally opened, the sight of the peeling light-blue paint on the ceiling above greeted his arrival. He always wondered about the gun shaped peelings. It must have been a divine communiqué. His professor at the Islamic University, Dr. Ahmad Abu Halabiya, taught him that Allah kept sending messages to every devout Muslim. The ones who were able to decipher them and act accordingly would be assured of a place in Paradise. Mansour recognized the peelings for what they were—a message from Allah, an undisputed one. He got up, sat on his bed for one more minute before strolling to the kitchen. His grandmother was looking down at her cup of coffee. She didn't raise her head to greet him. She was deep in thought, some of which sneaking out of her mouth as she uttered partial sentences between sips.

Mansour peeked out through the kitchen window watching the orange sun slowly sinking into the Mediterranean. One quick finger inside his nose for a final clean up, he reminded himself—*I'd better hurry.* He gave his dark curly hair a quick comb-out, his short spruce beard and heavy mustache—a fresh run through. He wouldn't want to miss his mentor's greatly anticipated sermon. His good looks, dark brown eyes, and his five-foot-nine-inch size couldn't overcome the repelling powers of his appalling bad breath. It proclaimed his presence from ten feet away, a common condition in a society where dental hygiene was a rarity.

Mansour picked up his fully automatic AK-47 Kalashnikov, loaded the magazine, then held it in his left hand while feeling the trigger with his index finger. Satisfied, he moved two steps forward toward the bathroom. Lifting the gun in a picture-perfect posture, he took an admiring stare at the scratched mirror above the chipped sink next to the rusty toilet seat, then, resting the gun on the concrete floor, he emptied his bladder into the toilet. The rusty seat wouldn't complain. Absorbing a few drops wouldn't change its condition. He wiped his hand on his black jeans, then covered his head with his new red *kaffiyeh* (an Arab headdress), took one more admiring glimpse in the mirror, then charged through the graffiti-covered door into the narrow alley.

He turned around and started sprinting alongside the dense row of olive trees. His sweat was running down his neck wetting his white shirt. He could hardly hear the fading chorus of singing muezzins emanating from the other mosques surrounding him.

Mansour stole a final stare at the Martyrs' cemetery with its marble columns where the names of some of the martyrs who had died in defense of the city had been engraved. He admired them and worshipped their final resting place in the Southern outskirts of the neighborhood. One day, his name would be engraved on a column just like these. His thoughts and focus were centered on the path to *al-Omari* mosque. As he crossed the street, he could already hear the unique voice of Dr. Ahmad Abu Halabiya's oration throbbing through the loud speakers, wresting attention from every soul around him. Watching these people, he was gripped by the stillness of their bodies. They were all gazing up at the dimming skies, listening attentively to every word, nodding in acceptance, and echoing "*Allahu Akbar!*" (God is Greater) at the end of every phrase.

"Have no mercy on the Jews, Have no mercy on the Americans, no matter where they are, in any country. Fight them; kill those Jews and those Americans."

"*Allahu Akbar!*" Mansour joined the chorus. "*Allahu Akbar!*"

"They're all liars. Oh brother believers! They've butchered our children, orphaned them, widowed our women, desecrated our holy places and sacred sites. The Jews and the Americans—they're the true terrorists; they're the ones who must be butchered and killed..."

As the voice of Abu Halabiya reverberated through the streets, Mansour reiterated the mantra behind the crowd, "*Allahu Akbar!*" It was dark now. The orange colored sun had drowned inside the Mediterranean. The cloudless October skies were covered with shining bright stars, while the warm and humid air contributed to the smell of wet human sweat and body odor saturating the streets and the nearby alleys. Almost everyone around him was gazing up at the heavens in an ultimate effort to freeze the moment. There was nothing else but the thought of revenge, of hatred. It was utterly consuming.

Mansour came to an abrupt stop and listened to the words thundering out of the loud speakers.

"The path of Allah is to kill and be killed. Kill the Jews and their Christian allies. Kill the ones who unite against those who say, there's no God but Allah and Muhammad is his messenger..."

Mansour was about to move forward in the direction of *al-Omari* mosque, but the human wall in front of him was too thick to make it through. He was only two blocks away, but the objective seemed beyond his reach. In his edginess, he pulled out his gun, raised it above his shoulders, then fired three shots into the open sky. The people in his immediate path turned around. A veiled woman took command, yelled orders to her neighbors who opened a narrow corridor for Mansour to walk through. He made it to the next block, but was unable to proceed. The human barricade was solidifying again.

Abu Halabia's thundering voice kept booming. Mansour was getting agitated. He pulled his gun again, raised it as high as he could, then pressed the trigger for a long spray of bullets. The action had its impact; the adjoining mass managed to open a wide passageway around him, while the people in front of him backed off, parting the human sea just as Moses had done on route to the Promised Land.

Mansour was finally standing in front of *al-Omari* mosque. He could hear his teacher devoid of the electronics. He was living and breathing the discourse.

"Oh brother in belief! The Muslim loves death and martyrdom, just as the infidel loves life. The Muslim loves the Hereafter, just as the infidel loves this world. Oh brothers in belief! The beautiful brides, the seventy-two virgins in Paradise, are looking forward to your arrival. They'll comfort your soul and slave to your needs. They welcome you, but they command a precious price and dowry. You must kill and be killed. *Allahu Akbar! Allahu Akbar!*"

As Mansour was rushing up the stairs to the door of the Great *al-Omari* mosque, two guards of the *Hamas* local militia stopped him. After confiscating his gun, conducting a thorough body search, and scrutinizing his intentions, they led him inside and told him to wait in front of the door. There was hardly any room left around his temporary parking spot. Old shoes, new shoes, different color shoes — they were all arranged neatly near the vestibule where he stood waiting. Mansour watched the packed grounds inside. He examined the sea of white robes and bare feet, all cheering, talking politics, yelling, cursing, praising Allah. His thoughts were interrupted by a heavy squeeze on the back of his neck. He turned around. One of the guards placed his hand on Mansour's shoulder, then led him to a room downstairs in the basement.

He was standing face to face in the presence of the notorious local *Hamas* Captain, Abu Musa. Mansour had never before seen the face or even a photo of the great leader. All pictures he'd seen displayed a masked head. This time he noticed the thick scar running from Abu Musa's left ear down to his left jaw. Even the dense black curly beard couldn't conceal the memento that hid behind it and wrapped a fascinating story inside its past.

"You'll receive your instructions tomorrow," Abu Musa declared. "You'll come here to the mosque, and we'll take you away. Don't say a word to anyone. Don't say good-bye to anyone. You'll say good-bye in a videotaped message. Your family will be proud of you. Your nation will be proud of you. Your soul will enjoy Paradise forever. When you wake up in the morning, wash yourself and shave your face and your body. Wear your best clothes. You're going to a heavenly wedding. Remember, seventy-two virgins are awaiting your arrival."

They shook hands, kissed on both cheeks; Mansour took one more look at his new mentor. He was incapable of making out the eyes behind the dark sunglasses, nor could he acquire a firm memory of the face. The cigar smoke Abu Musa was blowing in Mansour's direction thwarted any attempt to catch a clear view.

It wasn't vital. Mansour had had his moment on the path to paradise. He was all geared up. He was on a mission from Allah, for Allah. He would become a martyr. He would rejoice in the company of seventy-two virgins. Yes, he would. That's what they told him. That was what he believed.

•   •   •

On October 27, two days after the illustrious sermon in the Great *al-Omari* mosque in Gaza, following Abdullah Mansour's suicide bombing at the heart of Tel Aviv, Abu Musa didn't return home. The notorious *Hamas* leader in the Gaza region, the mastermind behind the bombing, went into hiding. Abu Musa was a marked man, but he wasn't yet ready to die. He chose to delay martyrdom for as long as he could.

In Tel Aviv, Dan Carmel, the Israeli *Mossad* Director in charge of counter-terrorism strategy, swore to his new life mission; he would see to it that Abu Musa would reach his paradise destination and visit with his seventy-two virgins, sooner rather than later.

Chapter 3

October 27, 2002—Tel Aviv, Israel

It was supposed to be a joyful turning point, yet it turned into a sentimental tear-jerking juncture. At four in the afternoon on that event packed day, Major Arik Golan shut off his desktop computer and said good-bye to his colleagues, subordinates, and fellow officers. One by one, his team members in the IDF (Israeli Defense Forces) top-secret intelligence team came by his desk. He got up to greet them. They hugged, then stretched their arms while still holding on to each other for a final eye-to-moist-eye contact. The impending loss of not having Arik around, of not being able to find guidance, and of not being taken over by his enthusiasm, talent, and charisma, were hard to bear.

For the final day of his military service, following nine years of committed duty, Arik was wearing his customary military uniforms. It made him appear as young and as a fresh as an eighteen-year-old army recruit, though he'd just celebrated his twenty-seventh birthday. Yet, his manly comportment, his towering six-foot slim body, his tanned Middle Eastern features, accentuated by intelligence projecting, penetrating dark brown eyes, seemed to adequately compensate for any lack of seeming maturity.

Ten years earlier, he was only seventeen, just commencing his final year of high school, when he received a letter from the Israeli Defense Forces (IDF) Central Recruiting Center. He was invited to take the written exam that would determine whether he would be a candidate for *Talpiot—a program established as the IDF elite brainpower summit, tasked with altering the makeup of technological warfare. Arik felt particularly honored. He realized that* each year, tens of thousands of names were submitted to the IDF for *Talpiot* consideration by school principals and science teachers. This group would then be narrowed down to about five-thousand potential candidates who, for a period of about six months, would rigorously be screened. At the end of the evaluation period, only fifty candidates would be invited to sign up. Among this group, however, only thirty-five to forty would make it through the entire program and graduate.

One year later, Arik found himself at the Hebrew University in the company of a select group of gifted soldiers who began their military service in specially built barracks in Jerusalem. They studied for their bachelor's of science in physics, mathematics, and computer science, and took technological courses at an accelerated rate; covering about forty percent more material than they would've in a regular BS degree program. The academic studies were an addition to massive training in military strategy during what other students labeled as summer vacation.

During his second academic year, after a long summer of a wide-ranging military training involving hiking in the desert with over forty kilos of supplies plus a rifle on his back, jumping out of planes and helicopters, Arik was honorably mentioned when proving himself through a grueling series of tests. By the end of the year, upon his graduation at the top of the one percent out of the one percent, he was deemed a true whiz kid, the most capable among the exceptionally gifted.

At that point in his career, Arik joined the elite IDF military intelligence section of the General Command. He was in charge of designing and developing methods and systems for enhanced intelligence gathering and interpretation. One of his pioneering inventions had earned him an exceptional honorable mention reserved for those whose bravery under fire saved lives in the heat of battle. He utilized a newly invented wireless communications protocol, named *Bluetooth*, as one of the greatest spying devices ever concocted. The new technology was designed for exchanging data between appliances over short distances, overcoming problems of synchronization.

Arik devised a way to exploit *Bluetooth* as a vehicle for downloading and planting spying applications into another mobile phone without the knowledge of the unsuspecting phone-owner. The application, a Trojan horse, could be downloaded from a neighboring mobile phone, then installed in the victim's mobile phone's memory. Upon activation, the application, in its initial release, granted the spying agent access to the victim's phone from any location, allowing the spy to review the controlled phone's directory and call history. It provided the spying agent with the ability to listen in on calls, whether incoming or outgoing, to make calls from the victim's phone without leaving a trace, and to exploit the built-in microphone of the victim's phone to eavesdrop on nearby conversations. The first release of Arik's Trojan horse application could perform all of those wonderful tasks only when the victim's phone was powered on. In its second release, due six months following Arik's retirement from the military, the application was to be extended, per Arik's specifications, to include the same control over the victim's phone, even when its power was off.

Arik's invention contributed to one of the greatest intelligence breakthroughs Israel had ever benefited from. The amount and quality of the information gathered through Arik's Trojan horse application resulted in nipping terrorists' plots in the bud, even before they had come close to setting them off. The many people, whose lives were saved as a result, had never realized how lucky they were thanks to Arik.

Yet, notwithstanding persistent requests from his superiors, the military chief of staff, and the Secretary of Defense, Arik refused to prolong his military service. He had dreams of his own. Like many graduates of *Talpiot* before him, Arik yearned for forming a hi-tech startup with a particular focus on military applications. He wanted to tour the world, then start a family. He craved the civilian life that awaited his coming.

On that final day of service, the atmosphere in the restricted military intelligence section on the third floor of the General Command building — in the dun-colored military complex, located at the heart of Tel Aviv — was cheerless. It mirrored an end to an era. The beloved team leader would be gone in a few minutes, never to return. There was cake on the table opposite the door, but no one had touched it. Appetite fulfillment was the last thing on people's minds.

Rachel Levy was standing at the door to Arik's office. Her moist blue eyes turned red, letting a couple of tears run down her face in reaction to the sentimental good-byes. Her long and curly blonde-hair was pony-tailed, resting on her left shoulder, fully exposing her cheeks and the right side of her neck. She needed little if any makeup to cover that silky, color-filled skin. Her black jeans and dark green top accentuated her full-figured five-foot-seven-inch build. Rachel was a familiar face around this exclusive intelligence unit.

During her military service, which had ended just two months earlier, she was Arik's administrative assistant. She organized his papers, rummaged out his daily agenda, answered his incoming phone calls, and one week before ending her military service, she hooked him firmly by letting him know what her future intentions entailed. He waited patiently until her final day before asking her out for the first time. Their friendship was already firm and un-yielding; still, since that decisive moment, their love for each other soared instantly, resembling a rocket taking off on its long way to the stars.

Arik and Rachel shared a special bond tying them to their very early childhood. Both were born in the US to parents who had come to New York on Student Visas. Rachel was born when Arik was seven years old. His father studied for the MBA at NYU, while Rachel's dad was working on his Ph.D. in Psychology at Columbia University. The two little ones spent time with each other when the parents got together at Israeli-student parties, Passover Seders, Israel Independence Day celebrations, and occasional dinners. When Arik and Rachel started dating, they had no idea that they'd shared a common past. The discovery came unexpectedly when Arik expressed his desire to visit Bali, Indonesia.

"You can't go there with an Israeli passport. Indonesia and Israel don't have diplomatic relations," Rachel said on their second date.

"I know that. I'll travel with an American passport."

"Oh, you have one too."

"Too?" he wondered. "I see." It was a revealing moment. Without warning, he held her face in both his hands and pulled it closer. Looking straight into her eyes, he announced, "we're going together;

but first, we'll have our American passports reissued outside Israel, so as to conceal our bona fide homeland while in Bali.

"Why?" she asked.

"Precautions."

• • •

Arik was ready to come out of his office and greet the crowd gathering near the door, when his thoughts were interrupted by a familiar voice.

"Hey, I'm here." Rachel was accompanied by Arik's superior, Colonel Amos Friedman. He was standing next to her and to another unfamiliar person, anticipating an introduction. Arik turned to his left, surprised but happy to see her; he stepped forward as she moved in towards him for a meeting of the lovers. A warm tight squeeze, a quick kiss, and then, switching attention to the other visitor, he said, "Hello Amos. I didn't expect you here today. I was going to call later to say good-bye."

Amos smiled. "Well, I couldn't let you go without a handshake, and, just to let you know, we'll see and talk to each other regularly in the future."

A questioning look on Arik's face froze in place. He was expecting more. "Yes?" He then glanced at Rachel. Her emotions were still revealing. He approached and hugged her. "Hey, what's going on?" he said. "We're leaving this place together, soon. Come enjoy the cake." He turned back to Amos Friedman. "It was nice seeing you here. You saved me a trip," he said, embracing Rachel's shoulder with his left hand, offering his right for a handshake.

Shaking Arik's hand, Amos exclaimed, "I'd like to introduce my friend, Dan Carmel." He placed his left arm on Carmel's shoulders while nudging him toward Arik.

Arik took a quick glance. The short man, just about five-foot-three, grossly overweight, semi bald, but with plenty of gray, covering the remains of his dwindling hair, offered his hand for a firm grip. "Amos has told me a great deal about you," he said. He had a peculiar knack for speaking almost without moving his lips.

Peering at Arik with piercing eagerness, he said, "I have a serious career proposal for you to consider."

Arik wasn't ready to consider job offers. He had already formed his long-term agenda. At that moment, however, the only thought on his mind was an extended break lasting for about nine months, together with Rachel, exploring the wonders of the world. Every one of his high school friends had followed this Israeli tradition when arriving at this crossroads in their life's journey. That journey took them through high school, then on to the military, followed by six to twelve months of world tours, concluding with the commencement of adulthood. That settling down finale was still roughly a year away and far beyond the foreseeable horizon.

"I'm not there, yet," Arik responded. He was looking to his left catching Rachel's gaze, then continued. "Why don't you call me next summer? We can discuss it then if it coincides with my plans."

Carmel wasn't one who took rejections lightly. "It's crucial that you take the opportunity to consider my proposal before you embark on your trip to Bali next week." He paused, trying to assess the impact of his words. The revelation regarding his knowledge of Arik's plans carried the conversation into a new plane. "Let's get together tomorrow," he continued. "What do you think of lunch at *Rafael*'s, on the beachfront in Tel Aviv? I'll meet you there tomorrow at twelve o'clock sharp."

Arik found it difficult but not impossible to resist the unexpected assault. "You know, this is going to be my first day as a civilian. It's been nine years. I worked hard. I served with all my heart, lost plenty of sleep. I deserve a clean first day after." He studied the dumpy person in front of him; late fifties, a bumper belly announcing a progressive pregnancy of something unpleasant, like a skinny little person screaming to get out after being eaten; he was clean-shaven, with a rosaceous face, though his yellow teeth must have been stained by an excessive measure of nicotine. Arik turned to Rachel who kept watching, admiring her boyfriend's cool demeanor. "Let's go," he said, changing his grim facial expression to a warm smile. "We have a lot of catching up to do."

Carmel removed his bifocals, wiped them with a tissue he pulled out of his light blue shirt pocket, then pressed the heels of his hands against his eyes, massaging them as if he were trying to open a lane to the insides of his brains. "Wait," he broke off, visibly restraining a more hard-hitting response. He offered a courteous smile. "This isn't turning out the way either one of us wants to go. I strongly advise that we meet up tomorrow." He turned to Rachel: "Please tell your boyfriend to say *yes*. We'll limit it to a couple of hours. You'll own him for the rest of the day."

She blushed. The color change exposed Rachel's intimidated state. She didn't want to be the reason for impeding Arik's smooth transition or for standing in his way. Amos who was still standing next to Dan Carmel reinforced the intimidation by nodding '*yes*' in her direction. "Okay," she volunteered. "I can give him up for a couple of hours." Arik released his embrace. He didn't approve of her spontaneous response, but it was a little late. He felt awkward starting an argument, with Rachel on the opposite side.

"All right, tomorrow at twelve," Arik countered reluctantly. He turned to Amos. "It was great seeing you today." He shook hands again, turned to his former team members, waved good-bye, then grabbed Rachel's hand. "Let's go. It's getting late, and we still have plenty to cover."

Chapter 4

October 27, 2002—Khan Younis, Gaza Strip

Al Shahid, the most popular Café in the Khan Younis refugee camp on the southern tip of the Gaza strip was humming with people who had come from all over to celebrate. Cigarette smoke mixed with the smell of coffee, and narghile (water pipe) steam filled the air under the clear skies. Nearby, less than a kilometer away, one could see the lonely lights of the loathed Israeli settlements of Gadid and Neve Deqalim. The night was bright, with a full moon shining over the Mediterranean. Those foamy white caressing wavelets were reflecting back the moonlight before kicking the bucket on the sandy shore. The romantic landscape lay there forever wasted; not a soul was in the mood for love. Less than three kilometers away, inside the strip, the party goers were all hanging around, passing the time in anticipation of the arrival of the local hero, Abu Musa, the commander in charge of the latest victory over the loathed Jews. The talk of the town was the latest string of triumphant suicide bombings that took place throughout the month, with the latest, only hours earlier, in Tel Aviv.

Five years earlier, Abu Musa committed his first courageous act when he knifed his Jewish boss to death. He was working on a construction site near the Southern Israeli city of Ashkelon, making a living, getting friendly with the enemy. They developed mutual fondness and respect for each other. His Israeli boss trusted him; let him roam freely around the construction site.

Abu Musa had been working on and off in the Jewish town of Ashkelon for about a year before he met Dr. Ahmad Abu Halabiya in *al-Omari* mosque in Gaza. There, he learned more about the true meaning of *Jihad* and life in Paradise next to Allah's throne, life reserved only for those who sacrifice their bodies in the defense of Islam. He started dreaming about the promised afterlife, and as his dreams became progressively more frequent, he began fantasizing about the seventy-two virgins awaiting his coming. He couldn't help it any longer; thus, he indulged in the habit of masturbating nightly before going to bed, until that was no longer adequate. That night, the night before the dawn of his utter conversion five years earlier, he went to see Dr. Abu Halabiya who ordered him to get ready. Allah was waiting. It was time for action.

Born as Jamal Huseini in Gaza in August 1967, two months after Israel had occupied the strip as a consequence of the Six-Day-War, Jamal Huseini grew up in Khan Younis, one mile away from the Refugee Camp. He got married at the age of eighteen, and nine-months later, following the birth of his son—Musa, everyone in town nicknamed him: Abu Musa (Musa's father), and the new name had stuck ever since.

Abu Musa's parents moved to Khan Younis from Egypt after the 1948 war between Israel and the seven Arab countries that had attacked it—Egypt, Jordan, Syria, Lebanon, Saudi Arabia, Iraq, and Yemen. They became 'refugees deluxe' following the UN Relief and Works Administration (UNRWA) acceptance of a situation that recognized any destitute Arab in Palestine as a refugee, letting them have refugee facilities and aid in their own home regardless of whether they were actual refugees or just local residents.

Abu Musa didn't grow up a poor kid in the refugee camp, neither had his parents been Palestinians before 1948. He was neither a refugee, nor a refugee's offspring. He matured as a relatively educated young man, who studied languages, the Koran, and above all, the Islamic version of the history of Palestine, which included no Jewish presence ever, not even since the times of Abraham—Father of all Arabs.

Since the time of his birth, Abu Musa knew no other governmental authority but the reviled Jewish one. He was a refugee at heart, and was determined to fight the occupiers all the way to the gates of Heaven, where he would enter Paradise and they'd burn in Hell. Since his sixteenth birthday, Abu Musa spent a great deal of his time in the neighboring Refugee Camp, where he became a gang leader, harassing rival gangs, local residents, and Israeli troops. He acquired his notorious scar during a fight with a local gang over disputed territory.

In 1987 during the first *Intifada* (uprising against Israeli occupation), Abu Musa, now a twenty-year-old gang-leader, joined the *Hamas* movement to become a captain of the local Khan Younis militia. The *Intifada* years saw him rise in rank and in fame, particularly following his capture and arrest by the Israeli Security Forces (*Shabak*) in 1992. By the time the first *Intifada* came to an end in 1993 with the Oslo accord, Abu Musa was a true celebrity hero among his brother-Palestinians. Yasser Arafat included his name in his speeches—the Arabic version—and young children recited his name and bravery-laced lyrics before bedtime. He was let loose by the Israelis as a measure of good faith subsequent to the signing of the roadmap to peace and ahead of the Nobel-Peace-Prize triumph, crowning his master, Yasser Arafat, as the most devout peacemaker of his era.

Nowadays, Abu Musa was a wanted man for the second time. The Israelis were seeking him out, but Abu Musa was determined. He would cause heavy damage before those hated Jews captured him dead or alive. He would go and train, lead and plan, educate and preach in the name of Allah. His latest act was the most courageous and most victorious. He trained his human bomb and had him explode next to the Dizengoff mall in the heart of Tel Aviv. Twenty-nine dead and many more wounded—an imposing triumph.

It was 8 p.m. when Abu Musa climbed into his nine-year-old Jeep with his driver and two of his deputies. He was set to show up in the *al Shahid* café at around 9 p.m., offer his blessing to the crowd, then go back underground to prepare for his next conquest. The sun had just set, glowing with beautiful orange colors over the horizon, but there was still light over the sandy beach, and the weather was perfect for an evening drive in the fresh, open air. He instructed his driver to go parallel to the beach before entering the heart of the refugee camp in Khan Younis. He loved the sound of the sea—a whisper, where the water met the shoreline; he adored the salty smell of the gushing waves. *Paradise must smell like this*, he imagined. He looked up watching and admiring the moon when, suddenly, his heart dropped. He saw it coming down from the sky. "Stop the car," he yelled at the driver as he was readying himself for a dive. "Run away and..." He was unable to finish the sentence. The missile hit the Jeep and exploded in a huge ball of fire. He was out of the Jeep when it was hit, but the power of the blast threw him in the air, thirty-feet away from his position. He landed on the soft sand, alive and lightly wounded, split seconds away from Paradise. His driver and his two deputies were dead. They were burnt beyond recognition. He was the sole survivor.

The sound of the blast was heard in and around Khan Younis. Crowds arrived in no time at the site of the explosion. Abu Musa was lying on the sand when the first throng arrived at the scene. He suffered a mild concussion, a fractured left elbow and minor burns on his left thigh. They carried him to a minivan and sped off to the Khan Younis hospital. He was rushed to the emergency room for urgent treatment, and within two hours, he was back on his feet, weak, wounded, plaster casted, a bit shaken, but alive and mad as hell. Although he was now only a thirty-five-year-old man, he looked more like forty-five. His black beard was coated with streaks of gray, and his thick scar running from his left ear down to his left jaw had a pinkish blush making it more pronounced. His eyes were ruby red, and he looked exhausted and frustrated. "It's not safe for me around here anymore," he announced. "This time, Allah wasn't ready for me. He saved my body and my soul. He wanted me to continue leading the *Jihad* before collecting my spirit. I must leave this place and carry on fighting from foreign lands. *Allahu Akbar!*"

Midnight was approaching when Abu Musa called in two of his most reliable *Hamas* squad members, "I'm leaving the Gaza strip for Egypt in the morning through the new tunnel we completed yesterday, the one under the Israeli border checkpoint in Rafah," he instructed them. "I'll need two-thousand Euros, and water, sufficient for one full day. You get in touch with Hassan Naguib's men from the *Islamic Jihad* in El-Arish, Egypt. Tell them to wait for me at around 5 a.m. on the Egyptian side of the border beyond the checkpoint." He took in air through his pursed lips as if he were sucking blood through a straw. "The suicide bomber I've sent to Tel Aviv today will blow up tomorrow. You take care of his family. Pay them off," he ordered.

Chapter 5

October 28, 2002—Tel Aviv

The sun had been up for several hours. They didn't notice. Arik and Rachel had stayed in bed until eleven, making love, sleeping, talking, making love again, napping, talking, making love once more. "You better hurry," she said when they finally revisited the talking mode. She rose to a sitting position, her bare back to Arik. Looking out the window, the apparent beautiful day induced hunger for an outdoor activity. "Your lunch appointment is only one hour away. You'd better get up," she said. "Quit procrastinating."

"I haven't even begun procrastinating," he said. He yawned with his eyes still closed. A wide smirk painted his lips. "Can I skip it?"

"I don't recommend it." She turned her head around facing him, then turned her body, placed her right hand on his chest, and followed it with a soft rub. "I promised him. You'll grant him two hours, listen politely, and then you'll be free." She leaned over, kissed his forehead, then lifted her head and looked directly into his closed eyes. He could feel her stare and the warmth of her body above him, so close and cozy. He opened his eyes and watched her breasts. They were hanging just above his nose; he couldn't take his eyes off them.

He lifted his left hand. "Can I touch?"

"Please, but you must get up right after."

"Get what up?"

She giggled. "Arik!"

"Okay. You win," he moaned. "But I really don't like that greasy guy."

"Arik… Please. Consider it a free lunch in a great restaurant. I'll see you at two on the beach in front of *Rafael*'s." She paused for a long second before letting off a grin followed by a conspicuous, mischievous look. "Afterwards we'll take a walk, run barefoot on the sand along the beach all the way to Jaffa. It's a beautiful day and we could use the exercise."

. . .

He was there at twelve, waited outside the door, but didn't see Dan Carmel. He glanced at his watch. Yes, it was that time, sharp. Arik decided to wait one more minute, and then if no change, he would simply leave. The restaurant was located on the first floor of the Dan Tel Aviv Hotel building. He watched the Russian-speaking armed guard sitting amused, watching the passers-by in front of the locked revolving glass door leading to the inviting beach. He was about to signal the guard to let him out of the building and into the sun.

"How long have you been sitting here?" Arik asked the guard, trying to break the awkward silence, warming up for the next request.

"I pretend to work here and they pretend to pay me," the guard said, letting a thick grin out of his system.

A hostess came out the restaurant door. "Are you Arik Golan?" she asked.

"I see," he said. "Someone is expecting me inside, right?"

"Oh, you already know." She felt a bit awkward. "Please follow me."

Carmel was seated inside a private glass-walled cabin—a fishbowl. He got up and greeted Arik with a firm handshake that felt more like a crushing grip.

Arik glanced at the large hall. The restaurant was packed. The surrounding babble added to the feeling of privacy. The sound of their conversation would be confined to a couple of square feet inside their private chamber. Comprehension would be impossible beyond that area.

They both stared at each other; no words exchanged. Two minutes of still gaping had passed. Arik glanced impatiently at the terminally dull and self-important plump fellow across from him. He was ready to get up and leave. "Okay," he finally uttered. "I came. You saw me. We talked. Can I go now?"

"Why don't you check the menu, the food is really great." Carmel pointed to the chopped liver starter dish. "This one is delicious. You must order that unless, of course, you're a vegetarian."

Arik couldn't help but think — *Carmel must have substituted sex for food. He must have found it difficult to tie his shoes in the morning, get into his own pants.* Arik was becoming annoyed. "Hey, I didn't claw my way to the top of the food chain just to eat vegetables." His smile turned into acid. "And by the way, I could've enjoyed that even more if I were to share the moment with someone else."

"We can talk while we eat," Carmel said, ignoring the biting remarks. "I know you want to know why you're here with me. You'll listen better on a happy stomach. And by the way, the home-made breads here are the best in town, and the focaccia is a dream come-true."

The waiter came by. He placed on the small table an assortment of fresh bread slices — nut bread, pumpernickel, rye, thick and bursting with aroma. "Anything to drink?"

Arik looked up. "Cold water for me."

Carmel nodded in semi-concurrence, beckoned, then held his empty palm up. "Diet Coke here."

He must be on an eternal diet amid hefty bites, Arik pondered.

"Are we ready to order?" The waiter took out his pen ready to take a note.

"Oh, not yet," Carmel said. "We've not yet checked the menu. A couple of minutes will do."

As the waiter was leaving their table, Carmel picked up the menu and started reading. Arik watched him impatiently. "You know, I'll feel a lot better if you tell me what this is all about." He paused, "now if possible?" He continued watching Carmel who concentrated on the menu, seemed to be paying no heed to the comment, although he raised his index finger in an indication of '*I hear you; be patient.*' Arik was watching him impatiently. Carmel's hair, or rather, his lack of it, seemed more evident than the day before. His plump cheeks looked pink, and his yellow stained teeth were more appalling than Arik remembered. Arik peeked through the window. The beach was humming with joggers, walkers, swimmers, and other sun loving people. He pushed his chair back leaving more room for a quick up and out. "Okay, I'm outa here. See ya," he said while standing up, all set for a speedy exit.

"Wait!" Carmel pushed the menu back on top of the table. "Sit down. Please. We must talk before you go. I just want to finalize the order before we delve into business."

Arik hesitated for a moment. The hard-hitting approach caught him off guard. After all, he owed nothing to the dumpy, flabby old fart who'd been trying to exercise power over his freedom.

The waiter came by with the drinks. "Ready to order?"

Arik turned his head. "No. Not..."

Carmel interrupted. "We'll take the Tuna Steak; make it double." He turned to Arik. "It's really delicious; best in town. You'll enjoy."

"Is that all? Any appetizer?" The waiter had his list ready to develop further.

"No, thanks. That will be all," Arik broke off Carmel's attempt to embellish the order.

The waiter left their table, but Arik was still standing. "Are you going to tell me or do you want me to leave?"

"You need to relax. I'm going to tell you, but you need to sit down first. This conversation is highly confidential. It requires your full attention." He looked around to ensure privacy, waiting for Arik to pay heed.

Arik sat back down, but his legs were geared up for a swift breakout just in case.

"You may or may not know it," Carmel continued. "But you're one of a kind...Special."

"Yeah, I know. I'm unique, just like everybody else and their mother-in-law," Arik countered in a sarcastic tone.

Carmel took no notice. He wasn't smiling. He drew another breath, then paused while the hostess, followed by two women in their thirties, approached the glass-walled-cabin on route to the only available vacant spot next to their private room. He waited for them to settle down before continuing. "You were one of the best intelligence officers in the Israeli army. You speak perfect Arabic. Your IQ measures above 140. You grew up in a family that had escaped persecution and immigrated to Israel from Iraq in the early fifties. You absorbed culture and traditions common to the Middle East. And above all, you look the part."

"What part?" Arik glanced at his watch. It was only 12:35. He started sweating inside his shirt, already anticipating the response.

"The part where you go undercover, penetrate the Islamic terror network, rise in rank, then bring them all down," Carmel said. His voice trailed off. For a long time he was silent, letting Arik absorb the proposal. "And by the way," Carmel added. "Your trip to Bali is too dangerous. You can pretend to be an American, but you can easily become a target, even as an American, and once someone finds out the truth…"

"Look," Arik exclaimed. "I'm absolutely not ready for this conversation. I'm in love. I have my own dreams. Don't count on me to play the part or to redirect my life plan." He got up, faced the waiter who was standing next to him with a plate of fresh green salad in one hand and a long, hot, fresh out-of-the-oven focaccia in the other. Turning back to Carmel, he declared, "the answer is 'No Thanks.' That's not for me. I can't play that game. I have a life and I'm going to live it."

He turned back to the waiter, tore a piece of the focaccia, thanked the stunned fellow, then waved to Carmel. "Got to go, duty calls." "He, then, took off in a hurry.

• • •

Dan Carmel was boiling with rage. His rosaceous face was on fire. He looked as if he had just run home from the beach, either that or he was an alcoholic— neither of which was the case. The good news—he now had two, rather than just one, delicious tuna dishes waiting to roll up on his table. The other good news—his plan B was about to unfold. He looked around; privacy was not an issue. He was still alone and insulated. He picked up his mobile phone and dialed an international exchange number. The only sound emanating from the other end of the line was one of a forced cough. "Bad news," he announced. "Einstein is out on the loose." He took a breather, waited for another forced cough to resonate from the other end before carrying on. "*Operation Paradise* is on," he declared. "Unleash the snake. We've got no choice."

                              •   •   •

There was still an hour before Arik was to meet with Rachel, and the promenade along the beach was inviting. It was sunny, colorful, and the atmosphere was energizing. He would jog south toward Jaffa and back in time to meet Rachel in front of *Rafael*'s restaurant. He wasn't fully prepared for the workout. Except for a suitable black T-shirt with a front red and white print announcing, *The Dream Team Has Arrived*, he was wearing old sneakers and long blue jeans. It wasn't ideal, but still good enough for a casual jog.

Less than two minutes went by. Arik was doing fine when he spotted two men running east towards the American Embassy building, two blocks away from the beach. Another man was running ahead of them, apparently trying to get away. He looked young, less than twenty years of age, but quite frightened. His hair was short and black; he wore running shoes. His light gray coat extended all the way down to his knees, a remarkable sight on a hot day, which it was. The two chasers kept on yelling: "Stop! We're going to shoot." However, the runaway kid wasn't attentive. He sustained his flight. Arik joined the chase. He crossed the busy road separating the beach from the rest of the city, where a white Toyota Corolla almost ran him over. The driver started cursing, but Arik wasn't about to be bothered. He kept on running.

Two minutes into the chase, the security guard in front of the American Embassy was able to block the youngster who was running towards him. An explosion followed. Arik and the two chasers froze in place. It took a couple of seconds before the new realization hit his consciousness. Arik was about seventy feet away from the blast. His right shoulder was hurting, but he resumed his advance toward the two lifeless, torn cadavers slouched on the pavement in front of him.

The two chasers and Arik converged next to the charred bodies. One of them bent to take a closer look. The suicide-bomber's body was torn, his guts spilled out on the pavement. The dead guard next to him had his right arm ripped out of his body. It was resting on the street more than fifteen feet away.

Arik felt nauseated. He turned around, trying not to face the carnage. One of the chasing guards, a tall skeletal man in his late thirties, was standing behind him, just concluding a phone call to the police. "Why didn't you shoot him?" Arik asked. "Why didn't you shoot him?"

The guard lifted his hands in frustration. He had tears in his eyes. "I stopped him in front of the restaurant down there," he said in a Russian accent. He pointed to the beach. "He could've ignited the bomb, killing me in the process, but instead, he started running away. I thought he hesitated. I thought he had second thoughts. I wanted to save his life. He was a young kid, you know…God."

The guard wiped his tearing eyes, then stared at Arik for a full minute. His facial expression turned grim all of a sudden. "Hey, you're bleeding badly. Your shoulder… Let me see." He helped Arik remove the T-shirt. It wasn't easy. Blood was pouring out of the shoulder. A large nail, shot out of the bomb belt, must have struck that part of his body where the arm joined with the trunk. The guard folded the T-shirt and wrapped it around Arik's wound in an attempt to stanch the hemorrhage.

It only took a few more minutes before police, first aid, and a cleaning crew surrounded the place. Arik was still standing when the First Aid squad arrived. The dead were collected in a hurry, and the sidewalk cleaned from blood and debris. Arik was placed on a stretcher, taken to the ambulance, then rushed to *Ichilov* hospital. In twenty minutes, the place returned to normal. All evidence of the violent incident evaporated. The local TV crew arrived ten minutes later. They missed on most of the action, were unable to film anything other than a shot showing Arik being whisked away in the departing ambulance.

. . .

He had lost a great deal of blood, and was semi-conscious upon arrival at the hospital. It was dark outside when he finally opened his eyes. The ceiling above didn't look familiar. It was off-white with a little crack in the old paint. He didn't know where he was. His right hand was strapped to his body, restricting its movement. He tried to reposition it, but the pain was too sharp. He stopped. He thought of Rachel. *Did I just hear her voice?* He then remembered. She would be waiting for him on the beach in front of *Rafael*, not knowing why he was late... *Wait...* His memory started rebooting. *Dead charred bodies; blood—lots of it. Why am I here? My shoulder. I got hurt. Have I just heard Rachel's voice again? Where is she?*

Suddenly the room filled with people. His Mom, his Dad, more people. His Mom was crying. "Thank God, you're okay." She came closer, leaned over and started kissing his cheeks, his forehead, his cheeks again. She let go, turned around, and hugged his Dad. "He's okay, he's okay." Her curly black hair had more shades of gray than he could remember. Her eyes were moist; her thick bushy black eyebrows were in need of a trim. She was only forty-four, but today she looked years older. Sarah Golan married at eighteen and gave birth when she was less than nineteen years old. She was a few pounds on the wrong side of perfect weight, but still attractive. Arik was her only child. He had been delivered via a C-section, necessitated by last minute complications that put an end to her ability to bear more children.

Sarah raised her hand above the first row of people standing right behind her. "Rachel," she called out with excitement. "Rachel, come here. Arik's okay. Come." She pushed a couple of people Arik didn't recognize, and suddenly, Rachel's face was gazing at his.

"Hi, honey." Her smiling blue eyes transmitted an electric current. He felt it moving through his guts. He lifted his good hand and touched her hair, pulling her head closer to his. She met his lips and stayed glued for a long minute. "The Doctor said that you could be out of here in a couple of days," she whispered. "I'm so glad you're okay. We should cancel the trip. You may not be up for it."

"Oh, no," he asserted. "Don't cancel. I'll be brand new in a week. We're going."

"You sure?"

"Of course I'm sure. I feel fine. My shoulder is healing already." He paused, changed the subject. "What did they say on the news?" he asked.

"The suicide-bomber was a sixteen-year-old youngster. Abu Musa has taken credit for the terror act," she confirmed.

"He stared at her, frustrated. "I can't believe it. Last week when I was still at my desk in the military, I had him in my cross hairs. Since then, our men have missed this asshole twice. Both times, we held our fire because he'd surrounded himself with civilians. Where is God?"

Rachel leaned over and kissed him again. "You need your rest now. I love you."

As if on cue, the nurse came in and announced the end of visiting hours. The room emptied, the noise faded away. He was alone again. Exhausted, he closed his eyes and fell asleep.

Chapter 6

October 29, 2002—Egypt

It was an early autumn evening. Abu Musa was taking a stroll along the shady palm-lined beach of El-Arish. The sand was cool and soft. He took off his sandals and walked barefoot, leaving footprints on the moist sand. He was guarded by three Bedouins who carried their guns openly as they walked around him. The tourists who were still relaxing on the beach hardly noticed the armed gang and the bearded man with a casted arm in its midst. Most of them were collecting their belongings, preparing for a trip back to the nearby resort hotels after a long day of sunbathing. The small shops of Bedouin crafts that marked this northern sea resort town of the Sinai Peninsula were still open for business and quite inviting while the appetizing aroma wafted from the many restaurants lining the shore.

The leader among the three guards was walking about twenty feet in front of Abu Musa, as the other two, followed him from behind. Once they approached Fouad Zekri Street, the Bedouin leader noticed Hassan Naguib, the *Islamic Jihad* chief combatant, sitting on the balcony of the Sinai Beach hotel overlooking the shoreline. Naguib was enjoying the perfect weather while having a slow cup of coffee. He was wearing a white suit, a black shirt accessorized with a red tie, white socks, and white shoes. And although the sun had set an hour earlier, he was still wearing his dark sunglasses. It was in sharp contrast to Abu Musa, who looked worn out; his clothes in awful need of laundry; no socks over his bare feet, as he was holding a pair of old (used to be) brown sandals in his good hand.

The leader stopped walking and so did Abu Musa and the two Bedouin guards who followed from behind. He turned around, signaled to his followers to get close. "Mr. Abu Musa," he announced when they all gathered around him. "Mr. Hassan Naguib is waiting. You go and meet him. We'll leave after we see you on the balcony." The leader turned and signaled to the elegant, powerful, and rich looking man on the terrace. Naguib got to his feet, then hoisted his right hand in an inviting motion. Abu Musa responded in kind. The two had never met before, but the chemistry seemed to flow between them and touch both. They beamed.

• • •

It was 3 a.m. when the three Bedouin guards knocked on the door where both, Naguib and Abu Musa, shared a room that accommodated two unattached twin beds. "Wake up. It's an emergency." Naguib leaped out of bed and opened the door. Abu Musa got up as well, but his casted elbow slowed him down. With his right hand, he rubbed his eyes, trying to unglue the crust that kept them shut. He'd been submerged deep in sleep, dreaming about Paradise, when the three woke him up, returning him to reality. He was annoyed, but the adrenaline rush energized him and plucked him out of his dream world.

"The Egyptian police are on the lookout for you," the Bedouin leader declared. He stared at Abu Musa, then shifted to Naguib. "They've been asking questions. You must get out of town immediately before they find, arrest, and interrogate you. We have a car down in the parking lot. Both of you must go."

At the end of a three-hour drive through the desert, they arrived at the town of Ras Sudr where Abu Musa woke up. He had been napping for the past two hours while Naguib drove through the God-forsaken road crossing the arid land of the Sinai Peninsula. Abu Musa's fatigue was evident. For the past forty-eight hours, he'd managed less than three hours of comfortable sleep in a genuine bed. *Where are we?* he asked himself, rubbing his eyes and watching the blue waters of the Gulf of Suez fifty meters ahead. It was still early; the preliminary sunrays were announcing the new day. Several kite flyers and wind surfers were already in action on the sandy beach in the warm gulf, while Hassan Naguib was out near the waters, talking on his mobile phone.

Abu Musa got out of the car and started walking toward the waters. He noticed a fisherman's boat at some distance. It was an old vessel, brown and rusty. It wasn't moving; there was a man standing on its deck waving his hands toward Naguib, trying to get his attention.

Naguib ended the call, turned to Abu Musa who, by then, was standing next to him. "We're going to board this ugly boat," he said, pointing at the rusty vessel. "My friend will pick us up here in about an hour and take us in his little craft to the big brown boat over there." He removed his dark sunglasses and wiped the sweat off his forehead and eyelids. It was the first time that Abu Musa could actually see Naguib's green eyes. He was a good-looking man. His outward appearance projected a movie-star quality, enhanced by his green eyes, uncommon among natives of the Middle East. Still, Naguib considered his eyes' color a negative, a pointer to his ancestor-crusaders' origin, nothing to be proud of and the reason for his dark sunglasses.

"We can't use the port." Naguib continued. "We don't want paperwork or any other trail leading to our whereabouts. This fishing vessel will take us all the way to Sudan, where my men will be waiting. They'll pick us up at our landing site and take us to our clandestine training camp in the Sahara desert. Not even the Sudanese government knows about it."

"I didn't realize that you still have a Sudanese operation after the government kicked out our beloved Osama in 1995."

"This isn't exactly an operation," Naguib revealed. "It's simply a Bedouin camp in the desert. It's small and private, almost unnoticeable. We have experts in most aspects of guerrilla warfare tactics and methodologies. We only have a few select students. This is a private school, unlike the ones in Afghanistan. Here you get private tutoring and you earn your diploma in half the time." Naguib laughed as he went on describing the curriculum. "You'll be an outstanding student," he concluded.

Chapter 7

December 9, 2002—Bali, Indonesia

The trip from Tel Aviv to Bali took them through London where they spent an enjoyable week. They obtained new American Passports, then carried on to Denpasar, Bali, where Arik and Rachel landed at the end of a twenty-one hour journey. They were beyond exhausted. They took a taxi to their hotel—Bed and Breakfast. The brochure promised *"A nice and comfortable place, where you feel immediately at home and where you get good value for your money."*

It was early afternoon local time, but the only thought on their minds was sleep. They'd have plenty of time for sightseeing, hiking, eating, shopping, and vacationing throughout their stay. They'd spend a whole month in Bali, then move to Jakarta for a week, and explore Java for three more weeks. They'd then proceed to Sumatra, visit the Tanjung Puting National Park where they'd spend two weeks watching the slew of exotic animals.

They'd follow their three months in Indonesia with three more months in India, then return to Tel Aviv for a long joint journey through life.

It was nighttime when they woke up. "I'm hungry," Arik said. "Let's go out and find something to eat."

As they stepped out of the hotel, they were barraged by a mob of hungry drivers. "Transport? Transport?"

There were about twenty of them. Arik held Rachel close. He pushed past the first wave of aggressive drivers only to be confronted by another wave, in front of him, while the first group was following from behind. "Transport? Transport?"

Arik spotted a friendly face standing next to a black and white taxi. The driver was holding the rear door open, anticipating their quick move. They jumped in. He closed the door behind them. "Where we go?" he asked.

"Something to eat," Rachel said.

"Any specific?"

"How about a local authentic experience?"

"I take you to biggest night market — *Pasar Malam* — at Kereneng Terminal. You sit out under the stars and eat food is Javanese and Balinese. It's open till 10 p.m." The driver turned around. "My name is Ahmad." He passed Rachel a business card with his cell phone number. "I take you tomorrow to many nice places. You like?"

A bike swerved into their lane from the right without warning. The biker was trying to avoid a parked car on the side of the road. Ahmad reacted quickly, sharing the left lane with the oncoming traffic from the opposite direction. The traffic light in front of them was changing to red, but the biker must have considered that only as a suggestion. Ahmad paused at the red light only because he was trying to make a left turn. A leafy tree branch, intended to warn drivers about the large pothole, marked the road construction in front of them. Ahmad was constantly hooting his horn while trying to force drivers coming from the opposite direction to let him go through. He glanced in the rear view mirror trying to establish eye contact with Arik. "If I miss turn I must to drive far before turn back," he said.

Arik approved. "Fine." He turned to Rachel, "We'll get something to eat and then stop at a pub before walking back."

"I'm still tired," she said. "I may want to take a taxi back after we eat."

"Are you from Israel?" Ahmad asked. He'd heard them speak Hebrew. He then switched to the same. "I lived in Tel Aviv for three years. I learned your language. I took care of an old handicapped woman there."

Arik was taken aback. He hesitated. He just realized that he and Rachel had been speaking Hebrew. Earlier they'd agreed to refrain from using their most comfortable form of communication and resort to English. They were tired and weren't on guard. "We're

Americans," he responded in English. "Like you, we lived in Israel for three years, and we learned the language." The discovery of a common past warmed up the atmosphere. Ahmad seemed cheerful. "Hey, I like Israel," he said. "I had great time until authorities find out my visa no more good." He began singing *Hava Nagilah*...

"What happened then?" Rachel asked, interrupting Ahmad's performance.

"They deport me," Ahmad said. "No Problem. Now I'm back in Bali."

They drove five more minutes with no one uttering a word.

"Here it is," Ahmad announced. "Kereneng Terminal." He stopped the car and turned around. "I like you people." He winked, then produced a wise guy grin. "Call tomorrow. I take you nice places."

• • •

"Do you trust him?" Arik watched himself in the mirror. His face, covered with white shaving cream, provided a strong contrast to his dark-black thick hair, black bushy eyebrows, dark brown eyes, and tanned skin. He liked the picture. He regained his energy after a night's rest.

"Who?" Rachel, still in bed, turned on her side facing the bathroom. "What're you talking about?"

"Ahmad, the driver from last night."

"I like him," she said. "I like the fact that he spent time in Israel."

"I don't know, but there was something about him."

"I didn't see it. On the contrary..." She came over to the sink and stood next to him, watching him through the mirror. "In fact, I thought he was really nice. I can relate to him. After all, we have a common past," she giggled. "I would like him to be our tour-guide today."

He watched her through the mirror as well. She was wearing a see-through nightgown. Her blonde curly hair, wild and uncombed, covered half of her face. Her natural beauty needed no makeup. Her blue eyes watched him intensely. He turned and hugged her. "I love you. If you want to have Ahmad as our driver today, it's fine with me." Her nose and right cheek were now covered with his shaving cream. He smiled. "You look funny with soap on your face."

She picked up the shaving brush from the top of the sink and painted her chin, cheeks, and forehead with the white soap. "Now, if you really love me you should lick it off my face," she challenged him.

He tried to pick her up, carry her to the bed, but his sore shoulder and the associated pain, still endured as a result of the suicide bombing in Tel Aviv, precluded any further lifting. He abandoned ship; put her down quickly. Rachel recognized Arik's limitation. Reading his mind, she darted to the bed, let Arik pursue her as the game began.

An hour and a half later, they met Ahmad in front of the hotel. He was all smiles, ready to take them sightseeing around the island. Arik took charge. "We'll go west and visit the royal *Taman Ayun* temple in Mengwi and then the *holy monkey forest* near Sangeh and the famous *Tanah Lot*." He turned to Rachel. "This picturesque temple was built in the Sixteenth century on a huge rock one hundred yards off Bali's West coast and is surrounded by the sea during high tides."

She looked impressed. Arik had done his homework.

He continued with his instructions to Ahmad. "Later in the afternoon we want to see the *Mother Temple* in Besakih." Again, turning towards Rachel he explained. "It was built in the eleventh century at an altitude of one thousand meters on the slopes of *Mount Agung*."

"Wow, are you an expert? You should get a job as a tour-guide." She kissed him lightly on the lips.

"We'll do museums and some more temples in Denpasar tomorrow," he continued. "On the way to Besakih, I want to stop by the artisan villages of Ubud where we can watch stone carving. If we get lucky, we'll be able to watch local dancers perform a cultural show. Then, we'll go to the North coast, drive around, enjoy the views of rice terraces, and large plantations growing vanilla, chocolate, coffee, cloves, and wine grapes."

"Okay. I go by your plan," Ahmad said. He picked up his mobile phone and made a local call. Arik was able to decipher the contents of the conversation. Ahmad was reporting his itinerary to someone on the other end and was getting directions in turn. "Okay, we go now," he said. He started the car; they were on their way.

It took over thirty minutes of fighting traffic in Denpasar, but Ahmad was finally out of the city. The two-way road didn't provide much relief. Slow moving bicycles, horse carriages, and traffic from the opposite direction hindered their advance. "I go to Tanah Lot first," Ahmad said. "It's on way to Sangeh."

"Okay," Arik said.

They were moving along the Western coast when Ahmad made a right turn onto a side road leading to a roadside *Café and Gift Shop*.

"We don't want to stop here," Arik said. "We want to continue."

"Only couple minutes," Ahmad said. "I need cigarettes." He didn't wait for approval. He stopped the car, stepped out, and ran into the Coffee Shop.

"I don't want him to smoke in the car," Rachel complained to Arik.

"Don't worry, we'll make it clear to him when he comes back."

It was sunny and hot. The car was parked in the shade under a tree. A light breeze came in through the open windows. "Let's get out of the car, and wait outside," Arik said, as he opened the door ready to step out.

The car door was pushed closed from behind. Arik didn't have enough time to be surprised. Two men came from behind the car, one on each side. They opened the front doors, quickly moved in, then turned around, pointing their guns at Arik and Rachel.

Rachel moved closer to Arik, putting her hands around him in hope of getting more protection for both. She was terrified.

"Who are you?" Arik inquired. "What do you want?" His heart was pounding.

"Shut up," the older man screamed. "Don't move and no talking, or I shoot." He commanded the younger one in a local dialect to get going. He kept pointing his gun at both of them while the younger one turned around and started the engine.

Rachel was trembling. She held on tightly to Arik. He could feel and hear her wild running heartbeat.

"You!" The older one yelled at her. "You, move to right. No touch." He pointed the gun at her.

Rachel kept holding on to Arik, who kept staring at the agitated older man. "You move or I shoot," he yelled again. "Is last time I say."

Arik turned to her and kissed her on the head. "Rachel, do what he says."

They set out on the main highway, drove in silence along the West coast for the next five minutes, then stopped at a side road.

The two gunmen stepped out of the car. They opened the rear doors. "You get out of car!" the older one commanded. Arik hesitated; he waited for Rachel to step out first. The older man was angry; he had little patience. "You!" He hit Arik on his neck. "Get out!"

The instant Arik and Rachel stepped out of the car they were surrounded by four more gunmen who appeared out of nowhere. Two of these grabbed Rachel and pushed her into the backseat of an awaiting white car, parked behind several bushes along the edge of the road. Arik tried to protest. He made an unsuccessful attempt to free himself from his captors, move to rescue his girlfriend, but those men held him tightly. He struggled to get loose, but his grapple ended quickly. He felt a painful blow to his head just before plunging into darkness, losing consciousness.

When he regained awareness, he was lying inside the trunk of a moving car. He tried to reconstruct the sequence of events that had led to his present situation, but the pain in the back of his head distracted him. He was lying on his left in this cramped space, his legs bent, his left hand crushed under his body, his sore shoulder shooting distress messages to his brain, his right hand squeezed between his thigh and the trunk lid.

The car slowed down. He could hear the traffic noise surrounding it. They must have left the highway, entered a town or a village.

The car stopped. Arik freed his right hand and moved it to the back of his head. His hair was lightly caked with dried blood. It was dark inside the trunk, although a tiny crack next to the lock allowed a little light to pierce through, making the immediate area nearly visible to the adapted eye.

The car was moving again. The average pace was slow yet variable. Evidently, it was passing through dense traffic conditions. He stretched his hand to the edge of the trunk past his head. Moving it around he could feel the jack handle resting alongside the rim. Picking it up wasn't an easy task, but he managed. He turned around and was now lying on his back. His head and shoulder were hurting but he didn't mind the pain. He was intent on freeing himself at all costs. One more stop. He heard the car doors open, people stepping out. Arik hurriedly turned back to his original sideways position, pretending to remain in an unconscious state. The trunk lid was unlocked, then opened. He could hear two people discussing something, then the lid closed again. They didn't notice the change.

It took one additional minute; the car was back in traffic, moving slowly through busy streets. Arik stretched his hand again and grabbed the jack handle. He moved it close to his chest, then slowly turned his body, freeing his left hand from underneath. He placed the jack handle on the lid-lock and twisted. It snapped open. He quickly grabbed the lid with his right hand so as to prevent it from opening any further, or locking again. Waiting for the right moment and the proper car speed, he began to crawl out of the trunk; holding the lid with one hand, he pushed his legs out first.

It was an unusual sight. The driver of a Toyota minivan behind him couldn't believe his eyes. A man was coming out of the trunk of a gray Mazda in front of him. He started pumping his horn. People walking the sidewalks stopped their activities as they watched Arik's maneuvering himself out of the moving car trunk. All at once, grasping the new developments, the kidnappers changed pace. Attempting to pass the car in front, they crossed to the sidewalk. The frightened crowd, panicking, struggling to avoid being run over, opened a narrow passage for the car to pass through.

Arik's feet touched the ground, sporadically, intermittently. The wild ride slowed down as the gray Mazda hit a food stand, turning it upside down, spilling its content on the sidewalk. The accident made it possible for Arik to release his grip of the trunk lid. He fell to the ground instantly as the crowd hurried to check him out.

His left knee was hurting bad. The fall wasn't very smooth. In the meantime, the gray Mazda made its escape and vanished from the scene. A man stepped out of the crowd. He wore a police uniform. He bent and touched Arik's forehead. "Are you okay?" he asked.

"I don't know. They have my girlfriend."

"Girlfriend?"

"Yes, they kidnapped me and my girlfriend."

A short woman with graying hair stepped out from the crowd. "There is two men in car. No woman. I don't see woman."

"Please wait here," the police officer told the short woman. "I talk to you very soon." He turned back to Arik. "What's your name?"

Arik provided the officer with his American background and the unfortunate events of the day. Seeing the dried blood in the hair on the back of his head, the officer checked Arik's head for injury that might require immediate attention, but Arik dismissed it. He was concerned about Rachel. "She's been kidnapped. Please go look for her." He handed over Ahmad's business card, and asked the officer to follow through. The officer's nametag identified him as Subarto. He attempted to gain control over the agitated crowd. His efforts yielded fruit. He wrote down the Mazda's license plate ID, color, and year—1993-94.

More police cars arrived at the scene. Four officers jumped out seeking eyewitnesses and testimonies. Arik was getting impatient. He approached Subarto. "Please. I'm concerned about Rachel. Could you do something now?" He recognized that without further information, the officer couldn't initiate any meaningful search, but his anxiety was soaring; Arik needed action to relieve it.

"Where you stay?" Subarto asked.

"Denpasar."

"Okay, we not far. We in Kuto. We go now to police station. We look for car. We also look for your driver, Ahmad. You go with me to station."

"What about my girlfriend, Rachel?"

"You be patient. We look for car first, so we find girlfriend. Okay?"

Subarto let Arik take the passenger seat; they rushed to the station together. Once there, he led Arik to the reception area, then told him to sit and wait. The place was humming with people waiting, coming, leaving, crying with frustration. Arik closed his eyes, hoping that the scene would change and the nightmare would end. New arrivals and fresh yelling and screaming brought him back to the unwelcome reality. Two officers brought in five prostitutes. It wasn't clear whether these girls were criminals or victims. They were screaming at each other, crying, laughing, discussing something very exciting. Arik glanced at his watch. He'd been sitting there for thirty minutes, which felt like an eternity. He got up and walked to the receptionist.

"Can you check with Officer Subarto for the status of my case?" he asked.

The female receptionist didn't look at him. She continued watching her computer screen. "Subarto left for the day," she said without changing her focus.

"What do you mean? I've been waiting for him to investigate the kidnapping of my girlfriend." Arik's face changed colors. He thought he was going insane.

"I don't know." She finally raised her head and looked at him. "He left." There was lack of concern in her voice. It made Arik go crazy.

"Not possible," Arik insisted. He raised his voice. "He wouldn't leave without getting back to me."

"He left," she repeated, unmindful of his restlessness. She spread her hands. "I'm only a receptionist."

"No!" He wasn't letting her off the hook. "I need to talk to whoever replaced him on the case. You get someone here immediately." The strain was showing in Arik's tearing eyes.

The receptionist was finally responsive. "Okay. I'll find out. Please go back and wait in your seat. I'll let you know soon."

Arik went back. Sitting down, he was watching the receptionist as she was getting frustrated over the next several phone calls. He got up again; walked in the direction of her desk. He couldn't control his frustration; he needed to do something. Unexpectedly, Subarto came out of the door leading to offices inside the building.

"Come with me. We go to my office," he announced.

Arik felt thankful. Although he had no idea what had transpired, he felt better knowing that Subarto hadn't abandoned the case. "Is there anything new?" he asked as they made their way through the hallway.

"In my office." Subarto had no inclination for small talk or any business discussion other than the privacy of his office.

He opened the door, let Arik step inside, take a seat in front of a large desk filled with papers. Subarto moved to the other side, eased into his seat behind the desk, then faced Arik. He took off his sunglasses. Arik gazed at his eyes — dark, almost black, but nonetheless, matching his overall complexion. He was a short person with broad shoulders, clean-shaven, but surly, somewhere within the family tree he must have acquired scores of Indian genetic material. He had a dark mustache that concealed a scar stretching down from his upper lip to the right side of his mouth; it helped him project the tough image he strived to convey.

Subarto lit a cigarette, took a long drag, then followed with a longer puff. Arik was tense. He realized the news wasn't good; otherwise, he would know what it was by then. His hands were trembling; he was tapping his feet on the floor in rapid motion, calming his nerves.

"We find car. Is stolen. We not find men stealing car. We look for men." He took another drag out of the cigarette. "We find driver, Ahmad."

"Good, did he provide more information?"

"No. Ahmad say men steal car. He not know men. But we talk more."

"Is he here? Arik asked.

"Not here in Kuto, but we talk. We bring him here later."

"Now, we have message in Radio. From terrorist organization—*Jemmaah Ismaliyah*. Is say they get hostage, your girlfriend, Rachel Levy. They demand release of people bombing discotheque October 12, 2002. They say they want release Abu Bakar Bashir, Amrozi, his brother Ali Imron, Imam Samudra, Mukhlas, and Hambali—chief of *Jemaah Islamiyah*."

Arik knew the names. "Yes. Hambali, his real name is Riduan Isamuddin. He was the operational chief of *Jemaah Islamiyah*. He was also *al-Qaeda*'s 'point man' in Southeast Asia. He was arrested in Bangkok. He's in American custody and has not been charged in relation to the Bali bombing. The Americans were reluctant to hand Hambali over to Indonesian authorities because of the lenient sentence given to Abu Bakar Bashir."

"Yes you right," Subarto said. He scratched the back of his head, then leaning forward and getting closer to Arik, he employed the pencil he was holding as a drumstick while striking his desk. "They say they kill her if demands not met in forty-eight hours."

Arik leaped out of his seat. "Does the American Embassy know?"

"We tell American Embassy secretary." Subarto made a hand motion indicating he didn't know how effective the notification had been. "You go back to reception area. I have much work. I call you later when is more news." He got up as well. They walked together to the door. Subarto placed his hand on Arik's back, guiding him through the hallway into the reception area. "I call you when is news. You wait here," he said.

"I want to call the American Embassy," Arik told Subarto.

"Is late now. Only cleaning people in office."

"There must be someone I can alert or talk to. I need a phone."

Subarto paused for a second. "Okay. Come with me." He took him back inside, let him into a small office with a phone. "Call here. Is a number." He wrote the Embassy number on a piece of paper and handed it over to Arik. He left Arik alone in the room.

Arik watched the phone for a moment. He wasn't certain as to what he would say once connected. He would have to talk to a janitor, run over the events of the day. The janitor wouldn't be able to help. He would go crazy…He finally dared.

"Hello, this is the American Embassy. How can I help you?" The woman on the other side of the phone was polite, but all business.

"This is Arik Golan…"

"Yes we know about you. Are you OK?"

"No, but my girlfriend, Rachel…"

"We know. We're working on it. We want you to come over to Jakarta, to the Embassy. We're sending over a police helicopter to pick you up. Where are you?"

• • •

It was close to midnight when he arrived at the American Embassy in Jakarta. Gina McLloyd was waiting for him. She was the one he'd talked to on the phone. She had well groomed, brown hair with blonde highlights, a forty plus Caucasian whose fine-looking light brown eyes were covered by glasses with an ugly, pointy, green frame that added ten years to her middle age. Arik was exhausted, but the strain and the adrenaline were at their peak. He couldn't break away from agonizing about Rachel. Gina made a fresh cup of coffee, then served it with a smoked turkey sandwich. "You probably have not eaten all day." She sighed, sharing his grief with him.

"I'm not hungry," he said. "I'm upset. What happens next?"

"I don't really know. It's in the hands of the local police." She paused, mulling over a new idea. "However, since this becomes a case of international terrorism and the terrorists made demands on the US, we're getting involved. I called in Nguyen Van Nam. He will be in charge of the case. He will be in shortly to assume responsibility. You'll meet him when he arrives."

"What about the demands?" Arik asked. "Do you believe they are serious about their threats?"

"I'm afraid they're serious. They truly believe in their cause. These people are ruthless. They treat life cheaply, even their own. Their brains are sponged down with hate detergent, and they don't think rationally."

"We must do something to slow down their clock," Arik said, while pushing the small plate to the side of the table. He rose, started walking around the room. "Who's Nguyen Van Nam? What's he going to do?" he asked.

"Mr. Nguyen is our CIA man. He's well connected. He knows everybody. He has friends inside the Muslim world, China, Russia, Israel, and of course, in most of the US, Europe, and Asia. I'm sure he will find a way out of this."

"Does he know that Rachel and I are Israeli citizens as well?" Arik asked. He continued pacing nervously back and forth across the room.

"I wasn't aware of that," she said with a conspicuous air of amazement. "I don't think Mr. Nguyen does. That worries me." She appeared to have lost some of the self-confidence she'd possessed a minute before.

"I hope the kidnappers don't find that out," Arik said. He then repeated. "I hope the kidnappers don't find that out." The anxiety in his voice was apparent.

The telephone on her desk rang. She picked it up after the first ring, then listened for a couple of seconds. "Yes. Please come up to my office. I have Arik Golan here, waiting to see you."

Arik walked to the door, then looked out the hallway in anticipation of Nguyen's arrival. It was dead quiet outside the room. Some lights in the hallway were off, adding to the serene, but gloomy, atmosphere. The elevator door opened and out stepped an Asian looking fellow, with dark-skin; he was short and somewhat underweight. He glanced at Arik, then walked straight up to him with his right hand out for a handshake. "You must be Arik Golan," he said, grasping Arik's hand. "Let's get seated and go over all of the details." He had an Asian accent. Noticeably, he must have been a naturalized American citizen.

Arik followed Nguyen to another office. As they entered, Nguyen took a look at Arik. "You're Israeli, aren't you?" he asked semi rhetorically, then continued before Arik had a chance to respond. "Your name, Arik Golan, gives you away, but don't worry. We'll save her." He pointed to a leather couch in front of a large desk covered with papers that were stacked on the right side, then asked Arik to sit down while he moved around to take his seat on the other side of the desk.

Arik was puzzled by Nguyen's overplayed self-confidence. "What're we doing now?" he asked. He was still standing when Nguyen turned his computer on, adjusting his chair before finding a suitable sitting position. As he was picking up the phone, he pointed to the couch. "Please, Arik, sit down, relax, and make yourself comfortable. I'm taking care of the situation."

Arik couldn't bring himself to sit down. He was standing, watching Nguyen Van Nam, while the latter was being briefed on the phone by the Bali's police. Nguyen wasn't saying much except for an occasional "Uh huh." He was in a listening mode; Arik was unable to decipher the course the saga was taking. He approached the desk and touched Nguyen's hand. "What're they saying?" he interrupted.

Nguyen pressed on Arik's hand politely, signaling patience. It took two more minutes of anxious stares before Arik touched him again, only to have Nguyen duplicate his body language. Two more minutes went by before Nguyen laid down the receiver. He turned to Arik who was staring back anxious for news. "There's been no change since before you came here. There's been no new communication from the kidnappers. There's a lot of work I need to do to get the bottom of the case before moving forward." He got up, started pacing toward the office door. "Why don't you come with me," he suggested. "I'll have Gina find you a place to rest for the remainder of the night, while I dig further into your case."

Arik protested. "I can't sleep; I need to be on top of this. I want to be with you while you work it out." He stood in place refusing to follow Nguyen out the door and into Gina's office.

Nguyen stopped and turned around. "No way! These are sensitive negotiations involving the State Department, the CIA, Homeland Security, and some anonymous friends of mine. I can't let you in on this. But, trust me. I'll do my best and let you in on the good news as soon as I have any." He raised his hand, made a suggestive signal that Arik understood and abided by. He followed Nguyen to Gina's office, dropped on the couch, and closed his eyes.

• • •

It was 5:30 in the morning. Gina patted Arik on his shoulder, waking him up. Three hours earlier, he'd fallen asleep on the couch in her office. "There's a phone call for you. Pick it up on Line three."

Arik vaulted as if struck by lightning. "Who's it? Is it Rachel?" he was fancying a *'yes'*. He felt an adrenaline rush, taking him from semi consciousness to peak alertness. His heart was pounding at two-hundred beats per minute; his vocal chords dried up. It felt as if he'd swallowed baboon's hair that became stuck inside his throat.

He stared at Gina whose calm contrasted sharply with his excitement. "No. It's someone who says he knows you," she responded on her way out of the office. "I'll let you have your privacy while I go to the kitchen and fix us a fresh cup of coffee."

Arik picked up the receiver and cleared his throat. He held the receiver for fifteen seconds before managing to utter a word. "Hello, this is Arik Golan. Who are you?"

"Shalom Arik," the man said in Hebrew. "We were asked by the Americans to get involved. This is your old buddy from Tel Aviv, the one you snubbed in *Rafael*. Remember? It's Dan Carmel. We've not given up on you, and we're going to try to save Rachel and bring her to safety."

"How is she?" Arik asked.

"All indications are that she's okay. The kidnappers want to keep her in good condition for their own self protection as well as a bargaining chip."

"Is she in danger?"

"There's a definite risk, but we're in touch with some insiders. We're working with the Americans, and I'm cautiously optimistic."

"How long will it take?"

"We don't know. If we're unable to get closure within the next twelve hours, it may either take a long time before we secure Rachel's freedom, or it may be the end, but I'm optimistic. We already have some leads."

"How long? How long?" Arik wanted assurance. "Is there a deadline? They posted a deadline. Didn't they?"

"We're negotiating an extension. It seems to be working. They seem to respond to our pleas for extra time…Well…" Carmel seemed used up. It was after 1 a.m. in Tel Aviv. "I'll call you back in a few hours," he said. "No, I'm not going to sleep, if that's what you were thinking." He hung up before Arik had a chance to react.

Nguyen had called Dan Carmel for help, Arik concluded. Whom else did he call? What's he working on? Arik wanted to find out right away. He put down the phone and went out of the office looking for Nguyen. His office door was open, but he wasn't at his desk. Arik walked back to the hallway as Gina was returning with two fresh cups of coffee. "This one's for you," she said, handing it over.

"Where's Nguyen?" Arik asked, accepting the coffee cup from her. He was surveying the hallway; maybe the little Vietnamese man would pop up. It was still early and quiet. Other Embassy employees would start showing up in an hour or so.

"Mr. Nguyen went out two hours ago. He didn't tell me where to and why. I asked him, but he ignored my question." She reflected, watching Arik's evident frustration.

With nowhere to go for information, Arik strolled back to Gina's office, then settled down on the couch. She followed him, went behind her desk, then asked him to excuse her. She had to mind some paperwork before the dawn of another busy day. When scanning the office Arik noticed the woman's touch. A nice vase of flowers rested on a shelf to the left of her desk. A young plant was placed next to the window; a TV set was attached to the wall in the corner across from his couch. He closed his eyes, thinking about Rachel, how happy she was that morning when they ventured into their exploratory journey on the island of Bali. He was seeking to pin that vision into his memory when the office phone rang.

Gina picked up; ten seconds into the conversation, she turned the TV on and immediately switched to CNN. The local police in Bali was on the attack. The target was a suburban villa where

Rachel and her kidnappers were supposedly hiding. The gun battle was dying down when the TV crew started filming. The local reporter was telling the story of the kidnapping. He didn't mention Arik and Rachel by name, but referred to them as *The Americans*.

Both Arik and Gina were silent as they watched every pixel, listened to every word. Fire had ceased for the past five minutes but the local police were still positioned around the villa; they called for the occupants inside to surrender peacefully. Tension was mounting as no one came out the front door.

"Storm the house. Storm the house." Arik was yelling at the TV set. Tears were running down his cheeks. "What're they waiting for?" he moaned.

Gina didn't react. She was heartbroken, filled with overpowering sympathy. She was at a loss for words. The TV reporter was now interviewing the local police detective, Subarto, who was telling the story of the previous day, providing background and color. He added more details including names and a timeline. Arik was disgusted. "Do something! Stop talking and do something," he yelled at the TV.

As if they'd heard him, the police SWAT team started moving in while the camera followed their every move. It took no more than five nail-biting minutes for the news to come out—Two dead men and no sign of Rachel. Apparently, as some neighbors testified, they'd seen two cars speeding away from the scene minutes before the police surrounded the house. The reporter who'd helped develop the testimonies expressed a working theory—Rachel had been kept in the villa, but was hustled out by some of her captors in those critical minutes. "We missed her," he concluded sadly.

Embassy employees started arriving at their desks. Word leaked out that Arik was in Gina's office; although a few came over, trying to inject optimism and comfort to their apprehensive guest, many were glued to the TV watching the continuous coverage of the tense situation. It was midmorning when Gina's phone rang; Dan Carmel asked to talk to Arik.

"Listen Arik," Dan's voice sounded grim. He didn't feel like sugarcoating the real message with a standard small talk. He came straight to the point. "We lost track of Rachel. There's one unsubstantiated rumor, that she's been killed in retaliation for the slain gang members." Dan elected to break it all to him in one blow. "You better come back home and help us find her or her murderers from here. It will be easier and more effective than staying over there in the American Embassy, where there's nothing you can do to help the situation."

Arik refused to believe the sad news. "What about these rumors? Where do they come from?" he asked, his voice shaking.

"There's a web site these terrorists used in the past as one of their communications channels. It's not the most reliable one, but some of what it'd announced in the past turned out to be true."

"How did the police track down the villa?" Arik asked.

"Apparently, your driver was talking to some people in the bar about your whereabouts and your plans, including the stop at the gift shop. He told them you were Israelis. The local police interrogated him and the people he'd talked to. Moving through the chain, they were able to extract the intelligence. We and the CIA were helping as well."

Arik nodded. "What a screw-up," he moaned. "I warned Rachel, she forgot, and I got carried away. We spoke Hebrew. It's hard to break a habit when you do it repeatedly all of your life." He paused, then added. "Call me in an hour. I'll let you know what I'm going to do." After hanging up, he turned and faced Gina who was watching the breaking news on TV. The reporter had just confirmed Carmel's revelation concerning Rachel. She'd been declared dead. Gina was crying. She turned around and hugged him. They embraced, shedding tears on each other's shoulders.

"I'm going home," he said as he let go of her. "I'll hunt these animals down; make them pay for their crimes with the help of my friends in Israel. I won't rest until justice is served."

Chapter 8

December 12, 2002—Schiphol, Netherlands

At exactly 5.35 a.m. local time, KLM flight 810 from Jakarta landed in Schiphol airport near Amsterdam. It'd been a long, tiring, fifteen-hour journey, but Arik was all geared up for five more hours of airplane confinement that would take him to Tel Aviv. His thoughts focused on Rachel, his future without her, his anticipated undertaking, his new life mission, one that would bring closure to his craving to see justice done, while helping shape a better world at the same time. He collected his carry-on, stepped outside the Boeing 747, then walked straight past the gate into the airport "connecting-flights" corridor leading to the EL-AL gate.

"Keep walking but change directions, you have a change in plans," the voice behind him said. "You're flying to New York on KLM at 1:30 p.m." The talker was pacing behind Arik who stopped his advance, turned around to face his unexpected company. Arik's facial expression was one of a surprise. He didn't expect anyone to welcome him upon his brief stop in Amsterdam. The Schiphol encounter wasn't in the blueprint.

"Who are you?" Arik asked.

"Jerry," the stranger replied. "Dan Carmel is waiting for you in his rental outside, in front of the Arrivals Gate. It's important that you come with me now."

"I'll miss my flight to Tel Aviv, if I do get out of the airport."

"It's okay. Not to worry. It's all figured out," Jerry said.

"But why couldn't he meet me here?"

"He doesn't want to be seen in public together with you," Jerry said. "Dan is a branded figure inside the wrong circles; some jerk may take a picture of the two of you together." Jerry halted briefly, then moved his hand through his heavy dark brown hair. "Not a good idea."

Arik stared at Jerry — a skinny, tall person, about his height, about his age, a large, but well shaped nose. He had a beautiful smile, exposing straight teeth that must have been braced at a young age, light brown eyes with bushy eyebrows, a one, or perhaps two-day-old beard, thick, curly black hair bordering on an Afro, although in urgent need of a trim. Arik hesitated for a moment. *Is this a trick? Are these bastards from Bali seeking me out here in the Netherlands? No. Not possible. This Jerry guy, speaking English with a heavy Brooklyn accent, looks too much like a good Jewish boy from Yeshiva University.* "Okay," he finally muttered, then followed Jerry, past the passport check, outside the terminal.

The cold December air of a cloudy Northern European day greeted their exit from the terminal. Jerry moved quickly. He opened the rear door of a light blue Volvo, then invited Arik to step inside. He picked up Arik's briefcase, walked to the front door on the driver's side, opened it, placed the briefcase on the passenger seat, sat down, and made himself comfortable, then turned the ignition key.

It was warm and cozy in the back of the car. Dan Carmel, wearing a long black wool coat, offered his hand for a shake. "Welcome back, my friend," he said. He took off his sunglasses, replaced them with his bifocals, then smiled. His yellow teeth looked rather brown in the dim light of the moving car.

Why?" Arik inquired. "What's going on? Why here?"

"I want you to go to New York this afternoon," Dan Carmel said. "There's a critical change in the plan."

"Why New York?" Although he wasn't prepared, Arik was more forthcoming than at their initial encounter at the Tel Aviv restaurant. "What about the rest of my luggage?"

"I intend to tell you all about it, and don't worry about your luggage. It's being taken care of as we speak." Carmel stated. "Just listen for now."

"Okay." Arik was a bit anxious, but he realized that Carmel was now his gateway to the fulfillment of his new life's purpose.

Carmel leaned forward and spoke in a low voice. "We're placing you in a safe apartment in Manhattan at the heart of *Greenwich Village*. Before you board the plane to New York, you and I will go our separate ways. Jerry will be on the same flight with you, but you are not to acknowledge each other. You'll enjoy space, privacy, and comfort during the flight. You'll fly Business Class to the US. We won't meet face to face again until your mission is accomplished. In addition, I like your three-day-old stubble. You should continue to grow a beard and a mustache. The publicity you got isn't helpful, and you must distance yourself as far as you can from that identity."

"What about...?" Arik couldn't finish. Dan interrupted him in midsentence.

"Let me finish before you ask," Dan said. "You'll assume a new identity. You'll become Qassem al-Nasr, a Palestinian whose grandparents and their children moved to Iraq as refugees in 1948. That's where you were born. Your grandparents became Palestinian refugees—residents rather than Iraqi citizens, and over the years, one of their children, your father, got involved in local politics. Saddam didn't like your family, had them all executed, but you were able to escape their fate. You lived on the road and in hiding inside Kurdistan in fear of your life. You, Qassem, have no immediate family now. Your roots cannot be denied by tracing them back to the dead. You, Qassem, made your way to Cairo, Egypt, where you stayed for about five years before moving to the US. The details are inside this briefcase." Carmel paused. He picked up the heavy briefcase that was resting on his lap and placed it on Arik's. "Inside this briefcase you'll find a detailed history of Qassem's upbringing, pictures of your Iraqi parents, your new address in New York, keys to your apartment, five-thousand in cash and two credit cards with your new name." He paused, then added. "And by the way, Qassem al-Nasr was a real person, just in case someone decides to check you out." A slow smirk crept across his face. "We took care of him. He'd never challenge his stolen identity."

"Okay, got the picture, but what's the plan, the purpose, why am I doing all this? And more importantly, what about my parents, my friends, Rachel's family, don't they expect me back in Tel Aviv? Aren't they waiting for me at the airport?" He paused, looked down, then puffed in frustration. He lifted his head, gazed at Carmel. "Why America? It doesn't make any sense. I want to work on getting back at Rachel's abductors and killers; I can't do it in America."

"Yes you can," Carmel argued. "Here's the deal. It's come to our attention that Abu Musa, your old nemesis, has been hiding and operating outside Gaza. We don't know just where; we're still trying to find out. However, this arch terrorist, whom you know well, has forged a new pact with *al-Qaeda* elements. Their fresh purpose is to infiltrate Israel through Ben-Gurion, our international airport, by newly recruited agents, American citizens of European and Asian descent, most likely, Muslims from former Yugoslavia, South East Asia, including Indonesia, even Bali, who wouldn't raise too much suspicion upon arrival."

"And you want me to infiltrate this network, join the game, then expose them," Arik concluded.

"Precisely," Carmel concurred.

"But what makes you believe they can be successful if I do not play a part in your scheme?"

Carmel kept his cool. He was determined to make his way deep into Arik's soul, convert him into a willing *Mossad* agent. "Let me put it to you this way," he said. "We'll be a hundred times more successful if you come with us." Then aiming at Arik's sweet spot, he added, "And we'll have a significant chance of learning about the Bali kidnappers through your newly established American connections."

"Are you serious?" Arik was taken aback. "Are you telling me that I may find my kidnapper friends or their associates in the US? It sounds like a long shot."

"It may be a gamble, but it's a real possibility. More important, however, is the fact that you may be in on Palestinian or Iranian plots to blow up Jewish establishments in the US, launder large sums of money, including funding arms purchases and sending them over to the Palestinian territories. In general, if you get in on some of those terror plots, we may be able to help US' homeland security and trade information for other crucial benefits."

"You know," Arik said. "You're telling me...You're not asking me. You want me to forget who I am, forget my family, forget my friends, stop thinking about why I'm here, and then go on a lifelong, lonesome mission." He halted briefly, swallowed hard, watched Dan Carmel's attempt to interrupt his thoughts, then continued before the latter had a chance to cut him short. "I'm sorry," he threw in. "But this kind of a choice requires a better frame of mind. I'm not ready, and I'm not convinced that this is the best way to serve my present goals or even my country. I can't accept this mission. I'm going back to Tel Aviv," Arik said. He picked up the briefcase from his lap and handed it back to Carmel. "Hey, Jerry," he turned to the driver. "Please go back to the airport lest I miss my flight to Tel Aviv."

"No one expects you in Tel Aviv," Carmel declared. "We informed all concerned parties that you'd stayed behind in Bali looking for Rachel. In about a week, we'll have you "killed" by the terrorists. Your death will be announced on one of their websites. It will include an old picture that we distorted enough so that your face doesn't look at all like the real you, especially with your new facial hair. And, incidentally, we'll collect your luggage in Tel Aviv." Dan didn't even try to hide the extravagant smirk.

"Very funny," Arik countered.

"There's one more important piece that you should consider before saying No," Carmel stated.

"And what would that be?"

"If you refuse the mission," Dan continued. "We, i.e., the concerned Israeli authorities, will close the case. Rachel's abductors will keep on roaming through their landscape, and Rachel's whereabouts will never be known."

"The Americans wouldn't rest until they get some answers, and of course, the Indonesians will keep on looking," Arik argued.

"No. You're wrong," Carmel said. "The CIA has more than plenty on their plate. It's a matter of priorities. We'll tell them that we're not interested, and they'll drop the case for its diminishing value. The Indonesians will keep investigating, but without pressure from the Americans, they'll also amend their priorities."

"Still," Arik insisted. "I need more time to digest all this before embarking on a new and lonely life."

"No, you're wrong again," Carmel countered. "What if Rachel is still alive? What if time is of the essence? What if your acceptance of my request can save her life?"

"I thought she was dead, is she not?" Arik's eyes turned moist with excitement.

"We have no solid proof of her fate. Her body has never been recovered, and she's worth more alive than dead. There's a pretty good chance that she's still alive."

"I hope you're right," Arik said.

"You'd better believe it, and take up your new mission if you want her saved."

"Are you blackmailing me?" Arik asked.

"I don't call it that," Carmel said. Then, in the manner of Marlon Brando's Godfather, he added. "I'm making you an offer you can't refuse."

Arik held his breath. He wasn't amused. He was mad, offended at the thought that Carmel would let Rachel's situation deteriorate all the way to hell, unless he came through with a *'yes'*. He felt he was pushed to the wall. "Okay," he finally surrendered. "You win. I'll do it, but…"

"There's no but," Carmel butted in. "Just do it, and we'll do our part. Believe me, you won't regret it, and it won't be as awful as you think."

"So what happens now?"

Carmel picked up the briefcase from his lap and placed it back in Arik's. "Before we answer this question, there's more." Carmel pulled a cigarette from his coat pocket and lit it. "Excuse me," he said. "May I smoke?" He didn't wait for an answer. He took a long drag, then continued. "You'll use your credit card only for relatively minor personal expenses when cash isn't an option. You'll use your checking account just to pay off the monthly credit card balance.

You'll keep a small balance in your bank account and replenish it with cash deposits on a regular basis."

"Where does the cash come from?"

"Here's one key to a safe deposit box at the Bank of America branch at the *SoHo* on Broadway. I'm keeping the other key. The box will contain an average of half a million dollars in cash. It will be replenished on a regular basis. We'll also use the box for communication. You mustn't call anyone in Israel and must avoid Israeli friends or acquaintances. I'm talking about those who are not part of the team. The box is one way for reaching out to us and obtaining feedback. Inside the box, you'll find your new documents, including a new American Passport and your old Egyptian passport. You'll have a support system, including Jerry here, whom you'll be able use, as well for sending and receiving messages. And, of course, you'll find CDs with copies of the spying software you developed while in the Israeli military."

"You'll have a PC with built-in standard software. You'll use it only for your business—your fictitious business. You'll fabricate correspondence between you and some imaginary business associates and contacts. You'll write and you'll respond from a separate laptop PC that you'll purchase in New York. The email accounts have already been set up. You'll leave a trail full of beans inside your PC. The only purpose of this PC is to help establish your new identity and background in the eyes of those who'll want to either trust you or expose you by accessing it without your knowledge. You'll never use it for any personal or other purpose. You'll take care of all your other communications needs by other means. Particularly, your phone calls. In addition to diverting calls through international exchanges, so as to mask their origins, every call you make will have to be secured by a scrambler, built into your cell phone or the device you will find inside the safe deposit box. Anything under other circumstances—you'll figure out a way."

Arik closed his eyes. He needed a minute to himself to absorb the gyration his life was about to take. Carmel waited for him to come around before continuing.

"Your official residences in the *Village* and the safe apartment on the *Upper West Side* have nice closets filled with your new clothes. They're packed with everything you need. In addition to the PC, you'll have two mobile phones, Satellite TV, and plenty of other stuff. But back to our agenda." Carmel took a final drag before extinguishing his cigarette, then continued. "You'll have to establish roots and track records among the Islamic community somewhere outside the Middle East. New York and New Jersey are good places. You ought to rise to prominence and become a respectable leading figure in this community and beyond." Carmel leaned back and looked at Jerry who was driving around with no particular aim. He felt at ease and kept on going. "All throughout, you must live in the shadows; you must avoid publicity outside your Muslim community. You must become the invisible puppet-master in charge of terrorist cells, whether they're PLO, *Hamas*, *al-Qaeda*, or Iranian missionaries—members of *Hezbollah*."

"I guess you wouldn't mind if I spend some time looking for Rachel's murderers," Arik asked rhetorically. He knew the answer. It fit in well with his mission. This was the unwritten deal behind his recruitment. Carmel and the rest of the *Mossad* understood it.

"Of course…and we'll help you. This is part of the deal."

The car stopped at a red light. Carmel looked outside as if he were expecting to see someone familiar inside one of the adjacent cars. He turned to Arik. "You'll have our personnel support including extra safe houses throughout the US. "You'll find an essential part of your support system in the Starbucks Coffee on 39th Street. Jerry, here, is the main man behind the counter. He also manages one of the safe houses, the apartment I've mentioned earlier, on the *Upper West Side*. Jerry will set you up with additional training and opportunities. You won't be alone even if it felt that way to you." The car stopped in front of the main train station. Carmel pulled out another cigarette. "I'm saying good-bye for now," he said before stepping out. "Between here and New York you'd better study the material in the briefcase, memorize it, and then dispose of everything that may seem suspicious to those who try to uncover your true identity. The information inside the briefcase is limited to Qassem al Nasr's history and background. Nothing inside gives your mission away. Still, when you get to New York, destroy the stories but keep the pictures. With your innate intelligence, you'll be able to figure out on your own what your next move should be."

"Before you go, I wonder, what does Qassem do for a living?" Arik asked.

"It's complicated. You become a magnet for terrorists. The complete manuscript is all in the safe deposit box. And one more thing," Dan suddenly remembered. "Your next door neighbors in your new *Village* apartment are working for us. They don't know who we really are. They don't know that we're Israelis. All they know is that they work for us and do what we tell them. They're well connected to some people whom we want you to get to know and establish close relationships with. They'll also take care of some of your needs, as well as spying on you and let the "right" (he made a hand motion signifying quotes) people have access to your manufactured personal information."

Carmel opened the car door and placed his feet on the ground outside. Arik leaned toward him; they shook hands. Carmel turned forward and out, ready to leave, but then changed his mind; he turned back to face Arik. "And by the way, since you'll use your existing American passport for the trip to New York, you'll become Qassem only after you leave JFK on your way to your new apartment." He paused, then continued before Arik had a chance to respond. "And one more thing, use your perfect Arabic accent when speaking English."

"Oh. It's good you've told me. I wouldn't have figured it out had you not mentioned it," Arik said mockingly in English, employing that pure, unadulterated Arabic accent.

"Sorry. I didn't mean it that way, just that... Okay, enough said." Dan Carmel winked, then turned around, stepped outside, only to vanish inside the train station.

Jerry took off with Arik still wondering about his altered life plan. Jerry had been quiet after taking the wheel. He now peeked at the rearview mirror; spotting Arik's bewilderment, he tried to strike up a conversation. "You're going to be alright," he said. "It's not as bad as you think. Your life will be full of excitement."

Arik didn't respond. His thoughts were elsewhere, in Bali, with Rachel. He wondered how she was doing. *Is she still alive? Has she been tortured?* He tried to picture her face. She was smiling. She stared at him with love and admiration.

"We're back at the airport," Jerry's voice interrupted his thoughts. "Why don't you step out and check in to your US flight. You still have a couple of hours, but time flies inside the terminal."

Arik stepped out of the car and walked in. The airport was humming with people talking, running, saying good-bye, eating, drinking. His thoughts carried him, once again, back to Bali, to the great time he'd enjoyed with Rachel. He would never forget her and would never stop searching for closure. His new project was, after all, the perfect path to remedying his mental state. He needed a new life; he was lucky to reap it so naturally. He peeked at his watch, then went to the bar.

"One Heineken for the road," he told the bartender. *Last one before I become a devout Muslim*, he reflected.

Chapter 9

December 12, 2002—Bali, Indonesia

It was evening when Rachel and her two kidnapper-guards arrived at a remote village in Bali. She had no idea where she was. The kidnappers had placed her in the trunk of the car where she'd been slumped with her hands tied for a couple of hours or more.

Upon their arrival, they picked her up, dragged her to a small house, then pushed her into a tiny room; they didn't bother to untie her hands. They left the room and locked the door. The place was rather dark. A narrow beam of light sneaked in through the slit between the door and the wooden floor. As her eyes got used to the dimness, she surveyed the room, trying to become familiar with her new home. She noticed a torn, stained mattress stretched out on the floor in one of the corners. She pulled herself in its direction, and once there, she parked her fatigued, aching body on it in a sitting position. After one minute in the dark, she found herself lying on her left side. Her right ribcage and back were aching from the squeeze she'd endured inside the trunk of the car. She was weak and exhausted. She lost track of time and was suffering from dehydration and a severe headache. She closed her eyes; *no need to keep them open.* She let her mind drift off; it didn't take long before she passed out.

When Rachel opened her eyes, she was looking at a young twenty-year-old Asian woman who was giving instructions to someone whom she couldn't see, in a language she didn't understand. The Asian woman seemed agitated; Rachel couldn't discern the woman's attitude toward her. *Was she friendly, hostile, indifferent?* Rachel couldn't tell. She now regained her senses; her hands were no longer tied. This was one new, longed-for aspect of her new condition. She studied the woman who'd just draped her with a yellow sheet used for a blanket. The woman's hair and part of her face were covered with a head style abaya (a loose fitting, full-length, robe); she wore some weird bluish makeup, and she had a fresh red scar on the left side of her neck.

"Do you speak English?" Rachel asked the Asian woman.

"Shhhh." The woman raised her index finger to her lips.

Rachel tried to rise and sit up on the mattress, but the woman pushed her, forcing her back to a horizontal position. "Nooo," she whispered. She pointed her hand to the door leading to the next room. "Boom, Boom," she described a potential reaction coming out of that location.

For the first time, Rachel noticed the tiny room in which she was kept prisoner. It felt more like a full-size walk-in closet. There was an old light fixture hanging down from the ceiling in the center. It contained one light bulb generating no more than twenty-five watts of power. There were no windows, bare walls with no pictures or shelves; both the floor and the ceiling were made out of unfinished plywood. Although there was little light, she could still see the nails, some of which bent in, holding the structure together.

A young boy, somewhere between five and six years of age, entered the room. He was running barefoot as he approached the Asian woman. His bare chest revealed a striking degree of malnutrition; his ribs were showing through nearly transparent skin. He was wearing gray bottom underwear with nothing else. Rachel noticed some resemblance between the boy and the woman. *She must be his mother.* The young woman yapped at the young kid, then sent him out of the room.

A minute later, the boy came back with a glass of water. He handed it to his mother who picked it up, turned, then offered it to Rachel. When Rachel tried to rise and sit up before taking a sip, the woman pushed her back, took the glass away, looked at the little kid, then said something that Rachel interpreted as, "check to see if there's anyone in the other room." The boy ran to the door, peeked through it, then indicated that they were in the clear. Only then did the woman lend a hand to Rachel, helped her sit up and drink the water.

Rachel began to grasp the situation. *The woman could be friendly but she was probably afraid of the guards who treated her as their slave. And odds-on, they didn't take it lightly if she became too sociable with their prisoner.*

Since these men were outside watching the premises, Rachel felt safe asking again, "do you speak English?"

For the first time since she saw her, the woman put on a smile. "Yes," she said, then after a short pause, she added, "a little."

"What's your name?" Rachel asked.

"Tuti," she answered with a smile.

"I'm hungry," Rachel said. "Can you get me something to eat?"

Tuti rose from the floor, picked up her son's hand, then looked back at Rachel. "You stay here. I come back soon," she said, before mother and child withdrew to the other room.

Rachel was desperate for a bathroom break. The fresh water awakened her digestive system. She hadn't relieved herself since her capture, and at that moment, she was under heavy pressure. She got up and marched toward the door. The next room had a cooking corner where Tuti and her little child were busy working. The woman was cooking rice; the boy was playing with pots and pans on the floor next to her. The room had a table, three chairs, two couches and a TV set. A door next to the cooking corner was half-open; Rachel noticed part of a fixture that looked like a toilet seat inside. She coughed in order to draw attention; Tuti turned around and noticed her at the door that connected the two rooms.

When their eyes met, Rachel noticed Tuti's tense stare. Rachel didn't think of asking for permission. She pointed at the bathroom and said. "Toilet. I must go now." She started marching in the direction of the bathroom. Tuti froze in place. Apparently, she wasn't given definite instructions regarding the details of guarding the prisoner. She mumbled something in her native tongue but didn't impede the determined captive's advance.

Once inside the bathroom, Rachel closed the door behind her. She quickly relieved herself, then took note of the tiny room. The door swung into the bathroom when opened. Once a person was inside the little den, there was little space left for the door to swing open by more than thirty degrees. Getting in and out of that nook required some serious maneuvering around the door. On the other hand, the window above the toilet seat was large enough for someone like her to sneak through and break out when opportunity arose.

Just then, one of the guards appeared unexpectedly inside the house. He began talking to Tuti, then within less than fifteen seconds into the conversation, he started screaming, apparently upset about her letting Rachel go into the bathroom unsupervised. He followed his screeching by walking toward the bathroom door. Rachel could hear his approaching steps as her heart began racing. The guard opened the door only a fissure before Rachel's body blocked it. "You come out of there," he barked.

"You'll have to let me do it," she responded. "Please close the door so I can move aside before opening it wider." She knew he was waiting outside; if she tried sneaking out through the window, he would be able to open the door wide, then grab her from behind before she was out. The only choice she had at that point was cooperation.

Once she came out, the guard pushed her back into the tiny room in the rear, turned the light off, then locked the door. Rachel was, once again, alone in the dark, hungry, tired, anxious, and frustrated, nonetheless, mulling over an escape plan.

It took an hour before Tuti turned on the light from the outside and opened the door to Rachel's room. She was carrying a rice-filled bowl and a glass of water. Her little boy accompanied her. He was holding onto her skirt; his eyes were reddish and teary.

Rachel stared at the little boy and couldn't help but reacting. "Oh, you've been crying, what's your name?"

Tuti answered with a whisper. "His name's Budi. He cry. Man hit me." She lifted her skirt and pointed to a purple spot on her left thigh. "Man kill my husband. Take my home. I afraid."

Rachel stared at her; she now realized she had an ally. Tuti may help her escape, or better, all three of them might escape at the first opportune moment. "We must flee before they kill us too," Rachel whispered.

"No! Man watch outside house," Tuti murmured. "Man watch outside and inside on night."

"Is anybody inside now?" Rachel asked.

"No now. Man outside now."

"I need to go to the bathroom," Rachel said after drinking the water and chewing on the rice.

"Man said to leave door open when you go to toilet."

"Okay, I'll leave the door partially open."

As soon as she was in the bathroom, Rachel closed the toilet cover, then climbed on top of it and inspected the surroundings through the bathroom window. She was unable to get a full view because the house next door, about fifty feet away, blocked much of her visual field in that direction, while to her left and to her right, the view was constricted by trees and bushes.

She spotted one of the two guards sitting next to one of the bushes, smoking a cigarette, talking on a cell phone. He'd just concluded his conversation; he was prepared to stand up. His focus turned to the house. He seemed to be staring at it with something in mind; Rachel assumed that he was about to come in. She quickly stepped down from the toilet, left the bathroom, then hurried back to her little room. Tuti was watching her nervous dash, as Rachel bumped into her on her way back. "They're coming in," Rachel divulged before going in and closing the door. She was scared shitless and hoped to have as little to do as possible with this approaching beast.

Tuti scurried to collect her young son and hold him close before the approaching warden crossed the doorstep. The man entered but didn't take notice of the frightened little woman and her whimpering child. He charged straight ahead toward the door leading to the little room in the back. Rachel heard the approaching steps and instinctively retreated into the corner. She cowered there, anticipating her next nightmare.

The man opened the door and stood there. He didn't move inside, but rather let his eyes survey the room. He noticed Rachel, but his abiding rage didn't seem to be affected. He uttered something that Rachel interpreted as a curse, then closed the door and locked it. Rachel was alone again. The man continued cursing as he turned his attention to Tuti, then started hitting and cursing her at the same time. Rachel could hear the punching and the screaming that followed. *Poor Tuti,* she reflected, *she's being punished because she hadn't locked my door. We must escape together.*

The screaming and the beating stopped; they were followed by a long silence. Rachel kept her position in the corner of the room, frightened, and stressed. She didn't know what was happening on the other side of the door. *Is Tuti still there? Is she okay? Is she alone?*

Two or more hours passed, nothing changed. Rachel was getting thirsty. Although she'd eaten no more than a small bowl of rice during the past forty-eight hours, she didn't feel famished; she wasn't longing for food. She got up and walked up to the door that separated her from Tuti. She stood next to it and listened. The only sound she could perceive was that of an utter silence. She knocked on the door and called Tuti's name, but still, no reaction or new sound from the other side. She started pounding on the door and calling Tuti, but nothing happened. Rachel raised the volume of both the banging and the yelling, but to no avail, as the prolonged sound of silence reverberated all around her.

Suddenly, the two men rushed into the house. She could hear their racing blast as they approached the door. Rachel shifted her way to the corner, then stood there in terror, as the door to her room was being unlocked. Both men came in. One of them approached her, grabbed her left arm, and pulled her close. She could get a whiff of his tobacco-tainted breath. "You're mine now," he announced.

The other man didn't seem to agree with the grabber. "Hey, Guntur, no!" he yelled, then followed his words with some local dialect that Rachel, watching his body language, interpreted to mean, "Hurry up, we must get out now."

Immediately following the first man's objection, Guntur grabbed Rachel by her right arm, then both men whisked her out of the room. On their way out of the house, Rachel noticed Tuti's body slumped on one of the couches in the main room. Her face was smashed; her eyes and mouth were covered with dry blood; there was blood on the floor next to her. She looked lifeless. Her little boy wasn't in the room. Outside, the two men lifted Rachel off the ground and pushed her into the trunk of their waiting car. Rachel wasn't wholly certain, but she believed that she'd just seen Tuti's little son in the backseat of the car. Before placing Rachel inside the trunk, the second man picked up a bottle of water and handed it to her. "Be a good girl and be quiet," he said. "We go for a long ride."

Chapter 10

December 12, 2002—The Sudanese Sahara

Three weeks passed following Abu Musa's arrival at the training camp in the Sudanese Sahara, far away from the watching eyes of the Israeli and Egyptian security services. He was a devout Muslim before, but three weeks of five daily prayer services, mid-morning Koran studies, mid-afternoon indoctrination lectures, together with military along with weapons and explosives training in between, turned the apprentice into a professional. It was now time to prepare for graduation; this was when Hassan Naguib, his Egyptian mentor, who'd deposited him in that splendor, came to visit.

"You're no longer a Palestinian leader," Naguib asserted. "From now on, you're a Muslim chieftain. You must follow Allah's will and devote yourself to Allah's command. The Zionist regime in Palestine is only one of your enemies. Your biggest foe is the Americans and their allies. They're the reason for your suffering. They're the reason for everything you hate, for everything Allah outlaws. They're the reason for the Zionists' fleeting successes. They're the reasons for the flooding of our sacred lands with infidels. They're using our natural resources to come back and oppress us. They're trying to spread their corrupt culture in the Middle East. They're Satan's commissioners."

Abu Musa nodded in agreement. It was a hot day, a 95-degree Sahara desert sun hitting on his head from above. He was thirsty, had little patience for a lecture concerning the enemies of Islam. He'd learned this part before Naguib came to the picture.

"What's next?" he asked, grabbing a bottle of warm water and pouring half of it into his open mouth.

Sensing impatience, Naguib changed course. "In a couple of days, you'll depart on a journey that will eventually earn you a place in Paradise. You'll go to Bonn, Germany, where you'll meet your new brothers and form an Islamic cell. You'll integrate into the community and become a well-mannered resident. Your neighbors will only have praise for your cleanliness, helpfulness, and friendliness. You won't flaunt any of your true thoughts, aims, or Islamic devoutness outside your cell and your inner circle. You'll be careful with whom you associate." Naguib lifted his hand and touched Abu Musa's face before carrying on. "You'll shave your beard and mustache and wear European clothes, all with Allah's approval. You'll assimilate within the community in which you live, with the aim of ridding yourself of any suspicion."

Abu Musa glared at the elegant man in front of him. Naguib was wearing his habitual double-breasted white suit and red tie, an appearance that stirred up feelings of detachment in Abu Musa's mind. *This green-eyed, rich son of crusaders is not about to order me around. He has no clue and no brains.* Abu Musa had different objectives in mind. His timeline wasn't as long as Naguib had suggested. He was seeking to establish himself as second in command, and in mystique, only to the greatest one—Osama Bin Laden, not to Naguib. He wouldn't sit and wait to be assimilated. His aim was pressing, his tactics—daring. Abu Musa raised his right hand breaking off Naguib's discourse. "Do you have a passport for me?" he asked.

"That's why I came in person," Naguib responded. "You'll travel with two passports. The one you'll use to enter Germany draws on the name of Ahmad Abu Rmeiyeh from Qatar. Upon leaving Germany, you'll use a British passport under the name of Amin Shukri. These will be your new names until we change them, Allah willing. You'll also have two credit cards, one per new identity. You may be able to draw cash and pay for your needs with these cards."

"Why Germany? I thought that we had better opportunities in the United Kingdom. The Brits are just as evil as the Americans are. They should bear the consequences." Abu Musa said.

"The Germans are weak," Naguib countered. "If you ever get arrested for any reason, we'll always be able to get you out. Remember the Munich Olympic games?"

"You mean the release of the three brothers who were supposed to go on trial in Germany for the kidnapping of the Israeli athletes? Of course I remember," Abu Musa said. "After the hijacking of the Lufthansa airline in October, the Germans released our heroes in no time, and sent them to Libya."

"In fact, the October 29th hijacking that followed the Munich triumph was only a show, concocted by Germany and the PLO," Naguib said. "These German idiots released our brothers for fear that Germany's own shortcomings and mishandling of the hostage crisis would be exposed during trial proceedings. The staged hijacking provided a first-rate excuse for ditching the trial altogether." He placed his hand on Abu Musa's shoulder and continued. "But you won't get caught. We have good people in Bonn. They'll protect you, and you'll lead them to glory."

"Okay," Abu Musa agreed. "What really does Osama want me to do in Germany? Can you be more specific?"

"It's a long term plan," Naguib embarked on a wide-ranging lecture. "*Jihad* is not about killing a few people. Rather, it's about conquering the world to its entirety. It's about crowning Islam as the master religion; it's about having *Sharia Law* become the law of the land—all of the land; it's about subjugating the infidels, forcing them to a *dhimmi* status, having them pay high taxes and serve their Muslim masters."

Abu Musa looked bored. "Why are you telling me everything I already know?" he asked.

"Because you must understand that true *Jihad* takes time. It can take a hundred years or more. We can accomplish our objectives via immigration followed by a high birth rate. We can change the world's cultures and laws by utilizing democratic measures, and once we achieve a critical demographic mass in a Christian, Jewish, Buddhist, or any other land controlled by infidels, we resort to intimidation, then follow through with violence before the final putsch." He paused, smiled with satisfaction. "I learned that final part from Hitler. Germany is a good place to get started."

Abu Musa became impatient. "Look, I don't have any patience for theoreticians. I can't wait for any great grandson of mine to enjoy a world free of infidels. As far as I'm concerned, my *Jihad* is current. I am already at the final phase you've described—the Hitler phase. I'm going to Germany, but you'll hear about me in no time. Osama doesn't see it your way. He sees it the 9/11 way, and I'm marching to his drum beat." Abu Musa paused. He stared at Naguib's sunglasses, then in a sudden shift, he lifted his hand and removed them from Naguib's face, then glared at Naguib's green eyes. "You have German ancestors," he said. "I understand you perfectly, but no. This is not the mission that I have chosen. Unlike you, I'm pure. I'm Son of Ismail—son of Abraham, I'm ready to die for a cause. That's where I'm headed." He returned the sunglasses to Naguib. "When do we leave the camp and get on with the plan?" Abu Musa asked.

Naguib looked embarrassed and weighed down. He shrugged to himself. *Let him think what he wishes, the time for a lengthy discussion is over.* "Tomorrow at daybreak we go back to the Red Sea and travel by boat to Egypt. We'll land north of Ra's Gharib. A brother will be waiting for us and take us by car along the Gulf of Suez to Cairo International Airport, where you'll board your flight to Germany. After landing in Frankfurt, you'll take the train to Bonn, where a brother will be waiting. As you get off the train, you'll call this phone number." Naguib put his hand in his pocket, pulled out and flashed a piece of paper with handwritten instructions. He handed it over. "Don't lose it. That's your gateway to the world," he declared. "By the way, your Qatari passport has a three-week-old Egyptian entry stamp in addition to a Greek stamp, and a few others. If anyone asks, you came to Egypt from Greece as a tourist, on a boat via Port Said. The British passport will gain you easy entry to most countries in the world. Your new name when leaving Germany, Amin Shukri, is common in the UK. They have a large Muslim community there."

Chapter 11

December 12, 2002—Manhattan, New York

The apartment in the *Village* was located on the second floor on West 10th Street. It was functionally decorated, a queen-size bed in the main room, a thirty-two-inch TV in the living room across from a beige sofa and a modest coffee table with a matching couch to its left. The kitchen included GE appliances—a medium-size fridge, a dishwasher, a gas range and oven combination and a microwave oven. The second room had no bed; it was set up as an office with a desk and a PC next to the window, a printer/scanner/copier all-in-one combo, just below a hanging light fixture, which included a concealed video camera aimed at the street below. There were nine other disguised or obscured video cameras spread around the apartment, covering most of the floor space. They were placed in the walls, inside light fixtures, within the kitchen cabinet, enclosed in the TV, and inside a wall clock; all linked to a server in uptown Manhattan through the Internet via a wireless router.

Arik arrived at the apartment by late afternoon; as soon as he opened the door and walked in, he began settling into his new role. He was no longer Arik. From now on, he was Qassem—Qassem al-Nasr. He looked around, checked out the layout and the setting. *No surprises.* Everything was as described in the briefcase memo. All cameras were set to go. He could turn them off, all at once, by disconnecting the router. The refrigerator was stocked with fresh fruits, vegetables, and dairy products, just what he liked. Someone had taken care of him. *My gay neighbors must have had access to my apartment,* he reflected. He didn't fancy that, but took it in as an integral part of what he'd become.

It was getting late; the jet lag wasn't helping matters. He locked the door, worked his way to the bedroom. The bed was inviting. The quilt was green and soft. He sat on it, then leaned back and stared at the white ceiling above.

He was in deep sleep when the doorbell rang. The first sound of the bell was incorporated into his dream. Rachel was standing there laughing, holding a chimpanzee in one hand and a banana in the other. There was heavy rain in the background accompanied by a severe thunderstorm, then a doorbell ding. The second dingdong awoke him and brought him back to reality. *Where am I? Oh, this is New York...* Rachel vanished; instead, he was lying on his back alone, wondering whether there was someone at the door waiting to be invited in.

He slowly got up and walked to the door. "Who's there?" he inquired.

"You don't know us yet. We're your new neighbors. We saw you coming in and we wanted to welcome you to a party."

He heard two separate voices—two men. He unlatched the door chain, then pulled the door ajar just to get a peek. "Hi." They looked harmless. He closed the door, removed the chain, then opened it wide and invited them in.

Jon and Bob were evidently the gay couple about whom he'd been briefed. They brought flowers as a welcome gift. Jon, the taller of the two, wore a dark brown Stalin-type mustache. He smelled as if he'd marinated in cheap cologne for the past decade. His thick eyebrows matched his Beatles' hairstyle, with one notable distinction— it was dyed blond. Bob, on the other hand, with his shaven-head, short build, and big nose was a contrasting figure. Arik couldn't help but wonder what had brought these two together. They were going to get married to each other before the end of the year. That night they were talking about a party at a Park Avenue apartment owned by one rich dude, Hamad Suleiman, from Saudi Arabia, a second year foreign student at the New York Film Academy who was interested in partying and girls to supplement his extracurricular activities.

It's clever, he figured. *These people will connect me to the world I'm about to belong to.* He'd not had a chance to relax after the long journey from Indonesia, but Dan Carmel had already put him to work. What a *shmuck!* (Yiddish for jerk). Arik's brain was working overtime, chugging in overdrive. Things were happening sooner than he'd planned for. He decided to stall, pretend he had no idea of who they were. "Have you been in my apartment before?" he asked.

"Of course," Jon said. "Bob used to live here before we met. We then moved together to the one across the hallway. It has a larger kitchen."

"Do you still have the keys to this one?"

"If you really want to know, we're the ones who filled your fridge. We got a call from your cousin in Boston asking us to welcome you." Bob winked while grinning mischievously.

"Okay, thanks, but I want my keys." Arik tried to look serious.

"But these are my keys." Bob protested.

"Not any more. From now on you can't come in without my invitation." There was a bit of sarcasm in his voice. He knew that they'd keep a spare key. It was in their contract.

"Okay, if you insist." Bob pulled the keys from his pocket, and handed them to Arik. The mischievous grin was still there, as if to say, "you'll have to change locks if you're really serious," an expression Arik didn't fail to notice.

"Now, after we've settled that deal, can I join you tonight?" Arik asked. He figured that whatever look Bob was going for—he had missed the mark.

"Goes without asking, Qassem," Jon said. "I'm sure Hamad will be delighted to see a brother Muslim sinning in concert with him. Do you drink?"

"No, not really."

"Do you want to meet girls?"

"That depends. I'm looking for the serious kind only."

"You may not be Hamad's type, then." Bob declared.

"I may not be, but who knows. I may be able to hit his Achilles heel."

"Okay. Why don't you wash the crust off your eyes, freshen up, then join us in about thirty minutes. We'll take the subway. Our apartment is the one across the hallway. Ring the bell and we'll be out."

. . .

A beautiful girl of Middle Eastern extraction greeted them at the door. She was holding a purple drink in her left hand, while offering her right to the men who kissed it ardently. She had dark straight hair resting on her shoulders, dark eyes, and a beauty mark on her left cheek. She wore dark red lipstick, little mascara, and green eye shadow. Her dress had an open back and a good-sized décolletage showing some stimulating skin. Her tight black dress, high heels, and striking perfume added appreciably to her feminine lure.

Arik followed suit and kissed her right hand. "I'm Qassem al-Nasr," he introduced himself.

"Fatima," she responded with an inviting smile. "Let me introduce you to our host." She took his hand and led him to the man of the hour. "And this is Hamad Suleiman." She pointed to the man in the center of the room who was holding court, surrounded by eight males, who were laughing and admiring his jokes and words of wisdom.

The young man stopped his discourse and stared at the newcomer. He was no older than twenty-five. He was wearing a suit, an unbuttoned shirt, socks, and shoes—all white. He had dark hair with long sideburns, a thin, well-trimmed mustache on an otherwise clean-shaven face. His eyes were quite penetrating as he examined the stranger with utmost scrutiny. He didn't say a word; the men around him watched him in anticipation for a breaking remark.

It took another moment of silence and penetrating gazes before Arik broke the tension. "Qassem al-Nasr," Arik introduced himself. "Nice meeting you."

Hamad didn't respond. He continued to study the stranger. Arik wasn't sure whether Hamad's demeanor expressed hostility, curiosity, or mere suspicion. His sixth sense made him feel somewhat uncomfortable. *It wouldn't be easy to get close to this fellow,* he mused.

"Are you a Muslim?" Hamad finally connected.

Arik nodded, signaling a positive response.

"We need to talk. This party is not for you."

Arik looked around. There were about twenty people in the apartment. Except for Fatima, everyone else was white—local partygoers, a couple of politicians from City Hall, a local Congressman, business people. There were no wives or girlfriends. All females were young and attractive, busy acting as servers and hosts.

Arik wasn't about to give up so readily. He turned to his new friends, Bob and Jon; they were standing next to him, embarrassed and humiliated. "I'll take care of it. It's not your fault," he comforted them. He then walked to an adjacent room, a private study that was unoccupied, turned on the lights and waited.

Hamad followed him into the room, then closed the door behind him. He continued to scrutinize him before asking. "Why did you come here?"

"I didn't plan it. My neighbors, Jon and Bob, brought me over. They said that it would be fun. It's my first day in New York after a five-year stay in Cairo."

Hamad switched to Arabic. "What do you do for a living?"

"I'm a businessman," Arik answered in Arabic.

"What kind of business?"

"Information services."

"What kind of information?"

"The kind you may not be able to get anywhere else."

"Certain people?"

"That too."

"What else?"

"Stuff…I can't talk about it now." Arik decided to go on the offensive. "I'm not sure I can tell you. I don't really know you."

"Do you have money?"

"Plenty."

"Are you looking to donate to proper causes?"

"Always."

"Where's your accent from?" Hamad realized that Qassem didn't possess a typical Egyptian dialect.

"Iraq, I was born there." Arik responded without hesitation.

"Okay you can stay here and enjoy the party."

"Thanks." Arik figured that he'd passed the first test. Many more were yet to come. Following September 11, New York's Muslim community was under the scrutiny of the FBI and the NYPD. These security agencies had infiltrated the Muslim community, trying to trap members by setting up sting operations. Muslims became suspicious of those who displayed clear traits, characteristic of police informers: Those informers liked to talk politics. They tended to live solo in Muslim neighborhoods, had no local relatives or family. Furthermore, they had plenty of time to spare. Arik knew that he'd retained some of these characteristics; he tried to avoid the other few. He wouldn't discuss politics with strangers, wouldn't give the appearance of having plenty of free time. He would attract suitable members by making himself needed, thus becoming a magnet for those who sought help, assistance, advice.

When they came out of the study, Arik noticed the signal passed from Hamad to Fatima. She responded with a smile and immediately approached Arik, trying to win him over with her feminine charm. "Can I offer you a drink?" she asked while placing her right hand on his shoulder.

"If you have diet cola I'll take it," he responded with an approving smile.

"I see. Are you bound by alcohol restrictions?"

He noticed the sarcasm in her voice. "As a matter of fact, I am."

She moved her body and her face closer to his, paused to see his reaction. Arik didn't make a move. He was standing still even though Fatima was swerving and undulating to the rhythm of the music only an inch away from his nose.

"Are you gay?" she asked, realizing his indifference to her inviting gestures.

"No. In fact I'm quite attracted to you, but I don't want to put it on display."

"I see. You want to take me home?"

"Not tonight. I'm exhausted. I also have a lot of work to do to-morrow starting at six in the morning." He figured that looking busy was essential at this juncture. He recognized that she was doing her job. Her boss, Hamad Suleiman, wanted to check him out; Fatima was his bait.

Arik left around midnight. Jon and Bob stayed on. They weren't as tired. Before leaving the party, Arik exchanged phone numbers with Fatima; she insisted on giving him hers.

• • •

He woke up at five in the morning. Although he lacked sleep badly, he hadn't yet adapted to the time change. It was late-morning in Europe and late afternoon in Asia. His body was still somewhere between those two time zones. He got up, took a long shower, then followed it with a longer shave. An hour later, he was out of the apartment on his way to *al-Quds* mosque in Brooklyn. He'd never been there before; he felt that he should familiarize himself with the mosque and the Atlantic Avenue neighborhood, Arab-Brooklyn's main street, before launching into any meaningful escapade.

Upon his arrival at the Atlantic Avenue address, the unconventional site astonished him—a four-story converted warehouse building trimmed in orange and gold. It was intriguing. He decided to head inside, explore the interior where services were being held. He wasn't impressed with the purple and green carpeting that covered the narrow prayer rooms on the first three floors. They looked old and shabby. Leaving his shoes on a shelf outside one of the rooms, he walked in and joined the prayer service. A while later he resumed his exploration of the building. He checked out the upper floors that housed the Islamic School, then noticed the battered desks and chairs that filled the various offices. It was apparent that the place could use a significant upgrade. The community was less than affluent; that fact presented a potential opportunity.

It was Friday, and at the 1 p.m. service, a guest speaker, an Imam from Illinois, was scheduled to give a sermon on Islamic education in the US in the third-floor prayer room. Arik planned on attending but needed to take care of some urgent business first. He left the mosque without engaging in conversation with any of the worshippers, then took the subway back to Manhattan. At *Times Square*, he bought a small laptop and a carry-on bag, then took a cab to 39th Street, not far from Park Avenue. All the while, he made sure that no one had been trailing him. He walked in circles, made unexpected U-turns, stopped at reflecting store windows, watched his back. He was satisfied. If anyone had been tailing him, that person would've been none other than James Bond's coach, but then, such a guru wouldn't be human.

He entered the Starbucks Coffee, ordered a tall latte, picked up a corner spot next to an electric outlet, then logged in to the uptown server. The surveillance cameras in his apartment in the *Village* were working properly. They were configured to start recording whenever they caught a glimpse of a moving object. And they did.

At 8:35 in the morning, Fatima was seen entering the building. She must have come over knowing that he was out by then. At 9:15, she entered his apartment with Jon, who had indeed saved a spare key for himself. She was looking through Arik's drawers in the bedroom but found nothing she wanted to keep. Then she went for his briefcase, pulled out two pictures of him in the company of friends in the streets of Cairo, Egypt. The first picture displayed a view of the pyramids from the *Mena House* hotel. In it, Arik was hugging a woman next to a man-made pond along a driveway leading to the hotel entrance. The second one had been taken at the *Khan el-Khalili* bazaar, where Arik was standing next to an older man who wore a traditional dress. In the background, one could spot a large display of various spices and an Arab man inspecting them.

Fatima retrieved the pictures, placed them in her purse, then parked herself next to the PC. Arik had turned it on before leaving in the morning. She opened the email application and started scanning the *Inbox* and the *Sent* folders. She printed out some of the messages, then placed the papers in her purse. She left the apartment at 10:25.

Fifteen minutes later, Jon entered the apartment. He looked around for the briefcase, placed the two pictures Fatima had pulled out earlier back where they'd belonged, moved the chair back to its original position next to the PC, then left and locked the door behind him. Arik wasn't supposed to recognize that he'd been under surveillance.

It was time to head back for the mosque. Arik picked up his bag, left the laptop on the table, then took off. It took just about ten minutes for Jerry, the attendant, to collect it along with the carry-on and place them in a safe place. During the time it was left on the table, no one attempted to steal a glance, grab, or move it. Arik hadn't been stalked; Jerry was watching.

Following a quick visit to his safe deposit box, he arrived at the mosque a few minutes after 1 p.m. It was a bit late; there was little space left in the prayer room. After leaving his shoes with all the others outside the door, he was unable to secure a place inside the main hall; the rug was crowded with men kneeling side by side with no space separating them. He decided to join the ones leaning against the wall. The standing position afforded him the opportunity to observe the believers. One man caught his attention as he muttered and rocked endlessly as if handled by a puppet master; another had his face buried inside his hands, not realizing that the Imam had already taken the stage, appealing for donations, asking for help in fixing the mosque, the school, feeding the poor.

Everything seemed quite innocent, at least on the surface. Even the sermon on Islamic education failed to spark any fireworks. Arik waited patiently for the conclusion of the services, then without a word to any of the worshippers, he followed the Imam, who was accompanied by the guest speaker and several other mosque officials, to his little chamber. The group didn't become aware of Arik who was climbing the stairs right behind them. They were discussing the sermon before entering the Imam's office on the upper floor and closing the door behind them.

Arik waited a couple of minutes before knocking and inviting himself in. He could hear one loud voice behind the door. It argued against Muslim assimilation within the Judeo-Christian culture. The talker posited extreme views, advocating total separation that entailed secluded living quarters, exclusive use of the Arabic language, even a local militia serving as a substitute for police or other law enforcement agencies. The Imam as well as the guest speaker were trying to tell the loud talker that his ideas were unrealistic; they could only take place in an Islamic Republic, but *Loudmouth* wasn't listening. He continued with his line of logic until Arik opened the unlocked door without warning, hung in there, waiting for an official invitation. The loud ongoing discussion that had been taking place in the office dived into sudden death. All eyes focused on the stranger. The room was filled with an edgy silence.

"Sorry to interrupt," Arik said to the Imam in Arabic. "But I wanted to answer your pleas for donations." He opened his bag, drew five-thousand dollars in new one-hundred-dollar bills, held his hand out, waiting for the Imam to either ask him in or come over and accept the offer.

The people in the room were dumbfounded. They all stared at Arik without uttering a sound. Finally, the Imam broke the silence. "Of course, please come in and join us." He motioned to the others to make room in front of his desk.

Arik moved closer, then put the money in the Imam's welcoming hand. The Imam couldn't hide his astonishment. "How much money's here?" he asked.

"You count it later. This is an advance." Arik responded, then faced the group. "I'm willing to support proper causes. Please tell me that the money helps the poor and the deprived and I'll help. Allah is my witness." He turned back to the Imam who was still staring at the money in disbelief. "My name's Qassem al-Nasr. I'm a businessman. I've just come from Cairo and I live in Manhattan." He reached for his wallet and pulled several business cards with his name and his *Village* apartment address and telephone number. After handing them out to the admiring group, he said, "please call if you want me to help in any of your charity cases." He turned around and left the room.

Loudmouth caught up with him on his way down the stairs. Hassan Omar was of Pakistani origin, born in 1978 in Karachi, Pakistan. In his youth, he attended a *madrassa* (religious school) where he became an expert on religious matters and literature. He could quote rhyme and verse from the Koran and was proud of it. Prior to his arrival in the US, he studied in The King Fahd University of Petroleum & Minerals in Dhahran, Saudi Arabia, where he learned Arabic as well. He came to the US on a student visa three years earlier, continued his studies in Chemistry for two years at Brooklyn Poly, but dropped out one semester before graduation. He blamed one Jewish professor for his failure. The Criminal Jew refused to approve his request for an Incomplete or give him another chance at a term paper, but instead, honored him with an F. "The Jew-monkey declared that I was guilty of plagiarism, and an F was the easy way out for me," he grumbled.

"Well, did you actually lift ideas and contents from an earlier work?" Arik asked.

"No, I simply submitted an exact duplicate of the earlier work." Hassan Omar was grinning, then as if apologizing, he continued. "I didn't realize that this damn Jew-monkey would notice. The original work, which had been submitted more than five years back to a different professor, had earned an A."

"So what're you doing about it?"

"One day I'll avenge this insult. I swear to Allah that this wicked Jew won't live to see his grandchildren." He flaunted another smirk, exposing his broken front tooth.

"So you're basically a chemist without a degree. Aren't you?" Arik asked rhetorically. "Have you ever studied bomb making?"

"Yes I have. In fact, while in Saudi Arabia, I met an Indonesian by the name of Suparman. He was a student in my class..."

Arik interrupted. "Are you sure about the name?" Arik remembered the name as one of his kidnappers' back in Bali. He'd heard it before his escape when one man called and told the other to open the trunk and check on his condition.

"Yeah. The Bali police killed the guy as part of an operation. He was involved in the kidnapping of a Jewish American couple who had lived in Israel. This guy was really into bomb making. I learned a lot from him."

Arik's blood pressure shot up. The memory of Rachel was still raw and painful. He was worried that his body language would expose his agitation and betray his true identity. Hassan Omar could've seen pictures of him and Rachel before he became Qassem al-Nasr. Now, though, he was wearing a bit of a disguise in the form of a beard, he worried that it might not be adequate, especially if other clues led the suspecting jerk towards research and discovery. "And what happened to the couple?" Arik asked. This time he was careful to project calm curiosity.

"The man was able to escape. The papers claimed that he'd been killed later during a fire exchange with the kidnappers, but I still doubt it."

"And why's that?"

"They've never showed the body to anyone. I don't think there's been a body."

"How do you know all that?" Arik asked; the knot in his stomach set off a nervous tic in one of his eyelids.

"Oh, much of it was written up in the local newspapers. I read it on the web. But more importantly, I have connections." Hassan Omar winked and grinned, trying to buy Arik's respect. "For example, the papers and the local TV reported that the woman had been killed by her kidnappers. My information tells me that she's still in their hands. They intend to use her as a bargaining chip for a bigger prize. Of course, they'll kill her if they get desperate."

Arik made a note to himself. Carmel was right. *Clues to Rachel's condition could be unearthed right here in New York City.* Hassan Omar was someone he would call upon for more information. Hassan was on the ball when it came to bomb making. However, he possessed a notable Achilles heel, as he was no longer a student, and his US visa must have expired. He resided in New York City as an illegal immigrant, or better yet, as a Muslim illegal immigrant. Moreover, he could easily be recruited into a terror cell if he didn't belong to one already, since his mind and thoughts were surely already there. Hassan Omar was Arik's admission ticket to the wicked world that Arik was trying to penetrate.

When hearing about Rachel's whereabouts, Arik's adrenalin zoomed to new heights. His thoughts focused on ways to save her.

Rachel is alive! It's unbelievable! This is huge! He felt that he had to share this news with his handler back in Israel as soon as possible.

•   •   •

At five o'clock in the evening, it was already dark outside; Arik decided to disappear in one of his safe houses, the apartment on the *Upper West Side*. His laptop was already there when he arrived. Jerry from Starbucks had performed as planned. Checking for intruders in the *Village* apartment, he found no additional unauthorized visits. Things were quiet on that front. His voicemail, on the other hand, contained several messages—two from Fatima, one from the Imam, and one from Hamad Suleiman.

Fatima wanted to meet for dinner. She'd called twice. The second call had included a more detailed suggestion, proposing time and place. Arik sensed a little impatience in her voice. She wanted to meet him badly as if she was on a mission. The Imam thanked him for his generous donation, pleaded with him to visit more often; Hamad Suleiman, the playboy from Park Avenue, invited him over for another party in his apartment on Saturday night.

It was Friday, December 13. Arik was still enduring jet lag from his unplanned intercontinental trip. He'd call Fatima later and politely decline her invitation. *Not today*, he'd say. He realized she had an agenda. She was working for Mr. Playboy Suleiman who sought to qualify him, Qassem, as a loyal member of a trusted troupe. Arik didn't want to play anxious. He figured that things were moving at a rapid pace, faster than expected; rushing it further was unnecessary. It could carry the risk of hitting a bump on the road at high speed. He wanted to slow things down. He would meet Fatima again at Hamad Suleiman's party.

He didn't check his video recordings before leaving the *Upper West Side* apartment, heading for his official residence in the *Village*. If he had, he would've found out that Fatima had already been waiting for him at his neighbors' place. He was, therefore, surprised when she knocked on his door, seconds after he checked in. "Where have you been?" she inquired, as if he should've reported to her his every move first. "I've been waiting for you for the past hour," she complained.

Her attitude irked him. "I'm a busy man," he replied. "I have work to do." He didn't invite her in, but let her stand at the door, blocking her approach with his arm.

"May I come in?" she insisted, bending under his arm, heading in the direction of the living room.

He had no choice. Fatima was the aggressive type. "So what's the occasion?" he asked, watching her find her place on the couch in front of the TV set. She was wearing tight jeans and a white jersey top with an inspiring cleavage that accentuated her figure. He assumed that she was there at that time of day with a clear agenda— seducing him. Arik recognized it, but was in no mood for hanky-panky. Memories of Rachel were still warm; he wasn't feeling any affection towards Fatima. He also knew that her seeming draw to him was an act directed by no other than Playboy Suleiman. At the same time, he realized that Fatima was getting too close for comfort. The last thing he needed right then was a Muslim woman who followed his every step around the clock, trying to control his agenda.

"Listen Fatima," he said. "I'm not in the mood for any of this... if that's what you're having in mind. I'm very busy, and I can't be a great host right now."

Fatima looked disappointed. She stood up and approached Arik. She drew up as close as a few inches away from his lips. She wasn't going to give up so easily. "And what if I am in the mood? Is there any consideration for me?" she implored, trying to ignite a spark in Arik by using the entire feminine lure she could muster. She grasped his right hand, picked up his index finger, and guided it into her mouth in a suggestive motion.

Arik pulled his hand away from her mouth, took a step back, then turned to his right, abandoning ship. "Sorry Fatima," he countered. "Not now." He headed for the entrance, held the door open; making it obvious, he wanted her to leave.

"Okay, I understand. You either don't like me or you're gay," she griped. "But, if you're straight, I'll change your mind, and one day you'll recognize your mistake." She sneered. She felt insulted, tried to cover up her emotions. How could a man resist the temptation? She was beautiful, she was sexy, she was begging for his love and lust. He was the first man she'd ever failed to seduce. He was a challenge. Never again was she going to be so humiliated. *Qassem would have to take the initiative if he ever wanted me back.* She turned around, walked through the open door; she didn't look back.

Chapter 12

December 13, 2002—Washington, DC

It was eleven days before Christmas Eve. The streets were humming with people trying to grab hold of whatever they'd passed up since *Black Friday*, the grandest shopping day after the Thanksgiving holiday. Jack Devon was sitting in his office at 935 Pennsylvania Avenue, the FBI headquarters in Washington, DC, reviewing the latest from the Middle East. Jack, three parts Irish with Dutch and German snippets, was in his forties. A pipe smoking, handsome man, over six feet, with ice-blue eyes, white teeth that fashioned a disarming smile, including dense, prematurely silver hair—was Special Assistant Director (SAD) in charge of the FBI counter terrorism Division, which had been upgraded and rejuvenated after 9/11/2001, was about to join efforts with the newly established Department of Homeland Security (DHS).

The folder on his desk carried the title: "Middle East News and Analysis." It contained the latest, concerning activities of terrorist organizations rooted in that region; high priority was assigned to items that could spill over domestically and pose a potential threat to the homeland. One particular piece that caught Jack's eye was an article on a newly established training camp run by *al-Qaeda* types in the Sahara desert. The site had first came to DHS's attention two months earlier, after satellite photos had brought to light what looked like a small village that had just popped up in the middle of the Sudanese desert. Further analysis and further photos made it clear that the village wasn't an ordinary, or an innocent, resort area. There were palpable indications alluding to its true nature.

When the US government alerted the Sudanese, the latter agreed to look into the matter. Two weeks later, the Sudanese gave their final answer. The camp was an official military base, run by the government, and the US need not interfere with Sudan's internal affairs. The answer hardly satisfied Jack Devon. Ground intelligence confirmed his suspicions, and that latest report he was reviewing, implied that Palestinian terrorists were receiving military training in the camp together with other international *Jihadists*. The camp was becoming a magnet for a slew of fringe groups including Sudanese militias destined to put down the uprising in Darfur, cleansing the province from its non-Muslim rebels and their support base.

Jack buzzed his secretary, Jennifer, and asked her to come in to his office. Jenny, a middle-aged Asian American woman, a University of Maryland graduate, was one of Jack's foremost fans. She was exceedingly loyal and didn't mind staying as late as her boss wished her to. She would have even given herself to him had he asked for it, which he'd never done. Jack was happily married; he wasn't looking for affairs on the side. His wife, Judy, was only second in importance to him, solidly behind his job, and although he liked Jenny and trusted her, she didn't cross the threshold to the top five on his list.

"Set up a meeting in my office, please," Jack instructed Jenny. "I need to talk to Stanley and Jim as soon as possible."

"Okay, I'll check their schedule," Jenny said.

"No. Preempt their schedule and have them here within fifteen minutes."

"Okay, Jack. I'll do it," she responded apologetically. "I'll get them for you."

Section Chiefs (SCs), Jim and Stanley, were two of Jack's closest direct reports. Jim, a humorless individual from Indiana, had a Midwestern conservative taste in almost anything that touched his life. His daily routines were conducted by the book. He dressed conservatively, always wearing a jacket and a tie, even to informal BBQ outings, forever acting as his partner's opposite. Stanley, a transferee from the New York field office, where he'd worked as a Unit Chief, was a native of New Jersey, a practical joker, whose sick sense of humor and politically incorrect attitude were going to take him down at some point in the future. He despised formality, treasured T-shirts and sweaters but felt obliged to wear a suit and a tie when on duty.

He liked to chew gums and crack shaggy dog stories at meetings, but had intuition and smarts that were the envy of his competition. Both SCs admired their boss, just as many who knew him. His intuition and intelligence were an inspiration; his great sense of humor and acting ability made people feel they were sitting in a comedy club rather than at a boring meeting. That, however, was the legacy of the time before 9/11. Lately, Jack had been in a bad mood, and the pre 9/11 *Dr. Jekyll* had turned into *Mr. Hyde*.

"What the fuck is going on in Sudan?" Jack inquired. "Is it true that the camp in the Sahara is breeding new fucking *Jihadists* on a daily basis?"

The four-letter word used twice in a single paragraph pointed up Jack's lack of patience. He wouldn't have used foul language under ordinary circumstances. Jim was first to volunteer a response. He could become a target of Jack's frustration if his explanation were indicative of more ignorance than awareness, or if he were to tell Jack things he already knew. Nevertheless, he gathered the courage to face his boss and took to the stage.

"We've intercepted a phone conversation between Detroit and Egypt. They were talking about Abu Musa, a grand terrorist, *Hamas* leader sought by the Israelis, who'd vanished shortly after a recent suicide bombing in Tel Aviv." Jim paused. He examined Jack's reaction to the information, trying to assess whether or not his statement bore any news to Jack. Jack picked up his pipe and began puffing, signaling patience and an appetite for more. *A good sign*; Jim had struck a chord. He continued. "The implication was that Abu Musa found refuge in Sudan. He's been training there and has associated himself with international terrorism."

Jack pulled the pipe out of his mouth, then said, "It's an Israeli problem, or is it?"

"It's clearly an Israeli problem, but the fact that it's been discussed by someone in Detroit makes it an American issue as well." Jim took a breather, then turned to Stanley, looking for support for his latest argument.

Stanley felt the vibes and finally chose to participate in the discussion. "As you well know, Jim and I are doing precision guesswork around here." A chuckle. Jack didn't smile. "By our estimate, Abu Musa is about to turn into an international terrorist. We must be on the lookout for him, while at the same time, let the Israelis and the Europeans in on the latest news."

"Are you sure?" Jack asked.

"Confidence is the feeling you have before you understand the situation," Stanley said; his face cracked open in a smile.

"Okay," Jack countered, ignoring Stanley's sarcasm. "I'll call my friend Dan Carmel from the Israeli *Mossad*; let him in on the news. He may be able to shed some extra light on this trail."

Chapter 13

December 14, 2002—Manhattan, New York

The loud ringing of the telephone awoke him. He muttered a curse. "Motherfuckers! Don't they have manners around here? Do they have to wake me up in the middle of the night?" He slowly opened his right eye, glanced at the alarm clock next to his bed. It wasn't the middle of the night. It was unusual for Arik to stay in bed as late as nine in the morning, but this was Saturday; he always took a couple of extra breather hours on Saturdays. This time it was a necessity; he had to make up for his lack of sleep, kill his jet lag. The damn phone—I should've taken it off the hook.

"Hello," he growled into the receiver, his voice betraying his condition.

"Are you still asleep?"

"That depends. Who's asking?" Arik countered, his eyelids still shut.

"This is Hassan Omar. We met at the *al-Quds* mosque at the Imam's office."

"Yeah, I remember," Arik grumbled. *Loudmouth*, he mused. He was slowly coming around. "What's up?"

"I must see you. It's urgent."

"Sure." Arik was brief. He felt a burning need for a trip to the bathroom. His internal Niagara River was gushing prior to crashing into the Falls. "Call me back in an hour," he said before hanging up the phone.

It was already 10:30; Omar hadn't called back. Arik decided to go, check the safe deposit box in the bank before they closed at noontime, draw some cash and check for messages.

He was still inside the booth when his mobile phone rang. He was hoping that Omar would call and was delighted to hear the ring tone. The caller ID indicated a 'Restricted call'. *Loudmouth* doesn't announce his arrival, he reflected. "Hello, it's Qassem," he addressed the phone.

"Hi, remember me?" Her sweet voice left no doubt in his mind. Fatima was still after him.

"No, who is it?" he answered in a tone that suggested the opposite, trying to outclass her in her own game.

"Okay, Okay." She figured out his prank. "I just called to remind you about the party tonight. Hamad's expecting you at 7:30. He asked me to remind you. He wants to talk to you."

"I see," he replied. "So, the playboy's getting serious."

"He's no playboy. He's very serious," Fatima countered. To Arik's astonishment, her voice changed from sweet to assertive. It was as if her suggestive sexual advance had been snapped up by a hungry crocodile. "Is there anything you want me to tell him?" she asked in a business-like tone of voice.

Arik paused for a second, took a breath, shook off the evil thought he'd entertained, then said. "Tell him that I'm looking forward to a meaningful conversation."

It was already four o'clock; Omar hadn't called back. Throughout the morning and early afternoon, Arik spent his time in the New York library. He was seeking information on America's Muslims in general and their US capital of Dearborn, Michigan, in particular. After four hours of intensive research, he felt that he needed more time. There was a great deal more he wanted to absorb. He also felt an urgent need to unearth as much information as was possible on the Bali kidnappers. Hassan Omar was a potential source.

He picked up his mobile phone and began dialing Omar's number. He was about to press the Send key, when all at once, he changed his mind. He didn't wish to leave such obvious self-incriminating fingerprints. Omar, in addition to being an illegal resident might have been a potential terrorist in the making. Calling him from the mobile phone was simply too risky. He began looking for the first public phone that actually worked, but found it difficult to locate a public piece of equipment that had not been vandalized. He got lucky two blocks away.

The lady who answered the phone was extremely upset. "Are you his friend?" she asked. Then, without waiting for a response, she went on. "I knew I couldn't trust the son-of-a-bitch. He vanished without paying the rent."

"What happened?" Arik asked. "What do you mean by 'he vanished'?"

"Who are you?" she asked. "Are you his friend?"

"Not yet," he answered. He owes me money. I'm looking for him as well. Why do you say 'he vanished'?"

"The Immigration officers were here. They told me he was going to be deported if they could only find him. Apparently, Omar had spotted them on their way in, before they entered the building of his… my apartment; he escaped through the backdoor before they could snag him. I don't think he's coming back."

A minute after hanging up, his caller ID alerted him to an incoming 'out of area' call.

This time it was Omar. "Hey, Qassem. Can you meet me at McDonald's on West Broadway near the Cortland Street station?"

"Where are you?" Arik asked.

"Can't tell you, but will meet you there at six sharp. Just say Okay."

"Okay."

Omar hung up.

The McDonald's was jam-packed. It was dinnertime, but Omar wasn't there. At 6:10, Arik felt the vibration inside his pocket. Omar was calling again. "Meet me at 6:30 inside BLT Burger on 6th Avenue and 11th Street," he bellowed. Arik could hear the loud background noise surrounding Omar. *That joint must be a challenging place for a quiet conversation,* he reflected.

"I'll see you," Arik said, but the line was already dead.

He didn't see Omar when he entered the BLT Burger. Arik waited for five minutes, then decided to take off.

As he stepped out of the fast food hang out, he bumped into a bearded Middle-Eastern looking fellow. The bearded man looked

angry as he was gazing at Arik. Suddenly, he grabbed hold of Arik's
shirt just below the shoulders, and pushed him back toward the curb.
Before Arik could muster any resistance, the irate chap forced Arik
into the backseat of a parked Chevy that had its door open, in anticipation of his arrival. The move brought a flashback memory of
the Bali kidnapping. The assault didn't end once Arik found himself
lying supine in the car seat, facing the man who had pushed him
in. Someone seized his shoulders, pulled him from behind, making
room for the bearded man who nudged Arik's legs down to the floor
before getting himself into the car. As soon as he closed the door,
the Chevy took off.

Arik was now sandwiched between two men who helped him
straighten up. They were strangers. He'd never seen either of them;
now he had to endure their pungent body odor as well as their bad
breath. He could see the driver's face through the rearview mirror
and immediately identified him in spite of his dark glasses. *These,
just like mine, aren't the ultimate masking gizmo,* he reflected. The
man at the wheel, who went by the name of Khaled Abu Marzouk,
was one of the fellows he'd met at the Imam's office the day before.
The man in the passenger seat turned around, displaying a smile that
exposed his broken front tooth. That man, Omar, turned to the bearded fellow and charged. "Check him out before we get started."

"What's going on?" Arik asked Omar. "Why this way? Couldn't
we just get together at the restaurant, have a quick bite, then talk as
you've suggested?"

"He's clean," the bearded man announced. "Neither recording
devices nor weapons of any kind on him."

Omar felt no need for apologies. "Listen, Qassem," he said. "I
can't trust you. One day passed after I'd told you my story, and the
immigration dogs have already been after me." Omar turned back,
faced the road ahead. "You're a spy," he declared without looking
back. "I know how to take care of spies."

"You've got it all wrong, my brother," Arik said, keeping his
cool. "I made it to New York a few days ago from Egypt. I haven't
yet had a chance to get around. I have an agenda, I have a plan, and
I've got money to support it." Arik paused to check the effect of his

words. Surprisingly, the physical pressure from the two-man sandwich diminished a bit. "And besides, I had nothing to do with any of those immigration dogs."

"What's your agenda?" Omar asked. He turned, watched Arik intensely.

"I don't feel comfortable enough around here. I don't know you well enough. I don't feel I can share details of my business dealings with you and your friends. And I'm very uncomfortable here in the back."

"We're going to Brooklyn to Abu Marzouk's house. You'll talk there, and you'll tell the truth." Omar stated.

Khaled Abu Marzouk removed his right hand from the wheel, then tapped Omar on his shoulder. "You're welcome, my brother," he affirmed.

"Just to let you know," Arik said. "I have an important engagement later tonight. I want to be back in Manhattan at around nine."

"What engagement?"

"I'm meeting with Hamad Suleiman in his apartment," Arik said.

"Oh." Omar exchanged glances with his three comrades. "I know him from my Brooklyn Poly days. What're you going to discuss?" he questioned.

"Again, I'm not free to divulge any details. That's a business deal," Arik said.

"Now I'm sure," Omar stated. "You're a spy. You won't meet Hamad Suleiman tonight. You'll be dead by then."

"You must be out of your mind," Arik said. He drew another breath. "Here I am, trying to help the real cause, and you are accusing me of spying?" The pressure on both sides of his body grew, as the heavy-set man on his right tried to grow more comfy, giving himself more butt room by pushing bulk on Arik's right thigh.

"What's your agenda?" Omar asked again.

"We need privacy for such a discussion. How much longer is this ride going to take?" Arik couldn't wait to see himself out of the crowded backseat. His right foot was turning numb.

"Okay we'll talk later," Omar responded. An uneasy silence descended.

They had been riding for about fifteen more minutes when the Chevy stopped in front of a single-family house. "We're here," Abu Marzouk announced.

The brother to Arik's right opened the rear door. They all came out of the car, grabbing and pulling Arik out with them, when, suddenly, all hell broke loose. Three squad cars sounding their loud, intimidating sirens converged on the Chevy. Four police officers — two in the first car and one each in the other two — jumped out. They pointed their guns at the five, then ordered them to stop and hold up their hands.

Arik was the only one who didn't lose his cool. "What's the matter, officer?" he asked the one approaching him.

"Turn around and put your hands behind your back," the officer barked.

As the police officers handcuffed the five men, one of the officers stepped forward and scrutinized the five. "We got a 911 call claiming that this car was used in a kidnapping in Manhattan. The plates belong to one Khaled Abu Marzouk. Anyone by this name?"

"Officer, I can explain," Arik interjected. "Yes. It might have seemed like that to passers-by in Manhattan. I'm the one who was pushed into the car in front of the BLT Burger, but it was just a prank. No one was kidnapped. Everyone's fine."

One grouchy officer who was in a particularly bad mood, gestured to his colleagues, then nodded. They all moved quickly and proceeded to conduct a body search on the five. Unpredictably, *Grouchy* retrieved a pistol from Abu Marzouk's coat pocket. "And what's that?" he asked. "Do you have a permit for this gun?"

Abu Marzouk stared at him but didn't answer.

"Okay, you don't have a permit do you?"

Abu Marzouk turned his head, faced the pavement, but didn't answer. Arik watched, as Abu Marzouk was getting deeper and deeper into a hole. *His sole purpose in life is simply to serve as a warning to others, a canary in the coalmine,* Arik thought.

Other than carrying an unregistered gun, Abu Marzouk didn't have a valid registration for the Chevy. His insurance was valid and in effect, but his Yemeni driver's license had expired three months earlier, a fact the officer failed to decipher due to its Arabic script.

"I'll have to take you in," the officer snarled at Abu Marzouk.

The rest of the search didn't turn up anything deserving attention.

"Before we let the rest of you go, I want to see some identification," *Grouchy* stated, then gestured to his colleagues to take the handcuffs off the four, excluding Abu Marzouk who was led to one of the police cars and placed inside, still tied up. Arik, happy to catch sight of his hands again, used one of them to pull out his brand new NJ Driver's license, the one Carmel had furnished him with. Carmel had explained that a NJ license didn't require a picture ID; it was ideal for his present predicament. Omar seemed bewildered. He didn't carry or wasn't willing to show an ID, a fact that didn't escape Arik's notice. Moreover, Arik became concerned that Omar, trying to avoid deportation, might do something stupid.

"Officer," Arik took the initiative again. "These people are my friends and my guests. I know them for many years. We're law-abiding. You may hold me liable if any of them is in trouble. You can have my address and my personal details. Please let us go. We've done nothing wrong."

Grouchy was in no mood for arguments. "Shut up and show me your ID," he barked. "You Arabs, you're trouble makers. I don't like you." He approached Arik and took his NJ license.

At that moment, unexpectedly, Omar charged forward in a mad dash. He was over a hundred feet out before two of the officers began pursuing him. "Hey!" *Grouchy* roared. "Stop or I shoot!"

Omar wasn't going to bring his run to a halt. He kept on racing.

"Stop or I shoot!"

Omar didn't hold back. Furthermore, as the chase progressed, the gap between him and his pursuers grew wider. They didn't have a choice. *Grouchy* fired a warning shot, but that didn't stop Omar. The few onlookers ducked for cover at the sound of the blast. Omar, energized by his fear of incarceration, picked up speed.

Another warning shot didn't change matters. The chase continued; Omar and the two officers evaporated into the night. After several more minutes of a wearying hunt, Danny, one of the officers,
was losing stamina; he became breathless. He broke off his dash,
took aim, then fired. The bullet swished by Omar's left arm, but it
only made him more resolute. He was now loping as fast as a cheetah. *Grouchy* was losing stamina as well. He cut short his sprint,
aimed his gun, but Omar abruptly changed direction; he swerved
into a dark alley before *Grouchy* had a chance to pull the trigger.

"We lost him." *Grouchy* took a deep breath, then let out a long
sigh. He walked back toward Danny. "We've got the others." He
drew another breath. "They'll talk; we'll dig up this fucking..." He
gasped for air trying to end the sentence before concluding—"...
bastard." He spit on the sidewalk after uttering the word.

Danny grumbled. "Yeah, I don't have a good feeling about this
fucking bullshit."

Grouchy turned to Danny and scratched his head. "We should
notify hospitals in the area. I'm sure the fucking bastard took a bullet. He must be injured. He may need hospital care; we may be able
to apprehend him there." He paused, narrowed his eyes and savored
his *Eureka moment*, acting as though he were Archimedes, running
naked out of his bathtub, following his discovery of the principles of
density and buoyancy. "Danny," he blasted. "Radio the other guys;
have them issue an alert."

The squawking radio in one of the squad cars drew Ryan's attention. Ryan and the fourth officer, Tom, approached the cruiser and
listened to the report. *Grouchy* was telling them about his fucking
disappointment. The big, heavy-set, Arab man, Abdullah Hatib, the
one responsible for Arik's seizure earlier in Manhattan, turned petri-
fied; he started crying. "Officer," he pleaded, with tears covering his
chubby face. "I've done nothing wrong. Please, let me go."

Ryan was preoccupied with thoughts. He had no patience for
an Arab terrorist trying to grease his way out of confinement. "Do
they ever shut up on your planet?" he barked without turning toward
Hatib. Ryan and Tom, too preoccupied with the news, failed to notice Arik's careful maneuver; he was moving stealthily toward the

second squad car, then snuck into it. Abu Marzouk was there, still handcuffed; parked in the backseat. The car keys were in, the engine was running, the light bar was flashing. Arik took to the wheel, shifted to *Drive,* then whacked the gas pedal. The car lurched forward, its big engine roaring. It was gone in no time.

Ryan and Tom watched the blast-off in utter disbelief. They didn't know what hit them. It took a full seven seconds before they came to grips with what had just transpired. The two remaining Arabs, Abdullah Hatib, the bearded, crybaby gorilla, and Masoud Numairy, a short fellow with red hair and a beard, stood there, frozen in place, waiting for the officers' ruling regarding their fate. The verdict was slow in coming, but hastily announced once decided.

"You two, get into the police car," Ryan commanded, pointing to one of the cruisers. "Do it fast before I get mad," he barked.

Tom and Ryan took off in the only squad car left, in a futile attempt to chase after Arik, the vanishing fugitive. They were too late. The only contribution they could possibly make at this point was to alert the rest of the NYPD in Brooklyn to the breaking story—a double failure that demanded an uncompromising effort to redeem their lost honor.

After parking the police car a block away from the *al-Quds* mosque, Arik turned back to face Abu Marzouk who was still sitting tight in the backseat. "Listen," he said. "You're going to stay in the car and wait for the police to find you. Don't try to slip away. You're better off waiting for them than being snatched later and treated as a trapped fugitive." He paused to weigh the effect of his power of persuasion, though Abu Marzouk didn't surrender his thoughts; he kept quiet and seemed bemused. Arik went on. "As far as I'm concerned, I'll be doomed for life if they apprehend me. I'm topping the list of dangerous terrorists. I have no choice but to evaporate. Sorry I have to leave you here, but we may see each other in the future, and then I'll explain." Arik counted on the fact that under the pressure of questioning and threats, Abu Marzouk would sing. The music would make Arik a folk hero, a celebrity among potential terrorists. They'd try to seek him out, crown him as their new prince; his aim would have been realized. He stepped out, closed the door and walked away.

• • •

Fox was first to break the news. Qassem al-Nasr was described as a suspected terrorist big cheese. His picture, the one the police retrieved from his apartment, was displayed on TV. The public was warned that he was armed and dangerous. The picture showed him with a clean shave and short hair, the style that he'd never assumed. Though it bore a notable resemblance to his looks, it reduced the probability of his being identified by strangers in crowded settings. Qassem al-Nasr had, nevertheless, made it to the ten most wanted on the New York scene.

Arik was watching his own TV crucifixion from his safe hideout on the *Upper West Side*. His laptop was on; he was viewing his *Village* apartment at the same time; it'd already become a crime scene. Cops, investigators, and photographers were swarming around, looking for clues and information on his background and whereabouts.

Arik was monitoring the latest crime scene with considerable interest. His planted fictional biography, including his current illusory business dealings, retrieved from his PC hard drive, was about to become public folklore. It would be leaked, most likely, to the media; no *Jihadist* would ever question his authenticity or his motives. The first part of his mission had been accomplished, but now he was faced with an overriding issue. He was a fugitive; he could no longer trust those who knew him as Qassem al-Nasr unless they were tested under the new circumstances.

• • •

The front door opened; Jerry stepped in.

"Good job, good job," he greeted Arik. His sarcasm was palpable. "How the fuck did you manage to get both the NYPD and the FBI on your back?"

"The FBI too?"

"What do you think? It's a whole damn Homeland Security Indian dance. Everyone's in on the hunt for your fucking ass."

"It enhances my credibility among *Jihadists*. Don't you think?"

Jerry made a face. "Even those nuts will be scared of your shadow. You've just developed into a magnet for terrorist hunters."

"And so did Osama Bin Laden. Still, he's been king of his domain; he's not to be found; his fans treat him as their prophet from Hell."

"Yeah, but they have armies of supporters."

Arik stared at Jerry in astonishment. "What about you and what you represent? My support comes from an entirely unexpected place. Your DHS hunters will never look under your crib."

"Look," Jerry was getting impatient. "You're about to become a very experienced *shmuck*. Bad judgment is the best teacher, and you're full of it. You seem to have plenty of confidence," he added. "That's the feeling you have before you understand how deep in shit you are."

"I may not be perfect, but I'm all I've got," Arik countered. He pulled himself up, then added. "And by the way, I strongly disagree with your definition. What happened today has been the first genuine breakthrough since I came to New York. I was considered as a spy; now I'm a hero. Without question, I've become a veritable star. You must face jeopardy in this business if you want to get anywhere."

"Okay," Jerry gave up. "What's done is done. Someday, we'll look back on this, laugh nervously, then change the subject." He walked to the kitchen, picked up a glass of water, took an extended sip, then resumed. "I suggest that you stay under house arrest for the next ten days. That is, until your picture fades from people's memory and the great quest in your honor loses some of its steam. During that time, I'll take care of your needs. You'll just have to pull a temporary disappearing act a-la Jimmy Hoffa."

Chapter 14

December 15, 2002—Bonn, Germany

As soon as he got off the train in Bonn, Abu Musa turned on his cell phone. He was ready after replacing the SIM inside with a local T-Mobile chip. Upon his arrival in Frankfurt, he pre-paid for two hours worth of airtime, and now he was geared up for business. He pulled out the note with the brother's phone number, noticed the time, just about 1 p.m. *Amazing, the trip from Cairo to Bonn took just about twenty-three hours.* Had he not missed the direct flight, he could've been here yesterday evening. Spending the early morning hours in Athens airport, however, wasn't a total waste. He took the occasion there to clean, shave, and brush up on his German.

He dialed the number. It took two rings before she answered, "hello," in a heavy German accent.

Oops, wrong number. He glared at the handwritten note, then dialed again.

This time it took only one ring. "Hello, this is…"

He didn't wait for her to finish the sentence before hanging up. He was all set to call Naguib in Egypt and scream in frustration, but just then, his cell phone began playing Beethoven's *Fur Elise*—she called back.

Abu Musa noticed the caller ID. He hesitated. Not sure about what to do, he waited for a fifth ring before choosing to pass. It took less than two minutes; the phone buzzed with an indication of a new voicemail message. He hesitated, but then dialed the access number and listened. "Mr. Ahmad Abu Rmeiyeh. Hello, I'm Hilga," she said in English. "I'm here waiting to pick you up. Moreover, I'm looking at you right now. You can see me. Look for a shorthaired, honey-blonde with a green top, black overcoat, and a black skirt.

I'm wearing sunglasses and holding a *Der Spiegel* magazine in one hand. And oh, I forgot to mention. I'm beautiful." She giggled at her own admission.

Abu Musa lifted his head and scrutinized the small station vestibule. He saw her standing fifty feet away, near one of the exit doors that led to the busy street. They made eye contact, but he didn't react to her apparent acknowledging smile. Instead, he lowered his gaze, directed it to the floor. He kept on listening to the voicemail message. "I can take you to your destination. Just follow me when you're ready."

Abu Musa lifted his head, made one more eye contact with Hilga, then nodded in approval. She picked up the signal — a green traffic light at a forsaken intersection — then headed for the exit.

The cold December air hit his face the moment he stepped out of the station. He didn't spend time outdoors after leaving Egypt, and this northern experience was fresh. His eyes turned glassy; his mouth dried out; his coat — too wispy for the season. He lifted his hands in front of his face, then exhaled into his palms, trusting the warm steam to thaw his frozen nose, but to no avail. He was quite uncomfortable, except the thought of his mission made him put the uneasiness out of his mind and concentrate on Hilga.

As he followed her, he couldn't help but imagine what she would look like naked. He watched her from behind. He could notice that even her coat didn't conceal her attractive figure. She was wearing black shoes with high heels that put some commendable touches on her fine-looking legs; her enticing buttocks moved and shook with every step she took. Her honey-blonde hair carried the promise of a beautiful face, something he failed to notice, mostly because of the sunglasses she was wearing and the fact that he didn't have a chance for a high-quality intimate scrutiny.

They walked alone and apart for two blocks keeping a fair distance between them. She finally stopped at a tram station and waited. Abu Musa continued his advance; seconds later, he was standing next to her. Still, they didn't exchange a word, nor did they renew any eye contact. When the tram arrived, she stepped onto it, then signaled him to follow her. She held two tickets in her left hand, removed one, and handed the second one to Abu Musa, still no eye contact. He took it without a word.

Several stops later, she stepped down and signaled him to follow. They were standing in front of the *King Abdullah Academy*. She turned around and looked at him. "We're safer now," she finally said. She removed the sunglasses and for the first time he could see her eyes and face in the open. Hilga had ocean-blue eyes and an inviting smile. She wore little makeup, bordering on non-existent, glossy red lips; while the slight space between her top front teeth revealed vulnerability.

"Why do you say that? Why are we safer?" he asked. The transition from the heated tram to the cold outdoors made him once again uncomfortable. He was bouncing from one foot to the other just to stay warm. He couldn't stand still.

She looked at him, then flashed an endearing, sad smile. "After I get you a better coat, hat, and gloves, you'll feel at home here," she said. "This school was established in 1994 by Crown Prince Abdullah of Saudi Arabia," she lectured. "It offers a diploma modeled on the Saudi Arabian school curriculum. Initially it provided Islam-based instruction to children, whose parents were in Germany only for a short time, such as diplomats. But lately, the private school has accepted many children who hold German citizenship."

"Who are you? Why are you here? Why did you come to pick me up?" he asked. In his mind, she didn't belong. *Is she even a Muslim?* He was eager to go inside and get away from the weather, but felt an urgent need to clarify the unexpected role of his new sister before he could feel safe.

"I'm a civil rights activist. I converted to Islam a year ago," she said, realizing Abu Musa's anxiety concerning her background. "The German authorities have been harassing Muslims. They allege that the academy serves as a haven for terrorists with connections to *al-Qaeda*. That's nonsense. The authorities claim that the academy serves as a barrier to integration of Muslims in the German society because it offers only one hour a week of German, compared to six hours of Arabic and eight hours of religious instruction. This is nonsense." She paused. "They'd never harass the Jews this way after what happened in the Great War. This government is racist just like the ones that preceded it sixty years ago. Then it was the Jews. Now it's the Muslims."

Abu Musa was taken aback. He was impressed. "So what else do I need to know?" he asked while looking at the promising building he was about to enter.

"The authorities want to close down the academy and I'm fighting it. They already know me; I'm being followed occasionally. Back in the train station, I was trying to avoid linking you to the same dirty game. I didn't know who was watching."

He looked down thinking; *she didn't do a great job. Any professional armed with warranted suspicion could've picked up on the connection, but then, maybe not.* "What about here?" he asked. He looked around, studying the passers-by. He was watching the schoolchildren playing outside. Their high-pitched Arabic holler gave him a sense of home. Several women walked by. They were covered head to toe with head style *abaya* or full *khimar*; some other women and a number of men strolled around in traditional Muslim dress, just like in Gaza. They weren't dressed as heavily as he would've under the circumstances, yet none of these people seemed uncomfortable. "How long will it take to get used to this freezer?" he asked.

She ignored the question, then continued. "Almost everyone around here is Muslim," she said. "A German police detective looking around in this neighborhood is going to be noticed. They'll only do it around here overtly on an official call. If you don't see them here, they're not here."

"That's good to know," he said. "Where am I going now?"

"You'd better go to the mosque. They're waiting for you inside," she pointed at the mosque behind the school. "You have my phone number, just in case."

• • •

The five men next to the main entrance ended their heated exchange upon his appearance at the door. They examined the newcomer with utmost scrutiny. A bearded man came in from the shadows and approached him. "You must be Ahmad Abu Rmeiyeh," he said.

Abu Musa turned toward the bearded stranger and nodded in approval.

"I'm Abul Bashar, the Imam in charge of the community and the mosque. Hilga has just called and said that you were coming in," the Imam said. The two hugged and kissed on both cheeks while the five men resumed their heated deliberation. "Let me introduce you to our brothers. They're teachers in our academy."

Abul Bashar lifted his right hand; his gesture silenced the five men who ceased their discussion; they turned around to face Abu Musa. They were ready for the official greeting. One by one, they introduced themselves, then followed with a hug and three kisses, one per cheek, and then—an extra one.

"I told them to prepare their pupils for *Jihad*—a holy war," Abul Bashar told Abu Musa. "My teachers have been discussing the details of the message delivery." He said, inviting the five to participate.

The Imam took charge again. He signaled to the six men to follow him to a quiet corner. He then stared intently at Abu Musa. "We know who you are, and we're proud of you," he whispered in a hushed, nearly conspiratorial, tone. He looked around making sure that the conversation remained private, then added. "You can trust us. We'll continue calling you by your new name, Ahmad Abu Rmeiyeh, even though we know who Abu Musa is."

Abu Musa grew anxious. "Who else knows?"

"Nobody, not even Hilga." The Imam said. "There's nothing to worry about."

"I understand," Abu Musa affirmed. "I'm here to help." He turned to the five. "You invite me to your classrooms as a guest, and I'll deliver Allah's message to your pupils. The *Jihad* has begun already. It must widen to include the next generation. Your pupils must grow up preparing themselves to become soldiers in Allah's command. I'll show them the way."

It was getting late; the long journey from Egypt via Athens was finally catching up with him. After spending several hours in the

mosque, discussing holy war against the infidels, Abu Musa decided to go outside and investigate the reasons for the thunderous
booms he'd heard during the past ten minutes of his visit inside the
mosque.

The nice day that had welcomed him upon his arrival at the
mosque had simply vanished. In its place, he encountered a thunderstorm together with a freezing rain, an unusual prospect in
Gaza, Sudan, or Egypt, a place he'd just come from, where the
month of December was much warmer. He stood at the door of
the mosque waiting for the icy rain to subside. As he was surveying the outdoors, he noticed a man across the street, taking pictures with a large zoom lens. The suspicious camera operator was
wearing a dark blue raincoat with a head cover, but it looked and
felt as though he were taking pictures of Abu Musa rather than the
building.

Something's wrong, Abu Musa reflected. He went inside quickly,
picked up his phone and called Hilga. He interrupted her greeting
while expressing his apprehension. "I must see you right away.
I'm being followed. You may be able to explain why this is
happening."

"Ask Jamil, our Imam's driver, to take you to my apartment. I'll
be waiting."

• • •

Hilga's apartment was located on *Winterstrasse*, less than a kilometer away from the *King Abdullah Academy*. She was cooking
when Abu Musa turned up. His hair and shirt were soaking wet because of the rain. He was unprepared for it. The heavy suitcase he
was lugging impeded his dash from the car that took him to the
apartment building.

Hilga was not concerned, when Abu Musa asked about the man
with the zoom lens. "They always take pictures. This is part of their
routine harassment. This is why I'm fighting it," she explained.

""Okay," Abu Musa calmed down a bit. "They are not after me
in particular."

"Why don't you take your shirt off and let it dry in the bathroom? In the meantime, you can sit and enjoy this coffee. I'm making dinner for both of us," she said.

Abu Musa hesitated. He wasn't accustomed to taking his clothes off in front of a woman whom he'd met only hours before. But then, she was German, not an Arab woman. He let the distinction make him feel more at ease. He sat down.

"Please," she insisted. "You're all wet. That's the best way."

Her words turned him on. Once more, he watched her while trying to picture her without her clothes. His scrutinizing eyes went down from her face to her breasts, then farther down to her waist and below, then back up. She noticed and smiled. She moved closer to him and leaned over. He raised his head to meet her gaze; his eyes stopped at her unbuttoned top. Her young breasts were practically in full view from that angle; he was aroused. He took her face with both hands and moved it closer until her lips met his. She responded with a passionate kiss.

He pushed her one-step back so that he could stand up before picking her up and carrying her to her bedroom. Their lips were joined while she was unbuttoning his shirt on the way from the kitchen. They made passionate love for the next hour.

"You can stay here for the rest of the week if you want," she said after they wound up dinner. "After that I'll be going to Canada."

"Canada? Where in Canada?" he felt dumbfounded and disillusioned.

"I've been admitted to McMaster University in Hamilton, Ontario," she responded. "The semester starts in mid-January, but I promised my sister who lives there that I'd come before Christmas. She's due to give birth on New Year's Day."

Abu Musa didn't react. He was deep in thought. *Canada*. He always wanted to go there. *In fact, it would be cool if I could establish an Islamic cell over there, and then expand its reach to the US*, he reflected.

"What're you thinking?" she asked.

"Oh, I'd like to go with you." He uttered.

"Sorry, this is going to be impossible. You'll need a visa, and I don't know how long it'll take. They've been very difficult lately, especially when it comes to Muslims from Arab countries."

"I travel with a British passport. I don't need a tourist visa. Anyway, I don't think I can make it that soon, I have a job around here." His moist eyes let slip his emotions. The job, his devotion to Allah, and his prophet's vision exposed his soft spot.

She stared at him, noticing his reaction. She believed it reflected his penchant for her. She liked him, too, but decided to keep it to herself until the right moment. "You'll have me for the rest of the week," she countered. "Right now, you must be tired, and I am too. Let's sleep on it and start afresh tomorrow."

• • •

Abu Musa woke up at 5 a.m. It was still dark outside, but he got up quietly, careful not to wake her up. He got dressed, stole a quick look at her back and round buttock, as she was lying naked on her side, then headed for the door. Hilga was asleep. She was exhausted from the uncontrollable lovemaking they had engaged in until the early hours of the morning. Miraculously, he wasn't. He didn't have an early appointment; he merely wanted to fulfill his Islamic duty, pray before daybreak. *King Abdullah Academy* and the mosque weren't too far away. Hilga bought him a heavier coat while he was spending his time at the mosque the day before. Now he could take a walk and feel warm.

Inside the mosque, he found Jamil, the driver, who'd given him a ride to Hilga's apartment the day before. Abu Musa examined the young and cheery fellow. Shorthaired, clean-shaven, looked like an eighteen-year-old or less, enthusiastic about his job as a driver, eager to learn, eager to please. There was something about Jamil. His innocence was apparent, resembling a dog being taught to catch a Frisbee. Abu Musa was convinced he had a loyal follower. The youngster would be his first recruit. He figured he'd drawn Jamil into his orbit.

Following the prayer service, Abu Musa ushered Jamil to a meeting with the Imam, Abul Bashar. "With your permission, Imam, I wish to spend time with Jamil," he pleaded. "I can teach him how to be a better Muslim. I can show him the path to Paradise. I'll show him how to prepare himself for the final judgment day and how to devote himself to Allah's command. I'll tell him about the awaiting pleasures in heaven. I want him to help me in my holy mission."

Abul Bashar nodded in agreement. He moved his hand across his beard as his facial expression transformed from a fellow brother to one distinctive of great diviners. "You'll need more brothers for your mission." He said. "Jamil can help in your recruiting."

"I was counting on that as well," Abu Musa responded. "We have a lot of work to do. We'll see you back in time for the afternoon prayer."

"You have an important job to do," Abu Musa told Jamil. "Do you have friends or anybody you have total faith in, who owns or works on a big farm?"

Jamil was thinking for a moment before speaking. "Abu Baaqr, one of the teachers you met yesterday has a cousin who works in a company that sells products to farms all over the Rhineland." He paused, trying to retrieve the company's name. "Oh yes. I think it's some kind of an acronym for German words like Support, Agriculture and Fertilizer."

"Fertilizer? Perfect. How do you know about Abu Baaqr's cousin?"

"I heard him talking to other academy teachers about it. He was saying that it was an opportunity. That's all I know. I don't know what opportunity he was talking about."

Abu Musa made a mental note; Abu Baaqr was a strong candidate for his terror cell.

"Okay. That's good. Tomorrow morning, you'll go to Frankfurt and look for three vans. When you find any, you'll steal them. You'll take with you some of the most reliable brothers so they can drive these vans back to Bonn."

"I know how to do this, but what're we going to do today?" Jamil asked.

"We go to Cologne to check on the big Cathedral and its surrounding Square including the Dom Hotel, the Forum Hotel, and the
train station next door. I want to explore the best access points and
the best place to park the vans inside the Square, near the station and
near the Cathedral."

"Okay. I understand," Jamil glowed with admiration for his new
mentor.

"When we come back in the afternoon, you go and find Abu
Baaqr while I talk to the Imam." Abu Musa was now in full command; he was exercising his new authority with passion. "You tell
Abu Baaqr that I want to talk to him about his cousin. I want to
move on our project as soon as possible."

The drive to Cologne was shorter than expected. Traffic was relatively light. They parked their car two blocks away from the Cathedral on a small street, then walked to the Square. Jamil was growing
animated when he saw the street performer and the gathering crowd
in front of the Forum hotel. He stopped, started watching, but Abu
Musa got annoyed and grabbed him to the side. "Listen, Jamil," he
chastised. "We're not here as tourists. We're here on a job."

"Why here?" Jamil asked.

"You must understand that the purpose of terror isn't just killing
a few people you don't know. The true purpose is injecting massive
fear and anxiety that encompass the whole population. To accomplish that feat you want to have the entire media consumed with the
event for as long as possible. You want them to keep talking about
and analyzing the event. You want them to keep on criticizing the
authorities for not doing enough to protect the public. You want the
population to stay home sick with fear. You want the tourists to stay
at home sick with fear. You want the economy to spiral down inside
a black hole, and you want all that good news to last for a long
time."

Jamil was listening wholeheartedly. It was the commencement
of a true lesson.

Abu Musa continued. "Now, regarding your specific question —
Why here?" He paused; placed his hand on Jamil's shoulder. "Look
around. What do you see?"

Before Jamil had a chance to respond, Abu Musa interjected. "You see general calm, happiness, serenity. You see infidel crusaders celebrating their unholy but temporary triumph over Islam. This place, my brother, is the birthplace of the crusades; it's the heart of the city. It's the pride of the city. This place is the Mecca of the infidels' Rhineland. Look at this Square. Look at this Cathedral. If they happen to be damaged or destroyed, infidels from all over the world will pay attention, and more than ever if we execute on Christmas Eve. They'll wake up. They'll finally understand that Muslims may not wish to be oppressed, taken advantage of, and be discriminated against. They'll finally recognize that Islam is the only true religion and that Mohammed is the last and final prophet who carried Allah's amended message to the people. That's *Jihad*, my brother, and don't forget it. We'll either win or die as martyrs."

Jamil seemed to be absorbing the new truth. He was a good student. Abu Musa realized that momentum was on his side. He went on. "To accomplish our objective, we must have an impressive blast in an extraordinary place, at a distinctive moment. A small event in an inconsequential place or a mundane instant isn't going to generate a long-term impact. That's why I'm looking for three, rather than one, big explosions on Christmas Eve. And I want to set off these explosions simultaneously."

Jamil was finally on the same page. At last, he understood the plan Abu Musa had devised. That closing lesson was crucial to his conversion. He felt exalted at his discovery.

Abu Musa noticed Jamil's exhilaration. He took the opportunity, placed both of his hands on Jamil's shoulders, held him close, glared directly at his eyes, then pressed the point. "Jamil, my brother, if you want to become a martyr, if you want to enjoy the pleasures of paradise, if you want to have seventy-two virgins care for your needs, this will be your chance, my brother. That's your big chance."

Jamil's eyes widened. He felt as if he'd just been granted the promotion he'd yearned for. This was the second best day of his life. The best one hadn't yet materialized. It would transpire soon.

The trip back to Bonn took less than an hour. They didn't finalize the specific plans, but Abu Musa was satisfied. "We'll rehearse next week without the explosives. We'll need two getaway cars before and after the big event. You, Jamil, will rent the getaway cars from two separate car rental agencies. We'll use the cars initially for preserving two parking spots for two of the vans. We'll park them on the day before and leave them in their great spot overnight, thus preserving the particular location for the vans. The next morning, we'll drive the three vans in, remove the cars from their parking place, then fill the spot with the vans. I'll be working on the specific plan throughout the rest of the week."

"Wait, I don't get it," Jamil said. "Why two cars only? What about the third van?"

Abu Musa drew a breath. He paused, granted a polite smile, visibly restraining a less temperate response. His young student seemed slower than a herd of turtles stampeding through thick humus. Nonetheless, he was bound to being patient. "Two of the vans will explode on adjacent streets," he said. "The third van will be driven into the doors of the cathedral and explode there two minutes after the infidels finish their phony prayer and on their way out. You'll be inside that van. Those who got out a minute earlier will get caught by the street vans."

The afternoon meeting with Abu Baaqr didn't last long. He was somewhat amazed with Abu Musa's familiarity with his cousin's state of affairs. He'd never mentioned it in front of the new brother who'd just arrived from Egypt. All the same, he was impressed with the intelligence he confronted. "I'll talk to my cousin tonight," he promised Abu Musa. "I'm sure things can be arranged to your satisfaction, but we'll need a logistics plan. You'll have to take care of storage and delivery of the ammonium nitrate," he said.

"Not to worry, I'm taking care of it as we speak," Abu Musa said with an impish look in his eyes. "But I'll require some help from you and from other brothers. You should enlist assistance for the project."

Abu Baaqr nodded in conformity. They hugged and kissed. "*Inshallah*—God willing—we'll get it done," he declared.

• • •

As he was walking to Hilga's apartment, Abu Musa began enjoying the cool breeze. He started paying attention to the Christmas decorations, the miniature light bulbs dressing up the bare trees, the evergreens or Christmas trees as these infidels chose to name them, the apartment buildings with the alternating colored light. Bonn looked very different from Gaza with its crowded streets and poor housing, or the Sudan desert with its sandy hot air and light blue skies. The fresh cool air, the smell of it, the festive feel of the approaching holiday, the clean streets, the building architecture and color were all alien, but he was oblivious to it all. *This affluence was a direct result of oppression*, he reflected. *This must change.*

He finally arrived at *Winterstrasse*. Hilga's apartment building was located in the middle of the street. Her little balcony on the second floor was covered with bare pots that had been packed with flowers before the onset of winter. The apartment overlooked the street below, and although it was getting dark, there were no lights inside the apartment. There was a small truck across the street where two people were carrying boxes into the other building. Abu Musa chose to halt his progress, watch them work from a distance. He had some free time since Hilga was probably out somewhere; he didn't have an extra key to the apartment. A Muslim woman passed by; she wore a head style *abaya*. She was walking fast, almost running. A few children, aged about twelve, were still playing in the street near Hilga's apartment. One of them kicked a ball in his direction, then hollered at him, demanding its return. The kid was speaking German, but his accent was definitely Middle Eastern. Abu Musa caught the ball, then began walking in their direction.

As he got closer, preparing to kick the ball back toward the kid, he scrutinized the truck. A man had just come out of the entry hall and was about to open the door on the driver's side. Abu Musa took another glimpse. The man looked familiar, but Abu Musa couldn't put his finger on where, or even if, he'd met him before. Something about that man made him tense. He decided to go inside Hilga's apartment; *she might be in after all; she might be asleep; I would wake her up; we'd go out to eat.* He sneaked behind the truck to avoid eye contact with the driver, then moved quickly into her apartment building. He left the stairway lights off before starting for the second floor. Standing in front of her apartment door, breathing heavily as a result of the run upstairs, it took him a few seconds before he could locate the doorbell. He rang it twice. There was no answer even after he repeated the buzzing. He knocked, then turned the doorknob in an attempt to produce an added signal. To his amazement, the door opened. *Did Hilga forget to lock it when she went out? Where could she be by now?*

He closed the door and ran downstairs. As he stepped out of the building, he almost stumbled upon her. Hilga was about to walk in. Some of the groceries she was carrying fell on the sidewalk next to her because of the near crash. Abu Musa was so blissful at her sight that he almost let his enthusiasm show, but he stopped short. *A devout Muslim doesn't express his feelings of love or lust in the open,* he reflected. He wouldn't hug or kiss her even though he felt like she'd survived a near death experience.

"What's the matter? Is there anything wrong?" she asked, sensing his disposition.

Abu Musa surveyed the surroundings. The truck was gone. For some unfounded reason he felt more at ease, although still apprehensive about the unlocked door. "Where were you?" he uttered.

"I was at the university. There was a small public demonstration critical of the German government's discriminatory practices, and I was one of the leading voices."

"You never mentioned that before, why?" His tone was inquisitive. It sounded livid. He wanted her to report to him on her moves and plans ahead of time.

She felt the pressure and apologized. "I didn't want you to be there. There were countless police people. They took pictures."

"Do you know that your door to the apartment is unlocked?"

"Yes I do know. I couldn't find my key before leaving this morning. I thought that you'd taken it. I was in a hurry, so I just closed the door, left it unlocked. I didn't think anyone would walk in."

Abu Musa felt somewhat relieved. "And I thought..." he stopped. Staring at her quizzical face, he elected to keep his anxieties to himself. "Let's go inside," he said. "It's getting a bit chilly." He grabbed the shopping bag from her, bent and collected the groceries, cucumbers, and tomatoes, from the sidewalk, then put them back inside the bag.

Walking into the residence, he was still edgy. There was something different in the apartment; he could not pinpoint it immediately, but his sixth sense was working now. He rushed to the bedroom where he kept his suitcase, then promptly opened it and looked inside. As he examined its contents, he became more certain that his belongings and his papers had been examined; his possessions had been shifted inside. He looked up. Hilga was standing there, next to him, watching him getting agitated.

"Did you look inside my suitcase?" he asked.

She sensed his irritated tone. It felt as if he directed his ill feeling toward her. "No." Her puzzled face left no doubt. She didn't do it. But then, she was catching on to his next thought.

"Then, someone else did. Someone was in the apartment while we were out." He rose and charged to the balcony. The lights in the apartment across the street, the one facing Hilga's, went out once he crossed the threshold. He turned around, hurried back inside, only to meet Hilga's curious gaze.

His facial expression was filled with concern. He raised a finger to his mouth in a motion that suggested, "*no talking.*" Hilga gaped at him, trying to discern the reason for the odd conduct, while he kept looking for a piece of paper, on which he could write. He ultimately found a note pad next to the phone. He seized it, stirred to the kitchen table, then wrote—"We're being watched. The apartment is probably bugged. They can hear us when we talk."

She watched him with disbelief. *That was Bonn, Germany, not Fidel Castro's Cuba. How could that happen?*

"Do you know who lives in the apartment across the street?" he wrote while pointing at the darkened apartment.

She wanted to talk and explain, but Abu Musa raised his hand and placed it over her mouth before she had a chance. He pointed to the note pad and handed it to her.

She picked it up and wrote. "These people moved out last week. I think someone has just moved in." She was becoming terrified in reaction to Abu Musa's partial panic.

Although he was suspicious, another alarm zipped through Abu Musa's skull. His brain activity leaped through to nine on the Richter scale. He recalled the familiar face in the truck he'd seen earlier on his first day in Bonn. The man was there at the train station upon his arrival. He was there on the tram ride to the *King Abdullah Academy*. He was the one taking his pictures outside the Mosque. "Listen Hilga," Abu Musa groaned, then broke off before saying it out loud. He moved closer to her, held her face in his hands, then whispered in her ear. "I better move out. You're being followed, and now they connect me to whatever you're cooking." He paused, seemed to have made up his mind. He walked back to the bedroom, grabbed his suitcase, and moved toward the door. She swung next to him, all set for a good-bye hug. He didn't have to say it. It was evident. He pulled her head again and whispered. "I'm moving out. Don't call a taxi. I'll catch one down the street." He watched her perplexed, let down expression. "Don't worry," he comforted her. "You'll hear from me."

• • •

Although his forged passport wasn't in the suitcase, Abu Musa did have a booklet inside with bomb making instructions in Arabic. He was angry with himself for leaving it behind in the apartment, except it was too late to backtrack and do it right. He spent the night in Jamil's apartment napping on the torn couch after discussing the urgency of their mission before the police caught up with them. He realized that the police could've been on his tracks, or possibly on Hilga's tracks. He had to avoid overt contact with her, while concealing his movements, making it grueling if not impossible for the police to tail him.

It was after the Morning Prayer. The Imam took him aside, let him in on a new opportunity. Professor Hans Berger from Bonn University was about to leave for Argentina on a Sabbatical. He was looking for someone to rent and take care of his country house on the outskirts of the city while he was away. After reviewing the ad in the paper, the Imam realized that the residence would be available in a couple of days. It was fully furnished, fully loaded with housewares; it had a nice yard with a barn; it was secluded. In short, it was a perfect place for car bomb preparation.

Following that piece of news, Abu Musa had a short exchange with Abu Baaqr in the mosque. He made it clear that he didn't wish to have any direct contact with his cousin, the fertilizer man. People joining the project wouldn't have any contact with the real chief, only with his deputy, he argued. He handed the bomb-making booklet to Abu Baaqr and told him to study it carefully, buy all the necessary ingredients listed in the manual—like hydrogen peroxide, high solvency acetone, hydrochloric acid, baking soda. Once he acquired all of the ingredients including the ammonium nitrate fertilizer, he would bring it all to the newly rented country house. Abu Musa would then be in charge of constructing the bombs with Abu Baaqr's help.

Following his mosque activities, Abu Musa went out to check on his new temporary living quarters, one bedroom furnished apartment, on *Waldburgstrasse*. The Imam arranged it on his behalf. It was painted yellow inside, a color Abu Musa abhorred. It reminded him of his brother's apartment in Khan Younis before the Israelis had bombed it. The kitchen was very small, the sink was dirty, the gas range—archaic, the tiny cabinet above it—rusty. It wasn't a real kitchen. It was more like a cooking corner inside an Afghan cave. *It must have been a crusaders' bliss before the filthy infidels had ventured on their ill-fated escapade, back in the eleventh century.* However, Abu Musa didn't plan on food preparation. It didn't matter. He accepted his fate knowing that the stay would be short. He would leave in a couple of days once the country house on the outskirts of Bonn became available. It was good enough for a couple of nights; that was all about which he cared. It was located close enough to the mosque—a walking distance.

Following a short nap on the narrow bed and a mattress that felt more like a flat tire, he got up, stretched for two minutes, restored his back to its previous shape, then headed for the mosque. It was time for the afternoon prayer.

Jamil was already there waiting. He had been able to snatch three vans from Frankfurt, and had already replaced the license plates. "We parked them at the *Hotel Maritol*. It's simple and free, and it doesn't hurt if you know the bellboy."

"Okay. I don't have to know the details," Abu Musa said. "I'm glad you didn't park them on the street. They won't raise suspicion in the hotel parking lot even if parked for a couple of days." He pulled Jamil by his shoulder, then led him outside the mosque. It was cloudy and drizzly; not the most pleasant environment, but one that best suited Abu Musa's need for utmost privacy. "Tomorrow is rehearsal day," he explained. "You take your team to Cologne and secure the route, the timing, and the placement of the vans. I want you to plan a simulated evening explosion. By the time you arrive I'll be there watching you. Depending on your performance, I'll decide whether we need to modify the plan. If we do, we'll have to rehearse again before the real thing."

• • •

It was midnight, past rehearsal day, when Abu Musa turned off the light and slipped into bed. He didn't care for the blanket. It had a sickening smell. He imagined that it must have been wasted on wrapping dog shit before letting him have it. The mattress was saturated with stains, presumably leftover semen. That part bothered him only a bit less. He tried to keep his thoughts away from the apartment's conditions. The rehearsal didn't go well. He needed to make some major adjustments. The overall grade was unsatisfactory. Securing the perfect street-parking place for the vans proved problematic. He would have to figure out a better way for securing the spots. They'd go for another rehearsal next week. He began planning the next step.

Early in the morning, he would take possession of Professor Berger's house, under an assumed name. Abu Baaqr had already arranged for the ammonium nitrate to be available. Jamil and his colleagues would provide logistics. They'd load the vans with ammonium nitrate, transport it to the house on the outskirts, then unload and store it in the barn. Three weeks from now, they'd set off the fireworks. He would be watching it on the news from Canada, where he would turn up one day ahead of the big event. He felt better at that final thought. His mission in life was about to materialize; Allah was on his side.

He was deep in thought when multiple bangs on the door made him jump out of bed. His heart was pumping fast. *How could I not prepare for such an eventuality?* He already suspected that the police were on his tail. *Why was I so careless?*

"Wake up, Abu Musa, wake up."

He didn't move.

"Abu Musa, it's the Imam, it's Abul Bashar. Open the door."

Is this a trick? Can they even imitate the Imam's voice?

"Abu Musa, get up and open the door. It's important." The Imam sounded alarmed.

He was finally convinced. He opened the door and let the Imam in.

"Why are you here? What's going on?"

Abul Bashar was breathing as if he'd just seen the face of Allah. His graying hair, or whatever was left of it, required an urgent combing. He looked distressed. "You'll have to put your mission on hold," the Imam said. "The police believe that I'm organizing a terror event. They believe that I'm inciting the believers and turning them into suicide bombers." He paused, looked around the room; although it appeared as though he was about to offer an opinion, he dismissed that thought and continued along the topic he'd come to convey. "They'll soon discover what you're up to. I talked to Jamil and I know. This isn't the right time. The German government and the city administration are talking about closing down the academy and the mosque. You must hit the brakes. I even suggest that you leave the country as soon as possible, before they catch up with you."

"What happened that makes you say that?"

"They were in my mosque today. They asked me to come with them to the police. They interrogated me for hours. They told me that I could be a dead man—accidents happen."

"So, you'll be a martyr. Isn't that what you want?"

The Imam turned away, then faced him again. The look on his face was condescending. "It's not the right time; there's more to do before I find my place in Paradise. The community needs me here."

Abu Musa heard the words but sensed the mood. *The Imam is definitely spinning; he'll never sacrifice himself for Allah.* Abu Musa felt betrayed. He wasn't about to follow the Imam's directive.

"Stopping everything's going to be hard," Abu Musa countered. "We've already got the goods. We can't keep them in the open. It must be stored in a safe place. We have the vans. The *shahids* (martyrs) have been mobilized. I can't stop it."

"They've already stopped it. You don't have the goods. The German police found out something. They've questioned Abu Baaqr's cousin before he was ready to deliver. He's going to talk if he hasn't done so already. You must understand. I don't want to put everyone in the community at risk. The German authorities are on it. You better vanish before they place you behind bars."

Abu Musa didn't say a word. His only thought—*the Imam is deceiving me. I'll have to change plans. I'll have to leave Bonn as soon as possible before it's too late*—was cooking inside his skull. He knew. He would avenge this misfortune. He would return a favor when the time came.

As soon as the Imam left, Abu Musa knew he had to act quickly. He wanted to get in touch with Hilga, but dreaded the idea of her phone and her apartment being bugged. He would have to wait until she was out in the morning. He got dressed, then sat on his bed. There was really no place to go in the middle of the night. *Even the Imam wasn't to be trusted anymore.* Abu Musa was getting anxious about the apartment as well. It might not be safe, the Imam knew his address; he could possibly give him away in an effort to save his own skin. Wondering the streets at this time at night wasn't safe either. He decided to stay in for the rest of the night, then leave early in the morning. He would be monitoring near *Winterstrasse*, mixing in the crowd, waiting for Hilga to come out.

• • •

He spotted her early in the morning as she turned the corner into *Waldburgstrasse*. He came from behind and tapped on her shoulder. She was startled at first, but as soon as she realized who it was, her facial expression changed into a welcoming smile.

"I must leave the country," he said. "I want to join you on your trip to Canada. When are you leaving?"

"Tomorrow at 5:00 p.m. from Frankfurt."

"Perfect, I'll see you at the airport."

It was a cold parting. Hilga was left dumbfounded. Abu Musa neither kissed her, nor hugged her. He was businesslike with no hint of warmth. After what they'd been through together, she expected something else. It didn't come to pass.

As he turned the corner toward *Waldburgstrasse*, he noticed a police car parked in front of his apartment. There was no seeming activity around it; he couldn't recognize any police officers, just a squad car, but that was plenty. Abu Musa realized that he was a hunted man. They hadn't yet pulled the full press on him; he still had a chance of evading arrest if he acted quickly enough.

It was still early. He could take the train and make it to Frankfurt airport in time for the 12:50 p.m. flight to Toronto. He would buy a roundtrip ticket even though he didn't intend to return. He would use his Amin Shukri Visa card to pay for the airfare. His brothers in Egypt would shell out the money. He felt safe. The Canadians were still miles behind on their border security compared to the Americans. He would cross the border into their country unscathed. Professionals had crafted his British passport, and the German border police hadn't yet been clued in about him and his alleged mission. They'd let Amin Shukri go across without any difficulty.

Chapter 15

Saturday, December 14, 2002—Washington, DC

Jim and Stanley burst into Jack Devon's office before Jenny had a chance to slow them down. Saturday was a common working day around Jack's office. Jack was at the heart of reviewing the latest on the Sahara camp when the unexpected interruption occurred. He raised his head, watched the two of them with wonder; they looked as excited as if they'd just sold a thousand shares of *WorldCom* to some poor sucker for $60 a share. He got up and walked to the door that separated his office from Jenny's desk, just to make sure she was there. She was an efficient gatekeeper; that function took account of his direct reports as well. Jenny watched him and recognized his reaction. She spread her hands with her palms up. Her body language and facial expression conveyed the obvious—*I couldn't stop them. What else could I do?*

Before he could confront and challenge his men, they both rushed to the TV in his office and turned it on to CNN. "Watch this," Jim said without taking his eyes off the set. "A new player has come to town."

CNN correspondent, Debby Helms, was reporting from Brooklyn on Qassem al-Nasr's daring escape from police custody. Al-Nasr's picture was displayed on the screen while Ms. Helms was talking in the background, telling the story. There was one extra potential terrorist on the loose after fleeing from his two pursuers. The three men in custody didn't seem to have much information on Qassem al-Nasr. The name of the other potential terrorist hadn't been released yet. Police had raided Qassem's apartment in the *Village*. They talked to his neighbors, confiscated his PC. Ms. Helms pledged for more news as soon as it became available.

Jack turned off the TV and faced his men. "What do you have in mind?" he asked as if everything were cool. Then, as an afterthought, he added, "there cannot be a crisis today; my schedule's already full."

The two stared at him in disbelief. They felt as though they had been interrupted during sex, seconds before reaching the Promised Land. Jim finally gathered his nerve. "We came here to make sure that you're up to date on what's happening in our backyard."

"What I don't like is that the NYPD is after the people we were supposed to catch. Why didn't we know about this character, Qassem al-Nasr, before tonight?" Jack complained.

"Qassem al-Nasr came out of nowhere," Stanley grumbled. "He's been living in the *Village* for less than a week. His neighbors don't know where he came from. They've never met the landlord. They mail their rent in cash to a P. O. Box in Boston. We checked that one out. It belongs to a woman by the name of Dorothy Mainham; her address is the same one we searched in the *Village*. The NYPD is still looking inside Qassem al-Nasr's PC. They may find more information."

"The NYPD... The NYPD," Jack whined. "It should've been us!"

Jim shook his head slowly, contemplatively, "Well, apparently, the Qassem guy arrived in the city a couple of nights ago. He came from Egypt," he said, his voice steely. "The guy hasn't registered any terror act or conspiracy to commit one. He isn't officially a terrorist. His only crime is running away from potential detention by the NYPD."

Stanley barged in. "I don't see how he could've been on our radar screen." He paused, scratched his head, then added, "they should've arrested him, then accidentally slam into a telephone pole while driving him downtown." His face cracked in an open smile. "I actually like the NYPD," he went on. "They remind me of when I was young and stupid. God will forgive us all. That's his job, after all."

Jack took notice of the final comment. "Okay, forgiven," he said with a low voice and a grim face. "But from now on, you're going to monitor this darling chap. First, we find where he is, then we follow him. We don't yet engage the NYPD in our investigation, but we take any information we can from them and use it to our own benefit. We must figure him out. We must know who he is, who he's connected to, what he's up to, and whether or not he's dangerous."

As soon as they left his office, Jim turned to Stanley. "You know," he said, "you should turn down the volume. Your jokes aren't well received by Jack. He seemed pretty irritated."

Stanley wasn't the one to retreat. "Hey, you don't really get it. Jack's been in a bad mood lately. He needs to cheer up. If he can't do it on his own, I'll have to do it for him. He's in competition with the NYPD, the CIA, the NSA, the Justice department. He wants to do it all alone. It's a mistake. I can change his attitude only if I use humor."

"Be careful. Jack is running out of patience." Jim said, then turned around and walked into his office.

Chapter 16

December 19, 2002—Toronto, Canada

It was about eight in the evening when the Lufthansa flight landed on the Toronto runway. The disappointment Hilga had sensed from not seeing Abu Musa at the Frankfurt airport dissipated in the course of the seven-hour journey. At an earlier point during the flight, she even felt relief knowing that there was hardly any room for Abu Musa in her sister's small two-bedroom apartment in Toronto.

Midway through the flight, her next seat neighbor introduced himself—Kamil Awad, a Lebanese Christian who was traveling to the US via Canada to study for his Master's degree at the University of Michigan in Ann Arbor. He'd recently completed his Bachelor's degree in Economics at the American University in Beirut and planned to spend the holiday season by himself in Toronto, before heading southwest across the border for his ultimate destination.

When Kamil got up before taking a bathroom break, Hilga managed a long-drawn-out gaze at the handsome man who was standing in the isle next to her. He was slim and just short of five feet eleven inches in height. His olive shirt matched his Middle Eastern complexion and his big, dark-brown eyes. His smile exposed an array of straight and shapely white teeth; he had the body of an athlete— broad shoulders and a narrow but cute butt. She liked him.

They kept on talking after his return from his break. He told her how his family had perished during the civil war in Lebanon. His parents and two sisters were traveling in their family car when PLO gangs ambushed it in West Beirut. He had no relatives in the US or Canada, nor anyone to write to at home in Lebanon. Hilga told Kamil about her life in Germany, then she extended an open invitation for him at her sister's place lest he felt lonely in Toronto.

She came out of the gate after breezing through Passport and Customs inspection. Then, she sorted through a long line of taxi drivers who were holding large pieces of cardboard, each with their customer's name. Looking for her brother-in-law, her eyes rested on a true surprise—her nine-month pregnant sister, one hand behind her back, a cheerful grin painting her face. She charged toward her not noticing her brother-in-law who was waiting on the other side of the line. They cuddled for a full minute, then kissed for another. Hilga's brother-in-law was standing next to them when they finally loosened their hug. The moment she noticed him, Hilga embraced him as well. They kissed on both cheeks, then she turned back to face her sister who handed her the red rose she'd been holding behind her back.

Abu Musa, whose identity had been transformed to Amin Shukri, a British citizen, was watching the scene from a well-placed nook. He didn't want to have any contact with Hilga's family that would compel him to expose his old identity. Still, he chose to have a look at them without being noticed—a potential point of reference for future endeavors.

Abu Musa was preparing to leave the scene when all at once he noticed the young stranger who was waving his hands toward Hilga. She seemed to be familiar with the new arrival. Her facial expression conveyed joy upon catching sight of him. She invited the stranger over to meet her relatives who greeted him warmly. Abu Musa froze in place. *Who is this man? Is he an intelligence officer who befriended Hilga so that he could get close to her Muslim friends?*

Kamil Awad headed out of the airport after his first encounter with Hilga's sister. Abu Musa followed him and watched. As the attention-grabbing Kamil was about to step in the next taxi, Abu Musa positioned himself next to him. The driver stepped out of the cab; glancing at Kamil's two heavy suitcases, he elected to take a leap, offer his services to the next passenger in line who carried no luggage at all. "Where to?" he asked Abu Musa.

"Oh, he was ahead of me," Abu Musa said while indicating at Kamil. "You want to take him first."

The humiliated driver felt out of his depth. He turned to Kamil who stared at Abu Musa with definite appreciation. "Okay, mister," the driver said. "Where to?"

"The downtown Marriott at *Eaton Centre*," Kamil said.

"Wow. I'm heading there as well," Abu Musa interjected. He turned to Kamil. "Can we share this cab?"

"Of course," Kamil responded. "It'll be my pleasure."

The conversation in the taxi on the way to the hotel was exceptionally open. Kamil and Abu Musa identified each other's accent, then realized they were from the same expanse. They switched to Arabic as soon as the car left the airport area. Once he found out that Kamil was a Lebanese Christian, Abu Musa played along, acting to suit the ambiance, telling Kamil that he'd grown up in Qauza, a tiny hilltop village North of the Lebanese-Israeli border, home to a small Christian community. They realized that fate put them, all but blood brothers, together, on their holiday away from home. They decided to spend the next few days visiting and exploring Toronto together, keeping each other company.

For the first two days, as they were spending time together, Abu Musa did actually enjoy Kamil's company. Deep inside, however, he still hoarded a great deal of enmity and suspicion. On balance, he considered Kamil an infidel, a descendant of crusaders who'd invaded Palestine nine hundred years earlier only to be driven away by courageous martyrs like him. He never regarded Kamil as a potential heir to the early followers of *Jesus Christ*. This version had never comprised Abu Musa's history lessons. At the same time, he deemed Kamil a potential spy who was on the lookout for freedom fighters of the ilk of Islamic martyrs. Abu Musa felt it was time to talk politics and dig up these dirty secrets, exposing the pig for what he really was.

"So where're you headed to next week?" Abu Musa asked during breakfast on the third day of their fresh camaraderie.

"The University of Michigan at Ann-Arbor," Kamil responded. "I should get settled there before the start of the new semester."

"I see," Abu Musa said. "Does anyone expect you there?"

"No one specifically, just that I'm due on campus." He paused for a moment, took a sip from his coffee cup, then continued. "My student visa is conditional upon my attendance, I guess. The university is probably going to report on my arrival to the US Immigration office."

Abu Musa took note, then changed the subject. "Have you ever thought of going back to Lebanon?" he asked.

"Not really," Kamil grunted. "The conditions there are unstable. I don't like the situation with the Syrians controlling the political agenda, the Shiites down in the South heating up the Israeli border, the Sunnis, the Palestinians, the Druze—they all detest each other. All this internal fighting makes me sick. I wish Lebanon could go back to the times when it was considered 'Paris of the Middle East.' I'd like to see internal harmony, independence from Syria, and peace with Israel."

"Peace with Israel? Are you kidding?"

"No, I'm serious." Kamil seemed surprised at the elevated emotions displayed by Abu Musa; he went on, nevertheless. "I wish Lebanon was conflict free. I wish I could go back there and live without fear, without being terrorized; I wish I could worry about my future rather than be mired in thoughts of revenge and dwelling on questionable history."

"Wait a minute," Abu Musa interjected. "Don't you believe in justice? Don't you think that the Zionists and the Americans robbed the Palestinians of their land? Don't you see how the Americans fertilize their imperialist appetite by supporting the Zionists, and the corrupt regimes in Egypt, Saudi Arabia, Kuwait, Pakistan? Do you accept the status quo as a final and stable solution?" He paused, then glared at Kamil with skepticism. "I can't believe you mean what you say," he added.

Kamil realized that they were stirring towards an unpleasant confrontation. He moved to change the subject. "Look," he said. "I'm not into politics. Let's talk about what we're going to do today and tomorrow. And by the way, I met a nice German woman on the flight to Canada, and I want to visit her and her sister tomorrow evening."

A red light went off in Abu Musa's head.

Kamil went on. "I told her about you, and she extended an invitation, if you wish to come, of course."

"I'll think about it. I'm not sure," Abu Musa said. He was trying to recall whether he'd mentioned the name Amin Shukri to Hilga, but he couldn't be sure.

• • •

It was early afternoon when heavy snow started falling on the already icy Toronto landscape. Kamil and Abu Musa decided to call off their planned sightseeing and relax in their own rooms. Half an hour later, Abu Musa came down to the lobby looking for a public phone. Using a pre-paid calling card, he placed a phone call to Bonn Germany. Abul Bashar, the Imam at the mosque at the *King Abdullah Academy* wasn't too happy to hear his voice since he suspected the authorities of monitoring his line. He was talking to Abu Musa in code. "Check with *Delilah* on the 1999 used *Black Mercedes*. It's for sale. And by the way, my dog has been missing you," he added, implying the obvious—*the German police had been sniffing behind his back and around his neck, seeking information about Abu Musa.*

Abu Musa got the picture. *Delilah* was a code name for a particular Internet site used by Islamic terror groups. Abul Bashar's code name in the *"for sale"* chat room was *Black Mercedes*. As soon as he hung up, Abu Musa made his way to the business center at the hotel where he was able to surf the web and exchange information with his benefactors. The message was coded but unambiguous. He was to establish contact with Hassan Omar from Brooklyn, New York. Omar had been a fugitive for a week. He was no longer in the New York area. His whereabouts were unknown, but on Saturday, December 21, the day he was supposed to surface, he would leave a trace with *Delilah*. Omar's code name was *Karachi_81*—his birthplace and birth year—making it easy to commit to memory.

Chapter 17

December 21, 2002—Toronto, Canada

It was breakfast again and Kamil Awad was eager to talk about his visit with Hilga during the previous evening. She was nervous, he supposed. She said that two officers from the *Canadian Security Intelligence Service* (CSIS) had come over to her sister's apartment to interview her about a person she'd lived with in Germany—Abu Musa, who, they suspected, was traveling under an assumed name, like Ahmad Abu Rmeiyeh or something else, and was staying, by all accounts, somewhere in the Toronto area.

"What did she tell them?" Abu Musa asked, his blood pressure leaping to heights reserved only for heart disease sufferers.

"She didn't say anything concerning Abu Musa's whereabouts, or his assumed name. She said she didn't know." Kamil paused. He lowered his voice and leaned forward, then muttered: "She asked me about you, my friend, and when I mentioned your name—Amin Shukri, she nodded, but said nothing. I got the feeling that she knew the name."

Abu Musa glared at Kamil, thinking—*this guy is dicey*, then without further ado, he said. "How would she know my name? I never met the woman."

"I believe she was thinking she knew you." He paused, looked down, then raised his head and stared straight at Abu Musa's eyes: "Do you know her? Are you connected to Abu Musa?" he questioned.

That was a bit much for Abu Musa to bear. His whereabouts and his identity were about to be uncovered in spite of all the precautions he'd been taking. "No way," he countered, but then his brain was already plugging away. *This train must be stopped before it's too late*, he reflected.

Kamil beamed back thinking — *Yeah sure. What else could the answer be?* Nonetheless, he tried to conceal his genuine standpoint. "I didn't think so," he said. Still, his facial expression and body language revealed his thoughts, a sentiment that didn't escape Abu Musa's eye.

"We should go and visit the West Don River Park today," Abu Musa said, changing the subject. "It's a nice day, the sun is shining, the snow is melting, and that will be perfect for hiking." He glanced at his watch. "Let's do it after lunch. We can hike for a few hours without worrying about getting hungry."

Kamil agreed. "Sounds good. I need to make a few phone calls now. We can meet in a couple of hours, grab a quick hamburger with fries, and go to the park."

• • •

It turned a bit cloudy when they met again in the afternoon. Abu Musa came well equipped. He had brought a blanket with him, tied on top of a backpack, inside which he had "some useful goodies", as he explained. Kamil didn't carry anything other than an umbrella and a camera. Both were dressed warmly, prepared for an outdoors December excursion.

They walked along the river taking pleasure in the cool Canadian breeze and the beautiful nature surrounding them. There were very few people at the park, and after four o'clock, as the sun was about ready to embark on its quick descent; they were all alone, watching the freezing waters, the bare trees, and the threatening clouds.

"Let's head back," Kamil suggested. "It's getting dark and frosty. I don't want to start looking for the way back without the benefit of a touch of daylight."

Abu Musa nodded. "Sure. Let's just pause for a second. I want to take some water out of the bag." He stopped, then untied the blanket from the top of the bag, spread it open, then drew the baseball bat that he'd placed inside.

Kamil was watching the waters, taking some final pictures with his camera before it would be too dark and too late. He didn't notice Abu Musa's approach from behind. He never had a chance. Two blows to the head with the baseball bat and Kamil fell unconscious, striking the moist ground. Abu Musa played it safe. He looked down at the bloody head and then drove two more weighty blows into the broken skull, only to make certain that no life lingered inside this infidel's body. Next, looking around and ascertaining that he was alone, he spread open the blanket and dragged Kamil's body to its center. He sorted through Kamil's pants pockets, picked up his wallet and the key to his hotel room. Exploring inside Kamil's jacket he found his Lebanese passport.

Without further ado, he wrapped Kamil's body in the blanket, lifted it onto his right shoulder, then carried it to the waters. As soon as he reached the riverbank, he laid the body on the ground, unwrapped the blanket and pushed the corpse with his feet into the freezing waters. *By morning, it'll be swept away into Lake Ontario and swim with the fish until it disintegrates.*

It was utterly dark now. The thick clouds covered the full moon; Abu Musa, upon his return to the spot where the killing had taken place, took a quick survey of the vicinity. He wished he'd brought a flashlight with him, but nonetheless, he was able to fold the blood-stained blanket and stuff it with the baseball bat inside his backpack before heading back to the city where he dumped it in front of a steak restaurant that had its garbage bags out on the street ready for an early morning pickup.

After moving his belongings to Kamil's room, Abu Musa took a shower, changed into clean clothes, then went down to the lobby where he prepaid the bill, and arranged for an early morning checkout for his, Amin Shukri's, room. From that moment, he began assuming Kamil's identity. Amin Shukri would leave the scene and vanish, while he, Abu Musa, would take on Kamil's identity and stay in the dead man's room for two extra nights before heading to Ann Arbor, Michigan, registering there at the university, under the name of Kamil Awad, before the start of the new semester.

It was December 21, rendezvous date with Hassan Omar over the *Delilah* site. Abu Musa was about to leave the lobby, walk into *Eaton Centre*, where he would find an Internet Café and attempt to connect with Omar, when it suddenly dawned on him that he'd left Kamil's, now his, wallet upstairs inside his soiled pants. Once back in the room, he went searching for the missing wallet, but failed to recover it. He was growing upset. He remembered taking the wallet, the room key and the passport, from the dead Kamil. All of these items were here, with the exception of the wallet. He was walking around the room thinking through, trying to conjure up the detailed sequence of events leading up to the present state of affairs, when he suddenly heard a knock on the door. An uninvited guest was waiting in the hallway, expecting to be asked in.

He froze for a second; he then approached the door quietly, and stole a look through the peephole. Hilga was standing there, more beautiful than he could remember. She was wearing a new fur coat; she had freshly dyed blonde hair. He hesitated for a moment. Hilga had come to see Kamil. She would be astounded if he opened the door instead. He stood there for another moment watching her and trying to make up his mind. Hilga glanced at her watch; she looked disappointed, then she turned around and walked away.

It was a deciding moment. Abu Musa wasn't thinking. His emotions drove his actions. He opened the door and rushed to catch her. Before Hilga realized who it was, he turned her around, faced her directly, held her head firmly in both hands, and pressed his lips against hers. She was overwhelmed. She was unable to utter a word. She could only return a passionate kiss and submit to Abu Musa's lead that took them back into the room.

It was a passionate hour. They weren't talking, only moaning. When it was over, Abu Musa was still resting in bed while Hilga got up and went to the bathroom. When she came back to the room with a towel wrapped around her body, Abu Musa was already dressed, ready to leave.

"Are you still here?" he asked.

She stared at him somewhat puzzled by his reaction. "Where're you going?" she asked. She expected a warmer welcome after what they'd just gone through.

"I'm busy," he shot back. "You must leave now."

"But I—"

He didn't let her finish the sentence. "You must leave now. I said I'm busy." He came closer, took her arm, then led her to the corner of the room, to the floor near the window, where her clothes piled up after she'd helped him remove everything. "Get dressed," he told her. "And hurry up, I'm late already."

Hilga was confused. "Why do you treat me this way?" she asked.

Abu Musa was running out of patience. "Listen, woman. You better hurry up, I'm getting impatient."

Hilga didn't answer. She started getting dressed, then paused after feeling a bit less naked with her underwear shielding her feminine parts; she dared a challenge: "Where's Kamil? I came to see him. Isn't this his room?"

Abu Musa was getting irritated, but felt he couldn't let a question hang in the air for too long. Someone or even Hilga might try to pull it down, looking for answers. "Kamil—this wasn't his real name—left the country. He wasn't what you thought he was. He was a man on the run. He had no choice. I can't offer any more information at this point."

"Doesn't sound like Kamil," she muttered. "What're you doing here? Why are you in his room?" she asked.

Abu Musa brought his voice down. He was whispering as if trying to prevent unwanted eavesdropping from gathering the information he was about to dispense. "That's part of the scheme. I'm Kamil from now on. Remember. When you see me again, you call me Kamil Awad." He picked up her shirt from the floor and pushed it onto her chest. Then, louder. "Put it on already. I've been waiting too long."

• • •

As soon as Hilga left, Abu Musa went looking for Kamil's wallet, but for a second time, he could not find it. The wallet was neither in the room, nor inside the clothes he was wearing. It had simply vanished. Frustrated, he swore in Arabic, then went down to the lobby and out to *Eaton Centre*.

The Internet Café was utterly packed. There was only one station left unoccupied, but for a good reason—the PC was down. After purchasing a one-hour credit, Abu Musa walked around the isles waiting for a vacancy. The attendant approached and asked him to wait in line, just like everyone else.

At that moment, one of the users got up, collected his coat, headed for the exit. Abu Musa ignored the attendant manager; he immediately rushed to catch the available station. The young woman whose turn was next came over and complained. "You know," she said to Abu Musa. "This was supposed to be my place. I was here ahead of you. Would you please let me have it?"

This was a bit much for the one who wouldn't be intimidated by infidels, especially women infidels. Abu Musa turned his head, stared at the woman. He rose off his chair, glared at her with a scary expression, trying to turn her heart to red jelly, then positioned himself inches from her face, while his scar was changing colors. "Look lady," he said in a threatening tone. "Don't mess with me. Go stand in line. I mean it."

The intimidated woman turned around and gazed at the manager as if asking for protection. The poor guy, not geared up for confrontations, came over and reiterated. "Please wait for your turn. She was first."

Abu Musa turned his attention to the manager. They were standing opposite each other next to the Internet station. "I'm in a hurry," he said. "I must use this now." His tone of voice flaunted resentment.

"Everyone wants to use it now," the manager responded. "You should wait for your turn, and then you can use it for as long as you want."

Abu Musa didn't like the answer. A wave of red was rising from his neck to his jaw, his scar seemed more threatening by the minute.

He took a step closer to the manager, whose unsettled expression laid bare his anxiety, then all at once, pushed him hard. The manager stumbled and fell on the floor next to the kid who was working in the adjacent station. Abu Musa acted as if nothing had happened. He went back to his seat and started working on his program.

The place went still as the manager got up and wandered back to his desk. Abu Musa didn't bother. He logged on to the *Delilah* site, then searched for Hassan Omar under the id—*Karachi_81*. In the next ten minutes, he was able to communicate in code with the Pakistani fugitive. They set up a meeting in Dearborn, Michigan, at the *Abu Shakra* restaurant on New Year's Eve, at 10 p.m.

Abu Musa terminated his session and got ready to leave. He moved his chair back, making room for an exit path, but was unable to proceed. Two police officers were standing in his way, blocking his advance. "We understand that you were involved in an assault some twenty minutes ago," one of the officers said. He was well built, relatively short, with dark brown eyes, black hair, and a moustache. He could very well go for a brother Arab if he hadn't spoken English with such perfect Canadian accent. The other officer, who parked on Abu Musa's left, looked like a downright contrast to the potential brother. He had golden-blond hair with bleached highlights, tall, clean-shaven; his blue eyes added to his attention-grabbing qualities.

Abu Musa had no choice but to be polite—not his strongest suit. He realized that the two had bested him. Resisting or acting aggressively would result in his downfall; therefore out of the question. There was no choice but to cooperate; the potential brother cop might be soft and respectful once they were acquainted.

"Nothing of the kind, officer," he said after swallowing hard. "I was only trying to secure my rights. I was first in line and in a hurry; now I'm done."

"We have witnesses who say you jumped the line and caused a violent altercation. Is that how you secured your rights?" the potential brother cop asked, while the good-looking one was gaping from the left, calmly watching the dialogue, but all set for action.

"I had no choice. The manager, over there, tried to force me out of line," Abu Musa said, pointing at the manager who was watching intently as the dialogue was pressing on.

The *brother* cop seemed to be ignoring the comeback. "Can I see some identification please?" he asked. The blond-haired officer was still standing at the same spot, but now he had his tongue out wiping his upper lip in anticipation.

Abu Musa went for the pocket inside his jacket, drew a passport and handed it to the officer.

"I see, so your name's Kamil Awad from Lebanon," the dark-haired officer stated after reviewing the passport. "You're a guest in this country, yet you behave badly." He turned to his blond-haired partner. "Take a look at this passport and tell me if you see something."

Blondy picked up the official document without taking his eyes off Abu Musa. He then opened it and scanned the picture posted on its first page. He eyeballed Abu Musa, then shifted his gaze down to the picture. Up at Abu Musa and down at the picture. And then… one more time…

Abu Musa was getting uneasy. He'd overlooked the fact that a careful scrutiny of the passport picture in his presence might raise suspicion concerning his identity. Both he and Kamil had inherited Middle-Eastern genes, They both had darker than average (Caucasian) skin complexion including big, dark-brown eyes; except for Abu Musa's facial scar, which could've come about after the picture had been taken, they did resemble each other. The apparent discrepancy between the picture and Abu Musa's guise could be justified on the grounds that the passport had been issued seven years earlier; things change in seven years. Furthermore, Abu Musa had assumed that to most Canadians, all Arabs looked alike, even though, on balance, he and Kamil weren't related and the passport picture wasn't his.

Blondy handed the passport back to *the brother*, his partner officer. "I think we should take him in for further questioning," he said, smirking.

The two officers appeared to enjoy the moment, as Abu Musa was getting increasingly testy; the palms of his hands began sweating.

"No!" Abu Musa declared, losing his cool. "You can't take me in. You have no good reason. I have no time for stupid jokes."

The officers exchanged stares. Then *Blondy* made the move. In a sudden shift, he grabbed Abu Musa, turned him around, handcuffed his right hand, then his left, turned him back in the opposite direction, then looked him in the eye. "You come with us, you. We must talk," he asserted before cracking a grin at his partner. Then he let his prejudicial thoughts break out of his system. He turned away from Abu Musa and muttered as if to himself. "We should do away with all these '*Osamas*' and their friends. What do they come here for?"

"Abu Musa was overwhelmed. The surprise move didn't leave any opening for a challenge. The two officers hauled him away. He was their prisoner.

Chapter 18

December 21, 2002—New York City

A full week went by in self-imprisonment in the *Upper West Side* apartment in Manhattan. Arik was getting bored and anxious. There was no news concerning Rachel; he was growing increasingly concerned. He didn't know whether she was still alive or whether anybody was still looking for her in Bali or any other Indonesian territory; he blamed himself for doing absolutely nothing to help her situation at this point. He'd also lost contact with his Muslim acquaintances, and he was eager to reestablish himself as a key player.

The temperature in Manhattan on that December day was down to the teens; the icy wind carried it further down to a windshield index reaching the lower single (Fahrenheit) digits. Arik wasn't accustomed to North Pole frigid air. Tel Aviv was forty-degrees (Fahrenheit) warmer. He remembered jogging on the beachfront throughout December. It was his favorite jogging month. However, here in Manhattan, he could forget about it. Only polar bears and penguins were keen on the outdoors in this kind of weather. He looked out the window, turned around, then gazed at Jerry.

"Man, you look like Paganini on a bad hair day," Jerry said, as both were watching Katie Couric on the *Today* Show from Rockefeller Center. "You need to trim your beard and comb your curls," he continued.

"What for?" he answered. "Don't I look sexy enough for you?"

"Unless you want the cops to stop you for poisoning the environment once you get out of here…"

"Once I get out… that's exactly what I was thinking. I'm getting out… soon… today, in fact. It's time to launch my rebirth."

Jerry flinched. "I'm not sure this is a good idea. It's not quite safe yet. The NYPD and the FBI are still on the lookout for you, after you stole their cruiser and escaped detention."

Arik rose from the sofa. "I've checked already. My face's no longer front page." He began pacing around the small living room, brought his right hand to his head and moved it through his uncombed hair. "I dropped from the top ten news headlines down to about two hundred plus," he contended. "I can walk around with my hat, mustache, beard, and sunglasses. No one will pay attention."

"Or move to the other side of the street." Jerry, revealing his bone-dry sense of humor, grimaced and let out a lungful of air. "Where're you going?"

•   •   •

It was still cold outside, but during the two hours that had passed, the temperature had climbed more than twenty degrees. It was time to venture out and instigate some action. Arik got his yellow turtleneck, formal black pants, a heavy, though stylish, black coat with a matching hat and sunglasses, then headed out. He made his way to the King James Bar on Park Avenue, next to the *Waldorf Astoria* — one block away from Hamad Suleiman's apartment building. He ordered beer, then picked up a dark corner where he could sip it peacefully, bit by bit, while monitoring new customers who turned up through the doorway.

Minutes afterward, a man, cleaving to a peculiar posture, entered the joint. He was about five feet eight inches in height, just under two-hundred pounds in weight. His head slanted forward, as if it were trying to break away from the rest of his bulk. He was walking somewhat lamely, shifting his right foot in a weird fashion and limping as if the frog inside his right shoe could do with more room. Arik felt a shiver of recognition, like a mirage in the midst of a hot summer afternoon. That person was the same man he'd noticed walking next to the *Upper West Side* apartment one week earlier, the day prior to the unfortunate police encounter. In spite of the dimness, Arik could make out facial details. The man looked forty, sporting an athletic build, big nose, bushy dark eyebrows, typical Mediterranean features.

One tip was apparent. Had the man been working for the FBI or the NYPD, Arik would've been arrested by now. *There must've been a shady group operating behind this sleazy character.* Arik was contemplating his next move, when, all of a sudden, the man's phone went off in a loud ding. He picked it up, didn't say a word, just listened. He turned his gaze toward Arik, watching him head for the exit. Less than a minute went by. The man came out of the Bar. He stepped forward toward the edge of the sidewalk holding his phone close to his ear while surveying the environs in search of his vanishing prey. Without warning, Arik sneaked up from behind, and pointing the knife he'd picked up at the bar; he pushed it against the man's back.

"Don't move unless you want me to shoot," Arik whispered in the man's ear, acting as if the pointed object he was sticking the man with was actually a gun. "Who are you working for?"

"Hey, don't get too excited," the man said. He tried to turn his head toward Arik but changed his mind in midair. "Dan Carmel wants to make sure you're okay," he said with a heavy Hebrew accent.

Arik released the pressure, let the man turn around. "You should've introduced yourself," he said. "You made me nervous. What's the purpose of being so stealthy?"

"I guess, Dan wanted to keep an eye on you without your knowledge."

"Okay. I want you to take off. And on your way to your loft, you should call Dan and tell him that I don't appreciate his spying techniques. I'm a big boy," he said, then walked back into the bar.

At thirty minutes past five, Arik stepped out of the bar, surveyed the surroundings but couldn't spot any sign of trouble. The street was sparsely populated. He hailed a passing cab, then stepped in.

The cabbie didn't look back. "Where to?" he asked, ready to get going "Here's fifty bucks," Arik said, handing it over to the amazed driver. "Just go for one block and stop. I'll stay in the cab, waiting for someone."

The taxi-driver turned around, snatched the fifty-dollar bill, then followed Arik's instructions.

They sat in silence for about ten minutes while Arik busied himself scrutinizing the vicinity. Following the long wait, the cab driver broke the silence. "How long are you going to hang on?" he asked without turning.

"Here's another fifty," Arik offered. "This should last for an extra fifteen minutes of wait time plus another fifteen for a short ride."

The cabbie turned around and glanced at Arik. "Okay, man," he said. "Whatever you say…"

Arik detected a foreign accent; he wanted to make sure. He checked the dashboard; the driver's nametag was displayed for the pleasure of backseat passengers like himself—Eduardo Carlos Dos Santos. "Where're you from?" Arik asked; he wanted to confirm.

"Brazil," he said.

"How long have you been here in the US?"

"Two years and two months."

"I see," *Pretty neutral; nothing to worry about*, Arik concluded. The short conversation ended. Arik had no interest in further tête-à-tête. Serenity took hold again, as no other words were exchanged.

It didn't take more than five minutes before Arik saw her making the turn from 49th Street into Park Avenue. She walked alone. Her short skirt exposed beautiful, sexy legs covered merely with nylon stockings and ending with trendy high-heeled shoes that made her stride in short, sexually suggestive, steps. Her light brown fur coat was a perfect fit for her freshly dyed, honey-blonde hair. She held her purse in one hand and a small gift-wrapped package in the other. Fatima walked toward the cab, then overtook it as Arik was watching, admiring from inside the dark taxi. She didn't pay attention when he opened the rear door, stepped outside, only inches behind her back. She continued her stride toward her target apartment building entrance, a few more steps ahead on her left.

Then, in a sudden move, Arik grabbed Fatima's shoulders, stopping her advance, as the startled woman grew swamped with anxiety. Arik realized that she was about to regain her voice, scream for help. He placed his right hand over her mouth, pulled her head closer to his, then whispered in her ear. "Don't worry, Fatima. It's me—Qassem al-Nasr. I just want to talk. We're going inside the cab now." He grabbed her from behind through the open car door, moved inside, and pulled her in with him. Then, bending over her, he closed the car door.

She was finally able to see his face, as they both were sitting in the back of the car facing the driver and the road ahead. "What do you want?" she asked, obviously irritated, still unsure whether she should be worried, scared, unconcerned, or pleased to see him.

Arik, making certain that Fatima didn't step out of the car instructed the driver to start moving forward. He then turned to Fatima. Switching to Arabic, he said, "listen. Disregard what you've read in the papers about me or seen on TV. It's all lies and made up stories. I'm really on your side. You must believe me. Please." He didn't actually know what side that was, but hoped she would spit it out throughout the discourse.

"So what was all that fiasco with the police? Did it actually happen?"

"Fatima, sweetheart," Arik said, "I can't talk about it right now. I'll explain later, but for the time being I need your help." He touched her left hand, then held it gently for a short moment.

She fixed her eyes on him, then touched his grown beard with her right hand and caressed his face. "You look so different," she said. Her voice was calm and enticing, as her confidence in Arik's amity grew stronger.

Arik couldn't help it, but the feminine touch, the perfume, the sexy tone of voice, the intimacy of the cramped quarters in the backseat of a humming car aroused him. Fatima was an attractive woman, a potential affair in the midst of sexual famine.

Seconds later, he took control of himself as he regained his better judgment; he let the purpose of this meeting take over and stamp out his carnal urges. "Fatima, dear," he pleaded. "I must see Hamad Suleiman. I want you to arrange it."

"I don't think he wants to be seen with you," she countered. "You know, he works for the Saudi government. He works to change the image of Muslims and Islam in general, here in the US.

He studies cinematography. He's already working, producing documentaries about the plight of the Palestinians and life in Arab countries. After 9-11, all Muslims have become suspect of instigating and plotting insane terror acts. Some of us are normal people, looking for the same things all Americans want—a peaceful coexistence and cooperation between us, Arab Muslims, and them, American Christians."

"I know that," Arik pretended to acknowledge, while noticing the absence of Jews from Fatima's world of peaceful coexistence. "I'm an integral component of this mission," he added. "That's why a meeting between Hamad and me must be arranged and must take place clandestinely." He paused, picked up her hand again, then turned to the driver, changing to English. "Please go back to the *Waldorf Astoria*. We'll drop my friend off, right there where we picked her up."

They continued the short journey without speaking. They merely kept holding hands, staring at each other and beaming.

"Here we are," the Brazilian driver said, as they arrived at the *Waldorf*.

Arik pulled Fatima closer, kissed her on the left cheek. "I'll call you tomorrow. Don't worry; no one will be able to trace the origins of the call. And just in case someone listens, I'll be using the codename: Jack," he explained. "And please, I must see Hamad."

He let go of her hand, but she kept holding his. "Come here," she insisted. "Closer."

He couldn't resist her charm. Their noses were touching just before she turned and kissed him passionately on the lips. "I'll be looking forward," she said. "I'll be talking to Hamad." She stepped out and walked in the direction of Suleiman's apartment building. Arik was watching as she made tracks toward the structure. *What am I doing?* He pondered. *I can't have an affair with this woman. This is insane.* Then, grabbing hold of himself, he turned to the Brazilian cabbie. "Drop me off at the Lincoln Center," he directed. "I'm already late."

Chapter 19

December 21, 2002—Toronto, Canada

After spending an hour in police custody downtown, the Arab look-ing officer came over, handed Kamil's passport back to Abu Musa, then told him that he was free to go. To Abu Musa's bemusement, the officer never questioned the passport validity; he never asked him to produce any other ID. When handing over the document, the officer said that the manager at the Internet Café hadn't wished to pursue further charges, and that was that.

It was getting late; Abu Musa went back to the hotel. He was tired; it was, overall, an eventful day. He decided to go to bed, watch TV on the way to a dream world. The local News was boring; he was about to doze off, when unexpectedly the anchor interrupted the mind-numbing broadcast for a Breaking News Story. A body was found floating in the Don River. The dead body couldn't be identi-fied, but there was evidence of a violent homicide. The victim's head had been bashed in with a hard object. Investigation continued.

Abu Musa took note but didn't heed. He was accustomed to news concerning his doings. The numerous suicide killers he'd sent to Israel in the past year alone had served as a requisite schooling and had inured him. Ten minutes later, he was sound asleep.

The telephone ring woke him up at five in the morning. Hilga was all shaken. Abu Musa could hardly understand what she was saying. The police found Kamil's wallet. Inside they found her sis-ter's home phone number. They called. She told them that she'd met Kamil; that he'd been over for dinner, that she'd met him on the flight from Germany."

"So why are you calling me this early in the morning. What's the urgency?"

"They said they found the wallet not far from where they'd hit upon a dead body, on the banks of the Don River. It's part of a homicide investigation, they said."

"It doesn't concern me," Abu Musa said. "I'm going back to bed." He hung up the phone. He didn't go back to sleep. He got dressed, picked up his one suitcase full of personal effects, went downstairs, then sneaked out of the hotel without paying the bill for Kamil's room. As soon as he was out, he made a decision. His identity would have to change once more; he would become Amin Shukri yet again, for as long as he stayed in Canada.

Chapter 20

December 22, 2002—Toronto, Canada

The room in the *Cambridge Suites* in the vicinity of *Eaton Centre* had separate bedroom and living areas. It included a microwave, a mini-bar, and a refrigerator, for which Abu Musa found no use. He was going to spend the morning in the fitness center, then taste the tub in the spa, a first for him. Two hours afterward, he enjoyed breakfast before going back to his suite. He was worn-out and decided to take a nap prior to moving on through the day.

It was lunchtime when he awoke. He went down to the business center, checked the Internet for news on the latest murder at the Don River. Hilga's sister was quoted offering glowing remarks about Kamil Awad, but the more compelling part was the one about the Marriott hotel. Apparently, Mr. Awad had stayed in the hotel. Some of his belongings were still there, but the room had been undone. The bed, the sheets, and the bathroom pointed to someone having stayed there overnight. These findings added to the mystery. It was no longer clear to whom the dead body belonged. It required positive identification; the only persons who could identify it were Hilga, her sister, or her brother-in-law.

Abu Musa was glad he'd decided to change his identity back to Amin Shukri. Kamil Awad would be declared dead; Amin Shukri would become just one superfluous forgotten nobody. Case closed; at least for the time being.

However, one more detail chose to surface. It was shortly after Abu Musa rented a car under Amin Shukri's name, which he intended to use for crossing to the US the next day. He was watching the late afternoon newsbreak on TV, when *Blondy*, the antagonistic police officer, gave an interview to a local reporter, claiming that the dead body bore no resemblance to Kamil Awad. He said he'd arrested Kamil Awad late evening the day before, probably after the dead man had been killed. He also told the story about the circumstances leading to the arrest, implying that Mr. Awad wasn't such a nice fellow, thus contradicting Hilga's sister's characterization.

"We don't know who the dead man is. We want to talk to Kamil Awad," *Blondy* said, cracking a grin. "He might be able to shed some light on all this."

Abu Musa felt he had a slight problem. Kamil Awad was a wanted man, and although Abu Musa had changed his identity back to Amin Shukri, he still planned on crossing to the US with Kamil's passport and student visa. He could've taken a chance—cross into Detroit, Michigan—but crossing in Ontario might be too risky. The border police were probably cooperating with their Toronto counterparts; the name Kamil Awad could raise a flag. He would reduce the risk considerably by crossing near Montreal. The French Canadians might have a communications gridlock with their English-speaking comrades in Ontario—just as the Shiites and the Sunnis were repulsed by one another.

There was only one more thing to do before venturing on his longer detour to Michigan.

He went down to the lobby and called Hilga. She wasn't home; her sister answered the phone. The sister had the very same German accent and her voice was indistinguishable from Hilga's. Once she came back with "Hello," Abu Musa was convinced he was talking to Hilga.

"Hey," he said. "It's no longer Kamil Awad. From now on, I'm Amin Shukri... Again. If the police ask you to identify the dead body, you say you don't recognize him. Don't tell them anything else. I'm leaving for the US. Once there, I'll be in touch." He hung up the phone.

Chapter 21

December 22, 2002—Tel Aviv, Israel

It was after 3 a.m. Sunday morning in Tel Aviv, just ahead of 9 a.m. in Indonesian Java, when Nguyen, the local American CIA agent in charge of Indonesian affairs, placed a call to Dan Carmel's home in Tel Aviv from the American Embassy in Jakarta. Dan was accustomed to being awakened in the middle of the night. His *Mossad* contacts spanned the globe, crossing scores of time zones. This morning, however, he had a bad cold accompanied by severe congestion, which made it difficult to breathe and see clearly. His headache stretched to eight on the Dan Carmel one-to-ten pain-scale, and his speed of thought slowed down to the quickness of a loping turtle.

"Hey Carmel, are you listening?" Nguyen responded to Carmel's sigh, which sounded like a hum resembling a pathetic *"Hello."*

"Ugh, who's that?" Carmel could hardly speak. His sore throat was flaring as he was emerging from a fleeting blackout.

"Carmel, what happened to your voice?" Nguyen asked, after hearing the hoarseness in his timbre. "Did you swallow a chipmunk?" He didn't wait for a response. He was too eager. "Nguyen here. I have important news. Wake up."

"Ugh... Can't speak but I'm listening... Go!"

"Rachel's dead, and so is our inside-man," Nguyen said. "Sorry, I've just got confirmation. No sense keeping hope alive. We were unable to save them."

"Which inside-man?" Dan managed to have a word.

"I'm talking about Ahmad, the snake," he paused, then added for emphasis, "Your Ahmad, the Hebrew speaking taxi driver who transported Arik and Rachel on their critical journey to their

abduction point in Bali. Remember *Operation Paradise*?" He paused
again and listened to Carmel's heavy breathing. It sounded as if Carmel was catching on to the news. His gasping and puffing resembled
a train on its way to hell. Nguyen continued. "Your man, Ahmad, the
snake, had left a message before he was killed."

"What did he say?" Dan's blood drained out of his brain; the
needles in his right eye sought to pierce his cornea.

"The snake pointed to a new-sprung web site, credible as far as
we can judge. It's already shut down shop. This is a new method employed by the local Islamic gangs. It's consistent. They open a new
site; bring it into play for a couple of days before taking it down,
only to repeat the practice a couple days later."

"How the fuck did you let it happen?" Carmel was now in full
alert, though mad as hell. He ran his fingers over the side of his neck,
then flicked off the perspiration. "This was not part of the plan. I did
not want Rachel killed, just detained for a while."

"I know, but we've lost control." Nguyen sounded apologetic.

"You totally fucked up," Dan found it hard to control his anger.
"Now I have blood on my hands, you moron." He paused. "No. It's
you. You have blood on your hands."

"It's your fault rather than mine," Nguyen bounced back. "You
knew the risks before you'd planned the kidnapping. "We let Arik
escape as you'd wished. Everything went according to plan until our
inside-man, the snake, was killed during the police raid. We warned
him beforehand. He was supposed to have left with Rachel before
the police made it to their hideout. It's beyond me why he stayed
behind, fighting the police."

"No. He was supposed to be captured alive," Dan said. "It was
his exit strategy. Once captured, he was supposed to let the police in
on Rachel's whereabouts, where she was being kept, where the terrorist leaders were hiding. Didn't you understand that?"

"You didn't make it clear. I thought he was supposed to vanish
with Rachel. That's why we shot everyone."

"You are a moron," Dan said. "Still, stay on it. The news regarding Rachel may be wide of the mark. We must strive to confirm it
through other sources."

"Okay. Got it," Nguyen managed a response before hanging up.

Carmel turned the lights on and sat on his bed, trying to digest the news. He was contemplating the possibility of callously breaking the news to Arik. That would be his comeuppance. The bad news, on the other hand, might weaken Arik's resolve, since his efforts would no longer yield results for which Arik personally cared. *Should I tell Arik?* No. Carmel had no decision capacity at that moment. He would wait, sleep on it; he needed extra sleep anyway. His head would clear up by morning; he would know what to do by then.

Since his divorce fifteen years earlier, Dan Carmel had never missed a day in the office. However, that Sunday in December 2002 was going to be a first. The bad cold he assumed he had, turned out to be the infamous flu. It was the flu season, and the epidemic had quickly spread all around the country. Half the staff in his office was out sick; he was just another casualty. After an hour of rummaging around, not counting extensive breaks for catching up on his breath, Carmel managed to find a thermometer in one of the drawers in his bathroom. He hadn't used one in ages. In fact, he started believing that following his divorce, his former wife had confiscated it along with many of their joint belongings, some of which had been his personal ones, like the gold watch she'd given him for his thirtieth birthday, his favorite tennis racquet, his music album collection, even his electric shaver.

This morning, his fever reached heights he'd never experienced before in his life. He considered frying eggs on his forehead, but then his appetite was gone, as were the memory cells keeping the details of the call from Nguyen at 3 a.m.; subsequently, he dismissed the gastronomical inspiration as soon as it had been conceived.

It was after 7 p.m. in Tel Aviv, past 12 p.m. in New York, when Jerry called from the Big Apple, using secure communications, by way of a small chip planted inside his modified cell phone, encrypting outgoing and decrypting incoming calls, to and from Dan Carmel, respectively. "Where the hell have you been?" he asked. "I was looking for you all morning, i.e., afternoon—your time. You weren't in the office. No one answered the phone. I thought Sunday was a workday in Israel. Is there a new holiday I'm not aware of?"

Dan Carmel had just swallowed four aspirins. He was still shivering. His voice quivered in rhythm with his shuddering body. "H.e.e.e.y."

"What's that?" Jerry questioned. "Am I interrupting a blow-job?"

"It's the flu, moron. I'm dying here," he finally gathered enough energy for a response. "Any suggestion for the menu at my funeral party? Oh, and don't forget to call my former wife, Aliza, she'll come up with ideas for a supreme bash."

"I see you haven't lost your sense of humor." Jerry countered. "It's a sign, my man. Aliza will be deeply disappointed—you're going to live another day; no parties for you or even for her." He paused, sighed, then went on. "I'm going crazy around here with your dude," Jerry complained.

"The good looking one?"

"Yeah. That's the one."

"What did he do this time?" Carmel asked. He almost forgot his own moribund condition, but not for long. A rippling shiver overtook his body and mind. "Man, I'm freezing. Talk fast before my ears fall off."

"It's Rachel," Jerry whined. "Arik has been bugging me frantically. He complains that no one is doing anything to recover her. He even started making threats."

"Saying what?" Carmel grew alarmed, at once recalling Nguyen's phone call in the middle of the night. *Did it actually happen? Was it a bad dream?* He wasn't entirely certain.

Jerry realized he'd overstated his case. He toned down the message. "Well, Arik put across that he wouldn't be taking showers or brushing his teeth until he was satisfied that you hadn't forgotten your commitment concerning his girlfriend/fiancée."

"And why's that *your* problem?"

"Can you imagine having daily breakfasts with that kind of BO billowing in your face?"

"Tell him we're working on it. A progress report is due in a couple days. I'll call tomorrow." A pause. "I'm going back to bed... *Arrivederci.*"

It was Monday evening. The Starbucks Coffee was bustling with action when Jerry's cell phone sounded the theme song from the movie "A Summer's Place," a ring tone reserved for calls delivered via a particular New Hampshire exchange. He signaled to Susan, his assistant, to take his place at the counter, then he picked up and listened; there was no need to check for Caller ID. He'd expected that call. Dan Carmel had promised to follow up. "She's gone." Carmel's weary voice bore out the sad news. "Tell him as soon as... He needs to know."

Jerry hung up the cell phone, then turned to his assistant, "Susan," he said, "something has just come up. Got to split. You take over and mind the store. I'll see you tomorrow night."

Jerry didn't go to the *Upper West Side* apartment. Instead, he decided to take a long walk all the way to the East Side, to his private and official residence. He didn't relish the thought of seeing Arik's face when he delivered the dire news. Not tonight. He would do it tomorrow morning over breakfast, when both could spend a couple of quality hours together before embarking on their daily chores.

Once again, as a matter of habit, they were watching Katie Courik on the *Today* Show over fresh sesame bagels, cream cheese, and scrambled eggs. This time she was interviewing the Vice President, on the US position concerning Saddam Hussein's WMD development program. Arik was all but consumed by the situation. "The Americans should take on this SOB. What're they waiting for? Once Saddam goes nuclear, he'll be in a position to bully the rest of the world. Can you imagine living under that kind of a nuclear cloud?"

Jerry didn't respond. He was waiting for a suitable opportunity to break the news about Rachel. As of yet, he'd been unable to pick one good lucky break. He was extremely tense. His fingers simulated playing muted piano music on his right thigh. He thought he would wait for the commercial, but when it came, Arik rose and walked to the kitchen. "Hey, check this new drink," he said. Jerry watched Arik filling up his cup with cold milk, placing it in the microwave, then letting it cook for a minute and a half, while, at the same time, keeping busy searching for honey inside the kitchen cabinet.

It was a long commercial break. Jerry lowered the volume on the TV, then walked to the kitchen. Arik pulled the hot milk out of the microwave, grabbed a teaspoon filled with instant coffee, poured it into the hot cup, then added the honey and stirred for another thirty seconds. "Steal a taste," he announced, handing over his latest version of Latte. "Starbuck's under a major blitz. You'd better learn how to make this drink or else the competition is going to gobble you up."

Jerry wasn't in the mood. "Hey, we need to talk," he said. "Let's go back to the living room."

The commercial was over. The *Today* Show was back on. Al Roker was outside the NBC studio, holding court, entertaining the crowd before embarking on his weather report. As soon as they took their seats on their black leather couches in front of the TV, Jerry turned to Arik who was fixing his eyes on Al Roker. "She's dead," Jerry said. "Rachel is…"

"I know," Arik barged in. He didn't turn to look at Jerry, but rather kept watching the screen. He didn't wish Jerry to notice his soggy eyes. "I've known it for the past two days."

"How did you find out?" Jerry asked. "Why didn't you tell me?"

"Didn't feel like it. I had to get over it; I myself first." He turned to Jerry; the tears in his eyes were drying up, leaving in their wake plenty of red. "I checked the *Delilah* site; one brute had sent a pointer to a new temp site, which required special access including a member IP address."

"So how did you get in?"

"I accessed a Palestinian server in Gaza that I'd known from my days in the Israeli military, then logged in to the new site with a 'Kosher' IP address I'd borrowed from the Palestinian processor. Then I engaged in some heart-to-heart, and later, I brought up the subject of Rachel. Somebody jumped in and broke the news."

"How do you feel about it?" Jerry asked.

"What do you think?"

"Yeah, it's tough. I'm sorry, my friend," Jerry said. "I'm sure Carmel was doing his best to help." He got to his feet, moved behind Arik's couch, then placed his hands on Arik's shoulders.

"Don't worry," Arik said, turning around, looking in Jerry's eyes. "I'm more committed now than ever before. These barbaric *Jihadists* will soon savor the bitter taste of their own savagery. Their strategy will turn back on them like a sharp boomerang." He paused, took a deep breath, then concluded, "take my word for it. It will happen on my watch."

Chapter 22

December 23, 2002—Albany, New York

In spite of the icy roads and the cold weather, the Autoroute 401 leading to Montreal from Toronto was swarming with cars, trucks, and minivans. It seemed as though every Canadian in the entire Ontario province was seeking refuge in the French speaking arctic they called Quebec. They couldn't take the warm nights—merely ten to fifteen below freezing—any longer. These Canadian polar bears were seeking genuine vacation spots, sustaining temperatures not exceeding single (Fahrenheit) digits.

Abu Musa joined the throng in his rental. His ultimate destination was the border crossing in the environs of Montreal. On that Monday, two days ahead of the holiday, the start of the holiday week, he expected to see long lines of vehicles and jumpy drivers, a fact that would prompt border guards, on either side, to speed up passport inspection and let him through with little scrutiny. He realized that he'd been a sought after man in Ontario. Both his present identities—Amin Shukri and Kamil Awad, one was dead, the other, a potential murderer, without a clear indication as to who was whom—were under a haze of suspicion.

It was a long, drawn-out drive, but Abu Musa made it to New York State after darkness. His assumptions concerning hassle-free crossing proved correct. He presented his Kamil's passport including Kamil's student visa; the worn-out American border police guard asked him a couple of routine questions, looked inside his trunk, then issued a—"Happy Holiday. Drive carefully" greeting, complemented by a welcoming smile.

Abu Musa chose to go down Interstate 87 and spend an uneventful night around Albany, New York, in a small Motor Inn, just short of the city limits. He checked in as Amin Shukri and stayed in his room until morning.

He woke up late on Tuesday morning and after a quick shower, he shaved his one-day-old beard—not an ordinary event—dressed up, checked out, and drove to the city.

The two pizza-eating individuals sitting next to the entrance raised their heads as Abu Musa entered the joint. They were regular customers who, as a matter of course, had their daily brunch at Ismail's Pizzeria. The man at the counter, Mahmud Ismail, about fifty years old, with a curly lipless mouth, reddish hair and beard, was watching intently.

Abu Musa approached the counter and offered his hand, *"Salam Alaykum"* (Hello, peace be on you), he said in Arabic.

The man at the counter offered his hand for a shake, but didn't respond with a verbal greeting. Instead, he turned around toward the kitchen and called a woman's name, "Hajar, come here and watch the counter." As the young girl, no older than sixteen, drew closer, Abu Musa could see the resemblance between father and daughter. She had the same type of hair and carbon copy lips. The man turned back to Abu Musa, then, employing body language, he headed for the kitchen, inviting Abu Musa to follow him.

It was hot inside. In addition to the pizza oven, which raised the temperature in the small room by twenty degrees at minimum, the Shawarma grill was radiating heat in a straight line with its turkey and lamb meat mast. Moving across it, Abu Musa was struck by a heat blast that made him feel as if he were about to be roasted on his way to hell. He moved quickly to the far end corner where Ismail was standing in anticipation of his approach.

"I've heard about you," Ismail said. "I need help in acquiring a shoulder-fired missile. I understand you can get me a couple."

"And I heard you can get me a fake American driver's license and a new set of New York State plates for my Canadian rental." Abu Musa cracked a grin.

"Use the name Clarence Simpson," said Ismail, "This is one real identity I've purchased online recently. Clarence Simpson is a real person, and I can give you one of his credit cards as well. The only problem is that this Clarence fellow may find out soon that his identity has been stolen, so you can't use the credit card for too long."

"That's okay," Abu Musa said.

"All right," Ismail said. "I'll get you these things tomorrow." He sighed, looked around as if there was anything he hadn't yet seen, then turned his gaze back toward Abu Musa. "You get me a shoulder-fired missile?"

"I heard about you," Abu Musa said. "You are a stealthy member of *Jamaat-e-Islami*, a Pakistani-based Islamic organization. I know you've been looking for weapons like a shoulder-fired missile as part of your planning for using it to assassinate the Pakistani ambassador in New York City."

"You're right," Ismail responded. "You're well informed." Ismail sneaked an admiring look at his new chief, then wrapped it with a wide grin.

"This isn't an issue," Abu Musa responded in a collusive whisper. "One brainless Pakistani diplomat isn't what I'm after." He paused, looked behind at the kitchen door, making sure no one was there listening in on their conversation. "I'm after something much more dramatic, a little catastrophe, something of the 9-11 magnitude. I'm talking about bombing the New York City, *St. Patrick's Cathedral*, on a major infidel's holiday like Christmas Eve." He waited, trying to assess the impact of his words. Ismail was listening attentively. Abu Musa continued. "I'm looking for a long-lasting effect, something people will be talking about for generations to come, a turning point in the holy war against America."

"How do you get that done?" Ismail asked.

"We'll trigger coordinated multipoint suicide bombings in that famous place, holy to the infidels.

"Do you have suicide bomber candidates?" Ismail asked.

"You think about it," Abu Musa said. "You have children. I've just met, Hajar, your daughter, and you have a son as well. You do want them to enjoy life in Paradise. Don't you?"

Ismail clenched his jaw, then turned his face up toward the ceiling. There was a glow in his eyes; his facial expression turned dreamy. All at once, he spread his hands, grabbed Abu Musa's shoulders and kissed him on both cheeks, one at a time. "Thank you for coming," he said. "You're an inspiration."

Chapter 23

December 23, 2002—Manhattan, New York

They were sitting on the couches in the *Upper West Side* apartment, enjoying the frozen pizza Jerry had pulled out of the oven minutes before. "So here's the latest scoop," Arik disclosed. "Hamad Suleiman, my favorite Saudi playboy, wants to get together tomorrow. Fatima has arranged it."

"Where?"

"In New Jersey."

"Interesting."

"Well, he doesn't want to be seen in my company. The meeting is to take place in a house in Elizabeth."

"Let me tell you something about Hamad Suleiman," Jerry said.

"Go ahead."

"Since your interest in this fellow, Suleiman, spiraled, The *Mossad* has run meticulous research on the guy. They unearthed some juicy stuff."

"Sounds like *Lapin à la moutarde* in a French restaurant. Let's have it." Arik stopped eating. He was all set to absorb.

"Sounds like what?" Jerry gazed at him, pausing for enlightenment.

"It's a classic French bistro dish, a rabbit cooked in grainy mustard sauce with herbs and white wine."

"Okay," Jerry brushed it aside. He picked up one more slice, then began. "This fellow's working for the *Sawarin Media Productions,* based in Riyadh, Saudi Arabia. This company has been serving as a front for the Saudi General Intelligence Directorate. This is, incidentally, a small company. They earn about four-million dollars a year from producing and selling audio and videotapes promoting the *Wahhabi* version of Islam, which is Saudi Arabia's dominant religion, in case you didn't know."

"Oh, yeah. The *Wahhabi* version employs the most radical, conservative, strict adaptation of the Koran and the *Sharia Law*." I also heard of *Sawarin* during my intelligence work in the Israeli army," Arik acknowledged.

"*Sawarin* provides Suleiman with the tools, connections, and know-how, in addition to his studies at the New York Film Academy."

"Okay?" Arik was wondering why this was so crucial and inflammatory.

"We've learned that Suleiman has just produced a new film depicting a father and son caught in a cross-fire between Israelis and Palestinians. He directed the production."

"I'm listening," Arik said. "I hope there's a point."

"The twelve-year-old son is dead in the next episode, hit by bullets, while his grieving father is crying over the dead body of his twelve-year-old son."

"I guess the bullets are fired by the Israeli soldiers, whose thirst for Palestinian blood is exceeded only by their craving for Palestinian women." Arik's attempt at sarcastic humor elicited no smile on Jerry's grim face.

"This is not the end of the deal," Jerry interrupted. "The key to the whole film is that the Palestinians intend to use it as if it has actually happened. They're going to use it as a journalistic piece to be picked up by the foreign media as a factual story about Israeli brutality, during an Israeli incursion into Gaza." He waited for effect. Arik was listening intently. "And that's only the beginning. *Al-Qaeda*, *Hamas*, and *Hezbollah* plan to turn Hamad Suleiman into a major star producer for more films to come. Films he fabricates out of his sick mind, only to be used as authentic journalistic pieces at the proper opportunity."

"Blood libels for modern times, using modern technology and media hunger for drama," Arik concluded. "And Hamad Suleiman's the mastermind. Clever! Clever!" Arik rose and began pacing the room. "Can we do something about it now? Like expose it for what it is?"

"The only thing Israel will do is wait for the film's release, then expose the scam," Jerry said. "Sorry, but that's the Israeli government Foreign Ministry's official line."

"No! It'll be too late," Arik continued pacing and talking. He was growing agitated. "By the time you expose the deception, people all over the world will have seen the film, believe in its authenticity, and find more reasons to hate the Jews." He stopped his stride, turned to Jerry, then pleaded. "You must stop this blood libel, this genie, before it gets out of the bottle. You know, once it's out, there's no putting that toothpaste back in the tube."

"That ain't my call. And there's plenty more." Jerry continued. "Hamad Suleiman has been working for *Sawarin* for the past three years. And here comes your lucky personal break." Jerry took a short hiatus. "Man, this pizza's making me thirsty." He picked up a large bottle of Coke and gulped half of it down his throat.

"What's the break?" Arik grew impatient. He stopped his nervous stride, took his seat on the couch.

Jerry came closer, found a seat next to Arik, then placed his hand on Arik's shoulder. "This guy, Suleiman, has been helping finance the Bali branch of *al-Qaeda*. According to the *Mossad*, in the past year alone, Suleiman took a couple of flights to Saudi Arabia only to continue from there to Geneva, where he deposited one million dollars in a bank account controlled by Ali Ashrawi. Ashrawi is a Moroccan businessman and a longtime *al-Qaeda* associate, with close ties to the terrorists responsible for the Bali nightclub bombing two months ago. And incidentally, Suleiman traveled to Geneva on an aircraft operated by the Saudi General Intelligence Directorate, or GID."

Arik rose from his couch. "Fascinating, our guys sure dig out nifty information."

"There's more," Jerry divulged. "And listen to this..."

Arik started pacing again around the room. "What?" he inquired.

"You'd think that Suleiman's a foreign student, on a student visa, since he's been in the US for three years only. In truth, he's actually a 'diplomat.' He's working under the cover of the Saudi mission to the UN. In this capacity, he enjoys immunity from prosecution by US courts."

Arik was getting hot and bothered. He kept on pacing the room. "Diplomat?" he hesitated. "So tell me" he turned to Jerry, "is he working for the Saudi government, or is he conspiring to overthrow it?"

"Officially, *Sawarin* has been serving as a front for the Saudi General Intelligence Directorate, an official part of the Saudi government. So, technically, Suleiman's a Saudi government employee. We're all still somewhat mystified as to whether the Saudi government is in control of itself. It doesn't look that way. At the same time, it's not clear whether Suleiman has been working on his own or on behalf of *Sawarin*. If he is on his own, then the Saudi government isn't directly involved. If he is doing all this on behalf of *Sawarin*, then it's a life-size mess. The *Mossad*'s still looking into this one."

"What's the bottom line then?" Arik asked, but then, before Jerry had a chance to answer, Arik answered his own question. "I know," he concluded. "Hamad Suleiman's a sophisticated, behind the scenes, stealthy terrorist manipulator. He's camouflaged as a Saudi official; he plays with the American upper class, diplomats, celebrities, other playboys and partygoers; the *al-Qaeda* foot soldiers have no idea who he really is, even Fatima may not know who she's working for, and the Americans consider him an ally." He paused, gazed at Jerry. "Am I right so far?"

"Precisely. And there's even more." Jerry approached Arik and placed his hand on Arik's shoulder as if trying to be more intimate. "We suspect that Hamad Suleiman is attempting to recruit non-Arabs, innocent looking white guys to his personal *Jihad* against Israel. He accomplishes this feat with the many parties he throws in his apartment. Those characters would try to enter the state of Israel as tourists via the Ben-Gurion International Airport near Tel Aviv, then eject their sperm around, form terror cells inside the country, or commit these atrocities by themselves." Jerry rose; he kept his gaze on Arik's eyes. "You'll have to warm your way into these activities, identify those innocent-looking baby agents, so that we can take care of them before they're toilet trained."

"Understood," Arik said. "I've scheduled this meeting with Suleiman in Elizabeth, New Jersey, the day after Christmas. However, I don't trust the bastard. You'll have to provide me with some backup, just in case."

Jerry lifted his hands, rubbed both of his eyes, scratched his head, then shrugged before concluding. "You go and meet with him as planned. We'll provide coverage by wiring the place ahead of your summit. During and afterwards, we'll be hanging around in the vicinity, ready to move in, just in case." He made his case, then as an afterthought, he added, "And by the way, rumor has it that Suleiman has a special drawing to a particular Koranic verse. You may want to check out—Koran (9:73).

Chapter 24

December 24, 2002—Elizabeth, New Jersey

The ride to Elizabeth, New Jersey was smooth. Traffic was unusually light. They arrived twenty minutes ahead of schedule. They parked two blocks away from Suleiman's house or meeting place, then waited inside the car. Jerry reassured Arik, "the house has been wired throughout," he said. "Our men are surrounding the place at this very moment. I have five including myself. You're covered."

From their parking spot, Arik watched the street in front. It was tranquil, very residential, lined up with single-family homes along with nice-looking parked cars along the curve. There was no traffic.

It was time. Arik stepped out of the car and started to walk in the direction of the house. At the moment he reached the entrance door, it opened from the inside; a gorilla-looking brute was standing there ready to greet him. He wore a tight black T-shirt that said, *"Touch me if you dare."* Arik was about to crack a smirk when he saw him. The man he was staring at resembled a sinister version of *Mr. Clean* from the TV commercial. However, the big man, blocking the entrance, didn't appear to be in a festive mood. He shot back an intimidating stare, stood there for a minute, then slowly backed down, let Arik proceed and enter the house.

Halfway through the hallway, Arik paused for a glance at the structural design. It was a plain Colonial type, a formal dining room to the right backed up by a small kitchen. On the left, he noticed the formal living room with plain, old looking furniture, a family room in the back of it. He observed the stairs leading to the bedroom area in front of him. They were carpeted with the same cheap material covering the living room floor. There was no one inside that he could see other than him and the heavy-set man behind him. He wanted to turn around and ask, but the gorilla preempted the move. He placed his fat and heavy hand on Arik's shoulder, then led him through the kitchen into the attached garage in the back of the house.

The passenger door at the back of the parked car was open; the fat hand steered Arik in its direction. He bent and looked inside the car. Hamad Suleiman was sitting and waiting for him to come in. "Welcome, my friend," he said. Arik was about to set his foot inside, but the brute stopped him from behind. He held Arik's shoulders and pushed him against the trunk of the car, then moved his hands along Arik's legs, ribs, chest, and back, making sure he wasn't carrying any weapon. He removed stuff out of Arik's pocket, stared at Arik's cell phone, turned it off, then handed everything back. Subsequently, he pulled Arik to a straight position, turned him around, and told him to open his shirt. He was checking for wires.

"He's clean," the big man announced. "You may step inside the car," he told Arik.

Arik moved in. Suleiman offered his hand for a greeting, and Arik reciprocated. "This was an incredibly pleasant welcome, except for the busted suit," Arik said jokingly, trying humor to cool down the temperature.

Hamad Suleiman apologized. He turned to Arik. "Precautions," he said. "The house has been bugged. Either you or someone else has been playing spy games." He halted briefly, then turning his gaze away from Arik, he said. "I don't appreciate this."

"I don't like it either," Arik said. Reading Suleiman's intentions, he added, "Let's get out of here. It's not safe for either one of us."

Hamad turned back to Arik. "Are you telling me it's not you?" It wasn't really a question.

The beast took the driver's position; they were on their way out.

"Are you kidding me?" Arik expressed hurt at the mistrust. "I'm here to ask for your help and to coordinate our mission."

"What do you know about my mission?" Hamad asked. "And what're you trying to find out that you don't know…through spying, I mean?"

Arik felt naked and threatened. Jerry and his team had messed up. Somehow, the plan got derailed. Moreover, it could get worse if Arik's backup was following Suleiman's car right now, and then were discovered.

Jerry was watching Suleiman's silver Mercedes leaving the house and heading out. He realized that he might've been spotted earlier when he'd dropped Arik off. He turned his GPS tracker on, but Arik's cell phone was off. No signal came through. He had no choice but to order the rest of his team members, who were split among three cars, to follow. He gave them description of Suleiman's departing Mercedes, reminding them to alternate their quasi-visible tail among the three to minimize detection. He stayed in place, just for fear that Arik could still be somewhere inside the house, or lest he would come back to that address after a short ride.

Inside the Mercedes, Arik was trying to work out a speedy comeback. He was under strong suspicion and mistrust and had no idea where he and Suleiman were heading. "Wait a minute," he grabbed Suleiman by his hand. "How long ago has it been since you swapped the house for bugs? And I'm not talking about yesterday."

"Last time we checked, and it's been a while, the house was clean," Suleiman admitted. "Yesterday, in preparation for the meeting, I had the house swept up again. We found a microphone under the kitchen table."

"I'm convinced it's been there for a while," Arik concluded.

"What makes you so sure?"

"If it'd been done in my honor, then those who had it installed must have known about our meeting. They'd not have had the need for bugs. They'd simply come in and snatch me away... right now as I speak. All things considered, I'm still a wanted fugitive."

"Unless," Suleiman added, "they want to associate you with me, and they're trying to gather evidence so they can nail me."

"At this point, if they, whoever they are, are outside in the neighborhood, they've already gathered evidence. They must have seen me come in. It's enough to get you nailed." Arik countered. "Still, I'm their main prize, and I haven't been arrested yet."

Two minutes of edgy silence had passed. They were staring at the road ahead of them, thinking of something to say. "Give me your cell phone," Hamad said to Arik. "I want to call Fatima." Suleiman grabbed the phone and turned it on.

•   •   •

Jerry was sitting in his car two blocks away from the abandoned meeting place. All of a sudden, his GPS tracker came to life. He called Jack, his *Mossad* comrade, on his cell phone, "Hey, Jack," he said. The tone of his voice revealed excitement. I see Jupiter on my telescope. I'll guide you through your blind alleys from now on. Confirm with the other two. Where are you?"

"GSP 148N (Garden State Parkway going North, near exit 148.)"

"Increase the distance between you. Your rocket may crash into *Jupiter*."

•   •   •

"Fatima, Suleiman here," Hamad said in a bossy tone of voice. "Did you tell anyone about my meeting today?"

"Only those who need to know," she said. "I followed your instructions."

"Are you sure?"

"Yes boss. I'm positive. Whose phone are you using? Looking at the Caller ID I couldn't figure it out."

"This is Qassem's cell phone."

"Good. I'll keep the number."

Suleiman hung up, turned the phone off, then handed it back to Arik. "Don't turn it on," he said.

•   •   •

Jerry got alarmed. He'd lost signal on his GPS tracker. "Hey Jack," he yelled into the cell phone. "Can you spot Jupiter?"

"Not really," Jack answered. "Why? Did you lose it?"

"I sure did."

"That's very nice. Okay, we'll split three ways. I'll take 153 East, Dave will go west, and Gimmel will continue straight. One of us will spot it."

"Okay, step on it." Jerry said.

• • •

They were sitting in tense silence for about thirty seconds before Suleiman turned back to Arik. "What did you want to talk about?" he asked.

It was Final Exam time. Arik was worried that Suleiman was still highly suspicious of him. Nothing he'd said up to then was very convincing. Time had come to make it or break it, to impress the evil prince. There was no other choice. "Look, Suleiman," he said. "I know who you are. I know about your films, I know how you've helped fund the Bali operation, I know about your UN status, about *Sawarin*, about your agent recruitment plans, and I know how you connect to our command center in Saudi Arabia."

Suleiman was staring at him in disbelief but said nothing.

Arik kept on. "I need your help," he said. "I'm putting together a local *al-Qaeda* cell. I need funds, and I need your connections back to your command center."

Hamad kept staring. He was in shock. The idea that someone in the US could've unmasked his cover, made him exceedingly anxious. *Fatima had talked to this Qassem fellow before, but she couldn't have possibly told him anything of this sort. She had no knowledge of those details. Where did Qassem get all that information? This wasn't supposed to happen. Did the FBI get wind of this? Is that why I, Hamad Suleiman, have been under surveillance?*

"Why are you telling me all this?" he finally asked Arik.

"I simply wanted to convince you that I'm well connected and well informed; I had to put forth my credentials. However, as I've already said, I need your help, and I hope you'll say *yes*. Furthermore, if I can be of help to you, please don't hesitate."

Suleiman seemed perplexed. *Who is this Qassem? Is he a brother or a foe?*

Arik read Suleiman's state of mind. He remembered Jerry's tutoring about Suleiman's fascination with one particular verse in the Koran. "The word is: Koran (9:73)," he stated, then continued to quote. "O Prophet! *Jahidi!* ('Strive hard') against the unbelievers and the hypocrites, and be firm against them. Their abode is Hell, an evil refuge indeed." It was the Prophet's call for an all-out war against all infidels, a call Suleiman was in the habit of quoting in intimate settings, when accompanied by his loyal troops.

It worked. All at once, Suleiman smiled and nodded in acceptance, as if he'd just heard the voice of Angel Gabriel. He turned his attention to his driver. "Change of plans. Go to the city," he said, then turned back to Arik. "You'll meet them right now."

• • •

"How did it go with Suleiman?" Jerry asked. They were sitting in the living room in the *Upper West Side* apartment, wolfing down Chinese food they'd brought over from the China Palace restaurant on Broadway.

"You really blew it, didn't you?" Arik said. "First, you fell through the bugging of Suleiman's place, then to top it off, you lost me. From now on, I want details of your plan before you go and mess things up."

"Calm down, everything's cool." Jerry responded; his face burned with embarrassment. "Be happy you're here in one piece. Do you have something to tell me?" He stole a deep breath, closed his eyes for a few seconds, exhaled as if he were trying to blow away bad luck.

Arik calmed down. "Yeah, I do, he said. "Suleiman has recruited two European looking Muslims from Bosnia. I've met them. I took their pictures without their knowledge with this camera-pen." Arik pulled his camera-pen from his pocket and showed it to Jerry. "They're scheduled to fly over to Israel from Paris via Air France on Thursday next week. Their aim is sabotage. Here's the pen with the stored pictures, and this is the whole plan…" Arik handed over the pen and a four-page outline. "They were going to try to recruit two of their friends to help in *my* mission."

"We'll take care of them," Jerry said, following his short study of the plan. "We'll be waiting at the airport in Tel Aviv, take them out as soon as they show up." Jerry rose and headed for the door. "I'll have to report back to Headquarters. And by the way, The *Mossad* is putting together a new "Islamic" web site, *www.jihad1492.com*, portraying you as an Islamic superhero, greater than Batman, Superman, or Spiderman — all combined." He paused, turned to Arik, then added as an afterthought. "You've done a great job, buddy. Great job."

Chapter 25

Christmas Eve, 2002—Manhattan, New York

St. Patrick's Cathedral was exceptionally crowded during the midnight hour on this particular Christmas Eve. By the time Arik made it inside, it was standing room only. The full-bodied scent surrounding him was a cocktail comprising a blend of domestic and French perfumes. Men wore expensive suits; women were clothed in celebrated designer art.

Arik mingled in the crowd. He didn't look for anyone in particular; neither did he expect any big cheese to single him out. He felt undistinguished and took pleasure in his new identity. He admired the awesome calm and enjoyed the pipe organ music. He was in awe of the Cathedral's enormous size, the white marble, the artistic windows, the *Saint Jerry*, *Saint Louis*, and *Saint Elizabeth* altars. Looking and marveling, he wondered why he'd never seen a Jewish temple, which could claim parity in stature with this awe-inspiring structure. But then, he realized that once upon a time, two thousand years earlier, there was one. It stood proudly in Jerusalem on *Temple Mount,* until the Romans burned it down, killed most of the town resident Jews, and precluded the remaining ones from ever again visiting the city.

His thoughts were interrupted by the sound of a single word in Arabic—*"Inshallah"* (God willing). It came from somewhere to his left. He couldn't see the speaker. It was crowded and noisy all around, but the sounding of a well familiar tongue—native, but foreign and unbefitting in that particular Christian milieu, rang loud in his ears. He turned to his left in an attempt to catch sight of the person or persons, but was unable to set apart the particular individual from the crowd. The Arabic speaking worshiper simply melted away in the soup. There was no hint of any hook Arik could hang his hat on.

It was vital. The Arabic speaking person could be a tail. Arik felt he had to catch a glimpse of that particular individual. A reference for future spotting would be crucial. He turned to his left and started pushing on his adjacent onlookers in an attempt to carve up an exploratory path. A minute later, he changed his mind and directed his thrust toward the exit.

Once outside the Cathedral, he crossed the street toward the *International Building*, found a spot fit for observation next to the *Lee Lawrie statue of Atlas*, then waited. *If there were anyone on my tail, that individual would step outside as well; I might be able to spot him then,* Arik contemplated. He realized that if it were someone else, someone he had already met or seen, then he would have a better chance of catching sight of that stalker outside the Cathedral, on the street, where more space between people would make that individual more visible.

Five minutes outdoors in the cold night were more than Arik could bear. He was ready to give up, walk back into the Cathedral, when, out of the blue, he noticed Hassan Omar, the chemical engineer from Brooklyn Poly, the man who could run as fast as a cheetah when police was in his tail. There was one more fellow walking down the steps leading out of the Cathedral into the street. When they reached the sidewalk, they turned back and gazed at the building, then engaged in a heated conversation supported by a great deal of agitated gesturing.

Arik was watching them intently. *What're they doing here at this hour?* Then, he made a decision. He crossed the street and walked in their direction. They both turned and gazed at the approaching man. Arik drew near and offered his hand to Omar, "Hi, my lucky day," he said. "For some time I'd wondered how I could touch base with you, and here you are on Fifth Avenue, past midnight, on Christmas Eve."

Omar hesitated for a second before admitting, "Man, I could hardly recognize you with that funny beard." He offered his hand back, then turned to his friend. "Qassem al-Nasr," he introduced Arik. "You must have heard."

The friend nodded in approval. "The famous fugitive, the one who escaped custody by stealing a police cruiser," he said. "It's an honor to finally meet you in person."

"I'm not the only fugitive around here," Arik said, beaming at Omar, referring to his Pakistani colleague's flight during the same episode, giving credit where credit was due.

"What're you doing here at this time of night?" Omar asked.

Arik figured that these two were at the Cathedral on that particular occasion for a reason. He elected to test his hypothesis. "I'm here for the same reason you are," Arik answered. "Research..."

"So you're in on the same one," Omar concluded, but his tone of voice made it sound like a half statement, half question. "Incidentally, this is Mustafa," he continued while introducing his young friend, who looked no older than an eighteen-year-old. "Same time next year." Omar turned his gaze to the Cathedral. "*Pufff...*" He was beaming, then said. "These stupid Americans will never suspect this until it hits them. They only secure places, identical, similar, or equivalent to the ones that have been hit before. They don't trust our imagination." He laughed aloud. "They secure airports and airplanes, but they don't bother with trains, cars, shopping malls, restaurants, stadiums, theaters, and certainly, they never think of Cathedrals— until it happens. They must be exceptionally dumb!"

Arik pretended to take pleasure in Omar's humor. "Yeah," he said, then it suddenly struck him. "Do you work with Abu Musa?" he asked.

Omar smiled back as if he were running a grand show. "Of course," he said. "I'll be meeting with him in Dearborn, Michigan, on New Year's Eve, to be exact."

"That's great," Arik reacted. "As it happens, I'm going to be in that neighborhood around the same time." Arik needed more details. He had to milk them out of Omar. "Are you staying with me in the same safe house?" he asked.

"I have no idea about that," Hassan Omar said with a tone of surprise, then went on. "Are you staying at the *Red House*?"

Arik raised his eyebrow. "Can I trust you?" He asked.

"Of course, you know better than that."

"There are two *Red Houses*," Arik whispered, as if he wanted Omar to be the sole possessor of the latest information. "Are you staying at the one on Kentucky Street?" he asked. Omar had no idea. Arik had made that up on the spot. Arik knew Omar would try to set him straight.

"No," Omar said. "I don't know about that one. I'm talking about the one on East Morrow Circle."

"Are you sure?" Arik questioned. He was looking for the exact address. "It's not number 20 is it?"

"No, no." He approached Arik and whispered the number in his ear. Evidently, he was trying to be discreet, lest his young colleague, Mustafa, would get hold of the confidential information.

"Yeah, I know that one. I won't be staying there," Arik said. He made a gesture, signaling an end to the encounter. Then, as if changing his mind, he turned back. "Who else knows?" he asked.

Omar placed his hand on Arik's shoulder, then walked away from his colleague. Once they were outside Mustafa's reception range Omar offered the information. "I'll see you on New Year's Eve," he concluded.

"What about your friend here, Mustafa?" Arik asked.

"He doesn't need to know. You must be cautious around here."

"Right." Arik agreed."

"*Yallah* (Come on), let's get out of here. I'm shivering," Omar declared. He started running in place to keep his blood flowing. "I want to get somewhere where it's not so cold."

They shook hands, kissed on the cheeks, then departed. Arik smiled to himself. Only one more week, and he would meet face to face with the individual he'd referred to as the chief son-of-a-bitch he'd ever known. He sighed with satisfaction. Dan Carmel would've raised a glass had he known the plan. No, Arik would keep it to himself for now. Dan would learn about it, later, after the fact.

Chapter 26

December 26, 2002—Toronto

The day after Christmas was a busy day at the Toronto malls. Hordes of sober customers, regaining consciousness from pre-holiday shopping frenzies, converged on store checkout counters in an attempt to reclaim sanity and return useless merchandise for practical cash. Hilga was standing in the long line, which didn't seem to be moving. She watched the nervous woman at the front arguing with the store clerk. The woman was seeking to return a pair of used pants, which even to the naked eye gave the impression they'd been worn time and again in a military boot camp before being washed with an acid compound and left to dry under the Sahara desert sun. The unhappy customer didn't have a receipt, while the store clerk kept claiming that the pants had been bought in another store. "Not here." The situation seemed deadlocked. The line grew longer while progress was at a standstill.

Hilga had already spent two hours at the mall. Before leaving home, she told her sister that she would be back by then. Frustrated, she left the line, stepped outside the mall, called a cab, then headed back. She opened the door with her borrowed key and called her sister's name. There was no answer. Surprised, she looked all around the apartment, bathroom, kitchen, then the bathroom again. She couldn't understand. Her sister was very pregnant. She had no plans of going anywhere. *Where is she*?

She picked up the phone and called her brother-in-law. He was just as surprised. He had no idea where his wife was but wasn't worried. "She'll be back shortly. She may have gotten bored sitting and waiting for her water to break." Finally, Hilga chose to sit on the couch, watch TV, and eat popcorn. It would calm her down. She was anxious.

Thirty minutes went by; her sister wasn't home yet. Hilga was entertaining thoughts of calling the police and reporting a missing person when the front door opened and her sister stepped in.

Hilga jumped off the couch; she couldn't keep her breath steady. "Where have you been?" she asked. Tears ran down her cheeks. "I was so worried," she said while hugging her sister, kissing her repeatedly.

"The police came over. They picked me up and took me to the morgue. I was called to identify a body," she said.

"So who was it?" Hilga asked. She stared at her sister with beady eyes, still holding her close.

"It was good old Kamil, the one I'd met at the airport; the one who'd come to dinner in our house. He was dead." She sighed. "Poor guy, he came here to study at the university, to improve his life."

"What did you tell the police?"

"I said, I'd known him, I'd met him. They said they knew who'd killed him. His name's Amin Shukri. I told them that I knew."

"How did you know?"

"He called a few days ago, said he was no longer Kamil. He was once again, Amin Shukri. I told the police what the man on the phone had said. I also told them that he'd been on his way to the US." She paused, cast her gaze along the wall, then back at Hilga. "They said they wanted to talk to you. They said that you must have known the killer. That's why he'd called here."

"Oh, man." Hilga released her grip and walked back to the couch. She sank in and faced the TV. She wasn't watching. She held her hands over her face veiling the tears.

Her sister came over. "What's the matter, sis?"

Hilga didn't answer. Her sister came closer. She touched Hilga's hands, then slowly and gently moved them away from Hilga's face. "Did you love him?" she asked.

"I thought I did." She sighed. Tears came down, dripping on her pants. "I thought I did... I did." She caught her breath. "I do."

"Well, I'm sorry," the sister said. "He's dead. You'll get over it once you meet someone else."

"Not him," Hilga said. She rose and grasped her sister's shoulders. She took a breather, looked her in the eye, then let it out. "I'm in love with the killer. What am I going to do now?"

Chapter 27

December 26, 2002—FBI HQ, Washington, DC

"I've just stumbled upon this new site. I believe it's popped up this morning," Jim nearly yelled in excitement, his face glowing like a full moon on a cloudless night.

Stanley stared in amazement. "What's that?" *Have you found the Holy Grail?*

"Check it out," Jim said. "*www.Jihad1492.com.* The URL, (Uniform Resource Locator), or Internet Address, stands for *Jihad* in America. The year 1492 is when Columbus..."

"Okay genius, my little fifth grader taught me that last week. One of these days, I'll be as smart as he is. That will be miles ahead of you."

"Oh, yeah?" Jim sneered. "So why am I the one who finds all the good leads?"

"The word '*all*' is a bit of a stretch," Stanley rejoined. He actually took pleasure in annoying his colleague. "How about using the word '*seldom*' instead? It contains the letter *S*, which stands for '*Stupid.*'"

"Very clever," Jim said. "Have you found it?"

"It's on my screen now," Stanley said as he was browsing through the page displayed on his monitor. "Take a quick look. We were right about Qassem al-Nasr. He's the real deal."

"I can see," Jim said without taking his eyes off the monitor. Stanley was watching his colleague's plodding mental awakening. Then, after a few minutes of concentration, Jim lifted his head and turned to Stanley. "We should take that to Jack," he said. "This is an escalation; we need more resources to tackle it."

• • •

Jack Devon was actually pleased to see his two SCs rushing in, brushing off Jenny's attempts to slow them down. Seeing them all energized, he expected a discovery, a breakthrough of some sorts.

As they entered the office, Stanley and Jim pointed to Jack's computer screen. "Go to '*Jihad1492.com*' and check it out," Stanley charged. "Our crafty fugitive, Qassem al-Nasr, is baking headlines."

Jack stared at the two for a brief moment, then turned to his keyboard and typed the URL they'd specified. As the screen came into view, Jack signaled to the two to take their seats. It would take a few minutes for him to review the entire site including the video portion. Jim and Stanley were watching their boss' changing facial expressions as he was cruising through the pages. They didn't speak. They didn't want to disturb his concentration.

"Wow," Jack finally muttered. He lifted his head; the two appeared to be waiting for his directives. Instead, he had questions. "Where are we on Qassem al-Nasr? Have we made any progress trying to tighten the noose around his neck?"

"All we know at this point is that he's been in or around the New York City area," Jim said.

Jack wasn't comfortable with the thin response. He made it obvious. It was less than he'd expected. "How do you know that?" asked Jack, the tone of his voice revealing tension.

Stanley came to the rescue. "We came across a telephone conversation between two characters. The latter claimed to have seen Qassem on Christmas Eve in the city. He also mentioned a vital summit meeting on New Year's Eve, but didn't say where."

"Is the NYPD in on that as well?"

"We've not shared that piece with them." Jim stated, knowing the answer would satisfy Jack.

"Good. Proceed," Jack instructed, then posed one more question. "Did they say anything about the purpose of that meeting, or who the participants are?"

"They didn't mention purpose. The only name we uncovered was Abu Musa's name; they said he was on his way from Canada; they also referred to him as Amin Shukri," Jim added. "In fact, they didn't mention Qassem by name as one of the attendees; they were talking about the *Great Egyptian* instead."

Stanley eased out of his seat, then approached the screen next to Jack. "I have a hunch. Why don't you check the Toronto Times? A few days ago I read about Amin Shukri's adventures in the Toronto area."

"Where're you headed with this?" Jack asked.

"This dude, Amin Shukri, if he's Abu Musa, then he's a dangerous terrorist," Stanley said. "If the same person were in Canada last week, and he's about to attend an important high level get-together, then he may be inside the US by now."

"I see," Jack said, then pursued the thought. "Plus, Qassem al-Nasr and a couple of other heroes are going to be there with him." He paused, looked up at the ceiling as if in the hunt for the Holy Spirit, then proceeded. "If you guys could only learn where that jamboree is to take place, then, wow, we could snag the whole US *Qaeda* leadership by their balls." He rose, letting the two know that the meeting was over. "Check with the Canadians," he concluded. "They have some dog food that our puppies may want to chew on."

Chapter 28

December 30, 2002—Upstate New York

The weather forecast wasn't very promising. Upstate New York was expecting another one of those habitual snowstorms, but Abu Musa shrugged it off. He'd never before driven in one, but didn't believe it would become an issue. Furthermore, news reporters on TV weren't getting too hot or bothered. They promised continuous clearing of the highways; not anything to worry about; just a few inches; nothing out of the ordinary.

It was December 30, one day before the important meeting with the heads of US *Qaeda* in Dearborn, Michigan. Armed with a brand new driver's license and a new set of plates, Abu Musa ventured on his ten- to-twelve-hour trip from Albany to Michigan. The drive west on interstate 90 would take him to Syracuse, Rochester, and Buffalo in New York State, before crossing to Ohio, and driving through Erie, Cleveland, and Toledo, then taking interstate 75 up north to Detroit and Dearborn. Once in Dearborn, he would stay with a comrade in arms, Ahmad, a Palestinian from Gaza, a former *Hamas* member, who'd arrived in Dearborn two years earlier, and was able to form a small cell of Islamic extremists, dormant for the time being, ready to be activated when Allah called.

The dark gray skies and the airborne snowflakes greeted his entry to the interstate. These weather forecasters were right on the money. He turned on the radio, and once again was unable to chance upon music, to which he could relate. He hated rock, was doubly repulsed by the loud announcers. They were screeching into the microphone as if they were alone in a soundproof bubble bath, pleasuring themselves with a self-inflicted blowjob. He despised Country Music. It sounded more like a juvenile attempt to impress his

Austrian born teacher of the English class. He was revolted by Pop, couldn't understand a word of the lyrics. It was as if Elton John was experimenting with lyrics in Latvian—not his favorite lingo. Classical was categorically boring; it sounded increasingly like some kind of organized cacophony. He was unable to fathom its makeup. He was annoyed—one more reason why these Americans should burn in hell.

He longed for an *Umm Kulthoum* sound, the famous Egyptian who'd been shaping Middle Eastern music and culture since the 1940s. But *hell, those American infidels don't know better; they have no musical taste; they are riding a subhuman culture. They've never heard of the greatest artist who has ever lived.* He switched to AM radio. It irked him even more. Those right wing talk show hosts were driving him mad. *Why are they making up stories about Saddam Hussein? Don't they know he's merely a showoff? Don't they understand that if they remove him from power, the Shiites will take over? And Iran will rule the roost in Iraq?*

Road signs indicated that he was converging on Syracuse. Some of the airborne snowflakes started accumulating under his tires. Traffic was slowing somewhat. He was going sixty, down from seventy, a few minutes earlier. He turned on his windshield wipers; the snow was coming down more rapidly now, and visibility diminished considerably. He detested the weather. *What's so great about America? The weather sucks, the people are uncultured, the leaders are stupid...*He was convinced. He wouldn't live there if it weren't for his mission for Allah.

The road sign indicated an oncoming rest area. He decided to fill up his tank and take a short brunch break. Several minutes later, he was inside the food court. He glimpsed into the seating area inside the Sbarro restaurant. An exceedingly obese couple was sitting at the first table on the right, consuming what looked like half-baked dough, covered with melted cheese and too much tomato sauce. He watched as they were gulping the coke and taking big bites of the exceedingly thick slices. He immediately hated them. He'd never before seen obesity—American style. And here, it was so common. *They're consuming the rest of the world's food supply. No wonder there's hunger in Gaza. That's one more reason why they should all burn in hell.*

Burger King was a more familiar, closer to home taste. He ordered a whopper, fries, and a coke to go, then headed back to his car. It seemed as if the snowstorm was taking a breather. Nothing was coming down at that moment, but his car required a modest cleanup. The windows all around were covered with icy cold, fluffy white stuff. Abu Musa hadn't equipped himself with a snow scraper or gloves. His bare hands were the only tools in his possession.

As soon as he started cleaning up, another motorist approached and offered help with his snow scraper. Abu Musa stared at the friendly face for one long moment before accepting the offer. "Where're you headed?" *Friendly Face* asked.

"Ah, Ohio," Abu Musa answered. He didn't really want to go into too much detail.

"They say the roads are getting worse," the man said, "especially around Buffalo. Be careful."

"I'll manage," Abu Musa said, then he decided to terminate the encounter. "Thank you," he said. "I'll take the rest of it from here."

The side and the rear windows had been wiped clean; the only remaining portion was the windshield. Abu Musa stepped into the car, turned on the windshield wipers, and pounced on his fast meal. The chips were already cold and so was the hamburger. *Even the coke in Gaza tastes better,* he reflected. *These idiots around here don't know a thing about good food or tasty drinks.* He turned on the engine, then headed back to the highway.

• • •

It was clear all the way to Rochester. Parts of the skies flickered occasional blue through holes in the clouds. It looked like the rest of the way would be smooth. Abu Musa started singing to himself:

"Shake off US domination

Shake off Western colonization

We're gon'na shake off the cops and wake up our nation

Shake off the cops and wake up our nation

One by one or maybe all at once
It comes tumbling down and crumbling into the dust
Then stand up, shake it off and move on
And prepare for a new era finally to dawn."

As soon as he went past Rochester, the clouds grew thicker, and the mood turned darker. It was the middle of the day; cars and trucks turned on their headlights to compensate for the vanishing sun. Halfway through to Buffalo, at Batavia, traffic slowed to a virtual standstill. Snow was coming down briskly, wind was howling at high speeds, and snowplowing trucks were unable to operate through the packed snow-bound gridlock. Abu Musa stared at his watch. It was only 2 p.m. There was still a chance that he could make it to Michigan before dawn.

The next three hours turned out to be an unmitigated disaster. Nothing moved. People were getting in and out of their vehicles, children were crying in the car in front of him. All at once, the truck driver from behind decided to make it a go. He made use of his four-wheel-drive, then moved to the shoulder, where he would advance and make it through. Abu Musa watched as the truck disappeared. Two minutes passed; one SUV traveled on the shoulder, sailing through on the side of the stalled column of cars, which had jammed the multilane highway. Time was passing; more snow was accumulating. A police cruiser with its lights flashing passed by on the shoulder. There seemed to be no hope for an expeditious break in the status quo. Abu Musa had never before experienced life in a snowbound prison-like situation. He was getting jumpy and downright unprepared for such a predicament.

It was dark now — genuinely, categorically, dark. That particular slice of earth, Abu Musa was dwelling in, shifted away from the sun on its revolving path to the ensuing dawn; the moon was nowhere in sight. It was buried somewhere at the back of the thick intimidating clouds. Abu Musa resolved to take his chances with the shoulder. Following a fleeting maneuver, he was able to make a right turn, but he skidded and almost bumped into the car in front of him. He finally positioned his car on the shoulder, then started driving forward.

His promising scheme lasted two minutes, but then it was brought to an end by a police officer in a light-flashing, white and blue cruiser. Abu Musa was trapped. The large truck to his left masked his view of the highway; the only view he had was one of the huge fuselage to his left, the guardrail to his right, and the hungry, intimidating brute beaming a powerful light in his face.

Abu Musa, who had never lacked any contempt for official authority, didn't diverge from his elements. He fired up a string of curses in Arabic accompanied by grimacing that could be seen through the rear view mirror of the car in front of his. The officer stepped out and approached Abu Musa's vehicle. He came up to the front of the driver's side window, motioning to Abu Musa to roll it down. Abu Musa pretended not to comprehend. He stared at the officer, then stared at his police cruiser, then back at the officer, then back at the cruiser, waving his right hand in a way, which the officer interpreted as: '*move your fucking car out of the way*'. It was enough to ignite a dormant volcano. The officer pulled out his gun, aimed at Abu Musa's face, shrieking: "Step out of your fucking car."

That angry burst brought Abu Musa back to his senses. He realized that although the officer wasn't going to shoot, the situation could develop into an unpleasant encounter, further delaying his plan of making it to Michigan in time. He signaled compliance, as the officer stepped back, making room for the car door to open. He opened the door and slowly stepped out into the cold snowy air. The officer didn't show much patience. He was mad at the weather as well as at being stuck on the road. Abu Musa provided a pocket-sized outlet for his frustration. "Who the fuck do you think you are?" he barked, turning Abu Musa around, pushing him down on the snow-covered hood, and searching his body. He then turned Abu Musa back to face him. "I want to see your driver's license, registration and insurance."

Abu Musa looked puzzled. He pulled his wallet out, and handed his latest driver's license to the officer. "My other papers are inside the car," he said. "This is a rental."

The officer laid down the law, "go wait in your car," then turned around and ambled back to his cruiser. Abu Musa moved back to the passenger side of his car, and then it hit him. His car rental agreement was written for a car with different license plates — the original ones. What's more, the name on his driver's license was inconsistent with the same on his rental agreement. His mind was racing; a trickle of sweat ran from his armpit inside his shirt down to his waist. He was cold and trembling. He looked up, then straight at the police cruiser. The pig's interior lights were on. He could see the criminal infidel resting back in his driver's seat making radio contact with someone out in a cozy, heated room. Abu Musa started cursing again.

He came to a quick decision. He rolled down the driver's side window, moved to the passenger seat, removed his coat and threw it on the backseat, pulled out a utility knife from the glove compartment, and waited in the darkened car. Minutes later, the officer stepped out of his cruiser. He approached Abu Musa's car, looked inside the driver's side; it was empty. He hesitated for a second, but then, his eyes adjusted to the dim light and he realized that his "punter" was sitting one seat away, on the passenger side. He bent over, his head inside the car, "your rental agreement, I want to see it," he growled.

Abu Musa turned toward the glove compartment in an apparent attempt to unlock it and draw out the papers. He seemed to have some difficulty opening the compartment door. The officer bent further through the open window in an effort to take a closer look at the challenge. Abu Musa was waiting for the opportunity. Without warning, he grabbed the officer's collar with his left, drew his face a couple of inches closer, then slashed his throat with his right.

A torrent of blood gushed down the driver's seat as Abu Musa continued slashing and pulling. Once the body was mostly inside, he stepped out of the passenger side and pulled it further in. He then closed the car door, moved to the driver's side, opened the door, and pushed the rest of the stiff onto the empty passenger area. He didn't think anybody saw what had just transpired. It was dark all around. There was no car behind, and his vehicle was parking in a blind spot, obscured by the huge truck to his left. The only problems he faced were the officer's body, the blood lagoon coating both front seats, his clothes, his hands, and all else. The other predicament, the one Abu Musa was unaware of, was the video recording inside the cruiser, which the officer had turned on prior to stepping out of his police car.

Just then, traffic came back to life; vehicles began moving forward bit by bit. The next exit on the highway had been cleared; all were leaving the snowbound central artery in quest of a nightly refuge in and around Batavia. Abu Musa merged into the traffic and joined the slow moving column. Once in town, he spent two hours in the hunt for a place where he could dump the body. He found one garbage dumpster at a parking lot of a remote Holiday Inn, about thirty miles away from downtown Batavia.

It was 2 a.m. when he did away with his lifeless companion. At that juncture, Abu Musa needed a makeover. Even a professional killer like him didn't feel comfortable sitting on top of a drying blood pool, dressed in bloodstained clothes, and operating a blood smeared steering wheel with hands painted with dry blood. He picked up his bag from the trunk, found clean underwear, pants, and shirt. He didn't have an extra sweater or a spare coat, but that wasn't necessary. His coat, out of action in the backseat, was relatively uncontaminated, barring a couple of small, dark-red smudges. He wasn't bothered. He put it on, then picked up the officer's gun and put it inside his coat pocket together with his utility knife.

After ditching his dirty laundry in the Holiday Inn dumpster, he wandered around the parking lot in search of a suitable car he could use for the next phase of his journey. As he looked around, he noticed a metallic-gray Chevy Camaro, a twin sister of his rental, parked peacefully just about fifty feet away. His training back in the Sudanese Sahara had come in be handy all at once. He would need less than a minute for the car to surrender to him. He approached on foot, then began unlocking the door when the alarm went off. This was unexpected. His rented car didn't boast a warning system; he was completely unprepared. At three in the morning, the sound of the alarm seemed louder than usual. A light came on in one of the rooms on the second floor, while the siren sound didn't break off. It appeared to be getting louder. He stood there for a second, watching the surroundings, then spouted a string of curses in Arabic, followed by a quick decision—abandon ship.

He rushed back to his car and stepped inside. It had the unpleasant stench of a two-day-old dead fish; the blood on the driver's seat hadn't all dried yet. There was no time for self-pampering though. He turned the ignition key and left the neighborhood. He was gone in a New York minute.

Chapter 29

December 31, 2002—Buffalo, New York

The snowstorm had taken a breather. There were about four inches of snow on the virgin ground, and hardly any tire tracks to mark the existence of human civilization. Abu Musa was feeling the serenity of the after-storm as he was paving a path through the airy white blanket of snow. He was now on the main road driving west at a slow speed, searching for road signs pointing in the direction of the highway. With the storm over, he figured, the snowplowing trucks had been clearing the interstate, ahead of any other local priorities. By the time he returned to the exit, traffic would be moving, though speed might not be at the posted limit.

He made it to Buffalo at around five in the morning, exhausted and unable to carry on driving without taking a short nap, snapping off a tad fatigue. He turned into the New York Throughway 190 and proceeded toward downtown Buffalo. He found himself driving next to the Convention Center when he spotted the brownstone structure of the *Hyatt Regency*. He decided to survey the adjacent block before parking his car next to the *Seneca Texas Red-Hots*; only that early in the morning, *Texas* seemed cool and deserted; nothing like *Red-Hots*. He stepped out of the car, picked up his bag; not minding his bloodstained pants, he walked around the block toward the *Hyatt*.

"Lucky you," the receptionist responded to his inquiry. "We still have a couple of rooms left." She registered his credit card while he was filling out the registration ticket. He used Amin Shukri, the name on one of his credit cards, rather than Clarence Simpson, the identity on his new fake driver's license, that Ismail had provided in Albany. He was careful not to use the name on his fake driver's license since the murdered trooper might have announced that name on his radio prior to his fatal encounter.

He went up to his room. The bed was inviting. It didn't take a minute before he was dead to the world, sleeping with his clothes on. At six thirty in the morning, the cleaning crew arrived. Two housekeepers, who'd picked up their schedule at four in the morning, didn't expect a fully clothed stranger spreading himself all over the king-size bed. They excused themselves in a hurry, but not before waking him up. Abu Musa got out of bed and looked down through the window.

A police cruiser with its lights flashing had just made it to the main entrance door of the *Hyatt*. Alarmed, Abu Musa picked up his bag, came out of the room looking for the stairs. He wasn't going to use the elevator. It was a potential trap. He wasn't sure, but the situation called for added precautions. He was the only one in that stairway. Once at the lobby level, he opened the door slowly and surveyed the area. He had no view of the registration desk. He got out and looked for the nearest exit. Problem was that the only path available would take him past *Reception*. He walked slowly, peeking at the people staffing the position. The girl who had registered him wasn't there anymore. Her night shift was over. The new faces behind the counter wouldn't recognize him. The cop was talking to one of the receptionist who was listening while searching through the hotel database. No one was paying any attention to him.

New arrivals had just shown up while fresh departures were standing nervously in line, hoping for a smiling and available cashier who would gladly close their account and take their money. Abu Musa didn't look back; he kept on moving toward the exit, his pace accelerating as he drew closer and closer to the revolving door that would carry him out to the fresh cool air outside. There was no barrier in sight. The path was clear.

As he pushed the revolving door in a counter clockwise direction, another cop showed up, trying to move in the opposite direction. The two faced each other behind the revolving glass, and for a split second, Abu Musa's arteries were pumping like a broken fire hydrant on a hot summer day in the Bronx. The high-pressure blue skies outside, however, brought with it a cold realization of a winter not recognizable to Abu Musa. He didn't appreciate the single (Fahrenheit) digit temperature of dense air, blowing at high speed across his face. He was in an urgent need of shelter, and there was none in sight. He'd already said good-bye to his rental car, the cops were inside the hotel, and he was out in the cold, alone and chilled, like a meat inspector trapped inside a slaughterhouse freezer. He peeked inside the lobby; it seemed as if the first cop had just taken delivery of his ephedrine fix. Both he and his colleague cop were rushing toward the elevator, their hands feeling their guns.

There was only one thing left to do; Abu Musa was about to act. He had no choice. He was on the run.

The middle-aged couple, who, minutes earlier, had checked out of the hotel, paid no notice to Abu Musa when making their way toward their SUV. They were arguing with each other in an overture preceding a customary fight. The husband went ahead and unlocked the doors remotely. He seemed rather upset and didn't pay attention to his wife or to the man behind him. He placed the two-piece luggage in the back while the wife climbed into the passenger side before closing the door, passing time in her seat, waiting for the full service. The husband turned around; he was about to make his way to the driver side, when Abu Musa blocked his path, aiming his new gun at the frightened man's face. "You go open the door to the back-seat," he commanded. "You do what I say, if you don't want me pressing the trigger."

The frightened man's leftover gray-sprinkled hair seemed to be losing the last of its brown hue as his pulse was thumping at full volume at the spectacle of the death threat. His feet stuck to the ground; he was frozen in place, as if someone had just pressed the *Pause* button on his eventful life. Abu Musa was losing patience. The man wasn't obeying his order. He moved closer, then hit the man's head with his gun. "I said, you move or I shoot," he barked.

As blood was dripping down his cheek, the pain brought the terrified man back to his senses. He stared at Abu Musa while moving slowly, submitting to the carjacking.

"What took you so long?" then, in an alarming voice. "You have blood on your face," the wife grumbled as the bleeding man took his driver's seat; but then she realized that the guest in the backseat had his gun pointed at her.

"You shut up," Abu Musa roared at her. He then turned to the man. "Drive. You go where I tell you."

Chapter 30

December 31, 2002—Dearborn, Michigan

The safe house condominium on Colson Street was nicely furnished. There were two bedrooms. One master bedroom with a queen-size bed and another, used as an office, included a desk, a PC, and a small TV set. The walls were painted with earth tones, peach and beige, providing warmth. There were large windows, which let the sunlight in, something that was lacking in the Manhattan place where it always felt like midnight. Arik was impressed. He regarded the conditions and ambiance as refreshing. The kitchen was generous. In addition to the large refrigerator, it included a double built-in oven, a garbage compactor, a gas stove, and a large bar-style aisle. The space overlooked a modest size living room containing a black leather sofa, a love seat, another large TV set.

Tarek, the *Mossad* agent under the cover of an airport limo driver, who owned the limousine company, lived in his own condominium one building away. A Moroccan Jew who immigrated to Israel in 1950 after Israel's war of independence, Tarek was now in his late fifties. Balding and gray at the temples, in spots where short hair was still hanging on with little to spare. He spoke Arabic with a typical Moroccan dialect although his Berber, French, Spanish, and English weren't bad either. His Hebrew had a definite accent, and the two, Arik and Tarek, resolved to steer clear of it and communicate in English immersed in Arabic phrases. Tarek had been living in Dearborn for the past twenty years. And like Arik, he was living a double life. He was working for the *Mossad* while acting as a compliant Muslim. He wasn't married, but had a live-in girlfriend, a Mexican woman whom he'd met when she'd come to clean his condominium three years earlier.

His job as a limo driver offered numerous opportunities to meet frequent travelers, and other active people—wheelers and dealers, schemers and scammers, who tended to move around a lot. His gregarious demeanor was contagious; people opened up to him. Information flowed his way like water flushing a toilet. What's more, he was fun to be with.

When dropping Arik off, he mentioned that his place was an exact replica of Arik's safe house. He'd been taking care of the condo since the time the *Mossad* had acquired it—three years earlier.

It was lunchtime when Arik settled in. Tarek allowed him thirty minutes of privacy before coming to pick him up for lunch at the *Sahara* Restaurant on Cherry Hills Street in Dearborn Heights.

When he came back, he announced. "We're going out to lunch. We'll have some interesting company."

"Who?"

"Two brave men you'll be delighted to meet."

"Uh huh?"

"Hassan Omar will be there," Tarek said. "You know him."

Arik nodded.

"And then, this character—Dr. Imad Radwan, an electrical engineer. Six months ago, he visited Lebanon. I believe he's connected to *Hezbollah*. He's changed since his return. He'd become very militant; *Anti-Semitism* is a great fit for his middle name. Once you get to know him, you'll fall in love with him. The *Mossad* will appreciate your input. I suspect that while in Lebanon, Dr. Radwan received professional training by *Hezbollah*, probably by an explosives expert."

"How did you reach that conclusion?"

"Since his return, he's been talking about the bombing of Jewish targets in the US. He claims to know the associated technical details." Tarek turned the corner and stopped the car on the side of the street. "I guess you'll have to find out more once you become buddies with this electronics connoisseur."

"The Americans don't know all this?

"I don't believe they do. We've not told them. Not yet, anyway." Tarek held back a smirk that was about to come out. "Dr. Radwan's an American citizen. He was naturalized five years ago. Once American police confronts him, his attorney will expose the absence of proof for any of the allegations I've just let you in on. The only information we have is *Mossad* information. We don't wish to expose our sources in an American courtroom, plus we want to find out more about his connections to *Hezbollah* before he's aware that we're on his tracks."

Arik made a mental note. "What else?" he asked.

"This guy graduated with a Ph.D. from the University of Michigan some ten years ago. He's a major partner in the venture capital firm of *Eastern Partners.* A key component of their portfolio comprises investments in the Middle East. This venture makes it relatively easy for him to transfer millions of dollars to *Hamas* and *Islamic Jihad* under the guise of economic investments." Tarek glanced at his watch. "It's getting late. We're five minutes away from the restaurant. Let's go." He started the engine; before shifting to *Drive,* he said. "Radwan works with Hamad Suleiman, your buddy playboy from New York. Suleiman is a key investor in Radwan's firm. And one more thing—the Doctor has tried to win Fatima's love, but it hasn't worked."

"No," Arik grumbled. "We're not going to see these guys now." He turned and gazed at Tarek. "Stop the car."

"But why? This is a great opportunity to get inside the real deal."

"The FBI may be watching these guys," Arik said, as Tarek slowed down and parked the car. "Dr. Radwan could be under surveillance. With the Patriot act, all of his communication channels may be bugged—his phone, his Internet surfing, his email, and moreover, they could've bugged his home and his place of work, conceivably his car, as well." Arik put his hand on Tarek's shoulder. "You've not informed the FBI have you?"

"No. I'm sure we've not."

"Well, my pal," Arik countered. "I believe it's the other way around. The FBI may have been watching our friends for a while and they've not informed *you.* You're the one who has been misinformed. Moreover, that is the reason they've not yet detained our cousins. They're hoping these minor league terrorists will steer them to the big fish; Dr. Radwan may be exploited as an FBI guided missile. I can see the teeth of that jaw trap."

"I doubt it," Tarek said. He scratched his head, rubbed his eyes, concealing his discomfiture for being so casual about the meeting. "So what do you propose?" he finally asked, as if he were running a brainstorming session at IBM on a resort island retreat with all the key power players."

"We'll meet them later, but not in a public place, and not in a place of their choosing," Arik asserted. "We'll meet them when they don't expect us. We'll surprise them. That way, the FBI or whoever's trailing them, will be caught unawares as well. We'll just have to make sure that our snooping hyenas are not behind with their tracking devices."

"Okay," Tarek said. "So what're we doing now?"

"We'll sit in the car outside the restaurant and wait for Dr. Radwan to come out. We'll then tag along."

"What do we do after that? And by the way, I'm getting hungry."

"I'll tell you when I know," Arik said, ignoring the "hungry" part. "We might get lucky."

They waited inside the car for about an hour. They listened to music, news, weather, then more music. Tarek's stomach was emitting eerie sounds, hunger pangs that even the hearing-impaired could take pleasure in. No one emerged out of the restaurant. Tarek was growing impatient. "You know," he said. "I don't believe the FBI's in the picture. We should've gone inside and delighted in the good food."

"No." Arik turned edgy. "We're going to wait here." Then abruptly, he turned to Tarek. He had an idea. "Is there another exit? Could we have missed them getting out?"

"Not that I know of," Tarek said.

"You sure?"

"Almost."

"You know. '*Almost*' is barely good enough."

"Best I can do." Tarek was getting irritated by Arik's insinuation.

Arik didn't like that answer. "In this field, the difference between winning and losing is a hair-breadth miscalculation. You'll have to be more thorough next time."

"Okay, but…"

"Wait a minute," Arik stopped him short. His eyes became glued to the sight of the man who had left the restaurant a moment earlier. "This is Hassan Omar. Trail him."

"What about Dr. Radwan?" Tarek asked.

"Forget him for now." Arik turned around and surveyed the surroundings, trying to make certain they had no partners in their pursuit. "Omar will take care of that once we visit with him." He turned towards Tarek. "Can you spot any spying eyes around?"

Tarek scanned his rearview mirrors, turned around and scrutinized the vicinity. "Not that I can tell," he concluded with satisfaction. *Arik is just too paranoid*, he reflected.

Omar was moving leisurely in his car along Oakman Blvd. Traffic was relatively light; they had no trouble following him at a comfortable distance. Omar made a left turn onto Wyoming Street, then stopped and waited at the intersection of Wyoming and Joy Road, disregarding the green traffic light. The two drivers behind him blasted their horns to no avail.

"Shit," Arik grumbled. "I know what he's doing. He must have become aware of his tail."

As soon as the traffic light turned red, Omar took off, crossing the intersection at a squealing haste as if he were maneuvering a racecar at the Indi-500 on Memorial Day. The two cars behind Omar and ahead of Tarek and Arik stayed in place, waiting for the next green light, thus blocking the view and access from Arik and Tarek.

"We lost him," Tarek said. There was relief in his words, which Arik noticed.

"Not yet," Arik countered. "He's not very far."

Tarek turned to face Arik. "How are you going to find him now?"

Arik didn't respond immediately. He was tense. They were sitting there speechless, watching the red light, while Arik tried to recall his latest conversation with Omar and super-impose its details on the Dearborn map, which he'd memorized on the flight over. It took two minutes before the traffic light changed back to green. "He's going to make a stop before proceeding to his final destination," Arik said. "He'll have to make sure he's shaken off any suspicious shadow."

"So? What does that mean as far as our next step?" Tarek asked.

"Go *straight* on Wyoming; make a *right* on Mackenzie; make a *left* on Esper, then follow with a *left* on E. Morrow Circle. Go a few blocks and stop there. We'll wait. Omar's going to show up soon after."

"How do you know?"

"That's the safe house he's told me about," Arik said. His smile revealed self-confidence that Tarek began to appreciate.

"Man, you're okay," Tarek said. "How many times have you been in this area?"

Arik turned back to Tarek. He placed both his hands on Tarek's shoulders. The smirk covering his face transformed into a somber stare. "Never," he uttered. He paused for a few seconds. "But I can read and memorize maps. My photographic memory never fails. I've been blessed with this gift ever since I can remember."

Chapter 31

December 31, 2002—Washington, DC

Christmas decorations were still hanging around in their final hour ahead of their lonely funeral where they'd be converted into inconvenient—hard to dispose of—trash. Jack Devon had a weakness for the Christmas atmosphere. He was walking the hallway, watching the Christmas trees, their glittering lights, while humming Christmas songs. He was in high spirits after his secretary, Jenny, burst into his office with Jim and Stanley. She let them barge in to bring him up to date on the latest, before she returned to her desk, wearing a coast-to-coast smile.

Jack had a special reason to be jolly. It was as if *Santa Clause* had paid him a final visit early in the day before leaving town. The gift *Santa* carried was the information gained through Dr. Radwan's phone tap in Dearborn, Michigan, and an Egyptian government's intelligence report concerning Qassem al-Nasr.

Stanley and Jim couldn't conceal their excitement. "I'm glad I didn't take the week off as my girlfriend had demanded," Stanley said. "This news is better than a hot Jacuzzi with Pamela Anderson under the dessert moon," he gloated.

"Does your girlfriend know she hasn't made your top ten?" Jim asked.

"Right behind Pamela," Stanley countered.

"Okay, so what makes you squeal like hyena in heat?" Jack asked Stanley. His wide smirk revealed his perfectly shaped veneer coated teeth.

"We're going to get them all, all those mother-fuckers, tonight, right in the middle of '*Goodnight Irene…I'll see you in my dreams,*'" Staley answered. He stood there all set to rock, then turned to Jim, placed his right hand on the back of his colleague's shoulder, left hand on his waist, then began to Tango.

"Okay, I got it," Jack said in an attempt to stop the partying. "You two have just come out of the closet. Is that it?"

Stanley froze. He let go of Jim, then turned to face Jack. "Nah, it's getting better than that. It feels like I've just smashed a glass at a Jewish wedding."

"Yes?" Jack gave him a quizzical stare.

"Then you take your broom, wipe the floor, and gather all of the glass fragments together in one heap. You grab your vacuum cleaner, and *Swoosh*—you chug-a-lug it all in a single orgasmic squeeze. You look around, and the floor's sparkling clean, just like brand new," Stanley said.

"You need to get off your medication," Jack said. "Now, do we have our guys in place surrounding the *Abu Shakra* restaurant?"

"Yeah," Jim exclaimed. "We checked with the hostess. We know what table they reserved. These bandits may be armed, so we've reserved an adjacent table for two guys and two gals from the Detroit Resident Agency—they'll be celebrating as well." Jim found a seat across from Jack. He took it, then went on. "Those low life creatures will be surrounded before they get a chance to say '*Allahu Akbar!*'" He beamed.

"Just make sure," Jack interjected, "that the word doesn't get out. If it does, we're fucked."

"We have," Jim said.

Stanley was still standing. "And there's more news."

"Shoot."

"The Egyptian Intelligence has found Qassem al-Nasr's file."

"Sounds intriguing," Jack said. "What's in it?"

"Well, they've sent us a copy. We'll get it by tomorrow. It includes pictures. Apparently, this chap lived in Egypt for a short time. He joined the Muslim Brotherhood cult—a group of fanatic religious mother-fuckers, who pose a threat to the secular regime in Egypt." Stanley paused, glanced at the notes he'd carried into the room with him. "He vanished five years ago. The Egyptians believe that he moved to Gaza, then got caught and done with by the Israelis."

Jack stared at Stanley. His facial expression resembled a dog waiting to be fed. "Did you check with the Israelis?" he inquired.

"We did. They've got nothing on the guy."

"They may be hiding something, or they really have nothing on the guy." Jack reached for the top drawer of his desk, pulled out a cigar, then began sucking on its edge.

"Only, the Egyptians insist that the Israelis do have information," Jim butted in.

"Jack glared at Jim, then at Stanley. "You ought to know," he stated. "The Egyptians always try to spoil the party for the Israelis in D.C. They always strive to make us suspicious of the Israelis. I don't take the Egyptian claims to heart unless they provide proof."

"They say the evidence's in the file they've sent over."

"We'll see," Jack said. He lit up his cigar, then stood up, indicating that the meeting was over. It was a back-to-work moment they all recognized.

"We're going to stay here in the office till it's over in Dearborn," Jim said. "Do you want us to get in touch when the party gets underway?"

"You know the answer," Jack said. "Get the glasses ready, Stanley wants to break his, like the good Jewish boy he is."

Chapter 32

December 31, 2002—Upstate New York

Abu Musa wanted to avoid the interstate. He directed the frightened couple through side roads leading out of the city in a southern direction. No one was saying a word except for occasional spurts of—"Take this road. Go right…" The only sound was that of the commentator on the radio News channel, who was reporting on the massive traffic jams on interstate 90.

In less than two hours, they were in Jamestown, New York. The anxious woman turned around and looked at Abu Musa. "I need to go to the bathroom," she pleaded.

"Soon," Abu Musa responded. He didn't seem to be as rude as he'd been earlier. He continued directing the driver through the vast white pine forests on the hills overlooking Chautauqua Lake, then he led them toward Hidden Valley Camping area. As they stopped the SUV, Abu Musa ordered the couple to step out of the car. The place was deserted. No sane soul would want to spend time camping in the freezing temperatures of that New Year's Eve early morning. "You go to the bathroom here, and don't try anything funny. I'll be watching," he instructed the woman. "You can go too," he told the man. The blood on the man's face had dried, staining his left cheek and sideburns red.

Abu Musa stepped out of the car and watched the two heading off. He approached the woman. She was wearing a gold chain with a Star of David emblem around her neck. He took a close look, then his mood changed. All at once, he became enraged. "Jews," he barked. "Dirty Jews." He pushed the woman back into the side of the SUV, then with his left he tore the chain off her neck and threw it

to the ground. The woman was getting panicky. She started screaming, as the husband came back, concerned about his wife.

It was over in less then ten seconds. Abu Musa flashed his gun
and fired; two bullets to the head; first at the man, then at the woman. They didn't stand a chance. He then picked up their wallets,
cell phone, and some paper receipts including the hotel statement,
anything that might help authorities identify the couple relatively
quickly. He turned toward the SUV; all set to leave the bodies on
the icy ground and walk away, but then changed his mind, reversing
course. He stood there scrutinizing the dead bodies, his rage building up to a crescendo. He couldn't just let them die in peace. Punish-
ment had to fit the crime. These people were Jews, descendants of
pigs and monkeys, despised by the Great Prophet. Abu Musa pulled
his utility knife. He bent next to the man, carved the word *JEW* on
his forehead, then slashed his throat, almost to the point of decapi-
tation, but no. He let the head dangle on its last remaining thread.
It looked like an incomplete job, a warning to all Jews—*It will get
worse when it's all said and done.*

He, then, turned to the woman. The necklace he'd torn off her
neck earlier, lay on the ground next to her dead body. He picked it
up and examined it. It contained a small golden locket next to the
Star-of-David emblem. He opened it, stared at the picture of her
two-year-old grandson who stared back, smiling and happy. *These
little monkeys must be killed when they are young,* he contemplated,
before they grow up and contaminate the rest of the world. His rage
gathered more steam. He was sweating now. His facial scar turned
bloody red; it looked as if it was about to burst open and spew brain
fluid. He grabbed the necklace, wrapped it around the woman's
neck, then tightened it hard to the point where it began cutting into
her flesh. He continued tightening until her cervical spine was the
only part securing the woman's head to the rest of her bulk. He then
turned her head around, severing it in the process. The golden chain
with the emblem and the little open locket dropped into her bleeding, open throat.

He stood up, took one more scrutinizing glare at his latest
artwork, then, all at once, he was engulfed by a sickening wave of

nausea. *Dirty Jews, they make me sick*. He spat on the woman's severed head as that latest thought entered his mind.

He left the scene in a hurry, then climbed into the driver seat of the SUV and turned on the ignition key.

Minutes later, he was back in town. He drove along West 5th Street, turned right onto Jefferson Street, then parked in front of Baker Park. He stayed inside the car, took out his newly acquired cell phone, and dialed Hilga's number in Toronto.

Hilga answered the phone after two rings. "Hello," she said in her familiar German accent.

"Hey," Abu Musa paused. Hilga didn't respond. "Your electrician's here," he said.

"I know," she whispered. She didn't say more.

"Okay," he understood. *She is cautious; the phone line may be bugged.*

"Call me in an hour, if you want to make an appointment," he said. "You have my number."

She peeked at the caller ID. "Okay. One hour." Hilga understood. She would go out to place the call from a public phone.

• • •

It was minutes after 6:30 in the morning. Hilga was on the line. She called from a public phone. "You know, they placed me under surveillance," she said. "I'm being treated like a criminal around here."

"That figures," he said. "These pigs are out of control. They'll pay for this. *Inshallah* (God willing)."

"I can't stay here any longer. It's become unbearable." She sounded desperate. "Even my sister seems to like the idea of me leaving."

"I have a job for you. It'll solve your problem," he said.

"Good. What is it?"

"I want you to rent a car and drive to Detroit this evening. Go to *Abdul Parking* on Diversity Street and leave the car there. Ask for Ahmad. Once you see him, identify yourself. He will get you a cab and an address. Go there and wait for further instructions. Be there before 9 p.m." There was a pause, then he resumed. "Do you remember the names of the people I've told you about?"

"Yes," she said.

"You'll meet them tonight. They'll give you a message, which you should forward to me."

"Do you want me to call you back at this number?" she asked.

"They'll tell you how to get in touch." He coughed, then spit the green gravy in his throat onto the ground. "I won't use this phone any longer. It will be bugged pretty soon, once the pigs figure out where I got it from."

She glanced at her watch. It was 6:47 in the morning. If she started now, she would make it with plenty of time to spare. "Are you going to meet me there?" she asked.

"Not there. Not tonight."

"I don't know if I can cross to the US, with my current student visa," she grumbled.

"Think," he said. "Your sister can. She's a Canadian citizen. She must have some papers. You figure it out."

"Uh, got it," she muttered. "It's going to be a long day."

In the corner of his left eye, Abu Musa caught a glimpse of an approaching police cruiser. He hung up the phone and watched through the side and rear view mirrors. The cruiser moved toward his SUV. It slowed down considerably as it passed behind, while the police officer was scrutinizing the vehicle. There was only one officer inside the police car. He was talking to someone on his radio. Abu Musa touched and felt his gun. He was ready. The cruiser didn't stop. It continued on its way, then slowly faded from view.

There was too much he worried about, too many were looking for him. Abu Musa realized that he had become a hunted animal; his sixth sense alerted him to the fact that precautions were a high priority. It was time to let them know he wasn't going to make it to Dearborn on time for the meeting. He called one brother, Dr. Radwan, his contact in Dearborn, on Dr. Radwan's recent acquisition, pre-paid, safe cell phone. This time he used the phone Ismail had given him in Albany. "Brother," he said. "You won't see me tonight. But, you'll go to the *Red House* at

9 p.m. You'll meet my woman emissary; you'll pick her up and take her to the meeting at the *Abu Shakra* restaurant at 10 p.m."

At this point, Abu Musa was careful not to expose either himself or his closest, trusted friends, to unfamiliar encounters with untried terrorists. Instead, he preferred having his fresh ambassador scout, Hilga, whom he was willing to sacrifice if circumstances demanded it.

"All right, brother," Dr. Radwan said. "I'll see to it that she makes it to the meeting."

Chapter 33

December 31, 2002—Dearborn, Michigan

Arik and Tarek, his Moroccan limo driver, had been sitting in the car for over an hour. Traffic around them was relatively light. A few local residents left their homes, drove away, some came in. A neighbor came with his SUV, checked into the *Yellow House* across the street from the *Red House*, remotely raising the garage door, moved inside, then closed the door with his remote control. Arik stared suspiciously at that *Yellow House*. No lights were turned on inside. Tarek repeated his old complaint. "Man, am I really hungry! How much longer are we going to sit here in the car and watch this wonderful, boring neighborhood?"

"As long as it takes," Arik retorted. "Something's going on. Omar showed up for lunch because he wanted to tell me something ahead of this evening's meeting. It could've been important. It could've been a substitute plan for this evening." Arik put his hand in his pocket and pulled out a granola bar. "Here," he handed the bar to Tarek. "Take it. This poison will quiet down your hunger pains for a while."

Tarek seemed surprised. "Where the hell did you yank this from?" He didn't wait for an answer. He rushed to unwrap the packaging. Arik watched in awe as Tarek mauled half of the bar in a single bite, gorging his mouth to the limit.

"I'm going to check out this *Red House*," Arik said. He opened the passenger door, put his fedora on his head, set his feet on the ground, then stepped out. He turned around to view the quizzical Tarek. "Someone may be inside," he said.

Arik had just reached the driveway when, suddenly, a taxi appeared, braking behind him. Alarmed, he stopped abruptly, turned around, only to watch the young blonde stepping out of the car and heading toward the house. Seeing him, she broke her stride. "Hi?" she greeted him with a friendly, yet curious smile, stamped on an inquiring face.

"Hi," he replied. "Are you going in?" he smiled back.

"Yes," she said. "I'm Hilga." She offered her hand, but her face projected a perplexed frame of mind.

"I'm Qassem," he said. "Qassem al-Nasr. I'm looking for Omar. I thought he would be here by now."

"Omar?"

Arik realized she might not know who Omar was. "Yes. Hassan Omar. You know him?"

She stared at Arik, scrutinized his face; took a step back so she could have an all-encompassing view. "Who are you?" she asked.

"I'm Qassem al-Nasr," he repeated. "Can we go inside and talk?"

She seemed anxious. "Not until you tell me what you're doing here," she said in a heavy German accent. She turned her head and surveyed the street to the left, than to the right, noticing the parked car nearby, and the driver, Tarek, sitting inside. "Is that your friend in the car over there?" she asked.

"Yes, he's my driver," Arik said. "You have nothing to worry about. I'm a friend, a brother." He smiled, but didn't move. He realized she was scared. "I had no idea you'd show up here. It's completely unexpected. To tell you the truth, I'm confused." He figured that looking less aggressive and unsure would make her less scared and more trustful. "Could we go inside?" he tried again. "It's freezing out here."

"I still don't know who..." she said, than changed. "I still don't know why you're here."

"Look Hilga." Arik was searching for a way to calm her down. "I'm here in town for the meeting tonight. Do you know about the meeting?"

She was still suspicious. He could be an FBI agent looking for additional information. All at once, she felt the prongs of a clever trap closing in on her. "Who are you meeting?" she inquired. She was eyeing Tarek. "What's he doing in the car over there?" she asked, pointing, referring to Tarek.

"He's okay. He's my driver." Arik was shivering. He had his hands inside his pockets, then started treading in place in an attempt to keep warm. "I'll be meeting with Hassan Omar, Abu Musa, and their teams later tonight," he revealed, after concluding that no harm could come from disclosing this information to her.

"Abu Musa isn't coming," she suddenly said. "He asked me to represent him."

"Oh, really? That's truly disappointing," the slow smile creeping across his face made her think that he didn't mean it. It made her feel more comfortable. She smiled back. *There's a crack in her firewall*, he reflected. *She's opened up. Her trust level in me has taken a leap upward.* Still, Arik was actually disappointed. He did hope to live through a face-to-face with Abu Musa. He took his right hand out of his pocket and pointed in the direction of the house. "Can we go inside now?"

He turned and waved to Tarek as she opened the unlocked door to the house.

It wasn't very warm inside. The thermostat was set to 45°F, but compared to the subzero temperature outside, this was seventh heaven. The split-level house was decorated with a dark-blue carpet at the entrance, which opened to a large L-shaped living room, dining room combination. The L-shaped wall in front was covered with mirror tiles. A blue velvet sofa took center stage on the opposite wall of the living room. It was enhanced with an orange velvet couch at the far end and a glass cocktail table in the middle. A blue pull-down blind covered the large picture window facing the street. There were no pictures on the wall, just light blue paint.

Arik followed Hilga into the dining room. She was exploring the place. Her eyes kept wandering around. He did the same. She placed her hand on the dining room glass table and moved it along its top as if she were testing the purity of the material. He watched her and wondered whether this beautiful German understood the situation she'd been drawn into. She didn't tie in with the profile of a potential fanatic Islamic lunatic who would sacrifice his living soul for the honor and pleasures of the promised afterlife. She appeared to be an innocent pawn.

"Why are you here?" he asked. "What do you know about our struggle?"

She lifted her head and stared back at him. "It was a last minute call," she said. "My boyfriend told me to come and meet with you. He was unable to make it."

"Your boyfriend?"

"Amin Shukri, or as you call him—Abu Musa. He's my boyfriend."

"Are you sure?" Arik found it hard to believe. Abu Musa was a ruthless mass murderer. It didn't fit. "How long have you two been together?" Arik went around the table so he could face her.

Hilga moved in front of the dining room chair, then sat down. "It's a long story..." She seemed tired.

"I'll make the time."

"Are you really Qassem al-Nasr?" she asked. "Abu Musa mentioned your name as one of the persons I was to meet tonight." She paused and scrutinized Arik who was still standing across from her.

He watched her eyes shifting slowly away from his face and down through his pelvis, X-raying the rest of his body, then slowly backing up.

He quickly got over the raw animal excitement at the sight of this slow scan. He smiled. "Do you want to see a form of identification?"

She felt self-conscious. "Oh, no," she said as her face turned pink. "Abu Musa never mentioned how handsome you were." She giggled.

"I never met the guy, but really, my mother kept telling me the same thing," he said, adding to her awkwardness. "And by the way, are you hitting on me?" He kept staring at her, lasering her eyes.

She beamed, said nothing, then looked down, avoiding eye contact.

"So what's the story?" he persisted. "You and Abu Musa—how did it happen?"

She kept looking down, then slowly lifted her head facing Arik. She told him how and why she'd converted to Islam; how she'd met Abu Musa in Bonn, and how she'd seen him again in Canada. She told him how they'd accused him of murder; how the Canadian police hadn't left her alone, and how she'd crossed the border to the US, had left her rented car in a Detroit parking lot, had picked up the key to the house, then had caught a taxi for the final leg of the excursion. She left out the part about Kamil Awad.

There was a knock on the door.

They both turned their heads toward the source of the sound. They'd locked the door from the inside once they'd entered the house. Arik got up and approached. "Who's there?"

"Come on, Qassem," Tarek said. "Open it, time to go and get some real beef."

Arik turned toward Hilga, "You must be starving, let's go out and have a bite.

Chapter 34

December 31, 2002—Bali, Indonesia

Rachel couldn't tell how long she'd been locked up in the cramped basement. She no longer cared for the stench in the musty room. She got used to the rice and water rations, and was no longer feeling hungry in spite of her consistent weight-losing regime. In her new prison, she couldn't tell days from nights; no sunlight could penetrate the underground bunker in which she'd been imprisoned. She spent a great deal of time sleeping, conserving energy. Her captors visited once a day, bringing in the daily ration; they opened the door, set the rice and water on the floor, picked up the empty plate, then left after locking the gates. Tuti had been dead since before Rachel's captors moved her out of the earlier prison and into this most recent one. Tuti's little kid, Budi, was somewhere in the vicinity. At one point, Rachel had heard his voice. He had been crying, asking for his mom. The rest of the time, Rachel felt total boredom wrapped in an unbroken despair.

The basement cell included a small water closet with a door and no key. Rachel would go in and shut herself inside, feigning a need for privacy, even when she didn't require the use of the toilet.

It was Tuesday night when she heard the guards yelling and cursing one another. The sound of steps outside the door to her cell was drawing closer and closer. She waited for the door to get unlocked while crouching in one corner of the cell, hands and chin on her knees, expecting the usual daily ration. Guntur, the guard, appeared at the door. His shirtless body revealed a pink scar, which ran across his lower abdomen. He approached Rachel who kept gaping at him with terror in her eyes. He got close and bent over her. His face was

only an inch away from hers. He had a mischievous look on his face
and she could smell the alcohol on his breath.

He grasped her hand and said. "You're mine now." He pushed
her to the ground, pulled her skirt and underwear off, then went on
top of her. She tried to resist the assault, but he was stronger. She felt
him penetrating her. She almost passed out, when, without warning,
Budi, the little kid, came rushing into the basement. Once inside,
he came within reach of Guntur and began pulling him off Rachel.
Guntur, surprised at the boy's nerve, got to his feet, pushed the boy
down to the floor, pulled his pants up and started kicking the boy and
cursing him in a language Rachel didn't understand.

At that very moment, the other guard entered the basement.
Guntur took a short breather, just as Budi started coughing in pain.
The little boy was on the floor bending his knees and holding his
belly in an attempt to shield it from more anticipated kicks. Guntur
turned around and faced his colleague who was barking back at him
in disagreement. The two of them were cursing each other while
inching away from their prisoners. Rachel merely needed a fleeting
hiatus. She got up, picked Budi off the floor, ran into the toilet closet,
and closed the door behind. The screaming outside in the basement
continued for another minute before she heard the gunshot and the
silence that followed. No one tried to open the door behind which
she was hiding with little Budi. She felt anxious and tense.

She stayed inside the closet for an hour. All that time, she held
Budi in her arms, pressing him against her chest, as he kept crying,
holding her tight. She finally dared open the door to the basement.
Upon entering the dark room, she almost dropped Budi on the floor,
as she stumbled upon Guntur's body. She turned on the light, and
noticed the fresh blood on the ground. It originated from the corpse
and formed a narrow rivulet that ended in a kidney-shaped puddle
in the middle of the basement. She felt like throwing up. She put
her underwear and skirt back on, then moved toward the basement
door. She accidentally leaned on the handle, and to her amazement,
it opened. Rachel was stunned by the revelation. Guntur's killer, in
his exploding rage, forgot to lock it. This was her chance. She stared
at the dilapidated wooden stairs leading from the basement up to

the ground floor, as her heartbeat started rushing in response to the thought of the looming freedom.

Rachel dropped on her knees to face Budi. She gave him a hug, then moved him a few inches away, holding him by the shoulders. She looked him in the eye, paused briefly, moved her left hand to her lips, and signaled, *shhhh*... Budi nodded. He understood. His eyes conveyed fear and anxiety, but he was on to her plan.

It was quiet on the ground floor. She climbed a few steps and listened. She could hear no sound. She climbed one stair at a time, paused to listen, then continued all the way to the top where another door separated her from the Promised Land. Budi was following right behind her, waiting for her to make the next move. She was about to attempt opening the door when the sound of approaching footsteps froze her to her place. She couldn't move back quickly enough, fearing that the noise of their joint retreat would alert her guard.

Moments later, it was quiet again. Rachel was listening behind the door contemplating a breach. She peeked again; there was no handle. She waited about thirty minutes, frozen in place with Budi two steps down behind her, before giving the door a light push, just to effect a narrow gap. A chair and a bare table blocked her view. She pushed further and now she could make out the rest of the room. She noticed a sofa on the right, where her warden was resting with his eyes closed. The window above the sofa was open. For the first time in weeks, she could tell day from night. It was dark outside, the sun was down, but the moon was shimmering at half crescent. There was only one more door to slip through before she would be out of the building. Her watchdog appeared to be napping; she didn't know how deep his sleep was, if at all, but she mustered all of her courage, dropped on her knees and elbows, and started crawling toward the entrance with Budi following her every move. The catnapping man wasn't moving; he was snoring. She made it to the door, but now she had to stand up, unlock, and open it. She glanced again at the motionless man, rose to her feet, and placed her hand on the door handle. At that moment, the kidnapper turned to his side, his left hand on his bent knee and his right hanging in the air; his closed eyelids faced her, and his expression was that of a mad man. Rachel got scared.

In her panic, she hastily turned the door handle, opened it, and raced outside with Budi right behind, doing the same. She had no idea where she was heading next, other than running away from the small house, in which she'd been incarcerated. It was a crowded neighborhood, comprising many single-family private structures in very close proximity to one another, but the streets were deserted. She kept on running, holding Budi's hand, afraid of being pursued, until she found herself facing what looked like a small church. For the first time since her escape, she looked back. No one seemed to be following her, but her senses told her she wasn't safe yet. She approached the church entry doors. They were locked. She banged on the doors, calling for anyone to open from the inside. Budi, still clinging to her hand, began crying.

She stood there for about a minute waiting for a miracle while at the same time trying to comfort the little kid, but the door remained locked, with no angels coming to her rescue. Suddenly, she recognized her kidnapper's voice. He was shouting, calling her name from a distance. Her heart skipped a few beats. She grabbed Budi's hand, moved away from the door, went around the building, and hid behind a couple of bushes, with Budi enfolded within her arms. The screeching stopped, but the bad guy could still be too close for comfort. Rachel decided to stay where she was. There was no point in trying to run away. Her hiding place seemed practical under the circumstances.

Two minutes later, the church doors opened. Someone came out looking for the door-banger. She couldn't see the person, but she could hear him. She was still hiding behind the bushes next to the sidewall and didn't wish to bring herself to light, lest someone else, her pursuer, spotted her. Still, she felt fortunate. Someone was inside. She would try again later, when she felt safer.

It was dawn when she and Budi made it inside the church. The priest was an old man who was slow to comprehend her situation. When he finally did, he offered to find out the telephone number for the American Embassy in Jakarta.

Chapter 35

December 31, 2002—Dearborn, Michigan

The Burger King on Schaefer Road was bursting with young American Arabs and their considerable number of younger offspring. Arik felt like he'd just regained admittance to his old poor neighborhood in Iraq. After ordering double Whoppers, Fries, and Diet Cokes for everyone, Arik and Tarek followed Hilga who'd been able to secure a corner table where they could all sit and watch the racket. A young mousy looking woman at the table next to theirs was screeching in Arabic at her five-year-old, who'd pushed his younger brother to the floor, spilling his coke on his clothes in the process. His younger sister, whose running nose was pouring into her tiny mouth, was shrieking. She wanted an ICEE, but her mother was too busy disciplining the older brothers, ignoring her daughter's tantrum.

"Let's get out of here," Arik suggested. "I need some peace." He collected the leftovers and got up. The others followed behind. They were just about outside the entrance when all of a sudden Arik saw him coming in. "Hey Qassem," Omar greeted him. "*Ahlan* (Hi)."

Arik didn't seem surprised. "I figured you followed us when you came with your SUV and moved inside the *Yellow House* across the street." He scanned Omar. The latter was wearing a brown hat that looked more like a sock, dark sunglasses to keep looking invisible, and an aftershave that reeked more like bug spray.

Omar seemed surprised. "Right! We always acquire safe houses in pairs, one across from the other." There was an admiring twinkle in his eye. "How did you know?"

"Standard practice," Arik added. "You prevent someone else from spying on you while you keep a watchful eye on your own premises." Arik turned to Tarek. "This guy, Omar, is the son of

Houdini. He left the restaurant with a Chevy, then showed up with an SUV. That's what I call cut-rate magic."

Omar beamed in return. "And you must be Hilga," he said, turning toward her, watching her nod in agreement. "Abu Musa has a message for you," he said, then turned to Tarek. "Hello, brother. You must be Tarek. My friend had expected you and Qassem in the *Sahara* restaurant for lunch. We were disappointed you didn't show up."

"Qassem didn't want to," Tarek complained.

Omar turned to Arik. "Why?"

Arik didn't answer. "Let's go back to the *Red House* and talk. I don't like an open convention in the middle of the zoo."

"There will be no meeting tonight at *Abu Shakra*," Omar said. He turned to Arik. "I came to town early. I was looking for a way to warn you."

"Has the meeting details leaked out?"

"There's a concern," Omar said. "Someone asked about our reservation. He wanted to know which table had been reserved for our party." They were all sitting around the dining room table. Omar rose. "Let's go to the kitchen," he said to Arik. "This is just between us two," he added, facing Tarek and Hilga, implying—*you two stay here.*

"How did you get a handle on the leak?" Arik asked as soon as they were in the kitchen.

"I know the assistant chef at *Abu Shakra*; he warned me," he whispered back. "Listen, I don't trust this German woman. She's not one of us. She doesn't come across or dress up like a Muslim. She could be the source of the leak."

"That's possible," Arik agreed. "Did Dr. Imad Radwan know about the meeting?"

"He was invited," Omar said. "He's a crucial part of the plan, and so is Hamad Suleiman."

"Is Suleiman supposed to show up tonight at *Abu Shakra*?"

"I'm not sure. Suleiman's always in the shadows."

"Uh huh," Arik scratched his head. "How does Dr. Imad Radwan fit in with the scheme?"

"Dr. Radwan will be in charge of assembling the suicide belts, and manage the money for the operation; Suleiman's in charge of global *Jihad*. Do you know he's already recruited two Germans, to act as suicide bombers following their arrival in Israel?"

"What about it? Arik asked, playing seeming ignorance.

"Talk to Suleiman. He will fill you in."

"I see." He paused, drew a breath. "I'll have to find him."

The doorbell rang. Omar stared at Arik; Omar had turned from a confident conspirator to a cornered cat in a space of a heartbeat. He reached for his gun, moved to the window, carefully shifted the blinds, enough for a quick peek, then grumbled. "I met this man last month. It's Ahmad from the gas station. I wonder why he's here."

He turned to Arik. "I'll go open the door for him."

Arik stayed upstairs, waiting for Omar to return. Two minutes later, Omar was back. "Ahmad's here to pick up Hilga," he said. "They're going to Cleveland together to meet Abu Musa."

"I understand Abu Musa isn't coming to town tonight," Arik said. He looked disappointed.

"I guess not," Omar concurred.

"The belts—are they destined for the *St. Patrick's Cathedral* next Christmas Eve?" Arik asked.

"That's the one," Omar said. "Abu Musa's actually the mastermind."

"He likes churches, doesn't he?" Arik's tone of voice reflected sarcasm. "I don't like it," he announced. "Too trivial, little impact. Plus—if you pull that off, then Home Land Security, the FBI, the NYPD, and anybody who wants to put his balls on show, will pour money and men into finding out who was behind that little scratch, before you get a chance to yank the big one." He paused for effect, briskly rose from his chair, then went on. "I have a different idea." He halted briefly again, stepped out of the kitchen only to peek back at the dining room, watching Tarek, Hilga, and now Ahmad, having a good time chatting and chortling. The kitchen was too close in proximity. "Let's go upstairs to the bedroom area," he offered.

Once they were upstairs Arik turned to Omar. "We all know why we're here. We all know who the enemy of Islam is—the Americans and the Jews," Arik lectured. "We'll have Allah's will executed on American soil once again. 9/11 was only an introduction." He waited, then shifted his head and peeked downstairs through the entrance. They had their privacy. Hilga, Tarek and Ahmad were still on the go in the dining room. He shifted back to face Omar. "I came here for the purpose of team building. We're at the initial phase of duplicating the victory we pulled off on 9/11, only this time it's going to be bigger."

"What's on your mind?" Omar asked.

"How about ten thousand dead people?" Arik said, gazing at his comrade in search of a reaction. Omar just stared at him, seeking further motivation. "We have plenty of talent around this town and across the world." Arik got closer, closer than spitting distance. Confidentiality was crucial at that moment. "I can't tell you all of the details right now, still, I'll need your help," Arik said.

"Just ask," Omar asserted. "But can a brother spare a hint?"

"Do you know anything about *Sarin?*"

"Funny you ask," Omar disclosed. "I discussed this with Suleiman. Getting the stuff in is vital. Suleiman's in charge of that. He can get you anything you want. He has money and he has connections."

Arik moved his face closer to Omar's. "Where does he get it from?" he asked in a collusive whisper.

"I believe it's coming by way of Iran," Omar said in a soft voice. He paused, scanned the surroundings, making sure no one was listening in on his hush-hush tip, then continued. "Suleiman knows the details."

Hilga came upstairs. "I'm leaving now for Cleveland. Abu Musa's waiting." she told Arik and Omar. She approached Arik, kissed him on the cheek. "I'll see you soon," she said with a sad smile, then turned to Omar. "Abu Musa asked me about the blueprints. He wants to review the plan. Can I have it please?"

""It's not ready. Qassem, here, isn't in favor." Omar said. "Tell Abu Musa we'll all have to discuss it in person as soon as possible."

"Okay," she said, then turned around and left the room.

Arik watched her going down the stairs. *She has no idea what the plan she's been asking for is all about*, he reflected. He turned back to Omar. "I must talk to Suleiman," he said, then shifted his gaze to the window, watching Hilga and Ahmad step into a white Honda, then back to Omar. "I must see Suleiman as soon as possible; is he in town?"

"That's what they say. I'm sure his shadow is." He shrugged, spread his hands, casual on the face of it, but his face was creased with anxiety.

"How can I get in touch with Suleiman?"

Omar beckoned, then held his empty palm up. "You know, it's just occurred to me. He may show up at *Abu Shakra* later tonight; you may spot him in the vicinity if no one has bothered to tell him otherwise." He scratched his head, then clenched his jaw. "I was unable to deliver the news to him in person. I left a message on the *Delilah* site, but I don't know. He's very guarded; you never know what he's up to or where he can be found. Someone needs to warn him about the leak. Could you?"

Chapter 36

December 31, 2002—Cleveland, Ohio

The driving on Interstate 90 toward Cleveland wasn't too arduous. The snow had been cleared ahead of Abu Musa's advance and traffic was relatively light. He was heading for the safe house on E. 95th Street. Several blocks away at the Exxon Gas station, Yusuf, the attendant, provided him with the remote, which opened the garage door, and from there, he continued straight to the safety of the private, sheltered home. After 9/11, the international Islamic terror organizations always picked up secluded single-family homes as safe houses rather than apartments in crowded buildings. You didn't have to meet the neighbors; you could get in and out of your garage without anyone catching sight of your face, and you could be practically invisible.

Cleveland was situated midway between Detroit and Buffalo; Ahmad, from the *Abdul* Parking Garage in Dearborn, would drive Hilga to Abu Musa's place—a reasonable compromise. He expected her to bring over blueprints of the plan for the well thought-out suicide bombing next Christmas Eve in New York's *St. Patrick's Cathedral*.

It was after five in the afternoon when Abu Musa made it to 95th Street. It was already dark outside. The house, a three-bedroom ranch, was partly furnished with white bare walls, missing furniture in the living room, a wall-to-wall dark green carpet, covering the entire house, and two twin beds in every bedroom. The dining room had a small table with a white Formica top and four cheap wooden chairs. There was a large battery-operated clock hanging down in the kitchen between two wall cabinets—except the battery was missing. The electric oven was out of order but the small microwave and toaster oven were in good shape, yet soiled.

Abu Musa wasn't impressed, but he didn't care either. His animal instincts were preoccupied with the thought of food. He hadn't eaten for over twelve hours and the emptiness in his stomach was giving him a headache. He had neither foodstuff, nor aspirin, and all the drawers he opened were empty except for some fresh spider webs.

He remembered. On his way to the safe house, he'd spotted a *McDonald's*. Hilga wouldn't show up for another two hours. There was no point in waiting inside the house. He put on his coat and went back to the SUV in the garage.

The line around the take-out curve was short. He ordered two *Big Macs*, large fries, and a Coke. Although he planned to return to his hideout right away, his craving won the day. He drove to a dark corner at the customer's parking lot, and attacked the food.

He was in the middle of the unwrapping his second *Big Mac* when a police cruiser pulled up next to his SUV. Feeling anxious, he dropped the *Mac* on his pants; from there it made its way to the floor next to his right foot. In the bewilderment that followed, he stepped on it.

Two local troopers came out of the cruiser and headed into the *McDonald's*. They paid no heed to the stolen SUV parked next to their squad car. Abu Musa decided to split before they reemerged; he was back home in a jiffy. Once inside the car garage, he kneeled down, picked up the mutilated sandwich from the floor of the SUV, and rushed inside the kitchen. Two bites later, he no longer felt famished. The added dirt boosted the flavor, but made the *Big Mac* hard to chew on. He went into the master bedroom, lay down on one of the beds and closed his eyes.

The sound of the doorbell woke him. He jumped out of bed. It was dark in the room; he almost tripped when his foot caught the edge of the bed. "O' motherfucker," he barked. The sharp pain caused by the bang made him limp. He moved slowly toward the entrance. Leaning on it, he could hear Hilga's voice on the other side. "I hope he's in," she said to Ahmad. "Do you have the key?"

Abu Musa opened the door, then stepped back, inviting the two guests in. He noticed the white Honda in his driveway. "You drove this one?" he asked pointing at the car.

Ahmad didn't answer. That wasn't a question. "We've not eaten yet," Ahmad said. "Do you have any food in the house?"

"I can take you to my favorite *McDonald's*. I haven't finished my dinner either," Abu Musa said. He approached Hilga, gave her a hug, and kissed her on her forehead. "Let's go," he commanded." We'll use your car," he told Ahmad.

Abu Musa took the passenger seat, told Hilga to take the back-seat, and let Ahmad drive. It was a cold welcome. Hilga found it hard to stomach. She'd expected a gala, but instead it felt like an attack of diarrhea in a fancy restaurant on a rainy night. Her belongings were still in the trunk. She didn't even manage to take them out before leaving for their late supper.

"You've got the plan for the *St. Patrick's Cathedral* project?" he asked Hilga.

"No. I was told that Qassem al-Nasr had overruled it."

"What?" Abu Musa was getting upset. "Who told you that?"

"I met Qassem al-Nasr," she said. "He didn't like the idea."

"Who the fuck is he to overrule me?" Abu Musa was screaming now. "Did you see Hassan Omar?"

"I met Omar."

"What did he say?"

"He went along with Qassem al-Nasr."

"Motherfuckers!" Abu Musa turned to Ahmad who was doing his best to stay out of the fray. "Let's go," Abu Musa commanded.

"This isn't her fault," Ahmad pleaded. "There's no reason to get upset at her."

"What? Are you her attorney?" Abu Musa turned back toward Hilga. His long facial scar twisted to form an overpass to his lipless mouth. "What did you do to turn everyone against me? Did you fuck them?"

"Come on, Abu Musa." Ahmad said, trying to pacify his comrade. "She's innocent, and you know it."

Surprisingly, Abu Musa calmed down. His rage vanished as rapidly as it'd come. It was as if *Mr. Hyde* had left the scene and *Dr. Jekyll* came back to life.

Abu Musa ran through his earlier routine at the *McDonald's*. They picked up their meals at the drive-in window, then moved to the same dark corner at the customer's parking lot. It was New Year's Eve, and traffic at the *McDonald's* at that hour was light. They were the only customers.

Half an hour later, they returned to E. 95th Street. As they approached their safe house, they noticed the flashing red and blue of the cruiser's light bar from a distance. "Wait a minute. There are several of them—police cruisers," Abu Musa said. He was growing tense. Ahmad slowed down, then stopped at a safe distance from the night raid. Their safe house was no longer safe. Their home had just become a crime scene. *The police must have broken into the garage, found the SUV, then, connected me to another double homicide*, Abu Musa concluded. *Nice work.*

"Abu Musa turned around and faced Hilga. "Who did you tell about this place?" *Mr. Hyde* had just reappeared.

She looked frightened. Her stomach tightened; she struggled through the spasms, writhing and gasping. "I told no one." She choked as if trying to suppress sad emotions. "I didn't even know where Ahmad was taking me."

Abu Musa was upset. He turned to Ahmad. "Go! Go by the house, I want to take a closer look."

"It may be unsafe," Ahmad said. "They may stop us."

"No, they won't. Just do what I tell you," Abu Musa said. "And then keep going at the same speed."

"What are we going to do now?" Ahmad asked after leaving the scene and reaching a safe distance.

"We're all going back to Dearborn, but before that, we'll make a stop at the Exxon Gas station, where I picked up the remote control key for the garage door."

"This could be dicey," Ahmad suggested. He was worried that if the attendant had warned the police, then going back there would be like sticking one's head into a lion's den.

"We won't step out of the car. I want to see the traitor with my own eyes."

"That's too risky," Ahmad protested.

"You do what I say," Abu Musa charged in an unsympathetic tone. "Don't you ever question my judgment."

Ahmad was intimidated. "Okay."

They drove by the gas station. Abu Musa touched his gun, then grabbed it in his right hand and held it above his knee. "Drive around. I want to look for him," he growled.

They drove around from pump to pump. There was no sign of the attendant. Abu Musa stepped out of the car and peeked inside the station, then came back. "Okay this is his lucky day," he said. He seemed disappointed.

Once back in the car, he turned to Ahmad. "Go back to Dearborn," he ordered. He turned around in his seat. Hilga was sitting in the back. She seemed stressed and frightened.

"Are you sure? Dearborn is quite far," Ahmad protested.

"You question my judgment again," Abu Musa proclaimed, glaring at Ahmad. "I want to find out who this Qassem al-Nasr is to overrule my plans, and I want to find out who the fucking mole is—the one who turned me in." Abu Musa glared at Hilga again. She cowered in her seat, as if caught in a state of suspended animation. "You must have an idea," he stated. "Don't you?"

Chapter 37

January 1, 2003—Washington, DC

"Nothing! No sign of Qassem al-Nasr, Abu Musa, or Hassan Omar. Where the fuck did they all go?" Jack Devon was restless and frustrated after an entire night of unrequited anticipation. It was early morning, just about 5 a.m., when he came back to the office after a New Year's Eve party with his family.

The FBI agents inside the *Abu Shakra* restaurant left empty-handed at around 2:30 a.m. The place was being vacated after a mind-numbing New Year's Eve celebration. The agents were among the finalists, careful not to win first prize for being the very last ones to leave. The entire outdoor squad left an hour later, after the place had been mostly deserted.

"I guess that place, and Dearborn, in general, isn't a New Year's Eve attraction," Jim said, trying to ease Jack's mind with light humor.

It didn't work. Jack remained pissed off. "What kind of intelligence are you guys collecting?" He turned to the door. The source of the noise was Jenny; she materialized without warning.

"A call from the Cleveland police," she explained. "They say it's urgent. Do you want me to transfer?"

Jack stared at her. "Sure." He turned back toward Jim. "Where's Stanley? He asked.

"He will be here in a minute," Jim said. "Last I heard; he was on the phone with Cleveland when you called us in."

"I see. He must have transferred the call to my office."

Stanley came in as soon as Jack finished the sentence. "Can you put this on speaker?"

"Hi, it's Officer Bentley," the voice announced. "As I've already explained to agent Stanley Kramer, based on the tip we received from him earlier, we've moved in on the suspicious premises in Cleveland. There, we've turned up the SUV belonging to an older couple from Virginia whose dead frozen mutilated bodies were discovered a few days ago in Jamestown, New York.

Jack Devon glared at Stanley. "You haven't told me...?" His right eyebrow raised in a questioning look.

"Dr. Radwan's phone tap," Stanley clarified. "It was urgent, and you were out. I figured, you'd be informed as soon as you came in."

Jack said nothing. He returned his attention to the voice on the speaker.

"It looks like agent Kramer had solid information. We've found plenty of fingerprints, some clothes, some unfinished fast food. Early indications point to one of your top ten—Abu Musa."

"This is a federal case, you know," Jack Devon interrupted.

Officer Bentley responded quickly. "That's why I'm calling. It's your baby. We're here to offer help, but you own this one."

"Thank you," Jack said. "We'll get back to you shortly. In the meantime, you should contact the local FBI field office; have them take over this one."

"We've already done that. You'll probably get their input as soon as they come up to speed."

Stanley barged in. "Officer Bentley, the clothes you found in the house—how many people would you say they belong to?"

"One small suitcase and not a lot of clothes. But there was more."

"What was that?"

"Inside we found two passports—one belonging to a Kamil Awad, and another with the name of Amin Shukri.

Jim turned to Stanley. "It all fits perfectly."

"Thanks, we'll take it over from here. Just give Stanley here the details," Jack said. "We'll be in touch."

Jack turned to Stanley. "Did you put a tail on Dr. Radwan?" he asked.

"Yeah," Stanley said. "He stayed in his apartment. Didn't go anywhere on New Year's Eve."

"Keep watching him. He will show you the way to the hornet's nest."

Jim had an idea. "They canceled the meeting at the last moment. They must have suspected a tail."

"Yes," Stanley added. "There must have been a leak from within that restaurant, *Abu Shakra,* an inside job, revealing our preparations. I'll have to let loose the Detroit FBI on that joint. We may get lucky; who knows?"

Chapter 38

January 1, 2003—Dearborn, Michigan

They were driving on Schafer Road after dropping Tarek off on Lithgow Street. All of a sudden, Arik grew uncomfortable. "We're being followed," he said to Omar. "You could apply the same escape maneuver as the one you used the other day at the Michigan Avenue intersection before losing me."

Omar's expression was impassive, but Arik could spot fear and anxiety in those eyes.

"Are you sure?" Omar asked. He shrugged, placed both his hands on top of the steering wheel, seemingly casual, but tension creased his face.

"Yes, it's a black Mercedes; watch it in the mirror." Arik said. His cool thawed out. He felt the sweat running down his armpits. "Don't get nervous; just lose the damn tail." He patted Omar on his shoulder in an attempt to keep him composed.

"I wonder why they're following me. I don't like it. They're not supposed to know me around here," Omar said. He shook his head in disbelief. "Are you sure?" he asked Arik. "You seem to be quite paranoid lately."

"Right; and there's a good reason," Arik said. He too felt nervous. Omar slowed down in front of Osborn Street, ready to stop at the red light, when the black Mercedes approached from behind, then passed them on the left, and drove in parallel matching their pace. Arik felt cornered. He was unable to see the person inside the Mercedes. The windows were thickly tinted. If they pulled down the window, he would roll out of the car onto the sidewalk and duck for cover. He could hear the blood rushing past his ears; it felt like the sound of the deep-sea enclosed in a seashell, the sound he'd experienced in Bali during the kidnapping.

Omar turned pale. His breathing grew orgasmic, except the cause had nothing to do with sex.

The window of the Mercedes began sliding down. Through the corner of his eye, Omar could sense what was coming next. He pressed down on the accelerator and his car leaped forward. Arik was able to peek at the passenger, catch a glimpse of the driver, microseconds before Omar's take-off. Omar was moving now at full speed, trying to shake off his pursuer. "Stop!" Arik barked. "It's Suleiman and one of his Popeye Gorilla guards. It's our lucky day."

Omar was floating in space; he wasn't listening. The expression on his face was strangely vacant. He kept charging like a deer, after sighting a cheetah.

"Stop," Arik roared. "It's Suleiman. Wait for him. He wants us to follow him."

Chapter 39

January 1, 2003—Dearborn, Michigan

The small Mediterranean eatery on Colson Street several blocks away from Schaefer Road was hidden from view. If you hadn't known it was there, you sure would've missed it. To the naked eye, the place looked just like a residential habitat. In fact, it'd been one before being converted to a boutique style eatery. It was a small place by any measure. It held just five tables in three separate former bedrooms with room for no more than twenty customers on a busy day. The owner/chef, Mahmud Salah, reserved the whole space for Suleiman's privileged party. Privacy was guaranteed.

They all came together. Arik and Omar followed Suleiman's Mercedes; it included an additional passenger—Dr. Radwan. Salah greeted the party warmly, then led them to the largest room, an ex-master bedroom, holding a single round table seating five, or six in a less comfortable setting. The entrance door was replaced with a colorful, yet semi transparent curtain, a likely import from the old country, and the walls were decorated with two copper bowls, a machete, an oil jug, and a framed picture of a smiling, waving Sadam Hussein, in military fatigue.

"I've been tailing you since you left the *Red House*," Suleiman said. "You ought to be more vigilant. The Americans may seem naïve, but in fact they're better than most."

"Qassem noticed you," Omar said. "We were prepared to shake you off."

Mahmud Salah interrupted the exchange. He brought over the tray with the coffee jar and the miniature cups; at that moment, Omar's mobile phone came to life. He picked it up, listened, then his facial expression turned cloudy. He let out a lungful of air as sweat began bubbling on his forehead. Arik watched him; he grew alarmed. "What's going on?" he asked.

"It's Abu Musa," said Omar. "He's all upset about the changes in our plan. He's going apeshit. I don't like it when he's like that, the guy's borderline crazy."

Arik took a sip of the coffee. It was his first since early in the morning. He felt he wasn't in top shape. He couldn't put up with a condition where he'd be lacking caffeine and thus vulnerable. He gulped the rest down, then put the petite cup on the table. "Is he around?"

"Abu Musa is in town in the *Red House*, drove all night with Ahmad and Hilga, all the way from Cleveland. He told me that he was going to take a nap before seeing us," Omar said. He sounded worried. "He's mad. He wants to settle and finalize his plan. He doesn't like yours."

"What about you?" Arik asked.

"I support your approach," Omar said. "It's a better one." He took off his coat, placed it around the chair, then poured coffee into his miniature cup.

Suleiman was watching. He pulled out a cigarette and lit it. His face changed into a question mark. He wanted to find out what they were talking about. Suleiman's bodyguard, *Mr. Clean*, the Gorilla, rose and turned to his boss. "I'm going out to check the street," he said.

Suleiman nodded.

"So what's all this anxiety? What's the problem?" Arik tried to calm Omar; he was seeking a logical explanation for Omar's demeanor.

"Abu Musa's a violent person," Omar said. "He said he was coming to town to settle scores." He paused, took another sip, then continued, "If you know what I mean."

"I don't worry," Arik said, although he was getting a bit tense. The sociopath to whom they were referring was a loose cannon. He, Arik, would have to be prepared. Nonetheless, he was looking forward to seeing the notorious mass murderer face-to-face for the first time. Memories of the Tel Aviv bombing flashed through his head. It was personal, more than anyone would know.

Arik took a quick survey of the people around the table. Suleiman was doing the same. He checked Dr. Radwan. The grossly overweight man had a two-day-old stubble, tobacco stained yellow teeth, protruding ears and nasal hair; his heavy moustache bore more than a few remnants of the humus he'd consumed that morning for breakfast; his dark eyes were moist with either excitement or anxiety—Arik couldn't tell. Dr. Radwan was wearing a gray jacket over a white shirt, open at the neck, enough to expose an exceedingly hairy chest, yet he was balding. He was short; Arik had noticed that he was almost a full head size below his own face, when they'd walked from the car to the restaurant.

No wonder Fatima didn't like him, Arik pondered. He was surprised the man had gathered enough courage to make a pass at that woman. *He must have a high opinion of himself,* Arik concluded.

"I've heard so much about you," Dr. Radwan said in admiration. "You're a great hero to us all, a true fighter for the Muslim cause."

Arik shrugged.

"I'm so flattered for the chance to meet you," Radwan said, continuing his sweet-talking.

A professional suckup, Arik thought.

Suleiman glanced at his watch. He had other plans for the rest of the day. "Okay," he said. He turned to Arik. "Qassem, I guess you're the boss. Tell me what you need."

"I want to talk to you about *Sarin*," Arik said.

"*Sarin*? Who's that?" Dr. Radwan asked.

Arik turned to Dr. Radwan. "*Sarin*, also known as *GB*, is one of the world's most dangerous chemical warfare agents. It's highly toxic," Arik lectured. "About one droplet can kill many people in minutes. *Sarin* is more than five hundred times as toxic as cyanide. It's a manmade nerve agent, which is a clear, colorless, tasteless, and odorless liquid in its pure form."

"I'm listening." Dr. Radwan said.

Omar interrupted. "Qassem forgot to mention that the nerve agent can evaporate and spread through the environment." He paused, then turned to Qassem. "Am I right?"

"You're the chemist," Arik nodded. "Do they serve any water around here?"

At that moment, Mahmud Salah shifted the curtain from behind Arik and entered the room.

He carried a large tray with five large glasses and a large bottle of mineral water. "Ready to order?" he asked.

Suleiman turned to face the restaurant owner. "The usual," he said. "A nice appetizer of salads, humus, and tahini, followed by a grill plate, and four cans of diet cola." He turned to Arik, then to the other guests, testing the table reaction. They all nodded in agreement. "It's on me, today," he said, as Salah was getting ready to leave.

Arik turned around, facing Suleiman. "You told me that you had Iranian connections. We should try to import it into the US from Iran. Can you manage that?"

"Do you want a finished product?" Suleiman asked.

"Not quite," Arik said. "*Sarin* is made by blending—methylphosphonic difluoride or *DF* with isopropyl alcohol and isopropylamine solution or *OPA*," he explained. "When *DF* and *OPA* are mixed they react to form the nerve agent *GB*." Arik noticed that he was losing Suleiman. "Take notes if you need to," Arik said. "But then, you'll have to memorize it all before you destroy your notes later today."

"Do I need to understand all those fine points?"

Arik was unhappy with Suleiman's comment. "You actually need to understand the nuts and bolts of this operation rather than the mere highlights. The reason I'm getting technical is because we won't be dealing with the final product. We'll acquire the two ingredients separately. Dichlor—the immediate precursor of DF—has legitimate commercial uses in fire retardants, insecticides, and plastics. Isopropanol (rubbing alcohol) is a common industrial chemical. Acquisition of these compounds for legitimate uses could thus be used as a cover for the illicit production of nerve agents."

"Do you plan on mixing it all here in the US?" Suleiman appeared uneasy. "I don't know about that."

"Oh, no," Arik countered. "That will be done automatically during the implementation. The final product has a short shelf life."

"What do you mean?"

We'll produce specialized belts. These belts will contain explosives, shrapnel, and nail fillings; we'll attach a special shell including two syringe-filled chemicals that make up the *Sarin* gas when mixed; it's called by the professionals—a binary weapon system. It must be formed right before its utilization." He paused, then resumed his lecture. "Seconds before the belt explodes, the trained *shahid* bomber will arm the shell by pressing a trigger creating a tiny explosion which will break the barrier between the two compartments, enabling the contents of the two syringes to mix, resulting in potent nerve gas. When the belt explodes, the gas, *Sarin,* will scatter in the air, creating a huge long-term celebration." Arik turned to face Omar. "And that, my brother, will be your job." He patted Omar's shoulder while the latter smiled self-contentedly.

"I'll check on it. I believe I can get the ingredients you mentioned, and probably several binary systems as well, all shipped in separate containers, in distinct shipments." Suleiman rested his case.

Arik turned to Dr. Radwan. "I'm worried," Arik said. "You may be under surveillance, because of your foreign travels. You need to lie low; you'll have to assume that they're watching your every move, your telephone, Internet, email...everything."

"I'm extra careful," Dr. Radwan concurred. "And everyone else should be too."

"Do you understand your role?" Arik asked Dr. Radwan.

"No, what is it?"

"You, Dr. Radwan, will be responsible for logistics." Arik turned to Suleiman, then back to Dr. Radwan. "You'll work with Suleiman. You'll receive the deliveries, store them, put them all together, then make them available when we're ready."

The curtain shifted again, and an angry man with a big facial scar, Abu Musa, appeared at the entrance. He stood there in a state of suspended animation. They all turned to face him. The entire room went still, electrically charged, as if Dracula had jumped out of his dark cave. None of the characters around the table had ever met Abu Musa. Arik watched him meticulously. He was a tough looking king-size man. His thick scar, running from his left ear down to his left jaw, could be viewed as a TV commercial for *"Don't dare fuck with me."* His overgrown, compact, black, curly hair reminded Arik of a monster he'd known as a kid in Iraq who'd terrorized the Jews, had murdered his aunt after raping her, robbed his parents of their possessions, and slashed their mattress with a machete, transforming it into a useless piece of trash.

There was tension in the room. Omar was trying to break the frigid silence. "Where's Hilga?" he asked.

Abu Musa, still standing at the door, glared at him, his eyes cold. "What's your problem, man? What do you need her for?"

"Just asking. I met her earlier."

"Don't ask," he barked. "Who's Qassem al-Nasr?" Abu Musa was putting his intimidating posture into play. It was panache ahead of charging like a bull during the mating season.

Arik was watching the men around the table. They seemed quite unsettled. Even Suleiman appeared to be caught off guard.

"Hey." Arik rose from his chair; he shook his head slowly, but his mien couldn't lie. The spasm of rage that played across his face didn't leave any doubts. "Take a seat if you want to talk," he said, his voice steely. He turned his gaze to Suleiman, to Omar, culminating with Dr. Radwan. "These people are my friends," he said, keeping an eye on Abu Musa. "We're having a quiet lunch. You can join and be one of us, or you can leave, and work alone." He clenched his jaw, narrowed his eyes.

In the corner of his eye, Arik saw Omar nodding in agreement. Dr. Radwan looked intimidated. Suleiman seemed to take interest in the evolving open rivalry. He appeared amused. Abu Musa may have noticed as well.

Abu Musa turned to Dr. Radwan. "Who are you?" He figured that Arik was the Alpha male—the leader of the pack. A dogfight at that moment wouldn't be to his advantage. Most people around the table weren't on his side. Dr. Radwan, on the other hand, would be a trouble-free convert. Abu Musa was looking for a non-violent way to overthrow the current leader, usurp him before he ran out of choices.

Dr. Radwan was slow to answer. He just looked up to face the intimidator. Arik read Abu Musa's move. He interrupted. "I said— sit down if you want to talk."

Abu Musa glared but didn't respond. He picked up the only un-occupied chair, then took his seat.

One to Nothing, Arik mused; *a good start. We'll see who will take the trophy this afternoon.* "Bringing you up to speed…" Arik began, but was quickly interrupted.

"I know what you're up to," Abu Musa said, "And it's not going to work. I've got a better plan."

"Well, you want to talk about it?"

"I don't have to convince you. I am the authorized leader." He stood up. "You follow my command." The confrontation was heating up again. "And I know that someone in this room had informed the police in Cleveland on my whereabouts. Someone here's a snitch."

"You're out of your mind," said Arik.

"You!" Abu Musa, was getting irritated. "You're the one!"

"Sit down, commander." Arik countered. His sarcasm was obvi-ous to the crowd around the table. Arik rose as well. Now they du-eled at equal height. "Who appointed you?"

Mahmud Salah had the food ready on his tray, but was standing outside the room behind the curtain; He didn't wish to get involved in a dogfight, even though no weapons had been drawn yet.

Arik noticed Mahmud. Abu Musa didn't. He was facing Arik with his back to the curtain.

"Food is ready if you wish to join," Arik said.

"Fuck you, man, and all of you; you know where I stay. If any-one here wants to be a real hero rather than a fucking poet, dream-ing and talking, talking and dreaming, then I'll see you in my place at four o'clock. If you don't show up, I'll take care of things, and you'll eat shit." He turned half way, pulled the curtain, then bumped into Mahmud. The tray flew out of Mahmud's hands; the filled plates fell on the floor and shuddered in a noisy splash; the humus, tahini, olives, mixed grill, all jumbled together with broken ceramic plates, spread throughout a wide perimeter. Abu Musa didn't bother looking down. He pushed Mahmud aside, then marched through the narrow opening, and left the house.

Chapter 40

January 1, 2003—Dearborn, Michigan

On his way back to the *Red House*, Abu Musa stopped at a flower shop and bought roses. That would pacify Hilga after their earlier fight, just before he split for the lunch meeting. It was a one-sided fight. Abu Musa hit her hard, threw a fist into her face, pushed her down to the floor, kicked her stomach. He was mad. *It was her fault. She said she'd called her sister in Canada.* She said she hadn't told her sister where she was or where she was headed, but Abu Musa didn't believe her. He claimed that the Cleveland police had tracked him down through her phone call. Now he wanted to tell her he was sorry. His rage had boiled over, overtaken him. He still loved her.

Abu Musa was driving Ahmad's car. After arriving at Dearborn late the night before, he dropped Ahmad at his apartment, then borrowed the car for the rest of New Year's holiday. Ahmad said he didn't need it. He was going to stay home and relax throughout the day. The long drive from Cleveland had its effects.

Abu Musa parked in the driveway, then approached the *Red House* and rang the bell. He waited. There was no answer. He turned the door handle; the door opened. He grew alarmed. *Someone was here,* was the first thought that entered his mind. *Hilga is supposed to be inside with the door locked.* He peeked into the L-shaped living room, but didn't spot her. He called her name, twice, but heard no response. He stood there at the entrance for a short while, debating whether he should move in and search for her upstairs.

He shut the door, then locked it from the inside. He called Hilga's name again, and once more, there was no answer. He went upstairs. Everything seemed to be in order. If anyone had been looking for him, the room would've been turned upside down. He went downstairs, half a level below the L-shaped living room/dining room, kitchen level. No one was there. Hilga was nowhere to be found. *Where the hell did she go?*

Abu Musa didn't know about the safe house across the street. He had no idea Omar was using it as his hideout. Hilga did know about it. She had been inside for a few minutes after they'd all met Omar at the Burger King. She also knew where Omar hid the key. Following the morning fight with her boyfriend, after Abu Musa had left the *Red House*, Hilga packed her suitcase and moved across the street. She was badly hurt—black and blue around her eyes, bruises all over her body. She was scared and looking for refuge; she found it inside the *Yellow House* across the street.

• • •

Suleiman took off after their lunch together. He said he was to catch an international flight. Omar and Arik came back to the *Yellow House*. They parked Omar's SUV in the garage, closed the garage door, then moved inside, expecting no visitors. As soon as they entered the kitchen, Arik sensed something. "Someone's been here a short time ago," he whispered, looking at Omar.

Omar didn't answer. He looked unsure, anxious. Arik put his hand inside his pocket where he kept the gun Tarek, his driver, had provided him before they parted. He pulled it out to Omar's astonishment. Omar's gaze was a rowdy—"Man, I didn't know you had a gun on you." Arik understood. He stepped out of the kitchen, then slowly moved toward the bedrooms area. There was nothing in the first two rooms. He continued his dance in the direction of the master bedroom, tiptoeing, careful not to set off alarming noises. As soon as he made the threshold he noticed the woman lying on her belly in the queen-size bed, her face buried in the pillow; she was whimpering like a ghost with little sound. Hilga didn't notice him.

He moved closer, still slowly and noiselessly; he got ready to touch her shoulder when the noise behind him spoiled the surprise. Hilga turned on her back to face Arik. Omar was right behind; Arik approached as she turned over. He and Omar fixed their eyes on her for a long moment. She looked awful as if someone had painted a puzzle depicting numerous world flags on her face.

"Ugh," she emitted, then covered her face with her hands, trying to hide it from Arik and Omar.

"What happened? Who...?" Arik held his tongue. It was obvious; they both knew *who* and *what*. He turned to Omar. Do you have any first aid stuff around here?" Arik kneeled closer, then gently pulled her hands off her face. He wanted to take a closer look.

"I don't really know," Omar said. "I don't live here, but I can check." A minute later, he came back. I found something," he said, holding a box of band-aids.

"Arik took a look. "That won't do a thing. She'll need some rest, and some makeup later on."

Hilga talked for the first time after they'd come to the room, her voice frail and shaken. "I'm hurt all over. I can hardly move."

"You stay here, girl," Arik said. There was a hint of fury in his voice. At that moment, he'd almost lost it. His tone of voice conveyed his fury. He was ready to go next door and kill the bastard. He turned around facing Omar who didn't seem concerned.

"She probably deserved it," Omar said aloud; even Hilga could hear it.

Arik just stared at him, said nothing, then turned around and put his hand on Hilga's hair. "You need some rest," he comforted her. "Why don't you stay in bed, and I'll make you something to drink."

Omar was at the window looking out at the *Red House*. "Hey, Qassem, come here, take a look."

Arik approached. A car came to a stop in the driveway across the street. A man emerged and walked to the door.

"Dr. Radwan," Arik said. "Go figure these people."

Omar looked surprised. "And I thought he was going with your plan," he said in disbelief.

"I did too," Arik responded. "He still may. He may join both plans."

Omar stared at Arik for a few seconds. Arik eyeballed him in return, reading his thoughts. Omar appeared to concur with the concept. He was going to do the same.

"Look." Arik tried to preempt his action. "If you pull off a small operation like the bombing of a cathedral on Christmas Eve, you can forget about everything else. The Americans are not as dim as you think. They'll get behind the plot in no time."

"Why do you say that?"

"Abu Musa and his colleagues will leave plenty of finger prints behind. Everyone in America will go hunting. Chances are that with so much focus and so many resources no stone will be left unturned."

"I'm going over to the *Red House*," Omar said.

"Use your car; drive around before getting there." Arik said, conceding the argument. "Keep this place under their radar." He was getting frustrated. If it'd been one to nothing in his favor earlier, it was now one to two in Abu Musa's favor. "And by the way," he waited… "Ah, forget it. It's not important." He didn't say it, but the thought of contamination through Dr. Radwan entered his mind. If the police or the FBI had indeed monitored Radwan and followed him, then the *Red House* wouldn't have been safe any longer, and Omar would've been compromised as well.

• • •

As soon as Omar left, Arik called Tarek on his mobile. "Come quickly; pick me up at the *Yellow House*."

"The *Yellow House?*"

"Come quickly before they realize Hilga's here."

"They haven't yet."

"They soon will. And where's this confidence coming from?" He didn't wait for an answer. "Okay, got it." He figured it out. Tarek had the *Red House* bugged.

"I'm going over across the street," Arik said. "Pick up Hilga; take her to my apartment."

Chapter 41

January 1, 2003—The Red House, Dearborn, Michigan

Omar opened the door after Arik identified himself. "Come in my brother, Qassem," he said, wearing a friendly smile. "I hoped you'd make it here. We may need your help."

Arik moved in. The people inside were sitting in the living room, Dr. Radwan occupied the blue velvet sofa, Omar had his spot reserved on the orange couch. Abu Musa was sitting on one of the chairs he'd brought over from the kitchen. He'd assumed leadership and had been holding court before Arik came in, as the others had been facing him from their lowered position.

Omar was standing next to Arik, his hand on Arik's shoulder. "Qassem's finally here," he announced as the others were watching.

Abu Musa glanced, then turned back to Dr. Radwan in an apparent attempt to diminish the excitement over Arik's advantage. "Did you transfer the money?"

"I did it yesterday," Dr. Radwan said. "Hamad Suleiman will pick it up in Geneva tomorrow afternoon. He will deliver it then."

Arik stared at Dr. Radwan. "What's the money for?"

"This Norwegian guy, Dr. Adam Olson, he works for UNRWA — the United Nations Relief and Work Agency; he's traveling to Israel next Saturday, to supervise the delivery of humanitarian aid to Southern Gaza from Israel via the *Kerem Shalom Crossing*."

Abu Musa gave Dr. Radwan an irate stare. "Hey, what're you talking about? There's no such a thing as Israel."

Dr. Radwan, stared back, confused. "What?"

"There's no Israel. You're talking about Palestine; The Zionist occupied sacred land of ours," Abu Musa shot back.

"Okay, anyway," Dr. Radwan wanted to move on beyond semantics; Abu Musa walked to the kitchen in order to attend the art of coffee making. "We're going to ship 6.5 tons of potassium nitrate, hidden in sacks marked "sugar" and earmarked for needy Arabs in Gaza. Our brothers in Gaza will use the banned substance for the manufacturing of explosives and *Kassam* rockets. The bags will be marked as humanitarian aid from the European Union."

"Sounds good." Arik said.

Abu Musa came back from the kitchen. He turned to Dr. Radwan. "We're going to finalize the plan for Christmas. Do you understand what you need to do now?" he asked.

"If you're talking about the *St. Patrick's* bombing on Christmas, then I have a better plan," Arik interjected.

"Your plan's too complicated," Abu Musa said. "It takes too big of an operation and many more people must get involved."

That's exactly what I'm after, Arik reflected. "Not complicated if you know how to pull it off, which you obviously aren't capable of." Arik challenged. He spoke slowly as if he were the only rooster in the hen house.

Abu Musa shot back an icy stare; didn't say anything. There was a long silence, which neither one rushed to fill. Two minutes later, Omar turned to Abu Musa. "I think Qassem makes sense. Let's talk some more."

"No!" Abu Musa's inner temperature hit the boiling point. His face turned red; he bore down on Omar with his bony predator eyes.

They could hear a car engine in the driveway. Arik peeked at his watch. "My driver, Tarek, is outside waiting to pick me up. We have an appointment." He turned to Abu Musa, "How about tomorrow morning at nine? I can come back here."

Abu Musa watched the other two *Jihadists* nodding in agreement. "Only if you sign on to my plan," he said, staring down his other comrades to submission.

"I'll see you tomorrow," Arik said, then walked out.

Chapter 42

A day earlier, December 31, 2002—Bali, Indonesia

When Gina McLloyd received the phone call from Rachel at the American Embassy, she couldn't believe her ears. All she knew was that Rachel had been dead for some time, but then, there was always hope that maybe, just maybe, she was still alive and she would surface somewhere, somehow. And now, here she was—alive and actually talking, asking about Arik.

Gina had been given a clear directive from Nguyen, the CIA rep in the embassy. He'd instructed her to tell whoever was asking that Arik was dead, killed in action. Nguyen was acting on a direct appeal from Dan Carmel, his Israeli *Mossad* contact. He'd never asked Dan to explain. He'd empathized with the request. Although Dan worked for a different agency in a different country, he was a colleague—a member of an equivalent secret society. He'd been an active part of Dan Carmel's kidnapping ploy that wound up with Arik's undercover work and Rachel's imprisonment and apparent loss.

"I'll have Nguyen call you as soon as he comes in. In the meantime, stay put; hide inside the church. Don't call the local police; everything must be executed on the sly. We'll get you out of there safely."

Rachel, in shock after hearing the news about Arik, couldn't stop sobbing. She rejected the warm food that the priest attempted to serve. Nothing could make up for her loss. She was deeply depressed. Budi wasn't eating either. He was sobbing, asking for his mom. Rachel's attempts to comfort him were only partially successful. It took a while, but eventually Budi's sobbing subsided as he was slowly dozing off in her arms.

* * *

The Special Forces that surrounded the church where Rachel was hiding were waiting in anticipation for their kill. After searching the empty shack where Rachel had been imprisoned, they realized that the remaining kidnapper had gotten away without leaving a forwarding address. Still, they took precautions, lest some of the bad guys would try something stupid, like snatching Rachel out of the church.

Two hours after daybreak, when no other evil soul had surfaced, Nguyen sent out a car to pick up Rachel and bring her to a safe house in the outskirts of Denpasar. Budi and Rachel were joined at the hip at that point. Rachel's maternal instincts and Budi's needs for motherly affection were the glue behind the unsullied bond they felt for each other.

Later in the day, in the American Embassy in Jakarta, Nguyen's plans for getting Rachel on a plane out of Jakarta to London, where Dan Carmel would be waiting, hit a stonewall. Rachel refused to leave without Budi, and Budi wasn't part of the plan. The situation reached an impasse; adoption was out of the question due to rules, which disqualified Rachel out of hand. She wasn't married. She wasn't a Muslim. She hadn't been a resident of Indonesia for a minimum of two years. She was much too young according to their adoption laws, her thirtieth birthday was still clear of her vista. In addition, Budi had already reached his fifth birthday, the upper limit for legal international adoption in that country.

Late in the evening, Gina called a local social worker, who came over to take Budi away and place him in the care of a registered and authorized social welfare organization. It was a heartbreaking separation, but inevitable nonetheless.

Rachel decided to stay in Jakarta and visit Budi every day in the orphanage. She'd fallen in love with the boy. Arik wasn't there anymore, and that sad fact served as a catalyst for her decision. She wasn't up to going back home to Israel. Her plans were shattered, and her present emotional state was in tatters. She would make up her mind once she'd adjusted to her new reality. It would take a while, and throughout that phase, Budi's companionship would become her preeminent therapy.

Chapter 43

January 1, 2003—Dearborn, Michigan

"Anybody home?" Arik called as soon as Tarek dropped him off at his safe apartment condo on Colson Street. It was already dark outside, time for supper.

There was no response. Arik placed the fresh pizza pie he'd bought on his way home on the kitchen table, then walked to the bedroom looking for Hilga. She was there, in the dark, lying in his bed. She'd just awoken from an afternoon nap.

"Hi," he greeted her with a warm smile. "How are you feeling?"

"Much better," she said. She smiled back. Her face had lost some of its purple, restored with a pinkish, more natural color around the right eye. She was still in bed under the blanket, her clothes nicely folded on a chair next to her.

"I brought some food," he said. "I'm going to the kitchen. Get dressed and join me there. I'm starving."

He was two slices down; she hadn't yet turned up. He walked to the bedroom looking for her, then heard a sound coming from the bathroom. The door was half-open. He knocked. "Are you okay?" He could see her. She stood in front of the mirror, covering up the area around her injured eye with makeup and checking the bruises on her right leg and chest. She wasn't fully dressed, just bra and underwear. She turned her head, watched him and smiled. He couldn't help but notice; her bruises might have inconceivably served to enhance her physical beauty.

"I'll be there in a minute," she said, not minding Arik's penetrating look watching her shapely bruised body.

"Okay," he said, then walked back to the kitchen. He sat there watching the weather report on TV, waiting for her to join the feast.

When she came in, she was fully dressed. She wore dark red lipstick; her shoulder-length white-blonde hair was combed to cover part of her battered forehead; her black eyeliner and navy-blue eye shadow enhanced the splendor of her ocean-blue eyes. The purple on the cheekbone next to her right eye was well masked, almost unnoticeable. She was transformed from a miserable, bruised, homeless-looking living thing, into an eye-catching, attractive woman, the kind who could turn men into animals. What's more, she was in a good mood that was contagious.

Arik had never before realized that women played these tricks on men. Rachel had never applied much makeup. However, noticing Hilga's makeover, he realized that women could camouflage their God-given natural features and turn a bland looking, lackluster face into a *young Marilyn Monroe* in no time at all, by merely applying over-the-counter cosmetics and body promotion underwear. For sure, he now realized that better initial conditions greatly improved the end result, but still…

Hilga took a seat across from him. "Thank you for your hospitality," she said. "I'm so grateful." Her eyes became moist as she spoke. She reached out and touched his arm, then leaned over the table and moved her face closer to his, still not close enough for contact; the table and the partially consumed pizza between them prevented any further advance. "Can I give you a kiss?" she appealed.

He tilted, got closer. She shifted her hand from his arm to his neck, pulled him closer, then pressed her lips on his with her mouth closed. He tasted her lipstick. It was a friendly expression of appreciation, not one riding on lust.

She let go, then said, "I haven't eaten anything today. I'm famished too."

"Pizza's getting cold," Arik said. "Let's eat it before it turns stale and revolting." He picked up a slice placed it on the plate in front of her. "Let's see how you take care of this one."

She watched the slice, picked it up, then raised her gaze to match his. She smiled with joy, then bit off a large piece without saying a word, encouraging Arik to do the same.

It was getting late. The wind outside was harsh. The forecast called for a weather change with more snow expected to accumulate over night. Arik was a gentleman. "You go and sleep in my bedroom," he said. "I'll stay on the sofa in the living room." He walked her to the bedroom, kissed her on the good cheek. "Good night," he said. They stood there for a long moment watching each other, smiling and giggling like two little kids who got caught stealing candy.

"Good night," she finally said, then turned around, entered the bedroom, and closed the door behind her.

Arik was lying in bed, his eyes open. He was unable to fall asleep. The loud swirling winds outside and the thought of the upcoming business, sent his adrenaline sky-high. Then, suddenly, a different kind of noise, a banging near the entrance, shot an electric current through his spine. He jumped out of the sofa, picked up his gun, then, tiptoeing on his bare feet, he approached the window and pulled the curtain just enough to get a good view of the front deck leading to the entrance. There was nothing there. The few trees down the street, the ones within his view, were swinging from side to side surrendering to the blustery weather. An empty lidless garbage can was rolling down the street. It was his can. The pizza box he'd lobbed into it, was now out in the middle of the street, flying from one side to the other, looking for a corner it could use as a resting place.

Arik took another glimpse. The bang he'd heard earlier was the rolling garbage can, he concluded. He tottered back to the sofa, stretched out on his back and gazed at the ceiling. He kept his gun close, under the pillow, just in case. He closed his eyes, and was on the verge of dozing off, when the sound of slow walking feet sent another distress signal through his veins. He jumped off the sofa, gun in hand, facing the source of the sound.

Hilga was standing next to his bed. She wore a long shirt, which to him, came across as a super mini dress. He frightened her. She turned around and rushed to the bedroom. "Sorry," he let out. "I didn't know it was you." He put the gun back under his pillow.

She turned around, still somewhat frightened, hesitated, then drew near him. He stood and watched her making her moves. He felt trapped in a spellbinding trance. She opened her arms bidding his embrace while the unbuttoned shirt she was wearing shifted sideways exposing her breasts. He was a bit slow to respond. She moved closer and wrapped her hands around his neck, pulled his head towards hers, then hit him with a French kiss, to which he responded passively, then passionately, as he was getting hard.

He picked her up in his arms, carried her to his bedroom, then closed the door from behind with his foot.

He didn't look back.

Chapter 44

January 2, 2003—Dearborn, Michigan

It was nine o'clock in the morning, but the door was closed. The *Red House* was vacant. Arik walked back to the car and turned to his driver, Tarek. "Let's go for a fifteen minute ride, then come back. They may be late."

It was ten o'clock when they returned, but nothing had changed. Abu Musa, Omar, and Dr. Radwan were somewhere else; they were neither in the *Red House* nor in the house across the street. "Let's go have a bite, then come back and check it out one more time," Arik suggested.

• • •

It was around nine in the morning when Hilga got out of bed. Arik had just left; she didn't have a particular agenda for the day. Staying in bed a bit longer and rest after an eventful erotic night, was the best option. She was hungry, but there was no food in the house. She got dressed, then called Ahmad at the gas station. There was no one else she could think of. He could take off for a little while, give her a ride to a fast food place, a supermarket, or somewhere she could get a quick bite and procure extra foodstuff for later in the day.

After a quick breakfast at the nearest Dunkin Donuts, Ahmad took her back to the house; he didn't have time for more. On his way back to the gas station he phoned Abu Musa, his apartment guest, told him where Hilga had spent the night, then listened to Abu Musa's distinctive rage flowing from the other end, concluding with a summon to come over and pick him up.

It was 10:40 a.m. Both Abu Musa and Ahmad were on their way to Arik's place. It was a bright day, blue skies, no clouds, but deceptively cold, way down below freezing. Ten minutes later, Ahmad parked the car next to the house. He stepped out while Abu Musa stayed inside. "You go in, and leave the door unlocked," Abu Musa instructed. Ahmad approached the front deck, rang the bell, announcing his arrival. Hilga didn't expect company. She was in bed trying to recoup some of the lost sleep from the night before. Her hair was a mess, and her makeup lacking. She got up and approached the locked door. "Who's there?" she asked, then slid the curtain and peeked through the window.

Ahmad noticed her, waved, then signaled. She understood.

"What's up?" she asked when he came in. "Did you come to pick me up again?" she paused. "Good idea. Let me get ready," she answered her own question. "I can go to the supermarket and fetch some foodstuff for later on. I hope you have a little more time now. I'd like to do a little food shopping. Qassem may want to eat when he comes back." She was with her back to the unlocked door, and failed to notice Abu Musa who had just stepped in.

"No, he won't! You fucking slut. So, that's where you're hiding?" Abu Musa barked. "What're you doing in here? Where were you last night? Did you sleep with Qassem?"

Abu Musa's rage made Ahmad uncomfortable. "Hey, calm down, man." Ahmad said, approaching Abu Musa in an attempt to contain his anger. "You're scaring her."

"You stay out of this," Abu Musa growled, pushing Ahmad to the side, closing the distance between him and Hilga. "You! You fucking bitch. You fucked him. I can see it in your eyes." He pushed her toward the bedroom. Then, noticing the unmade bed, he concluded, "you did it right here, you fucking bitch. You did it behind my back." He pushed her, forcing her to the bed. She lost her balance; fell on her back. Abu Musa kept at it, holding her down, then all of a sudden, he pulled down her pants while going on top of her. "I'm going to show you who you should be fucking."

Hilga tried to resist, but Abu Musa held down her hands. She started screaming. Abu Musa released his left hand, hit her hard in the face, then brought his knee up, in an attempt to hold down her free hand, covering her mouth with his left hand at the same time.

Ahmad, taking notice of the screams, entered the room in another attempt to calm and slow things down. Abu Musa turned to him. "Get out and wait in the kitchen," he yapped. "I have some personal business to finish here."

"Come on, Abu Musa," Ahmad pleaded. "She didn't do what you claim."

"I said, get out of here before I get mad," he yelled.

Ahmad didn't move. He kept standing at the door.

At that moment, Abu Musa pulled out his gun—the one he'd taken away from the murdered police officer on the snowy road in upstate New York—and aimed at Ahmad. "Get out!"

When turning toward Ahmad, Abu Musa shifted his knee, releasing the pressure on Hilga's wrist in the process. Hilga seized the moment. With her freed hand, she reached for the alarm clock on the night table next to the bed, grasped it, and as soon as Abu Musa turned back to face her she whacked him on his right cheek, under the eye, with all the force she could muster.

Abu Musa was overwhelmed. The bolt from the blue, the strike to the head, the pain, the blood, all served to halt the assault, even for a brief moment. He felt as if the entire scene became fused inside a freeze-frame. He lifted his hand and touched his face. It was bleeding badly.

He turned into a cherry, his rage boiling over, ascending to *Mount Everest* heights. And then it overpowered him. He turned his gun, pointed at Hilga's forehead; the whites of his eyes were bloodshot just before shrieking, "*Allahu Akbar!*"

And then, he fired.

The loud sound of the gunshot reverberated throughout the house. Ahmad came rushing to the bedroom. He didn't stop at the door, but continued, trying to take a better look at Hilga's shattered face. Abu Musa was watching Ahmad's mounting panic. He was still engulfed in rage and disgust. He couldn't control himself. He turned, aimed and shot straight at Ahmad's heart.

It took another brief moment. Abu Musa moved away from Hilga's body, stood up on the floor next to Ahmad's body; he leaned over, pulled out the car keys from Ahmad's pocket, then ambled toward the bathroom, urinated while humming the latest hit song by Diana Karazon, the Jordanian songstress, one of his favorites. He flushed the toilet, then picked up the remaining toilet paper roll, tore off a large piece, folded it, and placed it under his eye to stop the bleeding. He then went to the kitchen, but there was no food any-where; he stepped out of the house, left the door ajar, then stepped into Ahmad's car and turned the key.

Chapter 45

January 2, 2003—Colson Street, Dearborn, Michigan

The sound of the gunshot alerted one old neighbor, an eighty-year-old lady in a wheelchair, who was busy having her second cup of hot tea of the day. It was a familiar sound. Three years earlier, she'd heard the same kind of gunshot sound; it'd turned out to be a murder case she'd helped solve. Dina Shaker, first generation American Lebanese Christian, was a suspicious woman. She had a connection into the Dearborn police on account of her previous involvement. She wheeled herself to the telephone and called Officer Dembo. The officer was busy talking on another line, and the woman answering the call promised he would call back ASAP. Dina didn't want to leave a message; she insisted on speaking to the officer she knew. Thirty minutes had passed before Officer Dembo returned the call. It took another twenty before a police squad car turned up, and another twenty-five before Dembo and his partner discovered the gruesome scene inside Arik's temporary home.

The place was turned into a crime scene, a crowded flea market comprising squads of CSI teams, investigating officers, media TV crews standing next to their vans, hanging around in anticipation of anyone who would come out and fill the airwaves with the next horror story. A couple of ambulances stood by, ready to pick up bodies and transfer them to police custody for further investigation.

It didn't take much time for officer Dembo to figure out who the owner of the place was. He was sure that he would find out who'd been staying there as well. The CSI team had collected plenty of fingerprints, blood samples, men's clothes, quite a few personal effects, women's clothes, Hilga's papers and her sister's. It was time for further background information.

Dembo returned to his office. He turned on his PC, opened a new file, then recorded his impressions from the crime scene. He was careful to mention all of the details he could think of, including the ones he'd jotted down in his notebook. When he was done, he picked up the phone, made sure the recorder was turned on, then dialed Tarek's number.

Chapter 46

January 2, 2003—Somewhere in Dearborn, Michigan

"Should I answer the call?" Tarek, the apartment's owner and Arik's buddy and driver, stared at Arik, then at his cell phone caller ID. "This is not a good sign, I hate when that happens," Tarek said, trying to inject his sick humor. He'd never before received a call from the police on his cell phone.

Arik nodded. "Pick it up. Drag your heels. It'll take you time to get back in town if they want to talk to you in person. We ought to find out what it's all about."

Tarek picked up after several rings. "Hello, who's this?" He turned on the speaker.

"This is officer Dembo from the Dearborn PD. We've found two dead bodies inside a property of yours, a man and a woman." A cough. "We assume you know who they are. We'd like you to come over to the police station and identify them."

"Wow! That makes no sense." Tarek couldn't help but exhale the word. He regained composure at once, then stared at Arik as if wishing him to say it was only a dream.

Arik's heart sank. He was staring straight at the road, his eyes hollow. *This one's bad. It messes up the whole plan*, he reflected. He lifted his right hand, raised two fingers, then spoke devoid of sound. "In two hours."

Tarek read his lips, then repeated. "I can be there in two hours." He turned to Arik who talked using silent lips and sign language. Then back to the phone. "Do I need a lawyer?"

"Not if you're not involved," Dembo said. "You're not a suspect, not at the moment. I just need more information on who was renting this place."

"I can't hear you," Tarek said. "We must have a bad connection. I'm..." He hung up the phone, then turned it off.

"They'll find out anyway," Arik said. "They have my finger-prints. You'd better tell them it was I. You'll earn credibility for telling the truth."

"You sure?" Tarek had his doubts. "You'll become a hunted murder suspect."

Arik nodded. "It sucks, but we have no choice. I'm getting out of here, going back to New York," Arik said. "I'm glad I didn't leave any documents in the safe house. I always carry these on me." A short pause. "I'm taking your car. You get yourself a rental for now." He halted briefly. "You may be under surveillance for a while. Be careful."

"But what about your mission, your new amigos—Omar, Dr. Radwan, Hamad Suleiman...? And, oops, I almost forgot..." he paused, then spat. "What about Abu Musa?"

"I'll touch base with Omar before leaving after I drop you off at the car rental place." He leaned over, patted Tarek on the shoulder. "You may need an attorney after I disappear. They'll tie me to the killing. They may even connect you to it." He lowered his gaze. "It's all one fuck up. I want to cry." He lifted his head, stared at Tarek. "My heart is aching. This is the second girl who is murdered be-cause of me. I'm, beyond doubt, some kind of bad luck."

"No you're not," Tarek said. "Do you have any idea who might have done that?" Tarek asked.

Arik scratched his head. "The one who comes to mind is Abu Musa. He's crazy; he's a mass murderer. He has no soul; as far as he's concerned, killing a human being is like swatting a mosquito. Hilga left him; he may have gone mad and jealous." He paused. "But I can't be sure. The police will soon announce their suspects; I'll probably top the list unless this rat—Abu Musa—is involved. I'll pay attention."

They were sitting in silence for the next couple of minutes. Tarek made a turn entering the Avis car rental parking lot. He left the car running, opened the door, stepped outside, then leaned back and faced Arik.

Arik leaned over in Tarek's direction. They hugged, held each other for a long moment. "Good-bye my friend," Arik said, his eyes wet and glossy.

"Good-bye Qassem," Tarek responded. "You take care of yourself, you hear me?"

Arik didn't say anything. He just nodded, opened the door, stepped outside, went around the car, then scrambled into the driver seat.

Chapter 47

January 3, 2003—Washington, DC

The call came early at around six thirty in the morning. Officer Dembo was on the line from Dearborn, Michigan. At the FBI HQ in DC, Stanley picked it up.

"This is a Federal case," Dembo wrapped it up. "Qassem al-Nasr is your responsibility.

It became a media blitz. At the FBI HQ, following the latest from Dearborn, Stanley and Jim obtained Jack's authorization. Correspondingly, all major networks and cable news channels flashed Arik's picture on their screen. It was a younger Arik, a picture retrieved from his *Village* apartment in Manhattan. He looked clean-shaven, wearing a short haircut, pictured in front of an Egyptian background. In less than a minute, the same photograph made its way to Europe, Asia, and Australia. Arik had just turned into an international celebrity, Qassem al-Nasr, the most sought after, live terrorist on the planet, with a reward tag of two million dollars to anyone providing information leading to his capture. Someone would spot him for sure, though he bore little resemblance to that image they'd thrown on the TV screen. His beard, long hair, and sunglasses, minimized the probability of any quick discovery or detection. Still, he was front page for every law enforcement agency in the world, including Interpol.

Chapter 48

January 3, 2003—Dearborn, Michigan

It was getting late early. The northern hemisphere was still tilted away from the sun. It was the beginning of January on Earth's schedule; spring was more than two months away; daylight was gradually growing longer while darkness was still winning.

Arik was growing hungry. He didn't want to go near Tarek's condo, his former safe house on Colson Street; neither did he wish to touch base with Tarek. His friend was most likely being watched, monitored, and could even be jeopardized, if anyone could link him back to Qassem al-Nasr. The crispy clear skies and the cold air outside the car dried his mouth. He needed a drink.

The *Red House* was quiet. His radio receiver was on, yet silent. Abu Musa must have been out of the *Red House*. Arik was tired of the news; it was growing boring and repetitive. They had nothing new to report on Hilga's murder and the hunt for her killer. Arik switched to an Adult Contemporary FM station that better suited his musical taste, then searched for a place to quiet down his stomach. He passed by a Diner, almost went in, then changed his mind. *No! No need to drag down my face into a public place and talk to people at close range, not now, not so soon.*

There was a bottle of mineral water in the car. It wasn't full, but looked clean. *Beer could've worked better*, Arik reflected, *but what the heck, I'm thirsty*. He opened it up and gulped down the remaining liquid. He was both pleased and amazed when he noticed that the water actually eased his hunger pains, at least temporarily. Arik glanced at his watch. It was 7:32 p.m. already. A good time to check on Omar, pay him a visit at the *Yellow House*, making sure that Omar stayed within his guidelines, under his control and watchful eye.

As he entered 95th Street, his sixth sense made him slow down. Police cruisers with red and blue flashing lights sparkled, not too far away. There was a familiar odor in the air, the scent of an explosion, smoke, and fire. He stopped the car, realizing that police were swarming all over the area, guarding it and inspecting passers-by. He turned the radio back on, switched to the local news channel, and there it was. "The *Yellow House*…a mysterious explosion… one unidentified dead body…suspicions regarding possible explosives…an accident…" on, and on, and on—an open bar for the media frenzy.

Luckily, fire fighters were able to save a good deal of the house effects. CSI teams were already inside wearing their gas masks, collecting evidence. "Expect more news in the coming hour," the anchor announced. He sounded enthusiastic as if he were swimming in a hot tub filled with naked beauties. Anticipation for the next phase appeared to embroider his vocal chords.

Arik made a U-turn. His abrupt anxiety helped suppress his appetite for real food; his thirst was now focused on news. *What else were they going to unearth that will affect my plans?*

He continued to drive, then he parallel parked on a side street, in between two SUVs. He had little idea where he was. It was a residential neighborhood, relatively dim and serene. There were numerous cars parked along the sidewalk. He didn't stand out. He turned off the engine, left the radio on, rested his head on the seat support and closed his eyes. He fell asleep for about twenty minutes. He woke up as the anchorman came back on the air to announce, "We're awaiting a news conference in two minutes. Apparently, the house was used as a Safe House and a laboratory for a terror organization. More news after this commercial break."

Arik closed his eyes again. He was tense. A catnap wasn't possible. Although it was merely a natural surge of adrenaline, he felt as if he were high on caffeine, notwithstanding his empty stomach.

The news conference began shortly thereafter. Then, his name popped up over and over. They found papers inside a steel briefcase. Papers with his name inside; detonator drawings with his name on top; printed descriptions of binary *Sarin* weapon systems with his name scribbled on the side with arrows to particular paragraphs with question marks. Omar wanted explanations. He was doing his homework. Omar gave him too much credit. Arik didn't ask for it, not in writing anyway. *What was this son-of-a-bitch doing, ruining Qassem's good name?* It was a big mess, a huge blow. His whole mission was turned into a fiasco.

There was no way out. He was trapped. His Qassem's identity had become a nightmare. He considered shedding it before it was too late. It would become extremely difficult pulling off any mission under that identity. He needed advice, guidance, comfort, protection. Somehow, he wanted to hear Dan Carmel's voice, a voice that would tell him to drop it, to come home, to rewind his life back to the moment when he'd turned down Dan Carmel, in the Tel Aviv restaurant, before his venture into Bali, then replay it using a different script.

It wasn't going to happen. He was beaten, worn out, and it wasn't from lack of sleep. He was merely battle-fatigued.

Chapter 49

January 4, 2003—Jakarta, Indonesia (January 3, in the US)

The one bedroom apartment in Jakarta, one block away from the American Embassy, was small but comfortable. Rachel developed her daily routines around Budi. She visited him in the orphanage once a day, early in the morning. On Thursday, she took him out on her errands, then a restaurant, followed by a movie and some other suitable entertainment. She would nap for over an hour in the early afternoon, getting away from the heat and the humidity, then watch CNN before going to the Embassy, where she developed close relationships with Nguyen and Gina McLloyd, working part-time as Gina's assistant.

This afternoon, she couldn't sleep. She had her period; her head was throbbing. She called in sick, told Gina she wouldn't make it to the Embassy—Saturday was a slow day anyway. She returned to bed, turned on the TV, lay down and closed her eyes. The CNN desk had just advised its audience about a newsbreak bulletin; Qassem al-Nasr was being hunted throughout the US in the aftermath of a double murder followed by a huge explosion inside a house, in Dearborn, Michigan. He was suspected, in addition, of leading *al-Qaeda* cells whose purpose was—blowing up targets, acquiring WMDs in the US, etc. etc... "More, just in—The FBI had found evidence connecting Qassem al-Nasr to Bali, Indonesia. A small but a much-used pocket tour book with names of US Embassy employees and their phone numbers inside..."

Rachel opened her eyes. The mention of Bali with a link to *al-Qaeda* had sent an electric shock wave through her ears. She stared at the TV screen, almost passed out. A picture of Arik filled the right half, while the anchorwoman in the left window was calling him Qassem al-Nasr. Rachel remembered the photo. She'd taken it on one of their visits to the *Dead Sea*, in the Judean desert, a week before they ventured on their Bali tour. Arik was wearing his favorite blue T-shirt, had a small abrasion on his right cheek from a fall he'd endured minutes before the photo had been shot. There was no doubt in her mind. The photo must have undergone a slight alteration, though. Arik's face seemed a little blurry, slightly darker and vertically stretched. The distortion made him come across as more Arab looking than in real life, also less handsome than in real life. One could also spot the Egyptian Pyramids on the far horizon. *What's going on*? She believed he was, had been, dead for a while. *Did they lie to me? Did they make him…? No! That didn't make any sense, but he's alive, isn't he? Who would know? Who could explain*? She was agitated.

Rachel was going nuts. She disregarded her headache; her menstrual period seemed like history; her bad mood evaporated. She dressed, then quickly rushed to the American Embassy.

"I thought you weren't coming in today," Gina said as soon as Rachel entered her office. "Wow, you look like you've just come out of a garbage compactor. Sit and calm down."

"Did you see Nguyen? Rachel asked. She was out of breath.

"I think you need some Valium," Gina said. "What happened? Are you going to tell me?"

"I can't; I must speak to Nguyen. It's urgent."

"Nguyen's out. He will be back next week," Gina said.

"Where's he?"

"He doesn't tell me. It's some weird job assignment, I guess."

"I must call Dan Carmel in Tel Aviv," Rachel said. "Nguyen has the number. He was talking to Dan once when I came into his office unannounced."

"I can go into his office and look," Gina said. "I'll check his rolodex. He keeps names and phone numbers there."

"I'm going with you," Rachel said.

"No! You wait here. If I find it I'll have it for you." Gina got up, walked around her desk, passed near Rachel, patted her on the shoulder on the way out, smiled, then left the office.

Rachel stood there alone, nervous, anxious. She looked out the door in urgent anticipation; Gina was taking her time—too much time. It seemed as if every minute lasted an hour. Finally, just five minutes later, Gina came out smiling. She'd retrieved the phone number. "Let's call him from my office," she said.

Gina was sitting at her desk when Rachel, sitting across from her, placed the call. It took only three rings. "Hello, may I help you?" It was Dan's secretary.

"This is Rachel Levy," she announced. "I must speak to Dan Carmel."

"He's at a meeting, can I take a message?"

"No!" Rachel said. "It's more urgent than the meeting he's in. He must come to the phone at once."

"I'm not sure I can disturb him right now. I'd rather take a message."

Rachel was on the verge of losing it. "Listen, bitch," she countered, "I'm telling you that what I have to say to him is more critical than whatever he's masturbating on." Rachel brought up her hand, applied it on her own mouth. She realized she had to put the lid on it. Her self-control was gone; it'd gotten lost somewhere in Bali. She couldn't believe she'd turned into a hard-hitting spiteful bitch herself. Something had turned on that delightful trait in her. It'd never manifested itself before.

Gina moved to the other side of the desk, tried to calm things down. "Let me talk to her," she said, extending her hand, speaking in body language, pleading for the phone.

"This is Gina McBride from the American Embassy in Jakarta. I'm sure that Dan Carmel will agree with me that interrupting him now, and dragging him to the phone, is the right thing to do."

"I'm listening," Dan Carmel answered. "Gina McBride...And I thought that Rachel Levy was on the line."

"Oh, I didn't realize I was talking to you," Gina said. "Hold on. Rachel's right here."

"Rachel?" Dan Carmel tested the line, making sure he was talking to her in private.

"Yes. Hi Dan, What's going on? I've just seen..."

"Stop!"

The outburst startled Rachel. She froze for a short moment.

"You can't say a word about it, not on the phone, not to anyone. I hope you didn't tell Gina either," Dan said.

"But she can see for herself." Rachel raised her gaze and stared straight at Gina whose face expressed intense curiosity.

"No, she can't, unless you help her." He came to a full stop. "Listen, I suggest that you come back to Israel at once. We'll discuss everything. We can't do that on the phone. I'm sure you'll be pleased."

Chapter 50

January 3, 2002—Toledo, Ohio

Arik's plan appeared to be derailed. His mission struck an iceberg; he was the Titanic. He got out of the Detroit metropolitan area, drove down Interstate 75, then shortly after, road signs indicated he was about to cross into Ohio near Toledo. His gas tank was close to empty. It needed a fill-up. His senses were dulled; he needed a shot of caffeine. He could obtain both at the upcoming rest area.

Only three of several gas pumps were occupied. He picked up the nozzle of one of the unoccupied pumps, inserted his new credit card, one supplied by Tarek on his first day in Dearborn, then realized that his gas door was located on the other side of the car. It was his first filling up; he hadn't paid attention before. He returned the nozzle to its resting position, got into the car, made a U-turn and ended up facing another pump on the proper side. He stepped out of the car for a second time and repeated his previous act. This time, however, the machine refused to recognize his credit card; it kept rejecting it. He was prepared to retry with the next pump when the attendant approached. "May I help you?"

Arik turned and faced the attendant, an immigrant from India, whose English accent was typical of people coming over from his native land—heavy and melodic. Arik accepted his help. "You can pay cash if you wish, or I can take it inside. This pump has a problem with credit cards," the attendant said while jotting down the license plate number, before inserting the nozzle into Arik's gas tank.

"Cash is fine," Arik said.

When it was over, Arik offered the attendant thirty-five dollars, four in excess of the total bill. "Keep the change," he said. He turned the ignition key, drove to a parking spot on the lot, then strolled into the cafeteria for a short coffee and cake break. As he entered the premises, he turned around, only to notice the Indian fellow. The latter was following him; he seemed like a little kid trying to catch a better glimpse of a new toy. Arik pretended to ignore the possible tail; he kept at his quest for coffee. Once he reached the order point, he turned around but the Indian fellow was no longer there. Arik left the coffee line; he walked back looking for the Indian. Following a short skimming through, he spotted him in a small corner, making a phone call out of a public phone. He was with his back to Arik. Arik moved closer, making certain the Indian didn't notice him. He got close enough, stopped and listened. He could hear the words 'Qassem al-Nasr'. It was obvious. It was time to split.

He drove for another ten minutes before exiting. The sign said—*Food and Lodging*. The restaurant sign said—*Sea Food and Grill,* the parking lot was packed. He was on the outskirts of Toledo. He drove around the parking lot before spotting a Toyota Camry. He stopped his car behind the other Toyota, reached for the glove compartment where he knew Tarek kept a couple of screwdrivers, then quickly exited his car and approached the Camry. He unscrewed the license plates off the other car while making sure no one was watching. As soon as the first part of the job was done, he heard the approaching steps of a happy couple walking in his direction. Time was running out. He couldn't possibly manage to unscrew and install his plates on the other car in less than two seconds. He picked up the stolen plates, made it into his car and drove off. He took the first highway exit, venturing into the city. He didn't want to stay on the highway for fear of being betrayed by his old plates.

The city of Toledo Ohio was an unfamiliar place. He wondered aimlessly until he came by a residential street where cars were parked in parallel next to the curb. This time he had no trouble swapping license plates. Arik replaced the originals, on a Honda he was working on, with the ones he'd walked off twenty minutes earlier, in the rest area. He then installed the latest pickings on Tarek's car. He was now less vulnerable but only until police figured out his ploy, something he assumed would take a couple of days at the most. In the meantime, he disposed of the original plates, placing them inside a black plastic bag, waiting on the side of the curb to be collected next morning by the sanitation department troops. He then called his colleague, Jerry, in New York. "Listen, don't talk. You know what happened," he said. There was silence on the other end of the line. "I'm on my way home."

He made it to the *Upper West Side* safe apartment in Manhattan three days after he'd cut loose from his pursuers in Dearborn. The trip from Toledo was uneventful. He abandoned Tarek's car in that city after Jerry arranged for a delivery of a Ford minivan rental to Southwyck Shopping Center on Reynolds Road. The minivan was rented by a *Mossad* aficionado, doors unlocked, keys inside, and dropped next to the Aladdin's Eatery. Arik drove it all the way to Philadelphia, where he left it in the parking lot of the Roosevelt Mall Shopping Center before Jerry picked him up for the final stretch.

He was disappointed. His mission had been only partially successful. He did fashion new relationships with some bad guys, but then, the thread was severed, and he was back to square one. He closed his eyes. He would figure out everything when he woke up in the morning.

Chapter 51

January 6, 2003—Tel Aviv, Israel

"I'm going to New York to look for him. Rachel told Dan Carmel. "Arik doesn't even know that I'm alive."

One day, soon after her return to Israel from Indonesia, Rachel confronted Dan Carmel who swore her to secrecy before telling her about Arik's mission. "He is working for us in New York," he said. When she asked him whether Arik knew what she'd gone through, Carmel shrugged, then advised that it would be safer if Arik were unaware. "He's in a critical phase of this mission. The kind of job he's doing, takes years before it bears fruits, but once it does, the yield is massive," he explained. "You shouldn't trash the great strides he'd made by infiltrating the terrorists' network. Exposing him now could place his life in danger as well."

Rachel didn't accept the explanation. She realized that the truth about her and Arik had been manipulated by the *Mossad* to make each one of them believe that the other had been killed. She resented that conduct. She was a human being with desires and feelings. She wasn't a hand puppet from *Sesame Street*, and Dan Carmel wasn't *Mr. Rogers*, or so she deemed. However, she hadn't gone as far as imagining that Dan Carmel would have dared play her as well as Arik in his cold gambit. She was going to do what she had to do.

Upon leaving Dan's office, she went home to her parents, asked them for a loan of $20,000. She called the EL-AL office, purchased a roundtrip ticket to New York from Tel Aviv, called the *New York Times* and placed a full-page ad to run on the January 19, Sunday paper edition, following her arrival.

DEAR ARIK
RACHEL IS HERE IN NY.
I AM STAYING AT THE SHERATON
IN MIDTOWN MANHATTAN
COME SEE ME.
FOREVER YOURS,
RACHEL

The ad included a large portrait photo of Rachel devoid of background.

Chapter 52

January 8, 2003—Manhattan, New York

Recent events pulled Arik off Center Stage. He felt he had to reconnect, re-enter the terror scene. Fatima, his best conduit, was living nearby, a walking distance away. An urgent rendezvous in her apartment seemed like a natural course of action. The entry hallway to the apartment building on Park Avenue was lit like Reliant Stadium on Super Bowl night. Arik had to shutter his eyelids, curbing the amount of light energy hitting his irises. The security guard/doorman was all smiles. He was short, balding, and a thousand pounds on the wrong side of fit. His eyebrows resembled a dirty broom, and his shaggy mustache looked like a badly installed, discarded remnant of a used rug. The look in his eyes rendered his erotic thoughts transparent before sending Arik upstairs. Arik was troubled by what he considered unwarranted fantasies this guard was projecting onto him. *This grossly overweight ugly idiot had never experienced a genuine dual party synchronized orgasm*, Arik concluded; *a do-it-yourself was a likely option.*

Fatima greeted him with a warm smile. She was wearing a pink robe, tied at the waist, exposing her thighs as she walked. She looked as if she'd come out of the shower a short time earlier. Her hair wet, combed backwards, no makeup, she smelled of fresh soap, shampoo, perfume, or all of the above. Arik wasn't sure. The strong scent made him sneeze three times in a row.

She handed him a tissue. "Would you like a drink?" she asked.

"Yeah. Hot tea will be appreciated. It feels like I've got a little sore throat," he said, then coughed twice as if to confirm his situation.

"You look sick," she said. She placed her hand on his forehead. "You're hot, got fever," she concluded. "Do you have chills?"

Arik stared at her. He hadn't been feeling sick before showing up here, but as soon as she felt his forehead, he started experiencing chills along with painful discomfort. He walked to the couch, his head spinning; he sat down, then shifted to a more horizontal position short of lying down. "I feel sick all of a sudden," he said. "Did you poison me?" He was joking. She hadn't offered him anything since landing inside her apartment.

"I can do it now," she announced on her way to the kitchen. "You should take aspirin to reduce your fever."

"That will help," he said. "With hot tea and lemon," he added.

Three minutes later Fatima came out of the kitchen holding a golden tray with two empty white cups painted with red stripes, a slice of honey cake in each matching saucer and a teapot, ready to serve. Arik watched her as she bent over, pouring the hot tea into the cups. Her young breasts were on view through the loose opening in her robe. He was sure she was aware; it was in her plan, but he was in no mood. He felt sick, achy, unsexy. He was under stress as well. *Someone was watching the building from the street down below*. He didn't know who and why. They might have realized that he was in the apartment, and now he might become a person of interest, not counting the great honor of making the top ten on the FBI list.

He was glad he'd come over. She would take care of him; nurse him through his flu or whatever germ he'd contracted. Being alone in his crummy *Upper West Side* apartment surrounded and attacked by hostile flu viruses was the last thing to which he was looking forward. Fatima's feminine touch was the best medicine he could beg for, for which he didn't have to beg.

"Fatima, dear," he said. "Come here, sit next to me." He sat up, made room for her, patted the top of the pillow, as if to say—*right here*.

She came over, sat next to him. She held two aspirins in one hand and a cup filled with hot tea in the other. Arik took the tablets, chucked them inside his mouth, swallowed, then picked up the cup, held it in both hands, enjoying the heat that the cup was radiating. Fatima turned toward him, her back straight, her neck high; she put her hands behind his head, pulled it closer, then pressed it against her chest in a compassionate hug.

It was soft, cozy, and sexy. However, Arik had other things on his mind. He put his cup on the cocktail table, turned towards her, removed both her hands from behind his head and nestled them warmly within his. Then, looking straight into her eyes hanging at a kissing distance, he said. "I must talk to Suleiman. How can I get in touch?"

"He is in Switzerland," she said.

"What is he doing there?" he inquired.

"I don't know," she said. "Suleiman doesn't let me in on details of his doings. I only buy his airline tickets, make hotel reservations, organize his suitcase with clothes and other travel needs, take care of his social parties. I don't get involved with the politics. I hate politics," she said. She returned to the sofa, sat down, moved closer, then ran her hand through Arik's hair. "You look awful, better get some rest. You can stay here over night on the sofa."

"Do you have any idea where he's headed after Geneva?"

"Let's see," she brought her right hand up, supporting her chin as she leaned on the cocktail table. "He's supposed to fly back to Saudi Arabia, immediately following his meeting with the UNRWA representative — Mr. Olson."

Arik realized that Fatima wasn't aware of Suleiman's next stop or the latest scheme he was involved in — the reason behind his meeting with Mr. Olsen. Arik's *Mossad* sources had spotted Suleiman in Beirut, Lebanon. She was simply not plugged in, not a true insider. He wouldn't be able to retrieve much information in this apartment. Still, she was good for other services. He offered his cell phone. "Why don't you call Dr. Radwan in Dearborn; tell him..."

"He's no longer in Dearborn," she said, interrupting him. Then after thinking it over, she added, "I don't have his new number. He's in New York together with another man." She waited; scrutinized Arik's bloodshot eyes. "You finished your tea. I'll make you more if you want." She rose, picked up the tray, then walked to the kitchen. She was out of the living room when all of a sudden the intercom buzzed. Fatima, startled, almost dropped the tray on the floor, but managed to hold on to it at the last moment. She placed the tray on the counter, turned back to the living room.

"Go ask who it is," Arik said. He was blasé, or so he seemed.

"There's an FBI agent here," the security guard announced. "He wants to come up and talk to you."

Chapter 53

January 4-8, 2003—Manahattan, New York

Immediately after their arrival in Manhattan, Jim and Stanley contacted Stanley's former FBI colleagues from the New York field office, Jason Lambert and Ruth Goldstein, who supported them with additional resources, including arranging for and ordering the usual wiretapping on Fatima's fixed and wireless phones. Verizon was very cooperative; got the job done within three hours. Except, following a day and a half of mind-numbing uneventful time, the great information they had gathered wasn't paying off; they decided to take more direct custody of the case. That change in operational modes didn't alter the results.

Fatima was going on customary normal routines typical of young single women in the city. She shopped for food, did her nails, lunched in small restaurants, shopped at Macy's—nothing that would make her more interesting than any Christian Fundamentalist on *Yom Kippur*. Her use of the phone was minimal. There was nothing, absolutely nothing that one could call stimulating, revealing, ground breaking; just boring, boring, boring.

That Tuesday night, a little over an hour following Arik's arrival at her building, Stanley settled on a more aggressive approach. He entered the lobby and approached the security guard. He introduced himself as an FBI agent to the admiring nincompoop. "Do you know Ms. Fatima Zahar?" he asked.

"Yes, she lives here on the ninth floor," he said. "In fact she came in just about two hours ago." The security guard was eager to cooperate. "Did she do anything wrong?" he asked.

Stanley, whose politically incorrect sense of humor was always up front and in the way, turned his head to the side pointing at the elevator, then through the corner of his left eye and over his shoulder, still facing the elevator, he tossed a slanted stare, aimed at the guard. "She's a Muslim, isn't she?" he said.

"She is, I guess," the guard said, but then he gathered some nerve. "Except that isn't a crime in this city." He wiped his forehead. His daring challenge made him sweat.

"Right," Stanley admitted. "It's unfortunate that ninety-nine percent of Muslims give the rest a bad name." He turned his head and faced the guard directly. It was supposed to be a joke, yet Stanley wasn't smiling. "Anything else you want to tell me?" he demanded with an intimidating stare.

"Well ah." The guard scratched his head. "She had a visitor over an hour ago."

"A visitor?" Stanley was growing animated. His team took pictures of all who'd come in and those who'd left the building. "What did he look like?"

"He was tall, had a beard and a mustache, wore sunglasses, said his name was Rudy."

"Sunglasses at night? Does that sound normal to you?" Stanley asked.

"I've seen it happen before," the guard admitted.

"Okay," Stanley moved on. "Tell her I want to pay her a visit upstairs. Give her a buzz."

Chapter 54

January 4-8, 2003—Brooklyn, New York

Following the explosion at the *Yellow House* from across the street where Omar had bungled the assembly of the suicide belts, Abu Musa had grown uncomfortable staying in Dearborn near the *Red House*. There was too much activity across the street; too many police, FBI, investigators from other agencies. He and Dr. Radwan decided to go to New York to start implementing their deadly project. From inside the car, Abu Musa was able to thumb a lift on some innocent surfer with an unsecured wireless network, whose signal projected resiliently from his broadband, wireless, G-router down to the street below. He turned his laptop on, logged in to the Internet chat room on the *Delilah* site, connected with Mahmud Ismail, the restaurant owner from Albany, then summoned him to New York City.

Three days later, all three men arrived in New York. They settled into a safe house in Brooklyn, two blocks from the Islamic Mission of America on State Street. The next morning, they visited Manhattan, toured *St. Patrick's Cathedral*, and mapped it out. They pinpointed ideal spots and timing for the suicide bombers and the explosions—one in the middle of the Cathedral and one near the exit, seconds later—where the frenzied crowd would rush outside for air immediately after the blasts, only to be torn to pieces by car bombs detonated from inside an approaching minivan. They'd need three suicide bombers, a minivan, two suicide belts, and plenty of high explosives. Abu Musa was confident he could bring it all to a cheerful conclusion in less than three months.

Back in their safe house, the three *Jihadists* gathered to discuss the details of the plan. Mahmud Ismail volunteered his daughter, Hajar, for the indoor job, Dr. Radwan was betting on one volunteer, a student of the Islamic school from the Dearborn Mosque he'd met after 9-11, with whom he was particularly impressed. They needed one more candidate to pull off the original plan.

"What about you?" Abu Musa asked Ismail.

The latter seemed buried in thoughts. "Once they identify Hajar's body, they'll come after me," he said. "They'll figure out the connection." He got off the couch, started pacing back and forth around the living room.

Abu Musa, still sitting on his couch turned to Ismail. "I didn't mean it that way," he said. "If you're going to drive the minivan, this problem will be solved. They can't get you when you're in Heaven."

"Right, but my job isn't done yet. There's more Allah wants from me before I see him in Paradise." He paused, scratched his head. "But I'll think about it."

Abu Musa rose. "You don't have a lot of time to think. I want to do this on Easter," Abu Musa said. He moved closer, held Ismail's shoulders with his hands; their eyes met. "I depend on you. The whole operation rests on your shoulders. You must comply with Allah's will. The reward is immediate. You'll sit next to Allah's throne, your daughter seated next to you, and seventy-two virgins attending to your needs."

Ismail grew animated. His eyes turned moist. "Yes, I know." He was choking with excitement, his voice hoarse and vulnerable. "I can do it," he finally declared. "I will do it."

Dr. Radwan was watching the two ailing down the labor issue. However, he wasn't prepared for the new date. "Easter?" He turned to Abu Musa. "Easter is too soon. We need more time. We may need Qassem's help." He pulled up a *Marlboro* from his pocket. "It's just too close. There's too much to take care of." He lit the cigarette, took a drag.

Abu Musa turned his mad gaze toward Dr. Radwan. He approached the couch on which Radwan was seated, laid his hands on Radwan's shoulders, then leaned down, his breath in Radwan's face. "Qassem's out of the picture," he said between gritted teeth. His face turned dark. "We don't need him. He doesn't need to know about the new plan." He took a breath, entertained a few evil thoughts, removed his hands from Radwan's shoulders, then straightened up. "Qassem's a spy. He's the one who's led the police into my safe house in Cleveland; he's the one behind Omar's death." He took a deep breath. "I don't trust him. You shouldn't trust him. We'll do it my way."

Chapter 55

January 8, 2003—Park Avenue, Manhattan, New York

"Hello, Miss Zahar?"

"Who's there?" Fatima answered the intercom. She turned to Arik, her facial expression quizzical. Did he expect anyone? She didn't recognize the voice. Arik got up from the sofa, moved closer to Fatima.

"This is Stanley Kramer, FBI. I'm coming upstairs. We need to talk."

Fatima turned and looked at Arik whose body language and facial expression signaled a full-sized *NO*. She turned back to the intercom. "It's extremely inconvenient. I just came out of the shower. I'm not set for a date."

"Okay, I'll give you fifteen minutes." He hung up.

"I have an idea," Fatima said. "Hamad Suleiman keeps two fully furnished safe apartments in the building, in addition to his own. They're under different names. I have the keys." She stared at Arik who seemed tense. She realized he didn't look forward to the encounter.

"Let's go, before he shows up," Arik said. He picked up his blanket; put his shoes back on while Fatima retrieved the key to one of the apartments, one floor above, and gave it to him.

Arik left. She peeked at her watch. She had seven more minutes given that the FBI agent would keep his word. She took off her robe, threw on a tank top and a pair of jeans, rushed to the makeup corner in her bathroom, stared at the mirror for a long second, then picked up the lipstick.

The doorbell rang.

"Just a minute," she yelled. "You're early." She continued turning herself into a fine-looking babe.

The doorbell rang again. *This FBI agent is a nervous jerk,* she reflected. She rushed to the door, opened it, looking almost breathless. Stanley was standing there, his FBI emblem up in his right hand. "May I come in," he said, as he was pushing through the narrow opening between her and the open door.

"Thanks for asking," she countered, watching him take a visual tour of the surroundings inside. She became conscious of him taking notice of the tray, the cups, the cookies. "You have visitors?" he asked while proceeding with his appraisal, moving to the bedroom, peeking inside.

"You have a warrant?" she bickered. "What's this? You burst into my apartment in the middle of the night, looking around for who knows what. Do you mind? I have rights, you know."

"Not if you're what I think you are."

Fatima stopped. She folded her arms on her chest. Her eyes narrowed. "What's that supposed to mean?"

"We know what you're up to," Stanley winked; he wasn't smiling. "You better cooperate or you'll end up in Guantanamo with the rest of your *al-Qaeda* friends."

Fatima couldn't tolerate it any longer. "Get out," she screamed. "Get out."

"Not before you answer a couple of questions," Stanley retorted. He moved to the sofa, parked himself comfortably on the same spot Arik had been sitting on moments before. "Where's your visitor?" he asked.

Fatima realized there was no sense in denying. "He left half an hour ago.... And besides, it's none of your business." She was still standing in the middle of the living room, arms folded on her chest, while the knot in her stomach and the nervous tic running through her lower jaw hinted at her state of mind.

"We've not seen him leaving the building." Stanley argued. "Is he hiding inside your closet?" He got up, walked to the bathroom peeked inside, then on to the master bedroom, to the closet; he opened the door, fixed his eyes on her hanging clothes, then down.

"Nice shoes," he said with what looked like a facsimile of a smile. He closed the door, walked back to his place on the sofa. "Where is he?"

Fatima reached a state of helplessness. She started crying. "I want you to leave," she almost begged. She walked to the kitchen, grabbed a napkin and wiped her tearing eyes. "I want you to leave. Please leave."

"Not so fast," Stanley said. He disregarded the crying; wasn't affected by it. "We can do it here and now, or we can do it downtown in my New York office; your choice," he stated, then stood up, watching her, anticipating a "here and now" answer.

Fatima closed her eyes; her lips quivered unconsciously. Seconds later, she opened her eyes and headed for the couch. As soon as she sat down, Stanley parked himself back on the sofa, ready for questioning.

"Look, lady," he said. "You're in big trouble. You'd better cooperate and tell me what you know. If you don't, it will take a long time before you see this living room again, if ever."

Fatima tossed a blank stare. She didn't understand where this was going.

Stanley laid down the facts. "Your boss owns two houses in Dearborn; you arranged for the closing just about a month ago."

She nodded.

"Well, as you know," Stanley leaned over and lowered his voice as if he were revealing state secrets about the latest UFO landing. "One of these houses was blown to smithereens by a home-made bomb that accidentally went off. Once we found who owned it, we discovered that the same person—your boss, owned the house across the street. We checked it out, found interesting fingerprints, Abu Musa, Qassem al-Nasr, and a couple of others, all Islamic arch terrorists. Inspecting further, we discovered that a local resident, a suspected terrorist—Dr. Radwan, had been in that house as well. Apparently, Dr. Radwan has vanished. He's no longer in his own house in Dearborn. We found more prints, but we haven't yet identified them," Stanley said with a chuckle. He pulled himself up, then walked behind Fatima's couch. She didn't turn her head. He leaned over from behind her, his face almost touching hers, his lips next to her left ear; he whispered. "You must know those people. Were any of those characters here tonight?"

Fatima was facing the sofa. She didn't turn her head. The expression on her face was strangely vacant. Her eyes hollow. There was a moment of silence, then she gathered her nerve and braved a response. "You've not read the *Miranda* to me. You haven't warned me that I have the right to remain silent, that anything I say can be held against me. You fucked up."

Stanley was about to lose his cool. "Look," he said. "The stuff you're in the middle of—it makes the blood run cold. I could arrest you, but instead, I'm making you an offer. I'm the nice guy around here. You cooperate, work with me, help me find those people, and I'll protect you, let you roam free." He turned and walked towards the door. As soon as he reached it, he turned around, issued a final warning as an afterthought. "If any of the people I've mentioned or anyone connected to terror is still in the building, there will be one more reason to nail you, throw you in a cell, and lose the key. You may not have realized it, but this is serious shit and you're buried deep in it. The only chance you have is cooperation." He put his hand in his pocket, brought it out flashing a business card. "Here's my card in case you change your mind." He left his card on the small ledge next to the door. "You have until ten o'clock tomorrow. If I don't hear from you by then, you may say bye bye to this apartment and hello to the maximum security prison you haven't even seen in the movies."

He opened the door, stepped out, then peeked back, his head half way in. "It's an offer you can't refuse. See you by ten o'clock tomorrow."

Chapter 56

January 8, 2003—Manhattan, New York

Jerry was watching the police buildup next to the apartment building on Park Avenue where Arik and Fatima were supposedly enjoying their evening together. He grew exceedingly restless after counting four police squad cars with lights flashing, and two unmarked cars he'd attributed to the FBI, converge on the building. *Arik isn't going to break out of this igloo as a free man*, Jerry figured. *The whole sting operation is going down the drain. Saving Arik after he's caught would unmask his identity, sting the stinger, expose the mission, and even embarrass the FBI and the NYPD, after they realize they've blown an opportunity.*

Jerry had no choice. He grabbed his cell phone and dialed Dan Carmel in Israel. "Sorry to wake you up," he said, "but we have a burning emergency."

"What're you talking about?" Dan was still under the influence of his delightful dream; his mind refused to leave the sandy beach and the sweet taste of the pricey wine he was savoring.

"Arik is trapped. The FBI and NYPD are about to nail him," he paused. "I give it less than two hours…They'll get him dead or alive." He sighed, let an anxious breath out of his system. "We've got to do something, and quickly."

"I can call Jack Devon, my FBI contact, let him in on Arik's true identity, but that's risky. It may leak out, endangering his life."

"You have no choice," Jerry said. "It's better this way than the alternative." He found he had to struggle to keep his teeth from grinding. "You don't have a lot of time," he said. "We've got to stop the madness and the buildup before the media learn too much."

The media herds were already hanging and sniffing around. The air was filled with speculations; rumors of terrorists hiding in the building were reinforced when a SWAT team showed up ready for battle. Jerry was biting his nails. Forty-five minutes earlier, he'd talked to Dan Carmel, sharing the gravity of the situation with him, but instead of having it fade away, it was progressively gaining momentum, creating an unstoppable, expanding bubble headed for a titanic burst.

Time was running out. Jerry clutched his cell phone and redialed. Dan Carmel's line returned a busy signal. *Dan should've been done by now*, he pondered. *What's taking him so long*? Every passing minute felt like an extra eternity. Jerry didn't mind the rain. He didn't even realize it was raining. He didn't care. At that moment, he almost turned religious. He was standing across the street watching the events unfold the wrong way. The only thing he could do was pray. He was feeling helpless, frustrated, anxious; no more genies were left in his bottle. He folded his arms over his chest for warmth, then raised his hands, covered his face, looked up to the heavens, and begged. "Please, God. Make them stop."

He couldn't believe he'd actually found relief in pleading, as if someone was actually listening. Jerry had never before turned to Heaven for help. This was his first. He was always making jokes about those believers. This time, however, his nakedness, his inability to rectify the desperate circumstances, spawned a 9.2 magnitude earthquake through his skull. He kept his eyes closed, his lips moving unconsciously; he did it again. "Please, God; please prove that you exist. Make me believe."

All of a sudden, as if God had been listening, the squad cars turned off their flashing lights, the SWAT team returned to their bus, the FBI vans turned their engines on, and the media paparazzi gangs were assembling their equipment. It was definitely the end of the show, the part where the audience stand on their feet next to their seats, after the applause had died down, looking for the nearest exit sign.

Jerry looked up; he searched the stars above for an answer, but they were hidden by cloud cover. *Creepy,* he thought. Then, he said it. "Thank you. I'll see you in the Temple on *Yom Kippur*." A tear developed in his right eye. He wasn't smiling.

Jerry's cell phone's ringtone interrupted his thoughts. Dan Carmel was on the line. "The FBI is in business," he said. "They want Arik to work closely with them on a large scale sting operation." He coughed twice, cleared his throat. "Get hold of Arik immediately and let him in on the new plan. Over and above his work for us, Arik is about to become an undercover FBI agent. You'll arrange for Arik to meet with agent Stanley Kramer in New York tomorrow." Dan Carmel went on, providing details of the meeting time and place. "And so that you know, The NYPD or any other PD is still on the lookout for Qassem al-Nasr. The FBI team in charge will hold his true identity close to their vest, lest it's unearthed and the whole operation turns into a fiasco."

Chapter 57

January 8-9, 2003—Manhattan, New York

Fatima was overwhelmed by the stark choices Stanley had laid bare in front of her. She wasn't a person who betrayed trust casually, yet she wasn't a terrorist. She'd only done a secretarial job for Hamad Suleiman. He paid her well; she was faithful and dedicated in return. She was aware of Hamad's involvement in terror activities, international scams, money laundering, funding of terror activities all throughout the world, but that didn't bother her, not on account of her values but rather by reason of apathy. She hated politics, didn't care much, if at all, about the consequences, as long as it didn't involve her personally.

Fatima liked Arik, whom she knew as Qassem al-Nasr. He'd played a key role in many of her sexual fantasies. She could have him now if she wanted to; he would forget his sickness once she slipped a cool hand under his shirt, then proceeded in a southern direction, her bare breasts next to his lips. Yet, she would have to betray him, play Delilah in the Biblical saga of Samson; she would have to tell the FBI about Qassem's whereabouts. Qassem would be captured, may be subject to torture, may even be killed in the process. No! She couldn't do that. She might try lying. She could simply not tell a thing about Qassem, while yielding information about everyone else connected with the terror network. But what if Stanley found out that she had been seeing Qassem, talking to him. She would lose credibility, they'd lift her immunity; she would go to jail.

Or maybe she could make a deal. Leave Qassem out of this manhunt, and she would give the rest of her admission one-hundred percent. No! Stanley wouldn't go for that. Maybe she could let Qassem know about the deal with the FBI, warn him in advance, let him decide how to handle it. No! He could warn the others. He could even have her killed. Too crazy; too risky.

She was baffled.

Fatima walked to the sofa; she started developing a headache. She didn't have the slightest idea what her next move was going to be. In the subsequent minutes, she lay down, closed her eyes, then dozed off. Any light movement near her could bring her back to life.

The sound of the doorbell startled her. She opened her eyes, peeked at her watch. It was past midnight. *Who would that be now?* She got up slowly, straightened her tank top, massaged her face with her hands, then tiptoed inaudibly towards the door, glanced at the mirror next to it; she looked fine. Her lipstick needed a fresh layer, *but so what?* She peeked through the peephole, then opened the door. Arik was standing there—still sick looking, his eyes bloodshot, his hair, an untreated lawn overlying his forehead—waiting to be invited in.

Fatima moved to the side, parting a virtual corridor for Arik to walk through. "Come in," she said in a somewhat reluctant tone of voice. "You look awful."

As soon as Arik cleared the threshold, Fatima closed the door behind him, then without warning, she advanced to within arm's length and started beating him on the chest with both her hands, crying uncontrollably. "Why?" she moaned. "Why are you trying to kill innocent people? What's the purpose of all those insane massacres? Why am I becoming part of this crazy movement? I don't even see eye to eye with it. I hate it. It makes no sense. It makes me sick. I hate politics. You! Son-of-a-bitch! Why?"

Arik grabbed her hands, bringing her assault to a halt. He pulled her closer, released her hands, while pulling her head onto his chest, hugging her tightly, preventing her from launching a second round of uncontrolled aggression. Fatima was slowly calming down. Her incessant sobbing smudged on his shirt. He shifted her head at an angle where his eyes met hers. "I told you before, and we both agreed," he said. "I'm not a terrorist." He took a deep breath, let out a long sigh. "It's all a big mistake," he added. "One day you'll understand my role. I can't explain it right now. But you must trust me."

Fatima freed herself from Arik's bear hug. She stepped back and stared at him. She was shaking her head in mistrust. "I don't believe this. Why's the FBI looking so hard to get you dead or alive?" She lifted her head, searched the corner of the ceilings for an answer, didn't find any, then lowered her gaze, met his eyes. "I don't know what to do," she finally said; she was still crying.

"You go and cooperate with the FBI," he told her. "I know that they've put you in a vise; it's okay. Don't worry about me. Tell them what they want to hear." He paused. "Just let me know what you've told them, so I can keep one step ahead, vanish before they get me."

Fatima's stomach tightened. *How does he know about the FBI?* She asked herself. *Is this a game? Does he work for them?* She turned angry. "Why should I do that?" she asked. "I don't know if I can trust you." Her breath became shallow as she fought her way through sudden stomach cramps. "And how do you know about the FBI?"

"It's all over your face," he responded. "They have plenty on you; they've come here tonight to blackmail you. It's natural, but I can handle it. I can even help you." He broke with a tentative grin. "We can start by having you arrange for Hamad Suleiman to get in touch with me. Rumor has it that he is in Beirut, Lebanon. You could find out what he's doing there. He may be talking to *Hezbollah*. I need to know."

"I don't know where he is," she said. "I didn't know that he was in Beirut."

"But you can find that out," Arik argued. "You can dig and find that out. You don't have to do it for the FBI, but you could do it for me."

"Why should I do it for you?" she asked.

"First of all, because I'm on your side, and second..." he came closer, put his arms out, grabbed her shoulders, pulled her closer. "If I'd felt better, I'd have kissed you," he said.

"Go ahead. Take me. I don't care," she said. "Your germs don't scare me. I've already contracted them anyway."

It was 5 a.m. when Arik got up after a busy night. He felt healthy again. The bug that had assailed his body the night before appeared to have surrendered. Fatima stared at his naked body. *Michael Angelo could've used this image for his David,* she contemplated. The glow on her face broadcast her triumphant stance. She finally conquered this fortress. Her fulfilled sexual fantasies turned out to be an understatement. Arik took her through an erotic journey that could've turned a colorblind self into a Van Gough. She wasn't going to dispose of this treasure. *This is what life is all about.* Qassem grew to be her distinctive brand of cocaine. She became addicted.

"When am I going to see you again?" she asked, watching him get dressed.

"You'll see me, but I can't tell you when. I don't want you to lie to the FBI. Remember, the less you know about me, the better you'll feel. You may even pass a lie detector test with flying colors, to which they'll no doubt subject you." He was done. "I'm leaving now," he announced. "Your homework for today is Hamad Suleiman, your boss. I must talk to him."

Chapter 58

January 9, 2003—Manhattan, New York

The early afternoon session took place in the *Upper West Side* apartment. FBI Section Chiefs (SCs), Jim and Stanley, were both in a festive mood. Arik had just turned into an undercover instrument with whom they could badly use. "Fatima likes you," Stanley admitted. "I interviewed her this morning, and she wouldn't turn you in."

"That's my girl," Arik said, beaming in satisfaction. "I may be able to trust her after all."

"As a matter of fact, she's not very accommodating." Stanley went on, ignoring Arik's comments. "She claims to know nothing about her boss's whereabouts." He turned to Arik, spreading his hands with his palms up. "Is she hiding anything?"

"She's innocent," Arik responded. "I'm saying that only because I've already figured it out." He paused, watching Jim's guarded look. "No other reason…to be frank…really," he added to no avail. "She's been loyal to Suleiman since that was her job. She's never really understood the gravity of her actions. She still doesn't." He rose, walked to the kitchen, stared at the hi-tech burnished-steel coffee machine claiming pride of place on the counter. He turned back. "Coffee anyone? I'm about to make a fresh pot."

Stanley glanced at Jim. "Anymore caffeine today and I'll go dancing the cucaracha," he said.

Jim nodded in agreement. "Do you have decaf?" he yelled in the direction of the kitchen.

"No problem," Arik yelled back. "No reason to go swimming in caffeine, I have no lifeguard on duty at this hour."

The two SCs remained sitting on the sofa surveying the room all around them, waiting for the hot beverage. A minute later Arik came back without the coffee. "It's brewing," he assured them. "There are some interesting developments, though," he slipped that in as he found his seat on the couch. "Abu Musa plans to sacrifice unwitting, mentally retarded suicide bombers on his *Jihad* mission. He wants to equip them with a remotely controlled detonation mechanism. I suggest you closely monitor the *al-Quds* mosque for the next few months. The mentally retarded victims are being recruited by the Imam through the mosque."

"We'll order comprehensive telephone and Internet traffic monitoring," Jim said. He turned to Stanley. "Other topics?"

Arik cut in. "Hamad Suleiman is the most dangerous of them all. There's a whole network, funds, and governments behind him. I'd get the CIA involved, then put a stop to his soul, send him upstairs to his beloved Allah and the promised seventy-two virgins." He rose again, "Coffee's ready; I'll bring some."

"We can't do too much about Suleiman even if he's a terrorist," Jim said. "He's, after all, a Saudi diplomat."

"In this country," Arik said, "you can pick him up and accidentally throw him over the GW Bridge while driving at high speed. Accidents happen, even to FBI agents." He headed back for the kitchen.

"You know," Stanley concurred. He stared at Jim disapprovingly. "Qassem, or shall I say Arik, here; he's got the right idea."

Arik came back with a tray. He placed it on the cocktail table in front of the sofa, then served the coffee, offering the filled cups to his new buddies. "I'll figure out Hamad Suleiman," he said. "I need a little time. You must be patient."

"Now that we're unaided we can talk," Stanley said in a low voice, almost whispering. Although they had complete privacy in the apartment, his eyes kept wandering around as if he were talking to Larry King during a commercial break, making sure the camera crew wasn't eavesdropping. "This stuff is highly confidential for the simple reason that we're careful not to instigate mass panic." He glimpsed at Jim who nodded in approval.

Arik didn't say anything. He folded his arms across his chest, awaiting the beef to turn up.

"The CIA has intercepted some terrorist babble originating in Lebanon. Stanley continued. "After refining it, they picked out a communication mentioning *'The Black Cat,'* in conjunction with *'The Big One.'* One day earlier, the same source was discussing Qassem," he paused, then peered at Arik with edgy alertness. "That may be you," he said. "You may be closer to the information than you realize. We've also learned that *'The Big One'* is imminent. It may not be connected to the *St. Patrick's* situation; it could either reflect a change in plan or a brand new one," he concluded. "It's urgent. You've got to find out what's cooking, why it's *'The Big One,'* and who's the fucking *'Black Cat'?*" He shrugged; spread his hands, casual on the face of it, though his face was telling. It was wrinkled by excessive strain.

"Suleiman's the *'Black Cat,'*" Arik replied. I don't know about the *'Big One.'* I'll have Fatima help me figure it out." He paused, sought approval. Both Jim and Stanley nodded. They were in agreement. Arik went on. "Why don't you set up a date at the *Waldorf* for the two of us? The *Waldorf* is next door to her apartment building, but Fatima doesn't want to meet in her apartment for obvious reasons."

Chapter 59

January 11, 2003—Manhattan, New York

At ten minutes before eight in the evening, Stanley dropped Arik at *The Waldorf Astoria*. The room had been booked earlier that day by the FBI under the name Jose Fernandez. It was standard procedure. The FBI employed many fictional identities, complete with history, documentation, medical records, driver's license, social security ID, and a non-existent address, particularly for the purpose of undercover operations. The name Jose Fernandez was allocated to Stanley; this was the twentieth time throughout his career that he made use of that particular fictional character.

Less than an hour later, Abu Musa, Mahmud Ismail, and a young combatant, named Mustafa, watched Fatima making her way from her apartment into the hotel. They were standing at the Park Avenue street corner scrutinizing her apartment building when she was spotted stepping out.

"She's a whore." Abu Musa turned to Ismail, his hollow eyes let slip out his inner rage; a wave of red rising from his neck to his forehead made his facial scar look like a lighthouse on a deserted Island. "I want to know who's invited her in." He pulled out a cigarette, lit it, drew in smoke, then puffed it out, the cloud masking his predator's glare.

"She's a traitor," Ismail said. He turned to Mustafa; the kid was Ismail's best student. "Remember the raid, yesterday, on the *al-Quds* mosque in Brooklyn?"

"Yes," Mustafa said.

"The police showed up minutes after Fatima had left the place."

Young Mustafa, no older than eighteen, was listening to his older, wiser coaches. He was wearing his holiday clothes. Mustafa had attended the evening prayer before joining the observation spot on the Park Avenue corner. "What did she do in the mosque?" he asked Ismail.

"Fatima brought a message from her boss, Hamad Suleiman, to the Imam." Ismail said. A spasm of rage and frustration played across his face. "Suleiman's arranging for *Sarin* components rather than Iranian made, modified Russian SA-18, shoulder-fired missiles."

"*Sarin* components?" Mustafa asked. He shook his head, sought an explanation; he wanted to learn. "Why did Suleiman change the plan?" Mustafa asked. "What was his reason?"

"The message Fatima brought over claimed that downing an aircraft with shoulder-fired missiles would require substantial training, which we don't have. What's more, the message from Suleiman maintained that the Americans have started checking out containers." Ismail paused, took a breath, then continued. "The Iranians are careful not to be exposed as the source."

"That's one monster bull shit," Abu Musa interjected. "I don't trust Suleiman. He's using delay tactics." He turned to Ismail, "You told me Fatima had another message; that's why we're here."

Ismail summed up. "Yes, she warned the Imam, told him to cease his suicide bomber recruiting immediately. She said the FBI was watching him. When the Imam asked her how she knew, Fatima didn't say; she just shrugged." Ismail paused for effect, then brought the house down. "And then, as if to prove her right, the police showed up and arrested the Imam, minutes after she'd left." Ismail made his case, just like Perry Mason at the conclusion of his brilliant analysis. "Now, you tell me what conclusions you can draw from all of this."

Abu Musa didn't respond. He folded his arms over his chest; it was cold outside; it helped keep him warm.

"She's a traitor," Ismail concluded. "She works for the Americans. It's all coming together, once you consider Suleiman's letter to the Imam, nixing our plan." Ismail clenched his jaw, then turned his face up, watching the heavens. "She's very friendly with Qassem. He must be a traitor as well," he concluded.

Abu Musa seemed determined. "She must pay for her crimes," he announced. He turned to Mustafa, "You're dressed nicely. You go inside the hotel, try to find out where she is, what she's doing there."

Chapter 60

January 11, 2003—Manhattan, New York

There was a knock on the door. Arik moved slowly, peeked through the peephole, then opened. Fatima looked nervous; she didn't jump to kiss him. "What's the matter?" he asked, as she walked straight in without acknowledging him.

"It's the FBI. They don't leave me alone." She turned around to face him.

"What happened?" He closed the door, walked toward her.

She reciprocated. "I can't take it," she started sobbing. She nestled her head on his neck, her chin in the hollow of his shoulder, holding him tight with both hands, her tears, warm and wet, were running off against his neck, drenching his chest through his open shirt collar.

Arik let her calm down before gently pulling her away. Gazing into her eyes, he noticed; her mascara and eye shadow were smudging her face, there was too much of it to begin with. It looked like a *Picasso* masterpiece with little sense of palette. "You must tell me what's going on," he said.

"Earlier today, I delivered a message from Hamad Suleiman to the Imam in the *al-Quds* mosque. The message had been delivered to me in a sealed envelope. I didn't even know what it was about when I delivered it to the Imam." She lifted her arms, wiped her tears. "Yesterday during my FBI interview they asked me about the Imam and his recruitment of retarded suicide bombers." She shook her head. "I warned the Imam about it. I told him the FBI was suspicious of his activities... I don't understand what's going on."

"Who delivered the letter to you?" Arik asked.

"I don't know. Someone left the package with the doorman in my apartment building; early in the morning, said it was urgent."

"Go on."

"As you know the police arrested the Imam, immediately after I'd left and then they discovered the message. Later, they came over to interrogate me." She let out a lungful of air. "They threatened me; they said I needed the best lawyer I could find. They said they turned the case over to the FBI. They said I'd spend the rest of my days in jail." She was out of breath.

A minute of silence went by. Arik was waiting for Fatima to calm down. Her tears were drying up. It was time for more questions. "What did the letter say?" he asked.

"Something about *Sarin*. The police investigator asked me to explain, but I had no idea; they didn't believe me." She paused, her eyes pleading for help, comfort, reassurance. Arik came close, placed his hands on her shoulders, then kissed her on her lips. She moved closer, tipped her body against his; pushing her pelvis against his crotch, she could feel him getting hard. She returned a passionate kiss. They stood, kissing, necking, touching, in the middle of the room, giving each other a body-to-body massage, when all at once Fatima's cell phone rang.

She pushed back and released herself from Arik's embrace, picked up her purse, retrieved her phone, then listened. A minute later she hung up, turned to Arik. "Hamad has a message for you," she said. It was as if all of her sex appeal had left her, gone away without leaving a return address. She turned into the typical, loyal, gray secretary. "You must see the Iranian ambassador to the UN. You must see him tonight. He will meet you at the 42nd Street self-parking garage on the second floor in thirty minutes. He will pick you up from there. You must go now."

"Is this your phone?" Arik asked. He wasn't sure whether that call was genuine or a set up, preceding an ambush. If it were her old phone, it had, in all likelihood, been bugged.

"Oh, this cell phone was inside the package with the letter. The note next to it said I should expect a call from Hamad…"

"How did he know that I would be with you?"

"He'd called earlier in the day, asked whether I received his message, then he asked about you; I told him about our meeting tonight. He said he would call later tonight. When the phone rang, I figured it was him."

"Where did he call from?"

"I have no idea. He didn't say. The caller ID displayed—*unavailable*."

"Okay," Arik concurred. "I'm going to 42nd Street. You wait for me here; I'll see you when I come back."

Chapter 61

Late evening, January 11, 2003—Manhattan, New York

Fatima was alone in the room. She looked around inspecting her surroundings. The mini suite at the *Waldorf Astoria* was an oversized, luxurious accommodation with a sitting enclave separated from the main room by French doors. The suite comprised one king-size bed, two bathrooms, a kitchenette, including a medium-sized refrigerator, two TV sets, and a window with a view of the city.

Ten minutes went by after Arik's departure; it was more than enough. She'd already taken a complete tour of the hotel suite, looked down the window; there was nothing exciting about the street below. It was a familiar scene—her own neighborhood. She turned around, surveyed the décor—an orange red carpet, beige love seat with two beige pillows thrown over the corners, occupying the limited seating space. All in all, the place reminded her of a movie set depicting the *Happy Days* of the thirties. She felt like going back in time, to the days of President Roosevelt who was a frequent visitor to this place.

She wondered about the basement. She'd heard that down under the *Waldorf Astoria* there'd been an abandoned train platform and a few cars, once used as a private entrance to the grand hotel by presidents and other important guests to the city. President Franklin D. Roosevelt, whose disability was being kept a state secret, would arrive at the *Waldorf* in his private train. The car would stop on the upper level of the underground train yard directly under the hotel. This enabled the president's aides to carry the paralyzed Roosevelt through a special door and then by elevator directly to his room, avoiding the public altogether.

For the first time, Fatima was feeling as if she were touching American history; she experienced an emotional sensation, poles apart from sentiments she'd ever harbored for anything American.

Little by little, Fatima was growing hungry and bored. It was time to act on it. She picked up her purse, stepped out of the room, into the elevator and down to the lobby, where she found the Modern and Elegant *Peacock Alley* restaurant.

Mustafa was watching the elevator bank when he noticed Fatima coming out, walking in the direction of the restaurant. He picked up his cell phone and called Abu Musa.

"Wait for her in the lobby and follow her upstairs once she's done," Abu Musa instructed. "I want to know what room she's in."

An hour later, Mustafa joined Fatima and another couple on their elevator ride to the ninth floor. Back in the lobby, he called Abu Musa with the answer.

Some twenty minutes later, Abu Musa knocked on Fatima's door. It was somewhat earlier than she'd expected. She figured that Qassem would be back by eleven or even later. She was anxious for his company. Being stuck in the hotel suite, although the atmosphere moved her, stirred her emotions; it was nonetheless monotonous. She didn't think twice before opening the door.

And then it was too late.

Chapter 62

Late evening, January 11, 2003—Manhattan, New York

The 42nd Street parking lot was fairly tranquil. The few available parking spots on the second floor looked deserted like a turkey farm on Thanksgiving Day. Arik found a comfortable rest area, inside a red Ford minivan he'd broken into. He monitored traffic and maintained early scrutiny of the incoming vehicles prior to the expected encounter. His Iranian contact would drive a black Mercedes SUV; that's what Fatima had told him. The license plate wouldn't be a diplomatic type but rather a standard New York State issue.

At exactly 10:30 p.m., the black SUV rolled up the corner. It moved slowly through the center lane. There were several open parking spots, but the driver of SUV avoided them as if they were not good enough for his majesty. It was obvious that the driver didn't intend to park and leave. Another car came up behind the black SUV. It left it no choice but to persist on its aimless path. When observing the passing SUV, Arik couldn't catch a glimpse of any other passenger besides the driver. It was a promising sign. *A perpetrated conspiracy is better executed with as few witnesses as possible.* The SUV disappeared from view, but Arik was certain it would reappear if Fatima's message had had any substance.

Five minutes passed. The SUV turned up for a second time. It traveled at a snail's pace, hunting for something, like a predator watching its prey, preparing for a final strike. It was time. Arik stepped out of the minivan and crossed the lane in front of the SUV, in full view of the driver. He pulled his hat, held it high, transmitting the agreed upon signal the driver of the SUV would recognize. The vehicle came to a full stop. The driver pulled down the passenger side window, anticipating a follow-up signal. Arik approached. They faced each other. "Cigarette?" Arik questioned.

"What kind?"

"Camel filters."

The driver unlocked the passenger side door. "Please," he offered, expecting Arik to climb in, "take a seat."

They drove in silence that neither one made any attempt to fill.

Arik broke the silence at last. "So why am I here?"

"I'm the driver," the *Camel-filters* man said. He stared at Arik, stone-faced. "Mr. Ashtari will see you shortly." There was silence again. Finally, the driver stopped in front of a residential building. "You go to the third floor. Mr. Ashtari's waiting for you in apartment *32.* You knock four times like this." The driver demonstrated the particular beat. "Mr. Ashtari will see you then."

• • •

Adnan Ashtari was middle-aged, balding, short, a bagful of pounds over the top. He wore tight pants, which pushed his belly out as if he were half-pregnant. He had polished manners, the style of a diplomat. He wore an Armani-looking black suit with faint pinstripes and a yellow tie; he seemed as if he were all set for a funeral in his uncle's honor, or for a board meeting at General Electric. The contrast was remarkable. Arik was standing, tall and thin, next to the Iranian. He was dressed more like a hip-hop artist; his hair was a habitual mess, his beard, wild and uncombed, hanging down like a damaged, post-hurricane, palm tree. He was waiting for a clarification.

Ashtari offered his hand. "Ashtari, Intelligence attaché," he said. "Please sit down; would you like some tea?"

Arik didn't want to spend more time than necessary. He wished to go back to the hotel where Fatima would be waiting. "No, thank you. What's this all about?" he inquired.

"Hamad Suleiman referred us to you," Ashtari opened. "We can take care of your nerve gas needs. In fact, we have every part of it available right here in the vicinity of the metropolitan area. That includes some sophisticated binary systems as well." Ashtari walked to the desk at the end of the living room, opened the top drawer, pulled a cigar box, then walked back and opened it next to Arik. "Cubans," he announced proudly, then gave Arik a long quizzical stare. "Would you like to try?"

"Not really," Arik said. "In fact, I'd prefer it if you didn't smoke."

His quizzical stare turned into a questioning look. Then Ashtari got the message. "Okay, back to business."

It was Arik's turn. "Why me? Don't you have your own people?"

Ashtari appeared surprised. "I thought you were looking for this stuff." He smiled, exposing his homemade Vegas-white front teeth. He gave the appearance of a financial executive nerd; except truth was, he was Evil, just like Mussolini in his glory days.

"Yes, I'm still looking," Arik said. "But I wonder why you bother. You have it all here for a reason. You obviously didn't have me in the picture when you'd put it together."

"We have it all here for defensive purposes, just in case the Americans dare attack Iran."

"Why should they?"

"They may try to stop our nuclear program. They may collaborate with the Zionists. They may try to bomb our peaceful nuclear facilities." He pressed his lips into a smirk, as if to say *Yeah, peaceful, my dick.*

"They're not really peaceful, are they?" Arik reciprocated with a curly grin.

"They're exceptionally peaceful. Wiping Israel off the map is the most peaceful purpose one can strive for." Ashtari chuckled. "The crusaders all throughout Europe and their brainless Pope will finally be brought to understand that Islam is the only true and final religion. If that is not peaceful, I don't know what is."

"You're quite right." Arik concurred. *The gene pool could've tolerated a little chlorine,* he pondered. "That's a Godly mission," he added. "Did you try to get in touch with Abu Musa?"

"Suleiman recommended *you*. He didn't believe Abu Musa could pull it off. He had a low opinion of the man. He didn't think that Abu Musa was reliable. And besides, we don't know where Abu Musa is."

"Okay," Arik said. "But I'll need your help pulling it off. I'll need people, cars, resources, etc."

"Just give me the list. I'll take care of it." Ashtari said.

"How do we get in touch in the future?"

"You call my driver. Here's a phone number." Ashtari handed a colorful business card to Arik. "You just say 'I want to go shopping'; he will pick you up within half an hour from Lincoln Center, take you to my next safe place."

Chapter 63

Very late in the evening, January 11, 2003—Manhattan

The scene in front of *The Waldorf Astoria* upon Arik's return was worrisome to him. The ambulance, the police cruisers, the agitated crowds—all signified bad news. Arik stood across the street, watching and listening. He had no idea what was taking place on the other side and why. He was careful not to cross; he was still a fugitive. Except for a handful of FBI folks, other law enforcement agencies viewed him as a cross between Charles Manson and Bin Laden. Arik watched as they carried a sheet-covered body into the ambulance. Although he wasn't exactly close, he detected an outsized bloodstain that made the white sheet look like a Japanese flag in an Olympic village.

Arik grabbed his mobile, called the *Skype* station at a *Mossad* safe house using a Toronto exchange number, then dialed the hotel via his Internet connection. The operator sounded stressed following Arik's connection request. "Who's there?" she asked.

"This is Agent Jose Fernandez, FBI," Arik responded. "Please connect me to room *913*."

"Mr. Fernandez," the operator said. She took a deep breath, let out a long sigh. "I understand this is your room. A woman was murdered in that room, just about an hour ago. I'm so sorry. You must have been related."

Arik found it shocking. "Are you sure?" He shook his head in disbelief. "This makes no sense." He drew another breath. "It's the third one," he said to himself. The sudden emotion he was swept by caused his teeth to ache.

"The third one?" the operator repeated. She overheard.

Arik didn't answer. He turned off the phone. The murderer could've been after him, he concluded. *But why? Who?*

•   •   •

Back at his safe house on the *Upper West Side*, Arik turned on the TV. The gruesome murder topped the news. "The CSI team collected plenty of fingerprints. The woman, Fatima, had her throat slashed. FBI agent, Jose Fernandez, who had rented the room, was the key suspect. He was believed to be a serial killer. This was his third woman victim."

Jerry came by. He hadn't yet heard. He wanted to know what the Iranian wanted. Arik just stared at him. He briskly rose from his chair and strode to the kitchen. "That's the third one," he whispered. "I've been cursed. I'm never going to see a woman again."

Jerry had no idea what Arik was talking about. "Hey. What's going on? Do you suffer from insanity or do you just enjoy it?" he asked.

Arik paid no heed to the sarcastic remark. He came back from the kitchen holding a glass of water. He glared at Jerry. "Fatima's dead," he said. "They slashed her throat. I feel like a serial killer. They even called it so on TV."

Jerry clenched his jaws. "Do you have any idea who could've done it?" he asked with empathy.

"They must have been after me," Arik said.

"No! They were after her." Jerry felt thirsty. He turned and walked to the kitchen. He came back with a glass and a bottle of mineral water. "Here, let me fill up yours as well," he said.

"Why are you so sure they were after her?" Arik asked.

"You said that they'd slashed her throat. It's the traditional execution style among fanatic Islamists. It's applied mostly to women. Had they come after you, they would've most likely used a gun."

"Good point, but not an absolute." Arik countered. "You ought to remember how Abu Musa killed the police officer. He slashed his throat; he's a fanatic Islamist as you know."

Jerry shrugged. "It was someone who had known her, or of her," he suggested. "It was someone who considered her a traitor, someone who would kill without thinking twice, enjoying it at the same time."

"I can only think of one — Abu Musa," concluded Arik. "He fits that description, but that's a long shot. I can't see the motive." He closed his eyes for a few seconds, inhaled deeply.

"We'll let the police investigate," said Jerry. "The truth will come out. In the meantime, you have one more fugitive inside your body. I don't know how long you'll be able to hide."

"Sometimes, I look forward to being captured," Arik said. "It's like when you dread and look forward to having a colonoscopy following one episode of hemorrhoid discomfort."

"I hope you don't really mean it," Jerry said. "You'd better take a sleeping pill; have a good night's snooze, because tomorrow you'll need all the energy you can muster." He turned around and left the apartment.

Chapter 64

January 12, 2003—Manhattan

Adnan Ashtari was talking on the phone when he opened the door for Arik. The safe apartment on 32nd Street looked almost identical to the one on 75th. Ashtari, in contrast, seemed different. He was casually dressed—a light blue polo shirt, tight blue jeans, white sneakers. The only unaffected element about his appearance was his Mount St. Helen-sized belly. Eruption seemed imminent.

Ashtari was all business. He listed material pick up details from fifteen different locations, at fifteen different times, using fifteen different passwords. It was all designed with utmost efficiency—an Iranian organization—German style. Altogether, Arik hoped to meet about twenty new friends—brothers in the *Jihad* for Allah.

"Where're you going to store all this material?" Ashtari wanted to know. Although they were separated by six feet of fake camaraderie, Arik could feel droplets of his spittle.

"That's my problem," Arik responded. "I'll manage."

Ashtari viewed the deal as a business transaction. "It'll cost you fifty thousand bucks," he insisted. "All paid in cash and in advance." He pressed his lips into a smirk.

Arik was astonished. He assumed Ashtari was an active participant. The business approach made him look more like an outsider. "I thought you were in it for Allah. Where're the ethics?" Arik said. He folded his arms around his chest anticipating a retreat.

"Ethics are as dead as is the Byzantine Empire," Ashtari replied. "We, Shiites, don't fight alongside Sunni infidels. We help, we assist, we facilitate, but we don't die together." He shrugged broadly. "This transaction is strictly business. Take it or leave it." He stood there, tossed a stony glare as though he was expecting Arik to fall in with his wishes.

"I'll be back," Arik said, "with the money." He paused, spread his palms, moved them through his uncombed long hair. "On one condition, though." He allowed a polite smile. "I must get in touch with Hamad Suleiman. You know where to find him. You'll have to arrange it."

Chapter 65

January 19, 2003—Manhattan

Jerry was first to notice Rachel's New York Times ad and decipher its significance. Blood rushed to his head, past his jaws, then tore ahead like a Tsunami storming a beach in Bangladesh. He immediately placed a red alert call to Dan Carmel, who turned around and called Jack Devon at the FBI headquarters in DC.

It was Sunday morning. Jack wasn't in the office; the operator transferred the call to Stanley who happened to be back in New York, guarding the homeland from his former office. Stanley wasn't aware of the history linking Rachel to Arik; nor did he know Dan Carmel. He wasn't in a hurry to comply with Dan's request for putting the *New York Times* out of Arik's sight. "He doesn't subscribe to the *Times*," he said. "He won't miss it even if I don't do a thing."

Still, Dan was restless. "Could you make sure?" he begged.

Stanley was noncommittal. "I have many other issues on my plate today. It's Sunday, most, if not all of my help is out of the office. I can't promise anything."

In the meantime, Rachel stepped out of her room in the Sheraton. She preferred the fresh air to the waiting, idling, nail biting across from the TV set. The chance of a lucky encounter with Arik in Midtown Manhattan was virtually nil. Still, hope filled her with energy; it was the only source of light, illuminating the dark wilderness of her wandering mind.

Following a five-hour aimless walk through the avenues and the streets, including a quick pretzel, New York style, and soda from a street vendor, she returned to the Sheraton. She was exhausted. Jet lag was only a small part of her predicament. The core crisis was the creeping despair that had been sneaking up on her from every direction.

The Sheraton concierge was polite but disappointing. Nobody had called her; not a soul had bothered to leave a message. *Arik has not seen my ad, not yet anyway. He may never see it, may never call me.* She was in a weeping mood.

Dan Carmel had told her that a very small number of FBI agents in charge of counter-terrorism knew about Arik, those working with Arik directly. He didn't provide names other than Jack Devon, warned her not to contact anyone for fear that Arik's true identity would find its way into the wrong hands, thus jeopardizing his mission and well being and even putting his life in danger.

Sitting across from the TV, she suddenly came up with an inspiration. She could try to find out who in the FBI was Arik's handler. She would stay in New York for one more day; if Arik didn't contact her, she would then travel to Washington, DC, and try to establish contact with the appropriate FBI personnel.

She looked out the window. Watching the snow flurries, she made up her mind. It was one of many roller coaster mood swings on its way up. There was no way she would just surrender. Declaring defeat was premature. Hope was young. The path to fulfillment was long, drown out, but she would ride it through, hop over the mines, then embrace triumph.

Her adversity in Bali had taught her a lifelong lesson—*no more a nice girl*. This time she was determined.

Chapter 66

January 19, 2003—Manhattan

Arik was walking North on Broadway. He changed pace, stopped at shop-windows, reversed directions, crossed the street numerous times, making sure he hadn't been followed. His visual field comprised nearly two blocks in every direction.

All at once, his breathing was brought to a standstill. A little over two blocks away, he thought he saw a young woman stepping into a yellow cab. *She looked like Rachel, but that vision, almost certainly, was a long distance hallucination. Rachel was dead;* he knew it. *Still, that woman bore a remarkable resemblance.* He wanted to get closer, take a better look. He began running toward the yellow cab. He ran across the street, this time his dash interfered with the traffic. A terrified driver in a gray BMW avoided running him over; he swerved, causing an accident. A police officer popped up out of nowhere, as Arik barely made it to the sidewalk. He came to life right in Arik's face, grabbed him, then forced him to the ground with the aim of ending his run.

The police officer was a big black man, uncompromising, potentially violent. Resisting arrest didn't seem like an option. He turned Arik over, handcuffed him, then called for assistance. *That's it,* Arik reflected. *I'm out and done with.* He actually felt somewhat relieved. "I'll have to take you in…" the officer didn't have a chance to complete his sentence.

The sound of shrieking tires meeting asphalt at extreme friction cut him off, terminated the incident. Four big, *Schwarzenegger-* type musclemen jumped out of a black van, two of them grabbed the police officer, who was overwhelmed by the sudden bewildering assault; two of them grabbed Arik and pushed him into the van. Seconds later, they were all on their way to Downtown Manhattan.

Arik was alarmed. "Who are you?" he gawked at the ones sitting on both of his sides.

"FBI," the Irish type to the right said. "Agent Stanley Kramer wants to talk to you."

They continued moving toward Federal Plaza where Stanley's provisional office was located.

"Can you guys remove my cuffs?" Arik asked. He felt at ease following the introduction.

"Later," the Irish type said.

"Gee, this could be really comical if it weren't happening to me," Arik said.

Neither one of the two found it amusing; they had nothing interesting to add. They rode in silence the rest of way.

• • •

Stanley felt jumpy, a nuclear reactor of nervous energy, his default disposition. He wasn't listening; he was lecturing. "And by the way," he added as an afterthought, "Just to let you know, I've talked to Agent Moses from the Dearborn field office. You're off the hook for the murder of your friend Hilga." Stanley beamed; he felt self-content as if *Santa* had just delivered his favorite toy. "DNA analysis of blood found on an alarm clock, on the bed sheets, on the female victim, on and inside her fingernails, proves without doubt that Abu Musa was the killer." He paused. "We also proved that he..."

"He killed Fatima, didn't he?" Arik finished the thought.

Stanley nodded.

Arik didn't smile. He stood there, silent, digesting what he'd already known. He didn't want to discuss that subject with Stanley. It was a private matter. He moved on to the business at hand, as if he didn't care for the news. He outlined the understanding he'd reached with Adnan Ashtari. "I need fifty-thousand in green cash. There's a good chance we're on the verge of forcing some major rats out of their holes," he wrapped it up.

"Have you downloaded your Trojan horse software into any of your *new comrades'* mobile phones?" The trace of a smile appeared at the corner of his mouth.

Arik did not realize that Stanley had any knowledge of his invention. "You know about it?" his astonishment was apparent.

"There are very few secrets the US and the Israeli intelligence communities do not share," Stanley said, his smirk fading away. "We are in the process of trading a squadron of Phantom jets in return for your spying application, the second release; the one due in three months, which includes the entire array of your specified goodies even when the power of the son-of-a-bitch's telephone is off."

"Okay," Arik granted. "There's still one problem, though."

"What is that?" Stanley's expression turned grim.

"None of my *new amigos* has a *Bluetooth*-capable phone. They don't have the latest models. I couldn't download my application into any of their phones." He paused, then added as an afterthought. "You should make the latest models available to these thugs at bargain basement prices, just as Israel has done in the Palestinian territories."

Stanley nodded. "How did you become so clever?" He raised his hand, implying, *I'm not as dumb as you think*, then said. "Here's something you could use." He reached inside his desk, pulled an attractive Italian diver's watch, then handed it over to Arik. "Wear it whenever you want us to know your location," he said, then smiled conspiratorially. "You can draw a map with this baby, connect the dots, then pluck those bastards off the tree to which they hang on, and ship them to daddy." He leaned back in his executive chair, looking triumphant; he'd finally regained traction. Arik was about to lead him into the Promised Land.

Chapter 67

January 19, 2003—Brooklyn, New York

The Pope announced that he intended to visit New York during the first full week in February. He would conduct Mass in *St. Patrick's Cathedral* on February 9, 2003. Abu Musa was watching the reports with great interest. He was craving for the opportunity. The Pope helped him settle on the date for Allah's revenge. *The cathedral will be packed, the cameras will be rolling, the infidels will be celebrating, the world will be watching.* It was perfect.

As he was watching and contemplating, CNN broke the news. "A Broadway kidnapping in broad daylight involving an unknown felon who had triggered a car accident, before being arraigned by a police officer, who had become the subject of an assault by the kidnappers, who in turn, disappeared in a black van." The video was taken by someone with a low-resolution cell phone camera. It captured Arik's face including two of the FBI assault team members, the van's license plate, and the police officer's bewildered expression.

Three minutes into the broadcast—a news bulletin. "It has just been reported that the kidnappers' van was a previously stolen vehicle. We still don't know who that man was, who those assaulting the police officer were, and why those perpetrators came to that man's rescue. Still, many questions remain unanswered."

Abu Musa and Ismail were watching in the living room of their safe house as the story broke. Abu Musa enjoyed the scene. He turned to Ismail. "Those stupid Americans," he said mockingly, "they are all below average." Then, all at once, the camera zoomed on Arik's face. It stayed on it for over five seconds. That was plenty. Abu Musa grew agitated; he thought he recognized Qassem; moreover, as he kept on watching, his face turned dimmer. Evil thoughts crept into his criminal mind. He turned to Ismail. "Qassem's dangerous. He has his own people; they guard him tightly. They're well organized," he concluded. "He doesn't like my plans; he will spill the beans. I knew I had to kill him in Dearborn when I had the chance." He paused, took a deep breath, then nodded as if he'd just won an argument with himself. "He turned to Ismail. "Tell our brothers in the other room to come in here. I have an important announcement."

Ismail got up, walked to the other room where Dr. Radwan and Mustafa were staying. In less than a minute, all four terrorists were congregated in the living room. Discussion was overflowing with excitement. They set the date as February 9, 2003, Papal visit day. They'd steal a van, fill it with explosives, recruit and train two suicide bombers, one retarded man from the Bronx, the other—Ismail's daughter, Hajar. Dr. Radwan would be responsible for acquiring suicide belts supplied by Suleiman's proxies, the Iranians. Ismail would be in charge of stealing the van, hiding it in the garage of a New Jersey safe house. Dr. Radwan would be responsible for converting the van into a bomb on wheels, fixing the suicide belts, stuff them with explosives, compliments of the Iranians. Mahmud Ismail would drive the van into the panic-stricken crowd following the bombing inside the Cathedral, then blow it up for maximum effect. Abu Musa would coordinate that part.

It was time to get moving. Abu Musa was satisfied. His legacy would forever be associated with the thrashing of the evil infidels and their unholy Pope. They'll learn their lesson. His ticket to paradise would be secured. Seventy-two virgins would be waiting in anticipation of his coming, Allah will be proud.

Chapter 68

January 19-20, 2003—Manhattan, Washington, DC

In her hotel room, Rachel was watching the CNN report. She didn't pay much attention to the pictures. Her mind was wandering in a dark wasteland. She wasn't focusing. Suddenly—a double-take. *The bearded man on TV, Arik, oh my God.* She was certain it was he. She wanted to take a better look at the picture, but the broadcast continued. The topic changed. She was unable to rewind.

She rushed downstairs to the reception area, but her efforts to locate a taped recording of the broadcast turned fruitless. There was no way she could watch the scene again, take another look. She went back to her room, sank into the bed, then she buried herself under the blanket and let out her frustration in silent tears.

The next day, she took the early Amtrak from Penn Station and arrived at DC in mid morning. The FBI building on Pennsylvania Avenue was closed to visitors who had no appointments, but Rachel was insistent. The guard, a chubby chap with a glowing, sort of horsey face, was unsympathetic. "Mr. Devon is not expecting you," he claimed after checking with Jenny. "He's at a meeting." Except, following her Bali nightmare, Rachel had changed. She was no longer the nice girl who would back down after a single blow, especially one coming from such a dolt. *He is so dense,* she mused. *Light would bend around him.* She turned away, then back to the guard with a fresh strategy.

"There's an imminent terrorist attack coming," she was pleading. "I must talk to Mr. Devon if you only let him know."

The guard leaned back in his chair; his body language said it all. He was looking forward to the game. "Okay," he said. It seemed as though he softened up; he called Jenny again. Following a brief clarification, *Horsey Face* turned back to Rachel, filled out the routine registration form, then told her to wait. Jenny would come down to pick her up.

Jenny was polite. "Mr. Devon's in a meeting," she said. "How can I help you?"

Rachel had the time; she could wait. "I want to talk to him about Arik," she paused. "It's extremely vital."

"Who's Arik?" Jenny asked.

"Mr. Devon knows. I'm sure he would make time for me once he knows what I'm here for." Her voice trailed off.

"I'll see what I can do," Jenny said. She had that kind of down-to-earth appearance, a jutting jaw with vertical contours running down through her upper lip. In her twenties, she must have been a Lucy Liu look alike, but with time, her face had hardened a bit. "Follow me," she said to Rachel, then headed for the conference room down the long hallway. Jenny rapped on the door, opened it slightly, exchanged a few words with someone inside, then a few seconds later she turned to Rachel. "You may come in. Jack Devon's ready for you."

Rachel stood at the door. It was a gigantic room. An entire Bedouin tribe could live there comfortably. Only three people were sitting around an outsized mahogany desk built with rounded corners, a fact that contributed to the perceived enormity of the room.

The three shifted their gaze. They broke off whatever they were doing, scrutinized the newcomer with part curiosity, part hostility. Rachel swallowed hard, inhaled deeply, then approached the three. "I'm Rachel Levy," she said. "I'm Arik's fiancé. I know you're handling him. I want to see him."

"Wait a minute," Jack Devon interrupted her. He seemed dumbfounded. He looked like he'd just swallowed a spicy turtle. "I'm Jack Devon. I know nothing about what's his name. Oh yeah…Arik…I guess." He rose. "I suggest that your assertions are erroneous, I'm sorry. I can't help you." He had this habit of speaking in a fastidious way, especially when he got mad.

Rachel didn't budge. "You have a choice," she said. A trickle of sweat ran down the inside of her top from her armpit to her waist, but she was determined. She gathered all the nerve she could muster, tried to project a daring disposition. "So you want to play *Let's Make a Deal.*" She waited for a counter offer; it failed to turn up. The three of them were watching her in disbelief. They didn't discern what she was up to. She clarified." Behind door number one, you have a sure thing, a fulfillment of my request, of my pleading, which you have the power to make happen. In contrast, there's a surprise behind door number two. You want a hint?"

Jack Devon nodded. He froze in place wondering what she had in store. The other two stared at him awaiting a response.

Rachel kept going. "The *New York Times, the Washington Post,* and the rest of the media will be delighted to have my story run on their first page," she said. "You can imagine the headlines..." She paused for effect, then carried on. "So, you've got yourself a choice; I recommend you play door number one."

"No! No deal," Jack Devon declared, his voice climbing to a crescendo . He was certain that Rachel had been bluffing. *She would never act as irresponsibly as she had claimed, exposing Arik to the danger of being compromised in the eyes of his Jihadist comrades. Had they known his true identity, he wouldn't have lasted until lunch.* "Be careful," Devon said. "I have an attitude and I know how to use it. I suggest you get out of here before we get you arrested for trespassing." He took a moment to think, then added. "And if you dare step through door number two, you'll risk everything that's dear to you, including your own self. So, you may get out of here on your own two feet, or you may be carried away by building security." He paused, a trace of a smirk appeared at the corner of his mouth. "You have a choice," he said. "In this case, I recommend the door to this building, whatever number it is in your book."

Rachel left, realizing that she had been outmaneuvered. Jenny met her at the door. "Wait here," Jenny said. She opened the door to the conference room to let Devon know that she would be escorting Rachel out of the building. "Get this woman tailed," Jack Devon whispered collusively. "I suspect she's headed for New York. Inform the NYPD as well. I want to know to whom she talks, who tries to get through to her, where she goes. She's a troublemaker. We must do everything we can to stop her and help her get out of the country to where she would live in peace." He flicked his hand as if he were a Russian Tsar ordering the execution of an arugula eating Communist.

Chapter 69

January 21, 2003—Manhattan, New York

Arik awoke Tuesday morning at 4 a.m., unable to eat or think. An old filling in tooth number 31, had broken and had left behind a bottomless cavity, stretching all the way to Australia. He couldn't take it any longer. It was a matter of Life on Earth or hell in Allah's paradise next to his cousins' martyrs. He favored Earth. He got up, shaved his beard, his mustache, his head. He looked so different; he didn't even feel related to the fellow in the mirror. He got dressed, gulped down five aspirins with three tall glasses of water, then went back to bed. He couldn't fall asleep. It was 6:40 when he got up. At eight, he was already in Chinatown knocking on Dr. Chin's clinic door. He was third in line. Sitting in the waiting room, getting used to the fishy odor wafting in from the grocery next-door, he tried to pass the time, reading some dated magazines. The only English language paper he could chance upon was a two-month-old *Newsweek*; the rest included Chinese magazines, Chinese booklets, outdated Chinese newspapers.

He was next in line when he noticed sections of the previous Sunday's *New York Times* under one of the seats in the waiting area. The paper was old news on Tuesday morning, but at that moment, it felt like sunshine in the midst of a thunderstorm. He picked it up, disregarding the oil stains. It smelled like a two-day-old sushi. *It must have been used as a lunch wrapper,* he concluded, except it wasn't that much worse than the odor enveloping the dental office area. *Get used to it, and you start thinking its Vietnamese deodorant,* he reflected.

Arik didn't have much spare time; it was his turn on the torture chair, letting the old, white apron-wearing nick, pound on his teeth.

Sitting down, he turned a page, glanced at the paper before letting it hang around, reserved for future appraisal. The dentist was getting ready in the next room; the dental assistant, a young woman with a cute high-pitch lilt, and a sweet Chinese drawl that Arik could hardly get a handle on, was busy priming the venue for her boss, the dental emperor, who would step in, perform his magic in no more than a Chinese minute.

Arik's eyes hit upon the full-page advertisement. He wouldn't normally notice those ads, but the names — Rachel and Arik, and Rachel's picture — bundled within a single page, no matter how stinky, blew his mind. After reading and digesting the information, he was swept by a sudden emotion that caused his throat to tighten. His eyes were flooded with blazes of alternating black and white dots. He had thought that Rachel was dead, but the ad she'd placed in the Sunday paper made him wonder. *Was this my Rachel? Was she here in New York looking for me? Am I dreaming? Am I really in this dental clinic, having a Chinese prince of darkness about to hover over my head?*

Dr. Chin came in. Arik wanted to skip the Novocain. He wanted to feel pain; he wanted to make sure his brain wasn't damaged, that he wasn't hallucinating, that the light in the midst of the thunderstorm wasn't just a high-voltage lightning strike.

He was done forty-five minutes later. The pain he'd endured throughout the procedure helped slow down his heart rate, put the brakes on his out-of-control, crazy, speeding train of thought; it interfered with his sense of caution. He paid the bill, thanked the doctor, then rushed out to the nearest subway station, a first for him, where he caught the next train going up to the Sheraton.

The brunette receptionist was polite. "Rachel Levy checked out this morning," she said. "No. She left no forwarding address, but I remember her." She looked up searching the corner of the ceiling, then back at her computer, at Arik, at the computer, followed by — "Let me go inside and check further," she said. "Wait here."

Arik waited. Three minutes went by; the receptionist didn't come back. He left the counter, began wondering around the various attractions inside the hotel. Seven more minutes went by; he began walking toward the reception area when he noticed four police officers crowding the counter. They were talking to his blonde receptionist. Her gestures suggested that she was almost certainly offering them a description of his likeness.

An ambush, he concluded. He was no longer certain. *Was it Rachel? Had she placed the ad in the New York Times?* He was no longer convinced she was alive. It didn't make any sense. Nevertheless, it was time to split, to vanish, but he couldn't just walk out, pass by those police officers undetected. They had his description.

Arik took the elevator to the eleventh floor and walked around; all doors were closed. He took the stairs down to the ninth floor. A housekeeper was busy vacuuming in room *927*. He went in, greeted her warmly; she smiled back assuming he was the honored guest. He opened the closet; it was filled with clothes, exclusively Ladies'. He turned to the housekeeper, asked her to leave, come back later; he needed privacy. Back at the closet, he grabbed a red scarf, a red hat, a red shirt and a white blazer. He entered the bathroom, where he found lipstick. He applied it on his lips, then admired himself in the mirror. He turned, removed the plastic bag from the trashcan, took off his shirt and blue sweater, stuffed them inside the bag, then dressed himself with the woman's garments. The hat and scarf covered a decent part of his shaven head. The blazer wasn't his size, short in length, wide in the front, fit for a healthy bosom. Still, it could serve as a temporary cover, a Halloween costume. He walked back to the bedroom, found an empty black carryon, placed the bag with his clothes inside, picked it up and left the room. Minutes later, he was out on the street.

Back in his safe house, Arik was priming himself for a rendezvous with destiny. Now that his new look was celebrated by the NYPD, he felt he had to change. Jerry had obtained some used Halloween items. A professionally trimmed beard and mustache that Arik could stick on his shaven-face, artificial eyebrows and a toupee, all dyed Irish red, blazing, fake, but adequate, his darker skin notwithstanding. He wore his new watch, called his friendly Iranian driver, set up an appointment for the next morning at 6 a.m., then followed it by a call to Stanley.

• • •

Following her encounter with the Jack Devon from the FBI, Rachel grew desperate. She went back to the Sheraton in New York, not realizing she was under intense surveillance. *Arik wasn't going to contact her*, she concluded, just as Arik was waiting down at the lobby, asking for her. She was getting bored and frustrated.

She would stay in New York for two more weeks. Then if Arik didn't call , she would go back home to Israel and weep.

Chapter 70

January 22, 2003—New York, New Jersey

The Iranian driver picked him up at the 172nd Street and Broadway intersection. This time, two more passengers were seated inside; one in the front, next to the driver, whose monkey face was proof that evolution could go in reverse, and another one in the backseat, an older fellow with dark sunglasses, whose acne resembled moon craters covered by a three-day-old stubble. Arik stepped inside, found a seat in the back next to the older person, who turned toward him immediately and began checking him out. He patted him up and down, both sides of his rib cage, moved down to his waist, then his back. Arik felt uncomfortable. He understood the purpose of the scrutiny, but the garlic breath was a bit too much for him to endure.

"Hey, I'm clean," Arik protested. He made an effort to move away. "You can check me out later when we step out, just to make sure."

Moon Crater was unmoved. He stared at Arik's watch for a short minute. It seemed like he was about to say something, react, but then switched and turned his attention to Arik's thighs, checking them as well for any concealed weapon. He asked Arik to remove the cell phone and the keys he kept in his pocket. He turned off the phone, then returned it and the keys. "He's clean," he announced following his inspection. He then picked up a black scarf, tied it around Arik's head, blindfolding him as a further precautionary measure.

They were now driving north. Although he was blindfolded, Arik could sense and calculate the general direction in which they were travelling. No one was speaking.

Down at Manhattan Federal Plaza, inside the FBI New York Field Office, Stanley was watching the monitor, where a video stream — fed by the drone homing in on Arik's GPS transmitter — was being displayed. The first time he could make out the details of the black SUV in which Arik was riding, happened to be when it traversed the upper level of the George Washington Bridge on its way to New Jersey. The tall buildings in the city were a major hindrance to zeroing in on a moving target.

Stanley turned to his fellow agent from New York, Sam Gordon, who was watching the same video display. "Thank God we're going to New Jersey," he said, flashing a genuine, appreciative smile. "Now we can see them in the open space."

The SUV continued to move down the NJ Turnpike. They stopped at the tollbooth, picked up a ticket before proceeding. Arik had a perfect idea of where they were and in what direction they were heading. About twenty minutes later, the SUV got off at Exit 13 toward Elizabeth. They traveled through residential neighborhoods before coming to a full stop inside a garage, attached to a single family home.

Moon Crater untied the headscarf, let Arik adjust his eyes to the dim light inside the SUV, before stepping out and walking into the house. The driver stayed in the car while *Monkey Face* led the way to the living room. They were all standing in the middle of the room, when the person they had come to visit turned up.

Dr. Radwan stepped in, as Arik watched in disbelief. "You?" he said. "What're you doing in here?"

"I live here now," Dr. Radwan said with a grin. "And by the way, it was you who nominated me back in Dearborn. I'm working with Suleiman. I'm responsible for logistics. Suleiman works with these guys." Dr. Radwan pointed at *Monkey Face* and *Moon Crater*. "They cover all aspects. You want methylphosphonic difluoride, they supply it; you want isopropyl alcohol and isopropylamine solution or OPA, they bring it over; you want binary systems, detonators, anything else helpful in putting together WMDs — you name it, they deliver."

"Do you have everything I need here?" Arik asked.

"Not yet," Dr. Radwan said. "Let's talk about your requirements; once I understand it all, I'll gather the material and place it in storage, at a place of your choosing."

Arik turned to *Monkey Face* and *Moon Crater*, asked them to wait in another room while he and Dr. Radwan finalized the purchase order. It didn't take too long.

"Are you still with Abu Musa?" Arik asked as soon as they firmed up the details.

"Yes," Dr. Radwan said. "Our plan is complete."

"Where is he?"

"I don't have his new address," Dr. Radwan said. "Since last week, we have split. He keeps his whereabouts very hush-hush, changes his SIM card on a daily basis; we only speak in code."

"Are those Iranians helpful?" Arik asked.

"They are," Dr. Radwan said. "We'll be able to pull it off thanks to those guys." He fixed his gaze at Arik with fevered intensity. "In fact, I'll need your help," he added.

"I'll be happy to," Arik said.

"You're good at detonators," he said. "I'd like you to assemble a hand triggered one for a car bomb, and another couple, remotely controlled, for the suicide belts."

"No problem," Arik said. "Do you use the standard explosives?"

Dr. Radwan nodded, smiled conspiratorially. "That and *Sarin* gas." He waited for Arik to react, but poker-faced Arik didn't surrender his thoughts. "The Iranians provided us with several different binary systems and the soup that goes in each of the compartments. The detonator switch you construct will have to be a two-phase design. The first phase will trigger a minor burst that will join the contents of the binary system, breaking the partition wall, let the chemistry do its magic, and engender *Sarin*. The second phase will trigger the major blast. In addition to causing conventional damage, it will help spread the *Sarin* over a greater distance."

"No problem," Arik pledged. "I'll take care of it."

"I need it by the end of the week," Dr. Radwan said, expecting a pushback.

I thought you were going to use it on Easter," Arik said.

"Sooner," Dr. Radwan pulled a cigarette from his pocket, lit it, took a long drag, then exhaled through his nostrils.

"When are you going to pull the trigger?" Arik asked.

"On Easter, But we need it sooner. There is a great deal of preparation. We can't wait till the last moment." He wrapped it up after a short hesitation. Dr. Radwan didn't reveal the true date to Arik who, at that point, had not been integrated into the implementation of the plan. Abu Musa had made it clear. "None other than those who actively participate in the execution of the *Great Revenge* should be privy to the information. The operational details of the *Great Revenge* are to be kept top secret, discussed only among those who absolutely need to know."

Reading Dr. Radwan's apprehensive twitch, Arik realized that he'd been tossed out of the loop. He took off his watch. "I'm allergic to this one, it gives me an itch," he said, scratching the spot on his hand where the watch had been. "I'm going to throw it away unless you…" He paused. He didn't say it. He let Dr. Radwan complete the thought.

Dr. Radwan stared at the watch. "A nice one," he said. "He picked it up, examined it. "I like it," he added, implying," *I'd love to have it if it bothers you.*"

Arik watched him; he recognized the transparent gesture, then nodded in approval. "It's yours if you want it," Arik confirmed. "It's a lucky one, got it as a gift from a holy man. Make sure you wear it to important events if you want to be blessed."

Chapter 71

January 22—February 3, 2003

Dr. Radwan loved his new watch. He had no idea that his hot little toy was a Trojan horse, facilitating the spread of Stanley's fishnet around the Iranian terror network. The GPS transmitter planted inside the little gadget was like a map-drawing instrument. Stanley too, loved the watch. He loved adding up dots to his crowded map whenever Dr. Radwan was making a stop. On those occasions, he felt like a New Orleans chef enhancing an already delicious meal, adding ingredients, taking it up a notch by pouring *Chateau Petrus en Magnums* into an aroma-emitting dish.

Following a weeklong of close surveillance, where the dots on the New York, Long Island, and the New Jersey scenes grew more crowded by the hour, the lull in activity was becoming apparent. Hardly any new dots were appended; any fresh discoveries proved ineffective. The meal was ready to be served.

Arik's small storage facility on Route 17 in Paramus, New Jersey, was packed to the brim with materiel and tools, all set for final assembly preceding the big — *Pufff*. There was no reason to wait any longer, Stanley concluded.

· · ·

Jack Devon wanted no publicity when arrests were made. "We've got to keep the Media out of this," he insisted. "Publicity will make the whole thing grow into an international scandal; some hotheads in Congress and in the Administration will demand retaliation on a massive scale against Iran. We don't want to force the President's hand. Let him make the decision as to how to handle publicity without the added public pressure for speedy revenge."

Stanley looked disappointed. He was looking forward to becoming a national hero, but his boss had made him shelve that thought. It was time for quiet action, and he was a good soldier. As soon as his meeting with Jack was over, he travelled back to New York and began making final preparations for the great harvest. There were nine separate targets, all fit within a common but loosely tied thread. Raids had to be carried out simultaneously; surprise was key. It had to be done during the day, where actors and accomplices could be snatched while seeing to their dirty work.

Monday, February 3, 2003 was chosen as D-Day. An army of FBI agents accompanied by police SWAT teams, equipped with automatic weapons, overran targets marked for cleanup in New York, Long Island, and New Jersey. Altogether they arrested thirty two individuals, most were illegal immigrants; more than half were Lebanese Shiites, *Hezbollah* agents; two terrorists were British citizens of Pakistani origin; three were Black Muslims from Chicago; the rest, including *Monkey Face* and *Moon Crater*, were Iranian nationals holding Green Cards. Adnan Ashtari and his driver were arrested in a separate raid on Ashtari's legal residence, taken to the airport, then put on a plane on route to Beirut, Lebanon. The operation was a resounding success, a gold mine with more gold than *King Solomon's*.

Dr. Radwan was not among those arrested in the raid. Stanley let him roam free for now. Dr. Radwan served as his guided missile. Stanley would pilot him toward the rest of the terrorists. By Stanley's calculations, there was still time before Abu Musa was to pull the trigger. Easter was more than two months away.

Notwithstanding measures taken by Stanley, word got out to the *New York Daily*. The titanic size headline covered the entire front page, left no room for particulars; those were really lacking, adding to the mystery surrounding the event.

Abu Musa got wind of the story as he was working on the final details of his project. Mahmud Ismail, the only person sharing his hideout, seemed edgy, perhaps overcaffeinated, after reading the paper that he'd bought minutes earlier. He began developing second thoughts. "These pigs have arrested people we've done business with," he said, his nervous tension showing. "They may talk; they may sabotage our plans."

Abu Musa stared at his colleague in disgust; his eyes narrowed; his face projected aggression fitting a hungry carnivore in quest of prey. "The Iranians don't have the slightest knowledge of our plan. They only know that they've provided the means for launching it," he said, "unless they've got hold of Dr. Radwan by now," he added a conclusion. "Dr. Radwan was dealing with these Shiites idiots throughout last week. He may be compromised now, but I'm certain of one thing. As of this afternoon, he's been safe and still on the loose."

Ismail wasn't satisfied. "Dr. Radwan met with Qassem more than a week ago," he said as an afterthought. "He may know how to get in touch with Qassem." He closed his eyes for a second, inhaled deeply.

"That's it," Abu Musa, suddenly energized, jumped up as if he'd just rediscovered the first law of thermodynamics. He stole an abrupt mouthful of air, let out a hiccup, shot an obscenity prevalent in Arabic, then turned and approached Ismail. "That's it," he announced. "That's it!" He leaned over close until his face nearly touched Ismail's; he placed his hands on top of his colleague's shoulders. "Who do you think led these FBI pigs into the heart of the Iranian operations?" he asked. He didn't wait for an answer. "I don't believe in coincidences," he said. "There was a mole; it happened shortly after Qassem became involved with these guys." He removed his hands from Ismail's shoulders, moved away, then approached the window. "We have to find Qassem and kill him. We have to lay a trap for him, make him surface without his bodyguards. Once caught, we send him to burn in Hell. No mercy for traitors."

Chapter 72

February 4, 2003

Following the raid on the Iranian network, Dr. Radwan felt insecure. He changed his address, then contacted Abu Musa, expressed his anxiety, and suggested a postponement of the cathedral bombing to a later date. "The Papal visit was fast approaching, and the Americans might have gotten wind of the imminent terror attack on their favorite cathedral."

Abu Musa quickly overruled Radwan's proposal. He had different ideas. He wanted to pull Arik into his orbit, then assassinate him amid all the brouhaha. "Does Qassem have knowledge of the date and time of our holy mission?" Abu Musa asked Dr. Radwan.

"No," Radwan said. "As a matter of fact, I've already misled him. He thinks it's to take place on Easter, rather than next Sunday, February 9."

"Excellent, Allah be praised." Abu Musa jumped out of his seat. He felt as if Allah had just blessed him, had given him the thumbs up. He turned to Dr. Radwan. "You tell Qassem that I need his help. He must get involved. Ask him to join in with the plan, but keep up the deception at the same time. Keep reinforcing the fake Easter date." Abu Musa paused. His inspiration gathered momentum. "Tell Qassem that we want him to be our real-time scout, controlling and directing the van to its destination, remotely controlling the trigger of the suicide belts, then blowing them up five minutes after the suicide bombers make their way into the cathedral. Tell Qassem that he will be acting as a maestro, conducting a Godly symphony."

Abu Musa exhaled, made it sound as if he were choking on poison gas, then pressed on. "Are you listening?"

Dr. Radwan acknowledged. "I've got it."

"But here is one essential detail," Abu Musa continued. He reached inside his soul and dug out his personal vendetta. "Qassem is a spy; he must die," he announced. "I want to set him up on our *Great Revenge* holy day. You'll tell him that the Papal visit to *St. Patrick's* on February 9 is merely a rehearsal and a training day before Easter, the "real" date, real is in quotes, Qassem should stay at a secure observation post—the intersection of 5th Avenue and 53rd Street. He should study the security arrangements around the cathedral on a distinct day like Easter. The conditions surrounding the Papal visit could provide him with a first-rate practice opportunity. This way, he would learn how to manipulate the outdoor van explosion, time it to the expected stampede that will result following the suicide bombing inside the cathedral. He will practice calling in the outfitted Ismail, the would be suicide driver-bomber, on his cell phone, and direct him into the eye of the storm, before breaking away from the scene into the safety of the crowded streets.

Abu Musa conveniently failed to mention one more crucial component of his contemptuous, dastardly plan. Qassem's role would be superfluous. It would serve merely as a set up. Immediately following Qassem's call to Ismail, while Qassem was still lingering, open to the elements in that particular street corner, a passer-by on a bicycle—young Mustafa—would be rushing toward him, knifing him down, ending his miserable life before he got his chance to fulfill his cowardly betrayal.

Chapter 73

February 9, 2003

Arik got out of bed at 4:30 in the morning. He was unable to sleep through the night. It was Sunday, the day of the Papal visit to *St. Patrick's Cathedral*, the day of the *Great Revenge*, a fact unbeknownst to him. Still, Arik found Dr. Radwan's insistence—having him rehearse his role on 5th Avenue and 53rd Street—rather suspicious. Radwan was not entirely convincing; his demeanor betrayed him; *something else is cooking. There is more to it than a mere rehearsal,* Arik mused.

During the five days preceding that critical Sunday, Arik had worked with Dr. Radwan on the underpinnings of the event. He rigged up wireless detonator-switching systems, as per Dr. Radwan's specifications. Dr. Radwan made Arik demonstrate them in his presence, by the use of simulation, short of the actual chemicals or explosives, guaranteeing their performance. Arik could, in no way, design faulty systems and then receive Dr. Radwan's seal of approval. Still, Arik managed to embed a secret code inside the car bomb detonator system that, if triggered from a short, *Bluetooth* range, would permanently disable the bomb in Ismail's van.

Dr. Radwan was to prepare Ismail's stolen van, and convert it into a huge bomb on wheels, timed to blow up at the perfect moment, when triggered by Ismail's mobile phone.

Everything was in place, ready for the green light. At that point, Arik insisted on seeing Ismail in person. He claimed that Ismail required training; Ismail's newly acquired *Bluetooth*-capable mobile phone required a minor reconfiguration to enable it as a triggering device.

Ismail was eager to learn. During their meeting, Arik had planted in Ismail's phone the unique Trojan horse technology he'd developed in the Israeli military, allowing him, through his mobile, to control Ismail's mobile phone remotely, after Ismail had powered it on. This capability let Arik listen in on Ismail's incoming and outgoing calls, view Ismail's phone directory, pinpoint Ismail's location, and make regular and *Bluetooth* calls out of Ismail's phone without leaving a trace and without Ismail's knowledge.

Arik's plan was simple. At the first opportunity, after Ismail connected the detonator to the bomb, Arik would issue a remote command through Ismail's phone, disabling the bomb in Ismail's van, He would then continue to monitor Ismail's movements and direct the FBI to its unsuspecting target. Unexpectedly, however, during the days preceding the *Great Revenge*, Ismail did not turn on his new phone; he merely kept using his older one when communicating. He dedicated the new phone solely for that particular deadly application; Arik had no way to disable the bomb remotely. *There is still time,* he pondered. *An opportunity will pop up between now and Easter.*

Arik was told that on that critical Easter date Abu Musa was to be Commander in Chief who would usher in the *Great Revenge*. He would direct the entire operation from his command and control hidey-hole, of which none of the key players, other than Ismail, had details. His foot soldiers would do the work—kill and be killed in the name of Allah. Mahmud Ismail would drive the explosives-filled van from New Jersey, would cross to Manhattan, then circle the streets around the cathedral and wait for Qassem's final go-ahead. Dr. Radwan would collect the suicide bombers at a location unknown to Arik, drive them to the cathedral, drop them off one block away, where Qassem would spot them and then send them to their heavenly mission. The plan called for radio silence between Qassem and Dr. Radwan during the operation. As a precaution, however, Arik was provided with Dr. Radwan's cell phone number of the Papal visit—rehearsal day. Dr. Radwan had been in the habit of switching SIMs on a daily basis for security reasons.

One more change, introduced by Abu Musa, in an attempt to seize control out of Qassem's hands, had Dr. Radwan replace the remotely controlled two-phased switches by mechanical devices under the direct control of the suicide bombers. Arik had no knowledge of the changes.

• • •

Stanley was calm. He was not worried about the imminent terror attack. Arik had let him in on the Easter date. Stanley was certain that Arik could preempt the holy warriors, upset their plans and extinguish their sick dreams before they seized their chance to launch their deadly act. Easter was still a long way away.

The NYPD was mobilized in order to secure the Papal visit. Its role was confined to managing traffic. Nevertheless, the NYPD was primed and ready for any emergency, just in case. Earlier in the week, Stanley had had AT&T-Wireless bug Dr. Radwan's access line of the day, which Arik had provided. The agreement with AT&T had included forwarding all incoming and outgoing calls from and to Dr. Radwan's phone to Stanley's FBI team, which included an Arabic speaking fellow agent.

• • •

It was minutes after six in the morning, when Arik's cell phone issued a high-pitched alert. Ismail had finally turned on his new *Bluetooth*-equipped mobile phone. He placed a call to a public phone in upper Manhattan. Abu Musa picked up. Arik was listening in. "I'm getting ready," Ismail announced. I've prayed to Allah. He is waiting for me. I'll meet Him later today. My seventy-two virgins are prepared for my arrival in heaven. *Allahu Akbar!*"

"*Allahu Akbar!*" Abu Musa echoed. "*Inshallah* (God willing), Today is the *Great Revenge* day."

Ismail took a few more seconds before turning off his phone.

Arik was stunned by the revelation but didn't lose his composure. At first, he attempted to use the opportunity to disable the car bomb, but to his frustration, Ismail was farther away from the van, too far for *Bluetooth* to be effective. The remote disabling of the bomb via Ismail's phone turned out to be unattainable at that moment.

Arik placed a call to Stanley, He wanted to alert the FBI to the budding emergency, but the agent did not answer his phone and his voice mailbox was packed to its limits. There was no room for new messages. In his adrenaline rush, Arik called Jerry for help. He briefed Jerry on the emerging attack. "I can't get a hold of Stanley," he roared. "Do your best to find and alert him, and get your ass and your troops in place around the cathedral, just in case the FBI is slow to act." He then, calmed himself down, walked to the bedroom, preparing for the evolving, potentially action-packed day.

Following his morning coffee, Arik couldn't help but shift his thoughts to the future, to life beyond his undercover work, beyond a mission he'd taken reluctantly, which was about to climax in a breathtaking crescendo. It was the proper time to fold, to go back to Israel, to live a normal life. *But life without Rachel wouldn't be normal,* he remembered. And then it struck him.

Rachel could be alive...

The thought that Rachel could've been for real, and, of all places, in the same city where he was presently residing, was mindboggling. He had no way of contacting her directly, but the mere idea was intriguing.

It was still dark outside when he made the call to Israel. He was mad at himself for not thinking of that move earlier. But then he realized that he'd never had any good reason to do it; she was dead — that was what he believed. Now, however, he had doubts. *Is she really dead? Was I misled by Dan Carmel?* He was done around here. His mission would be accomplished in a few hours. In his mind, he was already back home with family and true friends. He had to find out. *Is Rachel alive? Was she looking for me?*

It was noontime in Israel. Rachel's father answered the phone. "Hello."

Arik recognized the voice. He felt tense. He placed the call through a signal equalizer, adding bass and subtracting treble frequencies. He sounded like a talking elephant. "May I speak to Rachel?" he asked in Hebrew.

"Who's this?" her father asked.

"A friend of hers," he said. "My name's David. I understand she's in the US, I'd like to touch base with her," he added.

"I'm sorry, she's moving around. I don't have her contact number in the US," her father said. He seemed cautious. *Whether or not he had knowledge of her phone number, he refused to divulge it to a stranger*, Arik figured. *He did acknowledge, implicitly, however, that Rachel was alive and in the US.* Arik realized, for the first time, that after all, the *New York Times* ad might not have been fake. *Rachel did stay at the Sheraton. She came to New York to find me; I even spotted her near the Sheraton. She's still my girl.*

She was on her way back to Israel when Arik called her parents. They missed one another yet again.

Chapter 74

February 9, 2003—Manhattan

At ten minutes after eight on Sunday morning, the explosives-filled van made its way from New Jersey to Manhattan. The driver, Mahmud Ismail, arrived at the George Washington Bridge tollbooth. He paid the toll, then proceeded east on the bridge toward the city. He was exceptionally tense. It was going to be the most critical and most decisive day of his creepy life on Earth. His van was making for the city but his soul was on its way to heaven. He was a religious man. He closed his eyes in a silent prayer; let his lips do the talking.

It was inevitable. The big bang to his right brought him back to earthly reality. He opened his eyes, realized he'd just crashed into a white Honda. The woman driver who'd been hit was in shock. She wasn't physically hurt; she stayed in her seat sobbing helplessly. Ismail was a committed man. He was on a mission. He had neither the time nor the patience. He turned the steering wheel all the way to the left, away from the Honda, found an open lane, then bore down on the accelerator. The van lurched, its engine vrooming. It was nothing but a typical hit-and-run.

The helicopter pilot, monitoring traffic for *Channel 4 News*, witnessed the accident and its aftermath from his observation post in the cockpit, at several hundred feet above. He aimed his TV camera at the moving van, maintaining its focus; he alerted the police, thus, sounding an alarm bell. The van continued on its path toward Manhattan. It exited the bridge, moved south on the Henry Hudson Parkway. Then, realizing he was being pursued from above, Ismail exited at West 145th Street in an attempt to blend into the urban backdrop and lose its pursuer in the city's expanse.

In the meantime, Arik was growing frustrated over his inability to track down Ismail with his mobile phone. There was nothing, just dead silence at the other end. Arik found it impossible to make use of and control Ismail's phone to communicate a disabling command to the car bomb. Ismail's mobile phone was off. Abu Musa had planned it that way to frustrate Arik's attempts to contact Ismail as a planned part of his phony rehearsal. The second release of Arik's Trojan horse software, the one that would've let him control his victim's phone even when it had been powered off, could have come in handy at that point. Unfortunately, it was not yet available.

Stanley called. "Where is Ismail? Did you disable the bomb?"

Apparently, Jerry had been able to get hold of Stanley, brief him on the events that were about to unfold. Arik figured. "Stanley, we've got a problem," Arik said, his blood pressure skyrocketing, his pulse shattering the speed of sound. "Ismail's mobile phone's is off. This morning, he briefly turned it on, but was out of *Bluetooth* range from the car bomb, I made use of the opportunity to identify his location, but I couldn't disable the bomb through his phone. You could raid his place in New Jersey and arrest him, if he's still there. I can neither locate nor communicate with his van."

Five minutes passed since Ismail had exited the *Henry Hudson*. The helicopter pilot continued his pursuit from above, when Ismail's van suddenly vanished, gone from his view. The pilot continued circling over the area surrounding the latest sighting, in hope that the van would reappear. After five additional minutes, he gave up. Neither he, nor the NYPD had any idea that the hit-and-run driver inside the van was a dangerous terrorist carrying a ticking bomb on his way to a deadly undertaking. The pilot turned around, back to monitoring the traffic over the GW Bridge.

Fifteen minutes had passed before Ismail left the indoor parking garage he had graced with his presence. He paid for one hour of parking, then returned to his mission, resuming his advance toward *St. Patrick's Cathedral*.

Stanley was going mad. After his team had raided Ismail's place, only to find it vacant, he was considering a massive evacuation of

St. Patrick's and its vicinity, but instead, resigned to the idea of blocking all of the access points around the cathedral within a two-block radius.

The Pope was celebrating Mass at *St. Patrick's Cathedral*. The crowd in and around the cathedral was huge. Police surrounded the place; their mission appeared to focus on traffic and crowd management, but unbeknownst to Abu Musa, the force was primed to tackle his assault as well. Police brought in Special Forces, ambulances, SWAT teams, all geared up for any unexpected emergency.

Arik was at his wits' end. He didn't know what Ismail's van looked like. His head was swirling in overload. His headache generated an irritating, piercing buzz inside his right ear. For the first time in his *new career*, he felt helpless, guilty, stupid, mad... all at the same time. He was filled with extreme anxiety, prepared to do whatever it took to remedy the situation, risk his life, even pray to Allah if that could help. Except, those options were not on the menu. There was nothing on his plate but desperation.

Ismail remained on course, making his way through the streets of Manhattan. He turned left from Broadway onto West 59th Street, then right onto 5th Avenue. One minute passed. A police helicopter spotted a suspicious-looking van, fitting the description of that hit-and-run vehicle they had been looking for, speeding down 5th Avenue next to the 58th Street intersection, four blocks away before it would be stopped by the roadblock down at 53rd. Earlier, that intersection had been being evacuated of pedestrians. Police officers were running for cover away from the site of the impending explosion, where the van would be forced to end its advance.

Arik was watching his caller ID. Stanley had just called; he was making a desperate attempt to thwart the looming disaster. "A suspicious van is moving toward you, he already ignored one police officer who had tried to stop him," Stanley barked, his voice screechy, panic stricken. "You know what the driver looks like; if it's Ismail, then make yourself visible to him, make him hesitate, pause, or hiccup before he tries to blow himself up together with the van and you."

Arik turned his gaze towards 54th Street. The van was rapidly approaching the roadblock on 53rd Street. He rushed to the center of the intersection as the van rammed through the roadblock, maintaining its unbroken course. When suddenly noticing Arik, Ismail hit the brakes. Stanley was watching the scene from a safe corner, two blocks away, next to *St. Patrick's Cathedral*. For a brief second, it looked like an opportunity. A professional sharpshooter, positioned at an ideal point, could have ended the nightmare; unfortunately, no such luck. A less than perfect aim carried the risk of a reaction, triggering an explosion and a major disaster in its aftermath.

At that moment, Ismail turned on his phone. He was readying himself for his suicide mission. There was little time left before disaster struck. Arik grabbed the opportunity; he grasped his mobile phone. His close proximity to the van granted him direct *Bluetooth* access to Ismail's car bomb, bypassing Ismail's phone altogether. He quickly pressed *2#, his coded disabling command, neutralizing the bomb in Ismail's van. "You are too early," Arik yelled at the puzzled Ismail who had no idea what had just transpired. "You should have made it here some thirty minutes later at the end of the prayer service."

Ismail seemed confused, as Arik couldn't help but beam with great relief, having just managed to avert a massive catastrophe, saving hundreds or even thousands of innocent lives. Had the bomb exploded, and its *Sarin* gas content spread through the air, the death toll would have been colossal.

The brief pause in the van's advance allowed Police to catch up with Ismail. Three cruisers, their sirens screeching, surrounded the van from three directions as Ismail regained composure and began moving forward, ignoring Arik's attempts to make him stop. The driver of the cruiser in front of Ismail's van hit the brakes, swerved sideways, blocking the van's path, trying to force it into a full stop. Ismail wasn't intimidated. He gunned the engine, hit the cruiser with full force, made it roll on its side, but was unable to clear a path to his heavenly destination. The twisted cruiser was still blocking the way while two police officers approached Ismail's door, their guns in his face.

Ismail was trapped. In his final desolate moment, he flashed a wicked little smile on his pock-marked-face, lifted his mobile phone, put it on view as if he were Leonardo da Vinci displaying his *Mona Lisa*, then closed his eyes and pressed *1#, the code that was designed to detonate the bomb inside his van.

Nothing happened, but not for long. Immediately following the botched suicide-bombing attempt, the two officers emptied their guns into Ismail's face, sending him to his awaiting seventy-two virgins up in heaven on a nonstop Missile Express.

• • •

Channel 4 was first to break the news. They were able to link the accident on the GW Bridge to the explosives-filled van. The pilot reporter bragged about his courageous chase; the three officers described their heroic adventure. They highlighted their scariest moment—the instant Ismail used his mobile phone, in his attempt to set off the bomb. The neutralized explosives-filled van was towed away as explosives experts and a CSI team converged on its damaged body and fresh cargo.

Arik returned to his observation post on 53rd and Broadway, anticipating the arrival of the two suicide bombers in Dr. Radwan's rented car. Only one week earlier, he'd handed over to Dr. Radwan his newly engineered remotely controlled electronic detonator switches. Dr. Radwan was supposed to attach them to the suicide belts and make them available to the two suicide bombers, two retarded supermarket employees responsible for collecting supermarket carts from the parking lot. Ismail's daughter, Hajar, who'd been volunteered for the task by her father, had rebuffed the mission. She was more interested in following the latest on Brad Pit, than tagging along the madness, for which Allah was calling.

Abu Musa was all set for a celebration, but the bulletin transpiring before his eyes wasn't the one for which he'd been hoping. The anchor was talking about the botched bombing attempt by the driver of the van, analyzing the reasons for the failure, pointing up what police had referred to as a malfunctioning detonator switch.

Abu Musa ran mad. *Qassem is a spy; he was responsible for the faulty detonator*, he confirmed. *I've known it all along.* Abu Musa was pleased he'd made the changes affecting the suicide belts. However, his contentment was overpowered by his craving for instant revenge. Mustafa was a couple of blocks away from Qassem's observation post, all set on his bike, his machete thirsting for action, awaiting the *Go-Ahead* order. Nevertheless, revenge, Abu Musa style, wasn't perpetrated unnoticed, in the dark, but rather in front of the world to see. He was about to make sure that the killing of Qassem should take place simultaneously with the bombing inside the cathedral, in front of TV cameras. *It's worth sacrificing Mustafa in the process.*

As soon as the news of Ismail's failure broke, Dr. Radwan made a critical call. He pleaded with Abu Musa, asking to postpone the attack on the cathedral. "Even though we've changed the remotely controlled detonators on our suicide bombers the effect wouldn't be as great as we'd intended; the van wouldn't be there to finish it off, why bother then?" He argued. Abu Musa went ballistic; his rage all but engulfed him. "No way," he barked, then slammed down the phone. He was going to take over Radwan's job; he had two extra belts. He would collect the two bombers at the Columbus Circle, then take them to the Cathedral. He could no longer trust Dr. Radwan.

Following a couple of hours of radio silence, which had kept Stanley's anxiety level high, the tip of the hurricane came into sight in that single call from Dr. Radwan to Abu Musa. It turned out to be an important pointer. Shortly after, Arik learned about the change concerning the suicide bombers' detonators, and Abu Musa's phone number of the day, including the associated line. These were now tapped for the benefit of George, the Arabic speaking FBI agent on Stanley's team. Furthermore, AT&T was working to pinpoint the physical location of the origin of the calls presumed to be Abu Musa's. More airtime was required for that task. Abu Musa didn't disappoint.

Fifteen minutes of radio silence helped cool Abu Musa's nerves. He grabbed his phone and called Dr. Radwan again; there was no answer. Next, he called Mustafa and told him to be ready for the *"Go ahead."*

Abu Musa, eager and energized, glanced at his watch. *It will take less than an hour*, he reflected, *before America commits my name to eternal memory.*

• • •

Dr. Radwan had been under surveillance since leaving his safe house that morning. His Italian diver's watch served as a compass. He made it to the Columbus Circle, thirty minutes after talking to Abu Musa, in time to collect the suicide bombers. They weren't there. Abu Musa had already picked them up, a fact unbeknownst to Dr. Radwan. Immediately following Dr. Radwan's arrival, he was taken into custody by FBI agents.

Soon after Ismail's botched bombing attempt and the capture of Dr. Radwan, Stanley grew calmer. Although the suicide bombers hadn't been located, and Abu Musa was still at large, with his phone off the air, Stanley assumed that the bombing mission had been foiled since the suicide belts had been secured. They fell into his lap as part of a package deal, together with Dr. Radwan. Stanley failed to realize that Abu Musa and the two-armed suicide bombers were taking a toxic stroll on their way to the cathedral at the time of Dr. Radwan's apprehension.

Jerry and two of his *Mossad* colleagues were scrutinizing the vicinity around the cathedral. They were scouting the area for a possible encounter. Jerry was armed with pictures depicting Abu Musa and Dr. Radwan, taken by Arik with his pen-camera, during the meeting they'd held with Arik in Dearborn. Jerry had memorized their faces and so had his colleagues. They were wearing bulletproof vests under their coats. Two days earlier, Jerry had pleaded with Arik, imploring him to do the same, but *Macho Law* had prohibited Arik from admitting fear; he'd said "*No.*"

• • •

The cathedral was brimming with people celebrating the customary Sunday Mass. The Pope presiding over the celebration was wearing white. The air was suffused with energy. There was no urgency, no idea of a looming disaster, and no fear, just serenity, a sense of holiness and exhilaration. It was a day to remember, a day Abu Musa would never want to forget.

Abu Musa and his retards were now two blocks away from the cathedral. He turned on his phone, called CNN, introduced himself, then ordered their cameras into 53rd Street. He followed by calling Mustafa, giving him the *go ahead*, then turned off his phone. One minute later, he caught sight of Arik; he was more than a block away. Abu Musa stopped his advance, found an obscure observation post, sent the two suicide bombers on their mission, then hung around, awaiting Mustafa's assault.

Arik spotted Abu Musa and his two companions, but pretended not to notice. After learning about Dr. Radwan's capture and the absence of the suicide bombers at the Columbus Circle, he put one and two together. He called Jerry on his cell phone, from across the street, offered a description of the two limping fellows, who were making their way into the peaceful gathering. "Watch them," Arik warned. "These are Dr. Radwan's suicide bomber-retards."

As soon as the two would-be bombers crossed the street on their final approach, they became the focus of the two Israeli *Mossad* commandoes, who pressed forward towards them. Then, all at once, as if turned on by remote switch, the commandoes sprang into action, grabbed the bombers' hands, making it impossible for them to pull the trigger handle; they twisted the bombers' arms behind their backs, carefully pushing them down to the ground and disabled them.

Abu Musa missed that action. He concentrated on the fast moving biker a block away. Mustafa was speeding en route for Arik. He crossed the street toward Arik's position, parked his bike ten feet away from his intended victim, turned toward his target, then sprinted, his machete drawn; he aimed at Arik's heart.

CNN cameras were trained on the heroic act. Their cameras didn't miss a thing.

Following the assault, Arik regained his composure. In spite of his earlier refusal to admit fear in Jerry's face, he'd known better.

He did wear his bulletproof vest as per Jerry's advice. It prevented the machete from piercing his heart. It stopped the blade cold; it very nearly broke it. Mustafa was stunned. He stood there like a deer frozen in the headlights, unable to move, before Arik kicked him in the crotch, making him slump to the pavement, affording him with a blinding, paralyzing pain. Abu Musa, witnessing the failed assassination attempt, was losing it. In his fury, he failed to exercise logical reasoning; he began a mad dash toward Arik, shrieking "*Allahu Akbar*! He was twenty feet away when he pulled his gun, fired two shots at Arik before being hit with Jerry's bullet from behind, straight to the head.

Chapter 75

February 9-10, 2003—Tel Aviv, Israel

It was early evening in Israel when Rachel was watching the news streaming in from New York. She watched in horror as Arik took the bullets from Abu Musa's gun, then fell to the ground like a palm-tree in the course of a Hurricane. Stanley was starring as the person-in-charge in front of a gaggle of thirsty reporters who were gulping down his every word. He identified the dead man as Qassem al-Nasr. "He deserved his unfortunate fate," he announced. Abu Musa and Mahmud Ismail, two other top Islamic terrorists had been killed as well. Mustafa, Dr. Radwan, and two part-time supermarket employees had been captured, and an entire Iranian sponsored network had been put out of commission a few days earlier.

Moving images of the material events, including Qassem's assassination, were being displayed concurrently in a separate inset, as Stanley recounted his incredible triumphs. He conveniently forgot to mention the Israeli *Mossad* involvement; neither did he elaborate on the sting operation orchestrated by Arik. He failed to mention Suleiman or his Saudi roots and UN connections. Suleiman had simply vanished. He would be taken care of by the *Mossad* one day, not too soon.

Rachel called Dan Carmel who confirmed Qassem's loss of life. He would arrange for the coffin to arrive at Ben-Gurion, Israel's International Airport near Tel Aviv, on the next EL-AL flight back from JFK. Qassem al-Nasr and his life story had ended. There was no point in keeping the legend alive. Carmel wanted to make certain of that.

At Ben-Gurion airport, Rachel, her family, Arik's mother, and Arik's close friends from his former military unit, prepared for the inevitable. They were anxiously passing time next to the Arrivals gate. Arik's father, unshaven, all set for the Jewish custom comprising seven days of mourning *(Shiva)* following the funeral, was the only designee, chosen to identify the body. The women were emotionally drained. They did not want to stand facing the heartbreaking presentation.

Dad was hanging around the customs office where the coffin was to arrive, but the customs clerk was unaware of any casket on board the plane. *The clerk must have been misinformed,* he thought. *Dan Carmel knew better. He'd made arrangements. He'd said so.*

Rachel was unable to stop the tears, but then, she didn't want to. Arik's mother stood next to her, her eyes swollen and dull. She reached out to touch Rachel's arm, sharing her grief. The somber atmosphere matched the dark clouds overhead and the heavy rain pouring down outside the terminal. It was as though God was crying from above. *Why couldn't He rewind, do it over, change the ending, make it a happy one?*

They were all waiting, dressed in black, all set for a final goodbye, talking about Arik, crying, hugging, anticipating the casket's arrival, when, out of the blue—a vision, a dream come true. *No, it wasn't possible. Or was it?* Rachel could not believe her eyes. Arik's mom got weak in the knees, then collapsed. Someone splashed cold water on her face and revived her. It was as if God was working one of His alleged biblical miracles.

And there he was—Arik, the Customs doors behind him. It looked as if he were standing at the gates of heaven, all set to walk down the Long-Mile back to Earth. His left arm swathed to his chest; his smile, an attribute that had always drawn people to him like filings to a magnet, was splashed all over his face, stretching out through seven time zones.

It wasn't a dream.

Qassem al-Nasr was dead. Dan Carmel did not lie. Still, in order to keep the media at bay—for a day, perhaps for eternity—he omitted the second half of the happy truth. He had other plans...He picked up his phone and dialed.

Indeed, Qassem al-Nasr was no more. Arik was Arik again, back in Israel with Rachel and family, all primed to reboot, to bridge over an interrupted life...to start over.

He was back from the dead...

• • •

But then, his cell phone rang...